THE
RAVEN
AND
THE RUSH

THE BOOK OF ALL THINGS

USA TODAY BESTSELLING AUTHOR
SARAH M. CRADIT

ISBN-13: 979-8-76-800265-7

Cover Design by The Illustrated Author Design Services
Map by The Illustrated Author Design Services
Hardcover Art by Steffani Christensen
Evrathedyn and Rhosynora Portraits by Lauren Richelieu
Evra and Rhosyn in the Armory by Alexandra Curte
Evra and Rhosyn on Icebolt Mountain by Alexandra Curte
Editing by Lawrence Editing
Interior Design by The Illustrated Author Design Services

Publisher Contact:
sarah@sarahmcradit.com
www.sarahmcradit.com

SARAH M CRADIT
WEAVER of WORLDS

PRAISE FOR THE RAVEN AND THE RUSH

"Absolutely addicting! The Raven and the Rush is a dark, glittering gem of a book, full of political intrigue, unforgettable characters, and an epic romance."
~*Casey L. Bond, author of House of Eclipses*

"The Raven and the Rush is a decadent fantasy that draws you in from the first page. The characters are rich, nuanced, and you are quickly and completely ensnared as they dance across the story. Dark, thrilling, and with a burn that leaves you breathless, this book is an absolute MUST READ."
~*Sherry D. Ficklin, author of Queen of Someday*

"A book that I would want to read over and over again. Cradit is a master of words and my heart is so full!"
– *Candace Robinson, author of The Bone Valley*

"Intricate world building sprinkled with a romance wrapped in darker hues. The Raven and the Rush takes the reader on a thrilling journey through intrigue and empowerment."
~*Angelina J. Steffort, author of Shattered Kingdom*

"A masterpiece of timeless scope."
~*J.S. Craig, author of The Chronicles of Benjamin Bright*

"Sarah M. Cradit has once again layered subtle storytelling with rich world-building, complex characters, and imaginative lore to create a powerful new fantasy that will send your imagination spiraling."
~*Jodi Gallegos, author of The High Crown Chronicles series*

INTRODUCTION

There exists a kingdom set upon an isle, surrounded by a sea no one has ever traveled beyond. The Kingdom of the White Sea it is called, or simply the kingdom, for they have no other name for it.

The individual Reaches—Northerlands, Southerlands, Westerlands, and Easterlands—once ruled themselves. Two centuries past, the Rhiagains washed upon their shores, claiming to be gods. From gods, they became kings.

But the Rhiagains were not the first to come from Beyond.

Hundreds of years before this, there were the Ravenwoods. Priests and priestesses, both avian and man. First hunted, as a kingdom with an already tenuous relationship with magic feared them. Then, revered, as the men of the Northerlands came to their rescue, benefitting handsomely from the resulting arrangement. Magic, in exchange for protection.

The Ravenwoods built their castle high in the Northerland Range, into the side of a craggy peak of Icebolt Mountain. The men of the Northern Reach thrived under this treaty, while the Ravenwoods simply existed without assault.

Necessity begot tradition. Tradition birthed a new Ravenwood dynasty. One wholly reliant upon the women to deliver hope, in the form of consistency and stalwart loyalty. One that could so

i

easily snap under the pressure of even a single High Priestess refusing to do either.

The Ravenwoods didn't introduce magic to the kingdom, but their arrival strengthened the prevailing belief that anything not easily explained should not easily be trusted. The Consortium of the Sepulchre in the Skies—the ruling body on all things magic and the oldest extant institution in the kingdom—has fought for centuries to protect magic by regulating it.

But even that is not enough for some men, who would see magic banished for all time. Its practitioners burned.

Lord Aeldred Blackrook of the Westerlands is the most conspicuous of such men. His campaign of terror against "witches" has made the Westerlands unsafe for any born with gifts. He boldly sundered the alliance between the Westerlands and the Sepulchre, denouncing the august body as heretics, an act that alienated him from his allies in the other Reaches—particularly the Northerlands, whose protection of the Ravenwoods borders on treasonous.

It's pride Aeldred feels as he strikes magic from his borders.

It's death and ruin he's invited in its place.

Disease runs unabated in his Reach. Its destructive tendrils are beyond the curative powers of physicians. Without magic, his people are dying. He will soon become sick himself, succumbing to the very illness he alone has the power to assuage.

His second son, Evrathedyn, whiles his days away at university in Oldcastle in the Easterlands, blissful in his obliviousness to the horrors his father has wrought upon their people and land. He escapes into his dusty books, content in his powerlessness. His irrelevance.

I'm only a second son, Evra tells himself. *This has nothing to do with me.*

Farther north, a young Rhosynora Ravenwood tells herself the same thing. *My sister is the High Priestess. I'm nothing. Nobody.*

But time and fate have a way of correcting all things.

As Aeldred Blackrook takes to his sickbed, a storm of change is brewing in the kingdom. On this wind rides death, but also hope.

It begins in a small room, in a tower at Oldcastle.

But this is not where it will end.

WESTERLANDS

Lord & Lady:
Lord Aeldred Blackrook
Lady Fyana Blackrook (deceased)

Capital:
Longwood Rush

Lord's Children:
Astarian, 20
Evrathedyn, 19
Edriss, 16

Other Blackrooks:
Lady Alise, Sister of Aeldred
Lady Meldred, Mother of Aeldred
Lord Andarian, Father of Aeldred (deceased)

Stewards:
Aelric Tyndall, Leonarde Bristol, Roland Ashenhurst, Lewin
Wakesell, Walter Glenlannan, Oliver Richland, Tedric Blakewell,
Oswyn Derry, Rohan James

Other Westerlanders:
Lorcan James, Finnegan Derry, Kindra Bristol

Rush Riders:
First Rider Thennwyr Blackfen
Theomund Wakesell
Aldwen Tyndall
Meira Ashenhurst
Tearsten Everhart
Farrigan Falstaff

MIDNIGHT CREST

High Priestess & Priest:
High Priestess Naryssa Ravenwood
High Priest Aberdyn Ravenwood

Keep:
The Rookery

Priestess' Children:
Rendyr, 21
Augustyn, 20
Arwenna, 17
Rhosynora, 16
Vradyn, 14

Other Ravenwoods:
Avadora Ravenwood, Dowager High Priestess

MIDWINTER REST

Steward & Stewardess:
Steward Oswin Frost
Stewardess Ethelyn Dereham Frost

Keep:
Midwinter Hold
Steward's Children:
Thornton (Thorn), 20
Morwen, 17
Rylan, 5

Other Frosts:
Brin Eaton Frost, Wife of Thornton
Wystan Frost, Son of Thornton and Brin

Lord and Lady of the Northerlands:
Lord Dryden Dereham and Lady Asa Weatherford Dereham

KINGDOM
OF THE
WHITE SEA

SON OF NO ONE,
ONE OF MANY

ONE

TRUE FRIENDS SPEAK TRUE

Evrathedyn stole his first kiss, but Seven commanded the pause that followed. She rolled back on her heels with a pensive frown. Evra's heart pounded while he awaited her appraisal. His anxiety wasn't born of any great affection for her, beyond the friendship they'd enjoyed over the years in Oldcastle. He was after her honest assessment, and if Seven was anything, she was honest.

She was torturing him now, intentionally drawing out the moment of truth he'd been chasing with this bizarre experiment. Seven took this responsibility with the seriousness it deserved, but that didn't mean she wasn't enjoying prolonging his agony.

"You're perfectly fine at it," she said at last, as if they were discussing dessert. "That is why you asked me, no? You wanted me to evaluate your skills or lack thereof?"

Evra leaned forward, breathless. "Perfectly fine? What does that mean?"

"I wasn't bored. Nor am I crying out for more."

"Did I rush it? Should I have told you it was coming, right then?"

"No," Seven said, eyes cast to the ceiling. "No, I rather liked that I *didn't* know when it was coming. But I'm not a lady, am I? Nothing like the girls you'd court. That's why you chose me."

"I chose you because you're my best mate."

"You *chose me* because there's no chance you'd ever have feelings for someone like me."

Evra frowned in place of a fair response to that. Seven Thorsen wasn't highborn. She wasn't even from that class in between where most of the kingdom made their place. The gold that paid for her education came from a wealthy patron who maintained Seven's mother, in ways Seven didn't like to speak about. The benefactor had sent all eight of the Widow Thorsen's children to Oldcastle to get them out of the way.

Seven's place in society had nothing to do with his platonic feelings for her, though. There were few things he had less interest in than arbitrary hierarchies decided by the random fortune of a man's birth.

"I'm not courting any ladies," Evra countered. He rolled forward onto his hands and pushed to his feet. The stone was cold against his palms as he pressed them to either side of the fogged window. Beyond, the thatched town of Oldcastle lay blanketed in fresh snow. It was a hundred-year storm, they said, but "they" said the same last midwinter, and the midwinter before. Far as he could tell, midwinter always brought snow to Oldcastle. "And that's not why I did it."

"Why, then?"

"I knew you'd tell me the truth if I was terrible at it."

"Does that sound stupid to your ears or just mine?"

He half-turned, regarding her over one shoulder. "Would you believe you're the only girl I've kissed?"

Seven burst into laughter. She pressed her matted hair off her forehead with the heels of her palms. "You're nineteen, Evra. A lord's son. You expect me to believe that? And if I *did* believe such a thing, I would've tried to give you a more memorable experience. I thought we were messing about. I didn't know this was *serious*."

2

"Well, you are. And you'll be the last." He returned his gaze to the window and the town below. From his room, the dots of homes and pubs looked like toys. "I suppose I'm relieved it didn't leave you bursting for more, or me, for that matter. This might be harder for me if I'd liked it."

"Harder for you? What would be harder?"

"Giving it up."

"Why would you give up kissing girls when you've only just begun? You make no sense." He felt her head shake behind him. "You never have."

"I thought you liked that about me?" He grinned, but kept it to himself.

"I don't *hate* it about you. If you're not fussed about your disappointing showing, then what was the point?"

Evra turned and leaned into the icy pane. "I'm taking the Scholar's Path, Seven."

Her gasp was soundless. "But you... can you do that? You're a Blackrook. Your father—"

"My father has an heir already. Astarian will be everything he wanted and more when the time comes. Thank the Guardians for it, too. The only thing my brother ever did to help me was to be born first."

"That doesn't mean Lord Blackrook will let you live the life of a monk. And why would you ever want to? You could have anything. Be anything." Seven dropped her eyes. This same fate ascribed to him by the fortune of his birth wasn't available to her. He wanted to help her; to do something about this. But though she liked to frequently point out his ancestry, it meant little here and would mean even less once he became a Scholar.

Evra turned the emotion brewing in his chest inward, burying it. "I can. And I've made my choice. I've already had my first meeting with the Grand Master, and once I have my second recommendation, it will be all but decided. When I finish my courses in springtide, I'll trade this robe for another and begin my training in Riverchapel."

3

Seven sighed into her head shake. "Your father will never let you do it. He's been trying to pull you back to Longwood Rush for years. But this? He'll send every last Rush Rider in the Westerlands to stop you."

"He has no choice but to accept it," Evra said. "The law forbids even a lord from swaying a man from the Scholar's Path, unless that man is his heir. My father has an heir, and soon, Astarian will have one, too. He has to let me go." He pressed his tongue into his cheek. "He'll rant about it, I'm sure. I already know what his letters will say. But once he's put up a fair enough show about it, he'll let it go. He doesn't want me around any more than I want to be there."

"Laws like that don't apply to lords." Her cheeks flushed dark. Anger burned in her amber irises.

Evra sagged in defeat as he approached her. "I thought you were the one who'd be happy for me. That if no one else would understand, you would."

"I understand perfectly," Seven said. Her eyes were splotched with red. "I understand you think so little of yourself that even the idea of having a wife and children feels like a promise you don't deserve. But you *do*, Evra. You're more than what he's caused you to believe about yourself. You're so much more." She sniffed. "And if you take that for a sign I want you to kiss me again, you'll find my fist is more agreeable to the endeavor."

Evra softly sighed and wrapped his hands around the ends of her shoulders. He smiled. "You have it all wrong. I've never wanted that for myself, Seven. It's never been my path. And now, no one can force me to take it. This is the first real choice I've made for myself. Once I switch my robes, I'll be free. I'll no longer be Evrathedyn Blackrook of Longwood Rush. I'll be Scholar Blackrook, son of no one, one of many."

"You'll never be one of many," Seven responded, voice low. "You could sail to Beyond, and you'd still never be able to run from who you are."

He dropped his arms. "Who am I, then?"

"A man who would rather hide away than face his own greatness," she whispered. She wiped her eyes and pivoted away, feigning a laugh. "But you really are a terrible kisser, so I suppose you're sparing some poor girl a terrible fate."

Evra followed Master Quinwhill inside The Golden Castle. At this early hour, only the most committed tavern-goers held court in the dark corners, nursing either their first ales of the day, or their last of the night before.

He shivered as he shrugged off the cold. A hard, relentless wind carried down off the Eastern Range, pushing the snow high against the thatched businesses lining the main road. He rushed toward the roaring fire in the corner, eager to be free of the chill that ran straight to his bones.

"You pick the table, Pupil Blackrook. I'll pay for the ale."

"Sir," Evra replied. He sent one last longing glance at the hearth and then picked a small spot in the corner.

Quinwhill returned with the ale before Evra had time to think of what he might say to persuade his mentor to write his second and last recommendation.

The master slid one mug across the uneven wood to Evra. He pushed his own to the side. "There's been news from the Westerlands."

Evra turned his head to the side with a scowl. "I have no use of news from there, Master. My home is here. Has been for years. You know this."

"So you say," Quinwhill replied. "And what a privilege it is to have the choice not to care."

"I thought you asked me here to discuss my recommendation for the Scholar's Path?"

"Do you know, Pupil, how many have arrived upon the steps of the Sepulchre and the Reliquary, fleeing your father's men? Men near to death and reduced to ruin. The numbers are doubling daily. Soon, they will triple."

Evra crinkled his lips together to keep from saying what he wanted to say. "And what..." He swallowed. "What has this to do with me, Master?"

Quinwhill pressed both palms to the table. "You are the son of Lord Blackrook, lad! Son of the man responsible for *hundreds* of burnings. Good men and women ripped from home and hearth to be sent to the pyre. *Children.* Those with high enough birth have their heads taken to be lined upon the pikes announcing the entrance to Longwood Rush, reminding others that the only way to live is to shutter your truths. It's madness, is what it is. Someone *must* stop it."

Evra dropped back in his chair, arms crossed. He wore the face his master expected; one of apathy. But his stomach churned at Quinwhill's words. The horrors he described were the very ones Evra had fled, no longer able to feign alliance with his own blood. Lord Aeldred wouldn't hear a word against his crazed campaign, and Astarian was weak, cowing. Master Quinwhill was right to be angry, to be appalled, but Evra had no power in the Rush and never had. Here, he'd found something resembling purpose.

"Lords Dereham and Quinlanden have been trying to stop him for years," he said finally. "If men of their authority have no sway over my father, why do you think a discarded second son should fare any better?" Evra squinted to hold back the tears. "Worse, why do you assume I've never tried?"

"What about your brother?"

"Sewn from the same golden cloth."

"Your sister?"

Evra snorted. "Women have no power in the Rush. It isn't the Northerlands."

"Evra." Master Quinwhill never dropped formalities. "Someone must intervene, or there won't *be* a Rush."

"Perhaps if the men and women of the Westerlands would take heed and keep their magic to themselves, this could end!"

"You don't mean that," Quinwhill said. "That cannot be your answer for this terrible problem."

Evra tilted his chair back, rocking it on two legs. He shouldn't have come. Master Quinwhill was his favorite. A surrogate father who issued his greatest challenges, offering kinship as a reward for meeting them. But his subtle nudges for Evra to return home and somehow influence the madman leading the Westerlands were misguided. Evra should have known the pleas would escalate as he approached the end of his studies at Onyxcastle.

His chair slammed back into the floor as he rolled forward. "I have no answer, Master. That's what I've tried to tell you for years. You look at me, sir, as if I forsake my purpose, when I've spent the past decade searching for one that couldn't be taken from me. Taking the Scholar's Path, I see the good I could do. If I cannot aid my Reach, then I can aid this kingdom. I can leave my mark another way."

Master Quinwhill shook his head. He gazed into his untouched ale. "The lies we tell ourselves, Pupil Blackrook."

"You could never understand," Evra retorted. "Just as Seven could never."

"Seven Thorsen is a true friend to you," Quinwhill said. "True friends speak true."

"It's done," Evra said, holding his chin high. "It's decided. I leave for Riverchapel in springtide, and if you cannot offer me your support, I'll find it elsewhere."

Quinwhill pushed to his feet. "There's still time to do what's right." He reached inside his robe and pulled out a roll of vellum. "A letter arrived for you today, from your brother. It's not for me to read the contents, but I can guess at them. The news has already reached our towers. Better for you to hear this from him than from the fishwife gossip in the commons."

Evra let the scroll fall into this hand. If Quinwhill hadn't forewarned him, it would've joined the stack of unread scrolls under his bed.

"What news?" Evra asked.

"I will craft your recommendation for the Scholar's Path," Quinwhill answered. He pushed his chair in. It skipped across the warped boards. "No matter my misgivings, you have earned this placement. I won't be the one who denies you."

"You'll write it?"

"Yes."

Evra followed him out. "You're not going to keep trying to persuade me to go home?"

Quinwhill turned at the door. He pulled his coat high around his ears. "What would be the point, Pupil Blackrook?"

His master disappeared into the snowy morning, leaving Evra hollowed by his victory.

TWO

HE HAUNTS MY DREAMS

Rhosynora Ravenwood hovered at the end of her mother's bed, awaiting her sentence.

High Priestess Naryssa Ravenwood kept the contents of her heart sealed. Predicting her response was as precise as deciding the weather.

"How long has your brother been doing this?" Her mother stood at the other side of the bedchamber, facing away.

"Months. Months now, he's been haunting my dreams," Rhosyn replied. "But this... this intrusion started even earlier than that."

"Earlier? When?"

"The first time was after Arwenna's Langenacht. When she showed no sign of quickening. He came to remind me who I am, he said. Who I will become if she doesn't rise to her fate."

"Arwenna will yet rise," Naryssa answered too quickly. "She has two years to produce an heir from the time of the Langenacht. She has time."

Rhosyn didn't remind her mother of what they both already knew painfully well. That the prescribed two years lingered just

9

on the horizon, like a fickle lover who hadn't yet decided whether to stay or go.

"Rendyr knows his trial will end soon if the two-year mark comes. More, he knows the role will fall to me if Arwenna cannot fulfill her duty. He's determined, Mother. Determined to be the High Priest, not only as he is now, provisionally, but for all his days. He doesn't care that he must earn it, as all men must. He's prepared to demand it."

"Rendyr does not decide the rules. He is just as beholden to them as all of us."

"He doesn't see it that way."

"He tells you this when he visits your dreams?"

He shows me, she thought, but there were still some things Rhosyn kept locked in her own heart box. "*Please* let me go. Even for a short while. If I'm down there... his hold on my dreams won't work from afar. His magic isn't that strong."

Naryssa sighed. She bowed over her dressing table, heavy with the weight of all of Midnight Crest. Rhosyn was often struck with an urge to comfort her mother in times like this, even though she'd come to Naryssa seeking exactly that for herself. She didn't need to read her mother's mind, though, to know what plagued her. The gods had lovingly chosen Arwenna, as they'd once lovingly chosen Naryssa, and her mother, Avadora. As they'd chosen all the firstborn Ravenwood women. And if they'd chosen them, then they'd also decided their failures, hadn't they? If Arwenna did fail, and was cast down against the mountainside, wings clipped, then that meant the gods had decided her death was as inevitable as her birth, and where was the love in that?

Rhosynora had no love for the gods. No love for their restrictive and stifling ways. No love for any of it.

Her mother knew this, another secret she kept locked tight, for both their sakes.

"Mother," Rhosyn said, rising off the bed. "He won't stop. He's already decided Arwenna has failed. I don't even know if he visits her bed anymore. He tells me..." Rhosyn swallowed. She pressed

10

a hand to her throat. "What he'll do to me if I'm to have my own Langenacht."

Naryssa spun around to face her daughter. "If you're to be our next High Priestess, Rhosyn, and I very much hope you are not, for everyone's sake, then he will have no choice but to return to the beginning, with the other men. He will have to compete once more and win once more. If he does not, then his power does not extend to you."

Rhosyn crinkled her upper lip into a sneer. "I thought men had no power in Midnight Crest, Mother."

Naryssa's eyes flashed with frustration. "You know my meaning."

"I know that what we say and what we mean are always at odds."

"You're exhausting, Rhosyn." Naryssa approached her daughter with a weary look. "Yet I adore you, more than a mother should."

"A Ravenwood mother, perhaps," Rhosyn said, her tone cutting but her heart sad. "I've seen how the women of the kingdom are allowed to love their children."

Naryssa scoffed. "In return, they are cursed to be men and women. Even the great ones are not meant for true greatness. Not like us."

"Do you truly define greatness as this gilded castle high in the mountains that we cannot stray far from or risk our lives? As a world where the women are revered with one hand and subjugated with the other?"

"Rhosyn, why must you always be so dramatic? Why do you try me so? What would the others think if they heard me allowing you to speak to me this way?"

Rhosyn reached for her mother's hands. "I'll accept my fate if the time comes." *I'll never accept it. I'll die before I lay with another Ravenwood. I'll kill Rendyr myself if he dares touch me.* "But for now, can I have some peace?"

Naryssa looked down at their joined hands. She unlinked herself, as if her love for her daughter was a weakness. "You've always been so different." She reached a tentative hand toward Rhosyn's shimmering hair, tucking it behind each ear, one by one. Rhosyn was the only Ravenwood with silver hair, when all the others had hair that matched their raven feathers; a trait that was said to appear but once every few generations. Her mother said this made her exceptional, but it only reminded Rhosyn that she didn't belong here. "My special one."

"I don't want to be special, Mother," Rhosyn whispered. She pressed her tongue to the roof of her mouth to stay the tears. "I just want to be safe. If only for a little while."

Naryssa pivoted away, wrapping her arms around herself. "Oswin Frost has requested aid for his wife, who is in childbed once more. She's quite ill like the last time." She shook her head. "Foolish woman. She knew the risks. But we will do as we must and go to her. As with before, we must be prudent with our magic. We can assuage the worst of her ails using a whisper of our power, but if we use too much, we attack the child."

"I know, Mother. It was me who saw her through the last confinement."

"You and Arwenna, you mean. Naturally, your sister will not be there this time," Naryssa said. "I was going to send Augustyn, as he's not yet practiced his training on men, but if you think you can manage—"

"Yes! Yes!"

Rhosyn was already ahead of her mother's words. The Frosts! It was more than she could have ever hoped for. She would get to see her beloved Morwen again. It would feel... it would feel...

Almost like freedom.

"Did you even hear what I told you?"

Rhosyn wrapped her arms around her mother from behind, peppering her lips against the back of Naryssa's head. "Thank you, Mother. Thank you, thank you, thank you!"

"Be prudent with your gratitude," Naryssa said sadly. "For if the gods call upon you, there's nothing more I can do."

"When can I leave?"

"Now, if you wish." She winced through a smile as Rhosyn squealed in delight.

"What will you say to Rendyr?"

Naryssa squeezed her daughter's wrapped arms. "Nothing. Words would only stoke his cruelty."

Rhosyn raced from her mother's bedchamber, gathering speed with every spirited step as she made for the balustrades.

"Where are you going?" Rendyr called, his menace now so routine it no longer startled her. He hovered in the shadows, where he fed his strength and purpose. She wasn't surprised he was there. She'd come to expect it. "Rhosyn!"

Rhosyn, grinning, stretched her arms wide and tilted her face to the sky. She erupted into feathers, settling neatly into her raven form. She could still hear her brother's indignant screams as she caught the wind, aiming herself downward, toward Midwinter Rest, and freedom.

14

THREE
A SECOND VELLUM

Seven awaited Evra's news in the commons, but he didn't stop. He quickened his pace as he raced the endless spiral staircase, towering into the upper levels of the Onyxcastle dormitories. The faster he ran, the less he thought, and that was the irony of why he'd come to the university to begin with, wasn't it? He'd sought a place of thought to avoid thinking.

When he reached his room, he doubled over, panting through the remains of a burst of energy he'd regret later. The vellum nearly melted away in his sweaty palm, crushed under the weight of his competing fear and curiosity.

It wasn't the first time Master Quinwhill, or even the other masters, had tried to spur him toward involvement in his father's bloody crusade. None of them had a kind word for Lord Aeldred, and they made no secret of it. It went against all they stood for to suppress any knowledge, even something as ephemeral and misunderstood as magic. That they came to Evra at all, the throwaway son, showed how little they knew about the terror brewing in the Westerlands, and even less about Evra's relationship with his family. It was also a depressing reminder of what little power even the revered leaders of the university had against a lord of the realm.

Aeldred Blackrook had been a second son as well. Few had the audacity to remind him of this, though.

Evra placed the letter on his desk and pretended not to be interested in the contents. Were there words that would change *anything* for him? He'd toughened himself to the empty platitudes, had worked hard for the confidence he now had to say they didn't affect him at all. News, as Quinwhill had said, could be anything, but what was news to him, when his only power was to agonize and lose sleep over it? When he could *do* nothing?

Though it was still early, he slipped into bed and turned his thoughts toward his dreams.

Evra woke to fists pounding against his door. He stumbled onto the cool stone, still tethered to the remains of his fractured sleep as he reached for his Pupil's robe. He'd just shrugged the fabric down when he opened the door.

Evra adjusted his eyes downward. It was a page. He didn't recognize this one, but they were all boys too young for studies, sent by their fathers to gain valuable training prior to the commencement of their studies. Second and third sons, Evra thought, because they'd never be sent so far from the hearth if they were heirs.

This one was fresh. He stared up at Evra, wan-faced, hands trembling as he handed him a roll of vellum matching the one still sitting on his desk unread.

"Thank you," he said and moved to close the door.

The page didn't move. He nodded at the vellum. "I... I've been ordered to stay till you've read it. Cannae leave until I've confirmed it myself. Ye know, that ye did." A Southerland lad, then. Whitecliffe, maybe, from the softness in his accent.

Evra laughed. "Ordered? Who ordered this?" He ducked into the hall and looked left and right, expecting Seven to leap out. "Where is she?"

"And..." the boy went on, gazing now at his feet, "I ken I'm also to ask if you've read the vellum that arrived two days ago. From Lord Astarian."

"Lord Astarian? He flatters himself." He wasn't surprised to hear his brother styling himself this way. Only that he hadn't started sooner.

Spent of words, the page locked his arms in front of him, waiting.

Evra glanced back toward the desk and the letter Master Quinwhill had passed him in the tavern. He realized that he'd never planned to read it. That the conflict he'd set to stir within himself was only to ease his conscience when he confessed later that the scroll had joined all the others under his bed, unread and forgotten.

"Who sent you?" Evra asked, but the boy had nothing more to say. There could be only one answer, anyway.

Evra moved to the desk. The vellum hadn't recovered from traveling tight in his fist, bunched at the middle and frayed at the ends. The young page's heavy, anxious breathing was the only recognizable sound as Evra slipped the thread holding the scroll off one end. The letter half-unrolled in immediate response to the loss of binding.

Evra flattened the vellum against the desk and read.

Thedyn- I will keep this brief, as you are unlikely to read it, and any extraneous words would be wasted upon you.

The worst has, at last, reached our own doors. Father has been stricken with the sickness. We both know the outcome of such a terrible affliction, and I will need you in the coming days. While fully aware of your unnatural predilection for books and learning, duty must come first. I look forward to your urgent return to Longwood Rush.

Your Brother, Lord Astarian, First Son of the Rush.

17

Evra dropped the vellum on the desk. His rebuttal lived trapped in his chest, wedged next to the shock at Astarian's news. But why should he be shocked? The man who would let his own people succumb to the terrible but preventable illness sweeping the Reach wasn't immune from the same. Aeldred had no secret antidote he hoarded for his own brood. Some outcomes were inevitable.

"Pupil Blackrook? Are ye quite finished?"

Evra nodded without turning.

"Can I bring you this one to read now?"

"Sure." Sweat slid down his cheeks. A new letter, two days on the heels of the last. It could mean only one thing. There could be only one reason.

The page tentatively approached. He reached forward from behind Evra, only his small arm visible.

Evra took the vellum. "You can go now."

"I was ordered to make sure ye read this one, too."

"I will. When you're gone."

The page didn't leave.

Evra's groan faded to a sigh. Would it be easier or harder to read the words, knowing them already in his heart? Would the complicated relationship he'd always had with his father be resolved with the finality of Astarian's message, or would it live on, haunting him?

He opened the second scroll.

Dearest brother Thedyn, it is with unending regret and a shaking hand that I write to you this news, so agonizingly swift upon the news I'd only just sent you. This terrible disease moves fast, with impunity. It spares not even the great ones, and it is with unspeakable sorrow I tell you now that it did not spare our father. Lord Aeldred Blackrook of Longwood Rush has gone to the Guardians, his glorious promise spent.

I am left now to carry this burden, but I will not carry it alone.

18

Evra held fast to the vellum as his hands quavered.

For you, now, are my heir. The heir to the Westerlands. Your place is here until I can find the resolve to take a bride who will deliver me my own heir.

I will expect your return with the swiftness this request deserves.

Yours, Lord Astarian Blackrook, Lord of the Westerlands, Champion of the Rush, Father of the Western Reach.

Evra stepped back, dropping onto his bed.
You, now, are my heir. The heir to the Westerlands.
"No," he whispered. "I'm not."
"Pupil?"
"You can go now. Your orders have been fulfilled."
"There's... aye, there's one more thing."
Evra tensed his jaw tight to stem the emotion welling up.
His father was gone.
Memories flashed out of order. Aeldred showing him how to draw a bow, offering a small but powerful nod when Evra's aim was true. Aeldred taking him before the Council to shame him when he asked for more books for their library. Aeldred crying over his wife's dead body after she'd spent her promise bringing their third and final child into the world.
"How? How can there be one more thing?"
"Pupil... that is, Lord Blackrook. What should I call ye?"
"Just tell me and go."
"They say... that is, that ye should look out your window."
"What?"
He turned to look at the page, but the boy shrugged. He was a messenger. He'd delivered upon that promise and had nothing more to offer.
Evra pushed himself off the bed's edge. When he made it to the window, he heard the small steps of the page running off, his duty finished.

Evra exhaled as he laid eyes on the sea of crimson and silver. Of magnificent steeds and the greatest bowmen in all the realm. The jewel of the Westerlands.

The fight left him.

There was nothing left *to* fight.

Astarian had sent the might of the Riders of the Rush to bring him home.

FOUR
SILVER-HAIRED WITCH

Rhosyn was already running when her feet unfolded and hit the rough ground of the northerly road. Her raven wings disappeared, talons lengthening into legs as she hit her stride. She hadn't changed out of her jeweled boots, and they were a poor choice for the snowy hamlet of Midwinter Rest, but she hadn't expected her mother to give her such a gift. She'd asked for a day away, and her mother had given her weeks. She'd not squander a moment.

Her pace eased as she left the main road and passed through the mammoth iron gates announcing her arrival to Midwinter Hold. Here, the way was less tended; old snow had buckled against the sides of the long path leading to the imposing keep, but there was enough fresh snow to betray the inconsistent efforts to keep it cleared. The Frosts left Midwinter Hold only when they had to. Their provisions arrived monthly, enough to last until more arrived the following month. She knew this because Morwen had told her. It was only through Morwen she understood the world of men at all.

21

We're too far north, Morwen often said, her meandering way of answering many of Rhosyn's questions. Men of the kingdom had no business in the remote town, she said. Those who did had no business with them.

Rhosyn didn't know what the Frosts' business was, though it could only be something lucrative that supported their northern dominion, which competed with Wulfsgate Keep, the capital, in size and splendor. Their keep spanned as far as her gaze could travel, all stone and ramparts and windows that stretched so far she had to crane her neck up to examine the length. It was far too big for the handful of Frosts residing within the walls. Even The Rookery of Midnight Crest felt less assuming than the fortress the Frosts had built for themselves in the northern wastes of the kingdom.

Despite her questions, the answers didn't matter to her. The Frosts were kind to her. Rhosyn used to fantasize about what it might be like to be their daughter, instead of the daughter of the High Priestess of Midnight Crest. To be tucked into her bed each night with love and awaken to laughter and warmth.

But she was not.

Rhosyn enjoyed a vigorous imagination, but always, always tempered by the acceptance that hiding from reality made it more difficult to face, not less.

A smile full of delight and promise spread across her face as she made her way to the iron doors of the place she secretly wished was home.

Arwenna Ravenwood sat upon the icy throne in the center of the Courtyard of Regents. The midnight goats were asleep at this late hour, as she should be if sleep hadn't forsaken her. The curious little beasts formed a furry circle just beyond where the tips of her boots grazed the ice. When she was a girl, some of her fondest memories were of nestling into a plush pile of their silver coats as her mother perched on the throne, lost to the one place a High Priestess could be alone with their thoughts.

That had led to her first hard lesson. Thoughts were dangerous.

Words were worse. And anyway, she had none. Not anymore. No more than anyone had words for her, about what her failures had wrought. Least not the helpful kind.

She tapped the end of her heel against the ice. Imagined the impact birthing a splinter she could send through the middle, splitting their world in two, leaving her safe on her own side.

The low sound of Rendyr's heavy, purposeful steps didn't surprise her. He knew he wasn't allowed in the courtyard. He had no care for the lines separating him from what was his to enjoy, and what rules forbade him from.

He emphasized his footfalls for her. Without fear, his power had nowhere to take hold.

"You aren't allowed here," she said because she had to. Rules didn't matter to him, but they still mattered to her.

"I'm your husband. I'm allowed anywhere you are."

"You are *not* that. Nor are you the High Priest," Arwenna said, more cruelly than she intended. It wasn't for fear of hurting *him* that made her recoil after she'd released the words.

"I should be," Rendyr said. He closed in on her, casting a tall shadow over her chair. His black hair fell in waves over the leather that tightened across his muscular shoulders as he tensed. "I would be, if not for you." He pulled the corner of his mouth into a grin. "I still will be, long after you're frozen against the mountainside."

Arwenna was frozen in another way. All the words she wanted to say burned against the back of her throat, warned away from finding life, as she herself neared closer to death. It hadn't always been this way. Once, she and her brother had even been friends. Playmates. She didn't know when the light had died inside Rendyr, or even why, only that it had. He was much more content in the darkness.

"You have only yourself to be angry with," he went on when she didn't rise to his hatred. "It was not for lack of effort on my part."

"No," she agreed, swallowing down the hard memories of those terrible nights.

"Rhosyn will be more agreeable," he mused. "Or not. It's really no matter to me how she feels about it."

"Your confidence that the gods will choose you a second time, among all the other Ravenwood men who will cast their lot for Rhosyn at her Langenacht, would almost be amusing to me if I didn't think you meant it."

"The gods," he repeated, as if she'd said something funny. "There's no magic who decides which man will light the womb of the High Priestess. The magic is merely an illusion so that the High Priestess can be seen as having no choice in who becomes her daughter's High Priest, when in fact she's the only one who *can* choose. Mother chose me. Mother chose me for you. She'll choose me for Rhosyn."

The swell of dread in her belly surged outward. She'd always wondered if this was true; if there was any magic at all involved in the Langenacht, or if it was simply a ceremonial reason for the available Ravenwood men to bed the future High Priestess. But if it was true, then it would mean Naryssa had knowingly sent Arwenna to the two years of torture that followed her Langenacht. If a mother could choose for her daughter, then what did this choice say about her own mother? About her?

"She will not make the same mistake twice," Arwenna said. She forced herself to stand. He didn't move back to give her room, and she nearly lost her balance. When she tried to duck around him, he threw his arms out. *Like a child,* she thought, but that was wrong, all wrong. He'd never been a child.

Arwenna summoned her courage and looked him in the eyes.

"You may be right about me," she said. "I *am* weak. I've never been strong. Perhaps it's this weakness that has prevented a child from finding its way to me. But you're wrong about Rhosyn. She will not fall so easily under your wanton cruelty. Nor will she abide it."

Rendyr laughed. His hot breath tickled her ear, sending a chill through her. "I once thought the same about you. You used to want it, Arwenna. You used to want everything about it."

"Everyone wants something until they have it." Arwenna pressed on his arm and pivoted away. "Your lesson on this awaits you still."

Morwen Frost held her for so long, Rhosyn's face flushed with dizziness.

"I didn't expect to ever see you again!" she cried. "Not after..." She rolled her lower lip inward. "The Guardians must be fond of me once again."

"Once again? Had you angered them?"

Morwen laughed. "I expected as much when they took you away from me." Her joy faded. "You're not going to tell me you're just here for the day? Break my heart?"

Rhosyn had been coming to Midwinter Hold for years, but the last time she had spent with Morwen was over a year ago, when Stewardess Frost lost the child she'd been carrying. Rhosyn, under the instruction of Arwenna, tended her difficult lying in, and then her broken heart and body, in the aftermath. Once the stewardess' illness was spent, so was Rhosyn's reason for being there. That was the agreement that had held her family's world together for so long. They came when called upon. They returned to their own world when done.

"You're here for Mother again?" Morwen pressed when Rhosyn didn't recover from her reverie quick enough to answer.

Rhosyn nodded. The urge to cry was powerful, and she couldn't decide if the source was joy or agony. "Is it like last time?"

Morwen sighed. "Worse. The physician walks around like she's already met the Guardians. Father didn't want to ask again, but..."

"Why wouldn't he want to ask? You need our aid, we come. In return, you keep the foothills safe for us."

"Ah, now's not the time for such talk," Morwen said, brightening again. "You're here, and that's what matters." She landed a kiss at the corner of Rhosyn's mouth. "How is Arwenna? Hopefully by now a mother?"

Rhosyn shook her head.

Morwen's mouth parted in a soundless gasp. "Even a sign?"

"None."

"They won't really do it. Will they?"

"I didn't use to think they would. But now that the two years are almost here, they all act less hopeful and more resigned to what's coming. It's as if they've convinced themselves her inability to bring a child is akin to treason. Shutting their love off for her. They treat her like a ghost, already dead."

"What can we do?"

"Nothing," Rhosyn answered, hiding her fury. "There's nothing anyone can do."

"But that's preposterous, Rhosyn!" Morwen went to the fire, removing the now steaming water. "They cannot just *murder* their own daughter! And what if it's Rendyr's failure and not hers? No punishment for his deficiencies?"

Rhosyn had supposed the same thing, and she loved Morwen for thinking this, too. In her world, the women commanded the glory, but they also bore the totality of the shame. "Rendyr will never be held to account for any of his crimes. Expecting anything else is a path to heartache."

"When did this bitterness spread over you? It's new." Morwen handed her a mug of tea. She climbed upon the wooden table, bowing her face over the steaming liquid.

"Ah, so I've not done a fair enough job hiding it this time. Is that what you're saying?"

"Has so much changed in a year?"

"I'm about to lose my only sister, and instead of mourning her, I'll be forced to take her place. Sadness, shadowed by agony. And there's nothing, *nothing*, I can do about any of it." Rhosyn set her tea aside and joined Morwen on the table. "You remember what I told you last time? About Rendyr?"

"Still?"

"Still."

"Oh, Rhosyn."

Rhosyn shook her head. "Put your pity away. It only makes me feel worse. He doesn't dare touch me, not yet. But he haunts my dreams now. I'm his, he says, like I'm a prize, and not his sister."

"I'll never understand the Ravenwood ways," Morwen said. "But I'm not a Ravenwood."

"I *am* a Ravenwood, and I'll never understand." Rhosyn linked her hands over her lap. "But my strength must come from enduring the impossible, not pretending it won't ever happen. Right? I know what's coming. I can't hide from it. But I can be ready."

Morwen reached a hand over Rhosyn's joined ones. "You could run away. Wait, don't say it. I know what you think. That they'd find you. But they won't fly beyond the Northerlands. It's too dangerous. They're not protected beyond our borders."

"When Arwenna is gone, I'm all they'll have. The last daughter. Without me, the line breaks. I can't even fathom the chaos that would cause." Rhosyn laughed despite her angst. "For me, they'd risk it. Not for any love, mind you, but to avoid that very chaos."

"He can't hurt you here," Morwen whispered, eyes heavy. "For however long that lasts."

"How far along is your mother?"

"She has months yet to go, but they fear she won't make it that far. That her confinement will end soon, for good or ill."

Rhosyn hopped off the table. She pulled herself erect and wrapped her silver hair in a ribbon. "Then we mustn't waste even a moment."

The door to Ethelyn Frost's chambers was cracked. A thin sliver of darkness marked the center of the brightly lit hall.

Rhosyn kept her eyes on the stone floor. Her reticence did her no favors. The whispers traveled her way just the same. Not even the Frosts' hospitality could slake the curiosity of the grooms and chambermaids.

She slipped inside Stewardess Frost's apartments and moved to close the door.

"Open. Leave it open."

Rhosyn left the door as she'd found it. She rolled her hands around her upper arms with a shiver. "It's far too cool in here, Stewardess. You'll catch a chill. Can I at least light some candles? A lantern?"

"I like it this way." In the darkness, Ethelyn's face was distorted. "I know this voice. The tantalizing intoxication of the silver-haired witch. Rhosynora Ravenwood. Like a dream."

"Stewardess?"

"I thought they'd send one of your brothers. I passed these wishes to Oswin, but Guardians know he only remembers the most pleasing parts of what I tell him. Perhaps it was his idea to bring you back. He does adore you."

"They were going to send Augustyn," Rhosyn answered. She moved to each window, drawing the heavy curtains. The stewardess may not want the light, but she wouldn't miss the cold. "I offered to go in his place."

"Offered," Ethelyn repeated. Her hands hovered in what seemed midair, but then Rhosyn saw the blanket move. The stewardess' hands formed over the bulge in the cover. "Of course you did."

"May I approach?"

"You may."

Rhosyn stepped closer, and now the thin moonlight provided a hint of illumination. The shadows darkened the stewardess' crescents beneath her eyes, but enhanced the radiant flush in her cheeks. She was both dying and more alive than she'd ever been. Rhosyn had the power to help her take either path.

28

Rhosyn wrapped her fingers over the hard swell of the blanket. Stewardess Frost shifted under her touch, as if anticipating pain. Rhosyn's eyes closed, and she listened.

"Your child is well. You are not," Rhosyn said. She lowered herself to the chair at Ethelyn's side. "I can help you. I will help you. It is my only desire to ease both you and the child through what remains of your confinement, and to see you both back to your health after."

"I know you will. You were such a comfort to me the last time when..." Ethelyn's words finished in her sad eyes alone. "But now I must ask you to help me in another way."

"Another way? How?"

"Morwen." Ethelyn pointed to the wine at her bedside. Rhosyn handed it to her, waiting for the stewardess to quell her thirst. "Morwen," she said, stronger this time.

"What about her?"

"She's to be married soon. And to a good man at that. A Haddenfoot. She'll leave for Dunwoode in the south, as soon as the weather turns in our favor. At last, she'll be free of this wretched cold that so vexes her."

"How lovely," Rhosyn said with a feigned smile. "Every young woman's dream."

"One would assume so, Rhosynora. Would they not?"

"What does this have to do with me?"

"You know," the stewardess answered, "what this has to do with you."

She could continue boasting her ignorance, but that would be exhausting. "It's not me who'll be giving you trouble with this. I have my own marriage to make, one way or another, and sooner than I'd like. I wish Morwen only happiness."

"She hadn't stopped talking about you," the stewardess said. "No, not entirely. But she'd slowed to once a day, and we thought that meant it was time. Any sooner, she would've fought us. Any later, she'd be talked about. An over-ripened maid."

Rhosyn cinched a fistful of bedsheet in her hand. "I won't stand blocking the door between Morwen's wants and needs."

"Good. Good that we understand one another."

"I love Morwen. My love for her is more familial than it is what you assume it to be. Like a sister."

"That sisterly love is what would drive her to forsake a good life that awaits her, to save yours, when we both know it would be the task of a well-meaning fool," Ethelyn answered. "It is enough for me that you understand and will not come in the way of what she needs."

"I came not only for her, Stewardess." Rhosyn's toes curled in her slippers. Her heart traveled down to join them. "Sometimes I just find it easier to breathe on land."

Rhosyn felt a hand close over hers. She looked down.

"We all have our burdens, raven. It's not about finding a means to be free of them. It's about how well we can adapt to living in a cage."

When Rhosyn slipped into her bed that night, for once, sleep came swiftly.

But it was short-lived. Replaced all too quickly by the familiar, commanding voice of Rendyr.

Did you think there was anywhere you could go, Rhosynora, that I could not find you? Anywhere I would not go?

Are you here, then? Did you follow me?

Am I not a part of you?

Rhosyn bolted forward in the bed. She heaved a sob into both hands, covered in the sweat of her darkest fears, which were never far away.

FIVE
THE RUSH

Evra rode in the center of the pack of crimson and silver. Rush Riders flanked him on all sides, their longbows stretching from above their heads to a soft sweep just above the ground. He'd always been fascinated with the bond Riders shared with their horses, but that interest had boiled away to anger. They were no longer the mythical horse-lord bowmen of his childhood, but his gaolers. No longer the heroes, but the villains.

They'd traveled up through the south, first passing through Whitewood and then Windwatch Grove. Landmarks of his youth, when Aeldred would take both his sons on progress through the Reach. The ruddier colors of the southern stretch of his homeland faded, replaced by the lush verdancy of his home. Longwood Rush had the best of both worlds, dotted with ornately tressed hanging and terrestrial gardens, but close enough to the White Sea to enjoy the sand and shore.

They stopped in Windwatch Grove to water the horses and have a meal before they made the final push home. Crossing the capricious River Rush was better suited for early evening, and so around dusk, they resettled their provisions and made for the shallows.

As Evra's horse dipped its hooves in the cool water, a shadow pushed in from his side. *Probably thinks I'm dumb enough to make a break upriver,* he thought, until he saw who it was.

He hardly recognized her in her regalia. She donned the red leather of the Rush Riders, silver swashed at the cuffs and straight through her breastbone. Meira Ashenhurst. His dearest childhood companion and one reason for his father's many concerns over his fate and future.

"Why are you wearing *that*?" he asked. Evra's horse kicked up, but he gently eased her along the same path as the bowmen. The Riders' horses were at perfect ease. He imagined they'd pulled him a skittish one from the back of the stables to help keep him in line.

"Hello to you, too!" Meira exclaimed. Half of her red hair was gathered in braids atop the other half, which flowed long and free down the center of her back. "I've been very well, thank you. Oh, how I've missed this about you. Your love of small talk and pleasantries."

His stomach flipped to see her so grown; so confident. She wasn't the timid field mouse running about with the boys now. She was a warrior, her resolve carved into every freckle, every curve of her mouth and nose. He realized she wasn't tagging along, playing pretend in those clothes. "They allow women now?"

"Again, Evra! Guardians! Are you not happy to see me, or have the Scholars taken your joy, too?"

"They've taken nothing," Evra murmured. "I *am* happy to see you, Meira." He hoped she mistook the flush in his cheeks for exhaustion, and not this bewilderment making it hard to even look at her. "You're the only one I missed."

Meira clucked her tongue. She reached for his reins and guided both their horses safely across. "Now, that isn't true. Edriss will be so happy to see you."

Evra nodded. "I tried to send for her, to bring her to Oldcastle. Father refused. No doubt he's used the years to turn her against me."

"Let us get right to the point, then. Your father can't hurt you anymore, not where he's gone to. Lord Astarian is the Lord of the Westerlands now. It's your brother to whom we answer."

"So you really are a Rush Rider, then? How?"

"Fledgling Rush Rider. I haven't yet passed my trials."

"You will," Evra said, nodding. He groaned as his horse navigated up the steep, uneven bank. "You can tell me the truth. He'll spring a bride on me when I arrive, won't he?"

"I know very little about the doings in the Rush. I've done most of my training at home, here in Windwatch."

"Meira..."

She sighed in mild annoyance. "Rumors is all, and you know how much I value those."

He remembered. Rumors had cut a sharp terror through Meira's childhood. The girl so unlike all the other girls. "I can't walk into an ambush. I already feel like a prisoner."

"You're not a prisoner," she replied. "Your brother is worried, is all. You don't know what it's been like since you left."

"That's *why* I left." It was part of it.

"When most of us had no choice but to stay."

"I won't apologize for leaving a place I felt powerless, for one where I might find some."

"Did you, then? Find your power?"

"I was close," Evra replied. "Tell me. Please, Meira."

She pointed her gaze straight ahead, sitting tall in her saddle. "Word is, a man his age should have been married and settled by now. Word is, he fought it, delayed it, and now lives in regret of that choice, as the Reach balances on him alone. And now, you."

"Why would he delay getting married? Astarian could have any woman in the Reach. Could have his pick of them."

"Your use of the word 'woman' seems to be the problem."

33

Evra's mouth parted. The world of his past continued to come to life in ways he'd forgotten. "He can do what he pleases behind closed doors, but he needs an heir."

Meira laughed. "Oi, and now he has one. *You.*"

When he'd left Longwood Rush as a boy, Evra's final memory of his home had been the long walk down the path connecting the Halls of Longwood to the River Rush. Lined with trees providing easy shade from the noonday sun in springtide or shelter from the storms of midwinter. Despite his tumultuous childhood, it had been a place of beauty, even peace.

The trees were still there, but they no longer held court alone. Their glory had been pushed back from view, supplanted by pikes that started at one end of the path and guided them all the way to the broad steps of the Blackrook keep, the Halls of Longwood.

Atop these pikes were heads. Most rotting, a few freshly mounted. Some, he even recognized.

Meira passed him a look from his side that didn't require words.

Evra held his breath until they reached the steps. He readied himself for fresh air, but the stench, of rotting flesh and the remnants of fires not long dead, was even riper at the keep.

Gagging, he looked up to see Astarian at the top of the stairs, obscured by the sun. He took another step forward, and now Evra saw him clearly. His brother's blond waves rippled in a gust of wind, the boyish face Evra remembered now lined with horrors he hoped never to learn about.

Astarian seemed oblivious to the foul wind ripping across the Rush. "Thedyn," he said without smiling. Evra dismounted to join him, but the Riders hung back.

"This is as far as we go," Meira explained. "We did our part in bringing you home."

The little boy in him wanted to beg her to stay at his side. But he wasn't a little boy anymore, and it wasn't the task of a boy awaiting him.

"You'll be in the Rush a while longer?"

She nodded.

"Come by tomorrow?"

"I would like that."

Evra ascended to the rhythm of hundreds of hooves moving in tandem. Two pages scrambled for his bags and raced up the stairs ahead of him. Astarian had already turned to go back inside. Evra hadn't been expecting a warm embrace, but still deflated at the denial of one.

He rushed up to his brother's side and fell into pace beside him. Astarian kept his eyes straight ahead as they moved together down the hall. "You should have come at my first vellum."

"I got the second one the same day, As."

Astarian's jaded sneer was another new sight welcoming him home. "It happened that fast. And would it have mattered, Thedyn, if they had come weeks apart? It was never my words, or father's, capable of bringing you home. I had to send an army. For my own brother."

"Don't call me Thedyn."

"It's what Father named you."

"He named me Evrathedyn. I chose Evra."

"Evra is a boy's name. Do you want to remain a boy for the rest of your life, sifting through meaningless books? Is that why you stayed away so long?"

Perhaps Father hadn't told Astarian about that fateful, terrible night that had driven Evra away from Longwood Rush almost a decade ago. If Astarian *had* known, everything might have been different.

"You brought me home to insult me?" Evra countered. Even deep within the halls of the keep, the stench lingered. He imagined it lived in the thread of every garment; the mortar of every stone. He noted the cloying scent of lavender mingled in, and as

35

his eyes fell on the sconces lining the halls, he understood. They'd raided his grandmother's beloved garden, mixing her famed florals in with the wax to mask the revulsion.

"I brought you home for you to wed and bed and help me save this Reach. Both our brides arrive tomorrow, and we'll both do what we must." Astarian closed his eyes momentarily. "For the Reach."

Evra stopped walking. He waited for Astarian to do the same. "There's only one thing that can save this Reach. You and I both know this, even if you have numbed yourself to the horrors."

Astarian squared his jaw, rolling it back and forth. "To suggest what I think you are going to suggest is blasphemy. Treason."

Evra thought no better of magic than his brother or father; it was the campaign of terror that left him disgusted and disheartened. It seemed no one was safe in the Westerlands. To know magic was to die on the pyre. To be less remarkable was to be lost to the illness only magic could cure. A never-ending circle of doom and despair, with no winners. "He's gone, As. You don't have to be the lord our father was. You *can* choose another way."

"Do you even..." Astarian's nostrils flared. "No. You know nothing, Thedyn. You never did. You know even less now." He resumed his pace.

"Where are we going?"

"I'm taking you to pay your respects to our father."

Evra recognized every solemn face gathered around his father's body in the Great Hall. They belonged to the men who had a hand in raising him after his mother died.

She'd spent her promise bringing Edriss into the world. In his desperate grief, Aeldred had gone against his own unwavering principles and commissioned a healer, but his wife was too far gone. Magic doesn't work that way, the healer insisted, and then the healer had found themselves burning on a pyre, the smoke from their perceived crime part of the backdrop as Evra and his brother watched their mother succumb to ash. Aeldred's hatred for magic burned hotter than it ever had, and he vowed never to allow himself such weakness again.

Astarian held the infant Edriss, because Aeldred would not. He wanted nothing to do with the child he believed responsible for his wife's death.

Evra's aunt, Lady Alise, stood along the back wall, her true thoughts a mystery to all. Beside her, Evra's grandmother, Lady Meldred, slept in the chair they'd pulled up for her. Her occasional snore ripped across the cylindrical room.

The men looked up together, each presenting a reverent nod to their lord's second son. They hadn't liked him much as a boy. He expected nothing more from them now.

Steward Bristol broke away from the circle of men ringing his father's corpse. He wore the appropriate black for mourning, but the glow of ambition burned in his irises, as Evra knew it would in all the men. Each of them, plotting their land grab in the aftermath. Wondering who was friend, who was foe. Alliances formed where words should be. Enemies, too.

"Lord Thedyn. Allow me to extend condolences on behalf of all men of this Reach. Your father was a great man. The bravest in all the realm. His loss will linger upon this Reach for years to come."

Evra didn't correct the steward for the misused name. The slight was intentional. "Thank you, Steward."

They walked together. Their shoes echoed against the marble, bouncing off the stone columns in rhythm with his grandmother's snores. "You've come just in time to stand at your brother's side. Where you belong."

Evra said nothing. He kept his eyes forward.

"I want you to know I am at your service. Whatever you need, I can provide. Even those needs you may not yet realize you have."

"Thank you." Evra fought back a wave of nausea.

"As a father might," he continued. Evra realized the man hadn't stopped talking. "For soon, I will be as a father to you."

37

Evra turned. "What?"

"It's my Kindra we've selected as your bride. She's expected on the morrow."

"We?" The tingling that lived in his fingers and toes moved inward. Bristol had been the quickest vulture, then. What gifts did the others have waiting? "I wasn't aware."

"You remember Kindra, do you not? You must have played together as children. In fact, I'm certain of it."

Evra's memory of all things was coming back much faster than he was prepared for. "Yes."

"Then you know you will have fared better than most men in this Reach. Her hand has been sought since she was still learning her letters. I knew something greater awaited her. Now, I know what that was."

"Hard to think about marriage right now," Evra managed. The numbness spread to his tongue. "Or anything, really."

"No." Bristol exhaled, flicking his hand into a brisk wave. "Of course not. You've only just arrived. There's still so much to tell you. You've been gone far too long. Only a shame it took your father's death to rectify that."

More like fifty Rush Riders. "Is this safe?"

"Is what safe?"

"All of you, hovered around him like that, when he's just died of a horribly contagious disease?"

"You mean, can a dead man spread the sickness?"

I know a dead man can spread the sickness. I know this because of this education you all decry and belittle. "The men should step back a few paces. They can pay their respects just as well with a safe distance."

Bristol's brows knitted. "It will not do to have Lord Aeldred's own son stand back from the crowd."

"I'm suggesting we *all* stand back—"

"Not do at all," Bristol finished, ignoring him. He shook his head, already falling neatly into the role of disapproving parent.

Astarian's steps sounded behind him and then he was at Evra's side. "It's all right. I've been with Father day and night since he went to the Guardians, Thedyn. As you can see, I'm not ill. Nor are my men."

The circle of men parted. Evra's stomach dropped at the sight of his father's purple, bloated corpse. They'd let him lie there in decay, without so much as a shroud to preserve the last of his dignity.

Evra pressed his hand to his mouth to stay the retching.

"Ah, and there's our Thedyn! Our little lost lord returned home at last." Steward Ashenhurst, Meira's father, this time. The others had their words too, practiced and empty, and he let them run through their recitations as his eyes locked onto the grotesque bloat of the man who had once choked Evra near to death to make a point. Who'd watched Evra almost drown when he didn't take to his swimming lessons quickly enough.

There was no victory in seeing him like this.

There was nothing.

Lady Alise caught his eye from beneath her long mourning veil. Her grin was quick, subtle. The nod after was for him, too.

Aeldred's pale tongue hung from the side of his mouth. A fly landed upon it.

"I'm sorry. I can't do this," Evra cried, backing away. "I'm sorry, As."

He turned and fled.

SIX
THE HANGING GARDENS

Lady Meldred had always called them The Hanging Gardens, though only some of the flora were suspended above ground. Most meandered the dirt path in coordinated assault, arranged, in some places by their vibrant colors, and in others, by their function. Only the Blackrook women who tended the ancestral garden knew the name of every floral resident; only the women knew every use.

As beautiful as they were, few visited the gardens on their visits to Longwood Rush. Most avoided the welcoming arched trellises, often with a light chill as they passed by. Some paused along their way, looking to the Guardians in brief, silent prayer. Others, still, told of the ghosts that swept down the paths in aimless pursuit of nothing.

She liked these stories. Encouraged them, same as her own mother had. When men would recount their experiences, working through their tales with nervous chuckles, Meldred would smile her famous smile. Their laughter would fade, and next time they came to the Rush, they'd take the longer hall to avoid even a glimpse into the kingdom ruled by the poison mistresses of Longwood Rush.

Rumors were often born of fact, growing new life. *Let them fear us*, she thought. Her daughter, Alise, had used this same training to be rid of the one leaving bruises upon her body. Alise's husband disappeared, and so did the evidence of his cruelty. The whispers grew louder. The chills longer.

But it would be unwise to equate fear with power, Meldred knew. The women in the Westerlands enjoyed the least amount of freedom in the kingdom. They took what they could and devised the mettle to endure the rest. A delicate game of take, but mostly give.

Aeldred's campaign of terror made the whispers disappear altogether. For what were the deft hands of sly highborns against an illness that spared none? Against a tyrant lord who offered no trial or fair justice for even the hint of magic? Children, she'd seen burn. The heads of her oldest friends, lining the pikes along the once tranquil, once welcoming road to Longwood Rush.

"He won't come," Alise said. Arms wrapped around her waist, she examined what remained of the lavender after the men had sent their servants to pillage it. Too craven to even come get it themselves.

It would grow again. That wasn't the point.

"He does not want to come," Meldred answered. "But that does not mean he will not."

"He knows, Mother. He knows all about my brother's misdeeds. This was his reason for staying away all these years. I can't blame him, but nor should we look to him for anything but commiseration. He's only here now because Astarian dragged him by force."

"Your idea, and a fair one. You were right, he would not have come otherwise," Meldred said. "Evra didn't run from *us*. He ran from his father. His father is gone."

Alise aimed a bitter nod down the path. "Astarian is just like him."

"No," Meldred said, shaking her head. Her slippered feet kicked up small swirls of dust as she walked. "He's weak and timid, and therefore worse. My brother may have seen Evra's education as an affront, but we know it for what it is. You and I."

Alise nodded as she reached into the dirt to caress the splintered roots. "How much would be different if the women..."

"It *is* the women," Meldred asserted. She turned back toward the way they'd come. Alise was right, after all. Evra wouldn't come. He would be a better man than his father and brother one day, but not while he was still determined to stay a boy. "Perhaps he's with Edriss, then."

"Then let them have their time," Alise said sadly. She pulled back to her feet, regarding the carnage of her beloved lavender with one last solemn look. "For that is the one thing they can no longer make more of."

Evra clutched his sister's bony hand as she watched him with sunken eyes. Her smile, though cracked, was still radiant. All the guilt he'd stored away was for her, and it came rushing forth as he saw, with his own eyes now, that his sister was dying. Her death was imminent. Though she wasn't afflicted with the illness that had killed many of their people, and now their father, it shared a common problem. The physicians had reached the end of their ability. Without magic, there was no hope.

"You came," she whispered. Did she know how Astarian had brought him here? Did she care, as long as he was home?

"I came."

"Did As take you into the fields, then? To see the pyres?"

"I didn't need to see them, Edriss. I can smell them. I could leave tomorrow and fifty years from now I'd still smell them."

Her head fell to the side as she smiled at him. "Be grateful you have not lived through so much of it that you no longer even notice. The lavender in the halls makes it worse, not better. I'll have forgotten for one blessed moment, and then that sharp floral barrage stings my nostrils, bringing me back. But I suppose men have always laid roses on corpses, haven't they?"

"Does nothing but bring attention to the problem."

"Perhaps the men of the Northerlands have it right, with their tombs below the ground. Bury the problem, and at least you're not thinking about it at all hours."

"I could take you back to Oldcastle with me," Evra said, feeling as foolish and childish as he sounded. He might as well be in prison now. He was surrounded by enemies or budding ones. His brother's men now, all of them, and his brother was too much of a coward to face the coming days alone.

"I wish you'd stayed away," she said softly. "But I saw this coming. I first saw it years ago."

Evra's heart crashed in uneven beats. "You guessed it, you mean."

Edriss shook her head on the pillow. "You know what I mean. You know I can see things."

"I just thought... you know, sometimes children..."

"We're not really children anymore, and I can still see."

"Does anyone else know?"

"Aunt Alise."

Evra dropped her hand.

"You can trust Alise, brother. I sometimes imagine a world where she had been the mistress of Longwood Rush and not our father. Where gardens were still gardens, and the full heat of the sun still shined down upon us, not obscured by smoke and ash."

There was no point in explaining the dangers of trust to his sister. She deserved some contentment. "Astarian thinks I'm going to be wed soon."

"Kindra Bristol. She's very pretty, Evra. You could do worse."

"Why do people say that, hoping it brings comfort? It could be worse? Well, why couldn't we just expect better for once?"

Edriss closed her eyes. "What is your point? Or do you have one? Has being away so long spoiled you against reality?"

44

"I won't be here long," Evra said. He stood as the thoughts took over. "Astarian is the heir. He should have been married long ago, Edriss. That's not my fault, nor my problem. He'll marry soon, she'll do her duty by the Reach, and then I'll return."

"Please tell me you didn't truly go away to school only to become an even bigger fool?"

Evra recoiled at the sting. "I'm not the heir. Father has been exceptionally clear on that point since I was old enough to understand his cruelty. I wasn't raised for it. Trained for it. Prepared for it." He pointed both hands at his chest. "I don't have it *in* me. Nothing has changed. Astarian should have had several children by now. Why should I have to adjust my plans because he's been too slow to realize his?"

Edriss chewed on her bottom lip. "Astarian has no more desire to marry than you, Evra. His reasons might be different, but his repulsion for the task is no less real. He'll do it, anyway, because he must."

"You're defending him."

"I'm defending duty." Edriss cried out in pain, both hands tearing at the sheets. Soundless tears rolled down her cheeks while Evra looked for something, anything, to ease her. "Stop. There's nothing. They don't even send for the physicians anymore. Did you know that? Even my attendants do no more than sop cool water on my brow, as if that does anything other than make me wet."

"Duty," Evra said slowly, "is what has caused my sister to lie dying. If this is duty, Edriss, I want none of it."

"No, Ev," Edriss said. Her mouth twitched into another wince. "Duty is facing this and using it to birth the courage to do what you must."

"And what is it I must do?"

Edriss patted his knee. "I need rest."

Evra was tired, too. The day had been among his longest ones, and those following promised to be even longer. He should've

45

been finding his way back to his old chambers before one of the men, or even his brother, forced him into another conversation about duty.

Still, his feet found another path, to the place his grandmother had always called The Hanging Gardens, but Evra knew simply as the Ladies' Gardens. As a boy, it had been one of the few places that promised him freedom from the constant press of expectations.

As his feet left the stone, hitting dirt, he looked up. He'd always done this. He loved to watch the canopy of bowing blossoms as they closed in, leaving him feeling as if he'd entered another world. The sense that he was being drawn into a broad hug pulled him forward still until he could no longer smell the rotting stench of the Halls of Longwood at all.

He meandered past the row of palms, greeted by the trill of birdsong. Hibiscus and jasmine peppered the wave of bromeliads, and these were names he knew only because of Grandmother and Aunt Alise. Flowers that did not grow native in the Westerlands, all green and rain and deep soil. They didn't grow anywhere anymore, but the Blackrook women had cultivated them from something, many years past, and they maintained them still, today.

There'd been an entire chapter about this in his studies at Onyxcastle. The Blackrook chapters in *The Book of All Things* were long, and it was there he learned that there were many things about the women's garden at the Hall of Longwood that defied understanding.

"You've come. See, Alise? It's as I said."

"Mother," Alise answered, a word bloated with all the rest she didn't say.

Evra let his grandmother crush him into her still powerful embrace. Life and years had worn the Dowager Lady Blackrook down to flesh hanging upon bone. Her mind would be as keen as ever.

"They say Astarian is the prince of the realm, but that must only be because you've been locked away for so long," Meldred said, appraising him with a half-turn. "I say the more handsome son is Evrathedyn now. What say you, Alise?"

"I say it's what festers inside a man that makes him rotten."

Meldred rolled her eyes to Evra alone. "She did not inherit this bitterness from *me*."

"Why all the secrecy?" Evra asked. He rolled his palms out. "Why did you want to meet here and not in the keep?"

"Have you smelled the keep?" Alise countered.

"Well, if you want to be precise, Thedyn, the gardens are in the keep. They are in the very center of it."

"Evra, Grandmother. Please."

"Evra, then. We're both so happy to have you home, dear one. The Halls have not been the same without you. Have they, Alise?"

"No," Lady Alise said. "Not at all."

Evra watched the women warily. They had always been good to him. He didn't trust either of them. "Why am I here?"

Alise tilted her head. "In the garden?"

"In the Rush," Evra said, too tired to mask his impatience. "Nothing happens here that you two don't have some hand in."

"Your father never thought very much of women, and I fear Astarian has even less regard for us," Meldred said, not exactly answering.

"Astarian has very different reasons for that disregard," Alise muttered.

"Do the reasons matter when the outcome is the same?" Meldred asked, still sizing Evra up. "Astarian was right to send for you, no matter how it pains you. Oldcastle was never where you belonged."

Evra backed away. "All of you, then! All of you, one by one, taking your turn with me, pressing your guilt over me like a shroud. I might be here now, but my stay is temporary. As will marry, and when his heir is born, I'll leave." He scowled. "If I survive these attacks from all sides."

"What of your own bride?"

Evra laughed. "That will not be happening."

"You think they'd let you marry Meira then?"

Evra flushed. "I have no intentions to marry anyone. Ever." His mortification shifted to a frown. "They? Who's they?"

"You think my brother's death changes things?" Alise stepped forward. She twirled her jeweled wrists in the air. "That all these terrible things he's done just go away?"

"Nothing so terrible could ever just go away. No one will ever forget what the Blackrooks did to their own people," Evra retorted. His cheeks burned. "If I could, I'd surrender that name. I'd rather be no one than the son of such a man. The brother of one who will keep these fires burning because he knows no different."

"Yes, I suppose that was your intention, choosing the Scholar's Path," Meldred said coolly. "But that will not be your fate, Evrathedyn. It never was. Your time away has strengthened your wisdom and dulled your wits. You'll need both for the days ahead."

"I'll need nothing but my patience while I wait for Astarian to do the duty he should have done years ago."

The women exchanged a private look that sent his rage straight to his belly.

"Edriss is dying," Alise said. Nothing on her face betrayed the sadness of her words. "Will die. I tell you this not because Edriss' life should be valued above the thousands lost to Aeldred's ignorance, but because it seems hers is the only one you actually care about."

Evra's nose curled in anger. "That's not fair. I care about all those lost to Father's madness. But what good has that done? What good has caring ever done?"

"None, I would say, from your dark little room at the top of a tower," Meldred said with a short laugh. "And the Sepulchre, only a two days' ride from Oldcastle."

Evra's mouth formed a shocked oval. "You shouldn't say that here."

"The Sepulchre?" Alise repeated, louder. She looked at her mother. "We should listen carefully. Evra aims to tell us what we should and should not say here."

48

"You both seem quite confident that Astarian won't send your heads to join your friends. I don't share that confidence in how he'd deal with me." He turned to look over his shoulder. He didn't think this was a trap, but it *was* a test.

"As your aunt said, Edriss is dying. This Reach is dying. There is only one prevention for both, and none brave enough to address it," Meldred said. "None brave enough to repair what their elders have sundered."

"You're not suggesting..." Evra gripped his chin as he laughed. "Either I'd be executed by my people for even thinking it, or dealt with at the steps of the Sepulchre by the witches themselves. That would be a fitting vengeance for what the Blackrooks have done to them, though nowhere near in evening the score. And even... even if by the luck of the Guardians they spared me, there's not a chance in the world that they'd help me. And even, even *if* they agreed, which would go against all the odds in the realm, the moment they stepped across our borders, Astarian would come to right that wrong."

"Witch is an old word, used only by the fearful. They are Magi," his grandmother said, ignoring all the rest.

"Are you even listening?" Evra looked at his aunt. "Have the two of you been into the elderwine?"

"I'm listening," Alise said. "I hear you spending more words on rolling through this idea than you've spent on anything else thus far."

"I'm trying," Evra said, "not to get us all killed for speaking blasphemy in a Reach that lives and breathes for that very thing."

"There will be more needless death," Meldred answered. "I do not need a seer's magic to know more of that is coming. But every one is preventable."

"I don't even know what the two of you are asking me. There's no sense in it." Evra again checked to be sure no one had joined them. "I don't know why I'm here. I know nothing, except that if you really saw the potential in me to do good, then you've taken me from the one place I might accomplish it." He bowed first to his grandmother, then to his aunt. "I *am* happy to see you both. You remind me it wasn't all bad. Not all of it."

"Evra."

He backed away. "But any power I have now is for show. It was always for show. And so I will bide my time, the dutiful second, until I can once again fade back into the irrelevance I was made for."

SEVEN
THE GODS AND THEIR ANGER

Rhosyn watched the storm from the safety of the fogged panes. She ran the edges of her satin sleeve over the glass for a better look. Snow and ice beat relentless songs against layers of the same, for the ground here never thawed before the next tempest struck. There might even be snowbolts this evening. These she'd only seen from Midnight Crest, hurtling past like boulders launched from the skies. Her mother said they were the angry tears of the gods. Rhosyn was weary of being told about the gods and their anger.

Heavy steps boomed in the corridor. She turned toward the sound and saw Oswin Frost embarking on the arduous task of layering furs to protect from the cold. His wife, the stewardess, was finally sleeping for the night, as was everyone else in the keep. Rhosyn knew what drew the steward out; why he waited until his world was at rest. She knew because she understood the power of being alone.

"Steward?" Rhosyn pulled her cloak tighter as she approached. The shiver traveling down her back was prophetic. She'd already seen herself follow him outside.

51

"Ahh, Rhosyn." Oswin fastened the strap connecting the furs at his neck. He tugged at his hood to secure it. "Forgive my lack of proper greeting on your arrival. It's been at the back of my mind since yesterday, but that's no excuse."

"Nothing to forgive," Rhosyn answered, smiling. "I've been with the stewardess. There wasn't time for anything else."

His expression hardened. He hesitated before continuing his dressing. "And? How is she?"

"Stubborn," she said, and this elicited a quick twitch from the steward. Almost a grin.

"She is certainly that," he agreed. He knelt to lace his boots. "Otherwise?"

"I'll tell you what I told her. Her child is fine. She is not. But this is why I'm here, and I'll do all I can to keep her safe through confinement and delivery."

Oswin nodded without looking up. "The reverse of the last time, then. Why does this keep happening to her?"

"I cannot say why the stewardess has lost as many children as she's delivered. We've healed her as completely as we can between these terrible times, and yet each time new challenges rise. But her three living children are strong and healthy. I see no reason there could not be more if the gods will it." She shook her head. "My apologies. The Guardians."

Oswin used the bench to push himself up. "You have your deities. I don't ask that you believe in ours, even when within our walls." He stomped to drive his feet deeper into the boots. "Was there something else you wanted to tell me?"

"Yes, actually," Rhosyn said. "It's—"

"Come with me," he cut in. He reached for the piles of furs and tossed one to her, though they both knew she was made from the cold. "There's something I should discuss with you as well, and you'll prefer we do it away from the many ears. Sleeping or no."

Rhosyn hustled out the main doors and into the snow, staying close behind him so she wouldn't lose the path. The white walls of the growing squall closed in all around her, but Oswin Frost was

52

not encumbered by the onslaught. He navigated his way smoothly from memory, never losing his pace.

At last, he heaved a grunt and a wooden door pushed inward. He pressed his hand to her back to ease her inside, then turned to secure the entrance.

She'd been inside Steward Frost's private smithy only once before. This wasn't the workshop his professional armor smiths used. This was his alone, for late nights and solitude.

The heat from the forge, recently fired, welcomed her, and she dropped her fur on a nearby bench. Her eyes scanned for evidence of what he'd been working on.

"Armor for Rylan," Oswin said as he shed the layers he'd worn for only a couple of minutes. "He's old enough now, no matter what his mother says."

"At what age did you receive your first armor, Steward?"

"Four," he answered. "A year younger than Rylan. But I was too late for any battle. The last was when my father was young. Thorn's age."

"Your father has been to war?"

"Yes," he said, then said no more about it. "The stewardess, then?"

"Ah. Yes." Rhosyn pushed herself up onto the bench to sit. "I will do all I can with my healing to bring her through this."

"But?"

"But I must be cautious with how my magic is used. I use too much, and her body will attack the child."

"I already know this. What's your point?"

"As we've agreed, she is quite stubborn. Insists on keeping her hearth cold and the darkness close. I was hoping you might speak to her about these things. The less I have to use my magic to sustain her, the better. She makes it hard for me to find the right balance."

Oswin nodded, facing his anvil with a thoughtful look. "I'll do what I can."

"I also wondered if I might stay on longer. See your child through its first year, just to be certain."

"You're seeking my permission? You know you're always welcome here, Rhosyn."

"If Steward Frost makes a formal request of Midnight Crest, then they cannot refuse you."

Oswin turned. "You know Morwen is leaving soon? A fortnight. Two at most. Her groom will arrive soon and then it will be done."

Rhosyn swallowed hard. "I know. This isn't about Morwen."

Oswin leaned back against the anvil, propping himself by his hands. "I believe I know what it's about. It may be the same thing I called you here to discuss."

"Oh?"

"Your brother came to see me this evening before supper." Oswin's upper lip twisted in a sneer. "The foul one. Rendyr, is it?"

"He came *here*?" Rhosyn's chest fluttered. "He was here? Today?"

"Found me in the stables. Told me he'd like to speak to me as a man speaks to a man, which I thought was strange, mostly in how he said it. He doesn't think much of men, does he?"

"No." Rhosyn rolled her hands around the wood of the bench.

"Well. I don't pretend to know very much about your world. I have always said, let men do as men, let Ravenwoods do as Ravenwoods, and it will all sort itself out. Our alliance, if you want to call it that, depends on that mutual respect, even if understanding could never follow. Am I making sense?"

She managed to nod.

"So when Rendyr tells me you have duties in Midnight Crest that await you soon, there's little I can say. When he tells me you'll be the next High Priestess, I have no rebuttal, for I don't even know what that means. Not really."

"It won't happen," she replied, breathless, wanting to believe the lie as much as she hoped he did. "Arwenna will come through in the end."

"Pray that she does. For to think of a parent who could allow such a fate for their child..." Oswin cleared his head. "He will return. When, I cannot say, but I witnessed the determination in his eyes. It goes against..." He coughed. "I promised not to judge. Those are your ways, not ours."

"They shouldn't be our ways, either!" Rhosyn cried out. The well of emotion swirling from the steward's revelation erupted, pushing her off the bench. "Steward, you say you do not understand, and well, perhaps that's because it defies understanding! It defies reason, and honor, and words I do not yet know but hope to learn. Perhaps once, once it may have been the only way to protect our magic and our blood, but now? Now, it is merely a way to subjugate both things!"

Oswin sagged into his sad look. "Dear Rhosyn. I didn't bring you here to upset you. I only wanted you to know what was said and what will be expected."

"It's not you who upsets me. The Frosts are..." *The family I wish I had,* she nearly said, but to think of this was to wound herself further. "I have wanted nothing more than to leave it all behind. And now that I've confessed this treason to you, I suppose you'll have to tell him?"

Oswin's eyes widened. "Rendyr? No. It was all I could do not to take my bow and pluck him from the sky when he flew away."

Rhosyn's fear melted into confusion. "What are you saying?"

Oswin stepped closer, but left a careful distance between them. His smile was warm; what she imagined a father's smile might look like if she had one with desires above duty. "I would protect you from him, Rhosyn, for as long as I can. I see he means nothing good for you, and if I didn't believe it would start another war..." He shook his head. "I will protect you for as long as I can. You are bound to aid my wife, and your brother knows this. But when the child is born..."

Rhosyn dropped her eyes, nodding at the floor.

Oswin sighed. "Would that you were my daughter..."

55

She raised her head and met his eyes. "But I am not. Wishing for what would be has done me nothing but harm."

Oswin watched her in silence.

She straightened her back and wiped the rogue tears forming under her eyelids. "I have always known no one is coming to save me. No one could. Expecting otherwise is foolish, and I will need my strength about me for what's coming, won't I?"

EIGHT
OUR LEGACY

Evra had only just slipped into sleep when the sound of boots against stone pulled him alert. Straining against the darkness, he attempted in vain to see the cause, but only made out a shadow dancing across the far wall. He reached for his unlit lantern on the nightstand, hand falling on his sheathed dagger instead, but a familiar voice stayed him.

"It's only me," Astarian said. He sounded small, no more powerful than the desolate men who came to the Rush seeking their aid. Wood creaked across the stone as he settled into a chair.

"What are you doing here in the middle of the night?" Evra blinked, eyes adjusting to the darkness. "And why are you sitting all the way over there?"

"You think I don't understand why you'd prefer the life you chose? Over the life you have here?" Astarian slurred. "You think you and I are so different."

"Are you in your cups?"

"I have always envied you, Thedyn. Always. You've known freedom in ways Father and I could never know."

Evra pulled himself up against the wooden headboard. He was awake now and could just make out the shape of his brother, slumped in the chair. "Freedom in having no authority, no influence is not the freedom you would desire, As."

"We don't even know each other anymore."

"We never did." Evra sighed. "You were always looking to the future, even as a boy."

"Have you been into the fields?"

"I haven't left the keep. You know that."

"The Whispering Wood used to come right up against the back of the Halls of Longwood. Trees tickled the stone walls. Do you remember how Father scolded the arborists for not cutting them back? Said it caused rot on the stone, though I don't think it did. Even on the parapets, you couldn't see beyond the forest. Do you even remember that? My children, your children, they'll never see beyond the fractured stumps. Those trees will take generations to again rise."

The stench of liquor mingled with sweat, both fresh and old, made its way to Evra. He knew he should say something to that drunken outpouring, but no words seemed right. He wondered if Astarian even knew where he was or how he'd found himself here.

"Nothing will ever be the same again. No matter what I do," he went on. "No matter what I do, this is our legacy."

Evra found his voice, groaning his frustration. It echoed off the walls. "Do you hear yourself? Nothing you can do?"

"You don't understand. You never did."

"How could I understand such nonsense?" Evra threw the covers back and started toward his brother, but Astarian jumped up.

"No! Don't come closer."

Evra eased back onto the bed with an eye roll. "There's no hiding your drunkenness. You could smell it in Wildwood Falls."

"You don't understand, *Evra*, because you haven't seen that the monster Father summoned is bigger than one man. He wasn't alone in burning our citizens! In pulling wives and children from beds by moonlight and sending them to the pyres, screaming! Do you not think that if it was as simple as *stopping* him, that his council wouldn't have been capable of doing exactly that?"

"Then you're suggesting Father was weak, for a council is just that. Steward Tyndall is not the Lord of the Westerlands. Steward Bristol is not the Lord of the Westerlands."

"Then you do not understand power, either," Astarian said, finishing his words with a soft sigh. "It is neither built on the back of one man, nor sustained by him."

"So get new men, As!" Evra wrinkled his blanket in his fists. He wanted to sleep. Only there could he be free of the madness that had fallen over the Westerlands. "They only have power if you give it to them!"

"You understand so little. And yet..." Astarian's voice choked. "Yet you would do that, wouldn't you? You'd release them all, not a whit of care for the revolt that would follow. The civil war it would cause. You might even prevail, and lay a fresh path for the Westerlands."

"It doesn't matter what I would do," Evra answered. "Only what you *will* do, Astarian."

"What I will do..." Astarian sighed. He ran his fist over his nose. "You're right. It's late."

"I won't marry Kindra Bristol, As," Evra said, finding his boldness in his brother's declining state. "I'll stay until you have a son, but then I'm leaving. You were born to this, and I was born to something else. I will stay to ease your mind as you build your own legacy, but not a day longer than I must."

"Good night, then, brother." Astarian tapped his knuckles twice against the stone, then stumbled out into the hall.

Evra's dreams that night were filled with women.

Edriss. Seven. Aunt Alise. Meira. Grandmother Meldred.

In a world ruled by men, it had been the women he'd taken his wisdom from. The women who understood what must be done, even if they possessed nothing greater than the desire for change.

Edriss. *Duty is facing my death and using it to birth the courage to do what you must.*

Seven. *You could sail to Beyond, and you'd still never be able to run from who you are.*

Aunt Alise. *Edriss is dying. Will die. I tell you this not because Edriss' life should be valued above the thousands lost to Aeldred's ignorance, but because it seems hers is the only one you actually care about.*

Meira. *You don't know what it's been like since you left. Most of us had no choice but to stay.*

Grandmother. *Your time away has strengthened your wisdom and dulled your wits. You'll need both for the days ahead.*

Together, circling him, repeating their words, their decrees on his character, his resolve, his courage. Their words, blending, until he could no longer discern one aspersion from another; until they were unified in their message, hands linked, closing the circle as his past and future came together to suffocate him.

Evra screamed, but the sound died in their embrace.

He was again thrust into consciousness by an intrusion, but this time it wasn't Astarian.

Many voices trickled in around him. At least a dozen, but enough that he had no grasp on the count. They shuffled into his chambers, whispering their words. Like the women in his dream, everything ran together, and as he struggled to sit, to wake, it wasn't their words at all that brought the situation to clarity.

He sat just as the men circling his bed dropped to their knees in uneven synchronicity.

"All hail Lord Evrathedyn, Lord of the Westerlands, Champion of the Rush, Father of the Western Reach! All hail Lord Evrathedyn, Lord of the Westerlands, Champion of the Rush, Father of the Western Reach! All hail…" Their words continued, droning on in refrain as the air left the room, his lungs.

"What? What is this?" He started to ask if this was a dream, but he knew it was not. Not even his nightmares brought such painful lucidity. "Someone tell me!"

Steward Bristol looked up from their reverent chant. The candlelight lit his macabre grin. "It is with great sorrow I tell you your brother, Lord Astarian, spent his promise in the night."

"No," Evra whispered. He choked on his next rebuttal. "No!"

"...Lord of the Westerlands, Champion of the Rush..."

"NO!" At last, it came out as a scream.

"We are ever so sorry for your loss, my lord," Bristol said, fading away into the sea of chanters, becoming one with the growing horror surrounding Evra's bed.

"...Father of the Western Reach! All hail Lord Evrathedyn, Lord of the Westerlands..."

Evra pressed his face into his hands, and, this time, his scream found its way.

SO FAR NORTH
OF ANYTHING GREEN

NINE
THE ESTEEMED COUNCIL

I really don't think this is a good idea, Evra," Meira whispered as he nudged her forth into his father's Council Chambers. He hung behind her a half-step, wearing her like a shield. Her groan traveled back to him. "We haven't even started and they're already whispering about me."

"Doesn't take a council meeting to make men whisper about a female Rush Rider."

"Your true feelings emerge." Meira aimed herself to the back of the room, to find a chair beyond the table, but Evra navigated her back to the center. He stayed behind her, steeling himself to face the men who already thought they knew him and would treat him according to that fractured knowledge.

"You're tougher than all the men in this room put together, Meira. They know it, and they'll never abide it."

"They have no choice but to abide me as Rider. But they'll never abide me as your counselor."

"Also not their choice," Evra said, shooting her a quick, tight smile over his shoulder. He'd forgotten how cavernous the room was. He'd last seen it as a small boy, weaving through the legs of what he once thought to be great men. Both views had come so far since.

"Wherever is our new lord?" Roland Ashenhurst quipped. "Surely that cannot be him, bearing such curves?" Roland ran his hands down his sides with a seductive glare.

Evra felt Meira tense. In his mind's eye, he saw her face darken at her father's cruel words.

"Ignore him," Evra said as he peeled out from behind her and took his seat. It was then he saw there wasn't another one for her, so he got up again, while she waited, stuck out in evaluation by the incredulous, mocking stares of the leading men of the Reach.

Someone beat him to the chair he reached for. He looked up to see Thennwyr Blackfen, the famed First Rider of the Rush. The noonday light streaming through the tall windows lit his silver and crimson armor. His dark hair fell in waves from the thin rope holding it back.

"I'll get another, Rider," Evra said, avoiding looking directly into the man's gleaming face. At least he thought it was gleaming. Time had only deepened his awe of the infamous Blackfen clan.

"For Rider Ashenhurst, my lord," Thennwyr answered, pushing the chair to Evra. He returned to the table without another word.

Wood screeching against stone was the only sound in the vast room as he pushed the chair to the table. Meira's small, uncomfortable sigh tore at his heart more than the disapproving looks from the men of the Great Families.

When at last they were all seated, Evra's eyes traveled an anxious path across the long table, pausing on faces that had been a part of the tapestry of his life. He didn't really *know* any of them. He never had. His father's men were now his men, but their assuming presence was a fear, not a comfort.

"She's not leaving?" Leonarde Bristol asked before Evra could find the right words.

"M... Rider Ashenhurst?" Evra asked innocently. His impertinent grin didn't match the churning in his belly. To speak to this man, in this way. *You're the lord now. Get over it.*

Leonarde turned to Roland. "You'll deal with this?"

Roland grimaced. He braced the table and pushed back, but Evra shook his head.

"No, Steward Ashenhurst will not be dealing with anything. It's not his matter to deal with. As Lord, I can choose my council, and Rider Ashenhurst is my first choice. Pray that when I am done choosing, you are all still sitting here."

Where had these words come from?

He would pay for this boldness later.

Evra choked down a gulp.

"But she's a woman, my Lord," Lewin Wakesell said with a weary sigh.

"Is she? I hadn't noticed."

"And we already have a Rider on your council."

"Is there a rule saying there can be only one?"

"No rule, no, no. Only we're already at our proper count. You will have to remove one of us to add her, or there will be one too many. And these are men who have served this Reach all their lives. Who have served your father since they were boys."

Ten councilmen, the lord the tie-breaker. He remembered now. With gladness in his heart, he went to train his gaze on the oily Leonarde, to dismiss him, but this was not a man he wanted as his enemy. Instead, his eyes traveled to Oliver Richland. "Steward Richland."

Richland threw his hands up and shoved back from the table. He looked at the others for help, but they'd all become fascinated with the dirt under their nails or the sunbeams traveling in lines across the floor.

"Do you really believe it is wise to discard of seasoned men when your hour has only begun?" Richland asked from the other end of the table. "When you have not even *lived* in this Reach for most of your life?"

67

"Seasoned men have let this Reach burn and die," Evra answered.

"And your ignorance will see it reduced to ash and wind!"

"Thank you for sharing your premonition with us all. Should we take that to mean you yourself are gifted with the magic required to possibly know such a thing?"

Richland's pounding boots echoed, followed by the slam of the door.

Thennwyr Blackfen didn't hide his grin as he watched the scene unfold and abruptly end.

None of this felt like a victory. In the end, Evra was still seated at the head of his father's table, taking on his father's burdens. Astarian was gone. There was no one else. Even if Edriss wasn't so ill, they'd never accept a woman running the Westerlands.

"*Well*, my lord?" Bristol asked, hands out. His slow blink was maddening.

Evra looked at Meira for help, but she was gazing at her lap.

"I want..." Evra cleared his throat. He needed something to wet his mouth. "We will speak of the troubles plaguing our Reach."

"Clever," Tedric Blackwell said, tapping his head. "Plaguing. My lord has a sense of humor." Some of the others laughed with him.

"I..." This couldn't be what the Guardians intended. Perhaps he would wake later, in his bed at university, and tell Seven about this awful dream that went on far too long. "Cleverness wasn't my intention, Steward Blackwell. For how could any of this be mistaken for amusing? The bones littering our forests and fields are our own people. We've either allowed them all to die or sent them to the pyres ourselves. If there's humor in that, I cannot see it."

"You're still so young," Bristol said with, Evra imagined, the same voice he used with his daughters. "How could you see it as we do? You've only just assumed this mantle, when we, all of us, have been fighting these battles for many years now."

Evra's cheeks flamed. "If experience makes what's happening in the Westerlands amusing, then I'm glad of my lack of it."

68

Bristol and Ashenhurst exchanged knowing looks, joined by most of the others. But Thennwyr wasn't smiling, and neither was Rohan James.

"The burnings will stop," Evra said, sitting taller. "Immediately."

"No," Bristol said, no longer smiling. "They will not."

"Excuse me?"

"The burnings will continue until magic has been eradicated from within our borders."

Evra almost laughed. "There are almost no people left within our borders, magic or no!"

"Then let us scorch this earth and begin anew."

Evra gaped at him. At all of those nodding along to this madness.

Meira finally looked up. "Lord Blackrook is not asking us to stop the fires. He's ordering us. As our lord, we follow his lead, not yours."

"Know your place, girl," her father barked. "Not that I'd expect you to grasp it, seeing as you've lost your way and stumbled into where you don't belong."

Meira's nostrils flared as she leveled a brave look at Roland. "My place is where Lord Blackrook says it is."

"And what of this plague raging unabated?" Osman Derry asked. "What is your plan, my lord, to return us to the good graces of the Guardians, to end this sickness?"

"The good graces?" Evra repeated, incredulous. "Not burning alive their creations might be a fair start!"

"The Northerlands have no plague." Thennwyr broke his silence, speaking in a low but commanding tenor that turned all heads his way. "The Easterlands have no plague. Even the fool-hearted Southerlands have eradicated it. There is only one thing they all have in common."

Roland rolled his eyes. "Heathens. All of them. Is that the reputation we want?"

"A sight fairer than the one we have."

"It isn't too late to make amends with the Sepulchre," Rohan joined in, emboldened by Thennwyr's declaration. "We're too late to save Lord Aeldred and Lord Astarian, but we might still spare others. What happens if Lord Thedyn follows them?"

"It is blasphemy to even suggest such a thing," Leonarde chastised. "To even *think* it. And if the Guardians will these losses, then... so be it."

"Madness," Rohan hissed. "When does it end?"

Leonarde licked his oily lips. "When the Guardians—"

"I answer not only to the Guardians, but to my conscience," Evra announced as he jumped to his feet. He watched the men watching him; sizing him up in their judgment, that was both fair and not. But all of them, even the reasonable Thennwyr and Rohan, saw in him a malleable boy, ready to be shaped to their agenda. While he may not know how to lead this Reach, he would twine himself to his own pyre before allowing them to turn him into their puppet. "The burnings stop. Today. Right now." He turned to Rohan. "I'll see you personally responsible for spreading this message, Steward James. Rider Blackfen can help you get the word out."

Rohan nodded. Evra thought he saw relief in his eyes as he bowed his head.

"As to the plague, I will let you all know once I've decided a way forward."

Bristol laughed. "Did your father teach you nothing?" He gestured around him. "This Reach does not answer to one man alone."

"No," Evra agreed. His skin tingled from head to toe. Fear flamed in his chest. He'd shown them he would not be so easily controlled, but there'd be a price. "But when I have further need of this esteemed council, I will call upon you."

"And my daughter? When will you call upon her?"

"I will not be calling upon her at all," Evra said. He stood. "The council is excused."

"Evra, wait!"

Should he have been surprised that Meira was the only one to follow him? That the rest had let him leave? They stayed to conspire against him. Of course they did. They'd started this on their way to his chambers to share the terrible news about his brother, and they'd taken no reprieve from it since.

Evra burst into the gardens and as the air reached his chest, he inhaled, throwing his head back. He panted through the floral assault, slowly returning to calm.

"What happened in there?" she asked. She spun around to the front of him, taking him by the shoulders. "Talk to me."

"They're complicit in these horrors," he managed as his breaths evened out. "All of them!"

"Most of them," Meira agreed. She let her hands fall away. "They thought they could control you, but they know better now. You made sure they knew better. Though I fear that won't work out as you hoped."

"As I hoped?" Evra shook his hand at the door leading back into the keep. "Nothing, *nothing* has gone as I've hoped, Meira!"

"All right, then. You don't have to throw a tantrum about it."

Evra's jaw dropped.

"Pick your face up. It'll freeze that way, my mother always said. And anyway, it won't do to sulk around amongst your grandmother's flowers."

"Sulk," Evra repeated. "You think I'm sulking?"

"I *know* you're sulking, and while you have every reason to, it will not serve you. Will it?"

"You're supposed to be my friend!"

"And you're supposed to be a lord now," Meira countered. "Standing up to tyrant men was a bold move, but it's not the one you need to take, is it?"

"What does that even mean? You think I should dismiss them all, make a new council with the rest of my childhood friends?"

"Not unless you want war," she answered evenly. "No, Evra. What it means is that if you want to fix what's broken, you cannot do it from here. You cannot do it with those men breathing down your neck, and then going back to the shadows, working against you. You think you've stopped the burnings? No. You've only encouraged them to be more devious about it."

"If not here, then where?"

Meira dropped her voice. "There was sense in what Rohan James suggested."

Evra stumbled back several steps. "The Sepulchre? You cannot be serious."

"I am serious. Very serious. There is no end to this plague without magic. The other Reaches know this, and they no longer suffer. The Sepulchre can help us restore the right balance."

"If you think dismissing those men will start a war, just what do you think consorting with our enemy will bring us?"

"*Their* enemy, Evra. Do not forget who you are."

"I think no better of magic than they do," he protested.

"You may not understand it, nor trust it," Meira answered. "But you would never harm someone for the practice of it."

"Of course not."

"Then what is the problem?"

He threw his hands up. "My only allies are you, Steward James, *maybe* Rider Blackfen, and the devious Blackrook women whispering in my ear."

"Wise women," Meira said with a grin.

"I can't do it."

"You won't do it," she corrected.

"Fine." Evra furrowed his brows. "I won't do it. If it makes you feel better to parade my flaws before me, then let us get it all out there. I'm a coward. A fool. And I'm not cut out for this."

"All right."

"All right?"

"Are you done?"

Evra sputtered.

"There is another way. A coward's way, I suppose, but if it saves your people, does it matter?"

"Say it already."

"You've heard of the Ravenwoods, I assume?"

Evra leaned against a trellis of brilliant orange flowers he didn't know the name of. "Heathens."

"You know who you sound like?"

"They're not even men, Meira. They fly around the mountains raining death, and the North protects them."

Meira pressed her hands to her mouth in a poor attempt to stifle her laugh. "You really believe that, don't you?"

"Don't act like you know any better than I do. When have you been that far north?"

"Never," she said. "But I know better than to listen to the same men who would destroy every inch of our Reach with their intolerance."

"So? What about the evil heathen sorcerers?"

Meira lifted one shoulder in a shrug. "You're probably right that the council would turn against you if you made peace with the Sepulchre. And if you tried to solicit what magic is left within our borders, no one would trust your intentions. No one would ever come forward to such a request. But what if you brought magic back to the Westerlands without them knowing?"

Evra shook his head. "We may as well send a summons into the Beyond, to the mythical Amberwood witches of Salvius, for as sensical as that is!"

"I'm serious."

"This is insane, Meira. You know that, don't you?"

"It's not the worst idea we have, is it?"

"It's a death sentence for whoever we bring."

"Only if they're expecting it. If they know about it."

"So, you're suggesting..." Evra pushed away from the flowers and paced. "That we go, we demand their help, and—"

"Demand? No, Evra. We demand nothing. We—"

"Borrow, then. We offer something they want in return. Whatever that might be... who knows with the sort they are. They come back, they quietly and secretly heal the Westerlands, and then all is well. No one is the wiser." He turned back toward

Meira, but the dark expression she wore chilled his growing excitement. "What?"

"Nothing," she said, avoiding his eyes. "It's a good plan."

"So you'll go north and take one of them? Sorry... borrow?"

"Me? No, Evra. That won't do at all. If you want their aid, it's you who must go. You must ask them yourself, as the lord of this land. You cannot leave this to anyone else."

"And abandon the Reach into the hands of those assassins? There'll be nothing left to return to."

"Leave the Reach in the hands of the men more likely to abide by your wishes. Steward James. Rider Blackfen."

"And you."

Meira finally smiled. "I didn't say I wouldn't go at all. Who else is going to protect you when you invariably insult the evil death-raining heathens?"

Evra went to say goodbye to his sister, but she wasn't alone.

Thennwyr sat at her bedsides, pressing one of her hands between both his palms. Tears sliced down his cheeks.

"I'm sorry... I didn't mean..." Evra started to say.

The Rider dropped Edriss' hand and stood, affording Evra the proper bow. "My lord."

"It's fine, Thennwyr. You can sit. I'll go."

"I wouldn't think of it," Thennwyr answered, aiming one last look at Edriss before slipping away.

Evra was reminded of the old rumors of his mother, Lady Fyana, and the Rider. Meira liked to say rumors were only that, but Evra had seen the birth of many himself. They always began somewhere real.

"What was that about?"

Edriss buried her cheek in the soft pillow. Her tears stained the linen. "Don't be daft. You know. Everyone knows."

"I know nothing, as my council is all too quick to point out."

74

"You know more than you'd like others to think you do, for then it would mean you might actually have to be good at leading, wouldn't it?"

"Don't make yourself sicker with all that venom in you."

"You're leaving," Edriss charged. "And you've come to say goodbye."

"How did you..." Evra swallowed. He knew the answer. "Please, Edriss, I beg you. Tell no one here what you can do. I can't protect you if I'm not here."

"As if I haven't been doing that already, all this time?" Edriss' cracked lips formed a smile. "I have bigger threats awaiting me than weak men like Leonarde Bristol. Though what will he say, Evra, when his beloved Kindra arrives and her groom is not here?"

"She's already here. And I'll never marry a Bristol. I told him as much myself in the council meeting, though I doubt he believed me," Evra returned. "You can tell him whatever you like. Tell him he's a boorish twat for all I care."

Edriss grinned deeper. "You shouldn't tempt me with such delicious thoughts." She grew more serious. "You will be careful, won't you? The Ravenwoods, they're not like us. But then, nor are the men of the Northern Reach. But they're not *beneath* us, Evra. And you mustn't let them think that's how you see them."

"You think I can't act right when the situation demands it?"

"I think you've left no one confused about how you see them."

Evra scoffed. He took her tear-stained hand and brought it to his mouth. "I will do *whatever* it takes to bring one back with me so that I can restore you to the way you were."

"Good." She nodded. "But not for me. For the Reach. You might believe a cruel twist of fate brought you to be our Lord of the Rush, but you're the only one who can change the path we're on. And I need you to remember this when you're stuck in your head, or feeling sorry for yourself, for there is *nothing* more important than you getting over yourself. Thousands of lives depend on you putting your boyhood behind you and stepping into the man you're to become."

An attendant helped Evra into his saddle. He watched Meira scale her own mare with effortless ease. Frowned.

"Are you certain you don't want to bring a more robust guard?" Meira asked him as she settled in. "It isn't too late to saddle up more Riders." She sighed. "Actual Riders, ones who've passed their trials?"

Evra shook his head. He threw his gaze over his shoulder, toward the Halls of Longwood. His grandmother and aunt watched him depart. They offered only a wave. "This is my burden." He rotated forward in his saddle and grinned at her. "And it was your idea, so now it's yours, too."

Meira settled into a smile. "Ah, well, I *have* always wanted to see the Wintergarden at Wulfsgate."

TEN
THE BITTER WOOD

"They say Dunwoode rarely gets snowfall, except deep in Midwinter. That it's sometimes even *warm*," Morwen was saying. They rode side by side through the narrow path that meandered The Bitter Wood. Or, Rhosyn thought, as she struggled not to slide off the horse Morwen had chosen for her, Morwen was riding, and she was spending the entirety of her focus on survival. But even hanging half off her horse, this was the happiest Rhosyn had been since she'd last spent time with the Frosts.

"Have you been there?" Rhosyn asked. She slid from one side to the other as her horse traveled with an uneven gait. Her knuckles reddened and then paled as she gripped the front of her saddle, holding her breath in hopes it might slow her inevitable fall. Her father had once said that only those not blessed with wings had the misfortune of riding other beasts.

"To Dunwoode? No." Morwen shook her head. Her dark waves fell down the back of her sapphire gown. "I've never been farther south than Wulfsgate. My father has, though. He said it's a lively town, being a border stronghold and all. They have fairs every fortnight, that men from other Reaches actually travel up to attend. Can you believe that? Men and women from the Westerlands and Easterlands, coming up here?" She affected an overly serious look. "The Haddenfoots have defended the Northerlands for centuries. It will be an honor to wed their future lord and bring a new generation of stalwart defenders."

"If I didn't know you better, I'd say those words were mere recitation."

"Really, Rhosyn. You cannot sit like that. Watch me. Yes, like this. Who taught you to ride? Those stirrups aren't for decoration, you know!"

"You taught me to ride," Rhosyn shot back, grinning. It felt good to smile. It felt good to *sleep*. Now that she'd gotten more adept at blocking Rendyr's nocturnal intrusions, she greeted her mornings rested and ready to face the day ahead. "Remember?"

"Me? Oh, well, that was your first mistake. I'm a *terrible* teacher." They laughed together. "I suppose they are recitations. I only have my father's word to see me into my future. He says Edelard is a comely young man, and what can I do but trust that? What would he know about it, anyway? He only has eyes for the chambermaids, and the Weatherford girl who brings us our furs twice a season."

"When does he arrive? Your Edelard?" Rhosyn had forgotten her habit of counting the hours, now that she was happy to exist within them. Had she been here days? Or was it weeks? When had Morwen's mother warned her off?

"*My* Edelard?" Morwen shook her head. "He sent a raven that he was on his way from Dunwoode a week ago, so he will either be here in a week or two, or perhaps three, depending on the weather in the Pass. If the Guardians still look fondly upon me, he'll get held up until springtide."

Rhosyn laughed. "I thought you wanted to be a wife and mother."

"Oh, I do. I very much do, but..." Morwen turned to her. Rhosyn was astounded at her ability to even do basic things in the saddle when it was all Rhosyn could do not to flip upside down. "It's only that I didn't expect to have this time with you again." She reached for Rhosyn's hand, but Rhosyn twitched her head in terrified rebuttal. "You silly girl. You're overthinking it. Riding's really not as hard as you're making it."

"This will be the last time I'm sent here," Rhosyn said. Her groan was a victorious one this time, as she found some temporary balance. "When I leave this time, my return to Midnight Crest will be a final one. Don't delay your happiness on my account, Morwen. I would never want that for you."

Morwen flipped her head back to face the forest path. "You could always come with me, you know."

Rhosyn groaned. "Not this again."

"I mean it!"

"And be what? Your lady's maid?"

"Rhosyn!"

"Your husband's plaything?"

"Why are you being like this?"

Rhosyn winced as she tugged a little too hard on the reins to slow her horse. "Because, Morwen! Fantasizing about what might be has never done me any service but sorrow. Do you not think I'd love to spend the rest of my days at your side, whispering into the night like we did when we were girls? Do you not think I'd escape what awaits me if I could? Do you think there isn't an hour that passes where I'm not wholly aware of my limitations?"

Morwen dropped her eyes. "I'm sorry."

"Don't be sorry," Rhosyn said, softening. "Enjoy with me what time we have. For I am. And it would hurt my heart if you were spending this same time thinking of what will be, instead of living here, in the moment, with me."

"Then I shall not waste another second in worry." Morwen lifted her face to the fresh sunlight spilling through the trees. "Though my bones are ice, it really is a lovely day, isn't it?"

79

Rhosyn followed her gaze. She closed her eyes, letting the momentary warmth wash over her face. "The loveliest."

Morwen picked the most wonderful spot for their picnic, a small knoll in a break of the forest. A canopy of trees bowed in to provide a reprieve from the snow, and this was where they laid their blanket down and passed around the food Morwen herself had prepared. That was another marvel of this world. Rhosyn had never even poured her own carafe of wine until she'd stayed with the Frosts.

"You look especially happy today," Morwen noted after her first glass of the garnet liquid. "There's a flush in your cheeks that wasn't there before."

Rhosyn nodded. She fell back on the blanket, staring up at the sky. It would storm later. But for now, it was only them and their refuge away from the rest of the world. "My magic regains strength the longer I'm here. It's as if... as if I have to relearn it when I'm away from Midnight Crest and The Rookery. But my nights are peaceful again, now that I've shut him out."

"I overheard Father telling Thorn that your brother came down here. Twice."

"Steward Oswin only told me about once."

"Father wasn't having any of it. He reminded Rendyr, once more, that you were here fulfilling your duty under the alliance, and that to send you home before completion of this duty would invite something unwise. That if he returned, we'd have no choice but to feel as if it was harassment."

Rhosyn grinned. "Your father is a good man. He's brave, standing up to my brother like that. No one else does."

"Or a fool." Morwen sighed with a shrug. "How long do you think Mother has?"

"Not long."

"Then let us—" Morwen's mouth stretched wide, her eyes following. Rhosyn felt the shadow before she saw it fall over the blanket. She flexed her fists and prepared to rise.

"Arwenna," Morwen whispered. "It's been so long, I nearly didn't recognize you! Although, I suppose there's no mistaking a Ravenwood, is there?"

Rhosyn rolled over and pushed to her knees. "What are you doing here?" This wasn't right. Something wasn't right.

Arwenna's harried eyes traveled between the two girls. Her chest rose and fell with fraught breaths. Rhosyn's dread deepened. "Morwen, it really is nice to see you, one last time. Steward Frost tells me you're to be married, and I wish you all the joy that can bring and none of the sorrow."

Morwen started to thank her, but the words died.

"Would it trouble you too much if I were to ask for a moment alone with my sister?"

"No, no, of course not." Morwen pushed to her feet, swaying from the wine. "I'll just... I'll just be..." She stumbled off the blanket, pointing into the forest.

Arwenna smiled long enough for Morwen to disappear. When she turned her face back to Rhosyn, a truth was etched so deep that Rhosyn almost screamed for her not to say it.

"It's time," she said. She reached for Rhosyn's hands. "And I will ask you, my sister, to not fill my head with pretty lies. These are our ways, and not even Mother has the power to stand against them."

"It's Rendyr," Rhosyn hissed. She backed away, dropping her sister's hands. "He wanted this. He *wanted* you to fail. He has issued your death warrant!"

Arwenna let her hood fall back. She shook her head. "He was biding his time for you, the silver-haired witch. The once in a century wonder. The real prize. But I fear the truth runs deeper than that."

"What are you saying?" Rhosyn's heart thrummed against her chest.

"Rendyr doesn't want to father a child with us, Rhosyn, and stand dutifully at our side as High Priest. He wants to stand where we do. He would bring down every woman in Midnight Crest to satisfy his desire for power."

"What does Mother say?"

"What *can* Mother say?"

"No! They cannot just throw you out like refuse, Arwenna! I don't care what tradition says! That's utter madness!"

Arwenna drew in a long, steadying sigh. "And this is what I have come to tell you. To say goodbye, Rhosynora, and to warn you. But also to give you one last promise of hope. Mother has shown me the magic I need to counter hers when she clips my wings, and I stand before our blood to accept my failure. They will heave me over the balustrades, like the traitor they perceive me to be, but when I am clear of the clouds, I will fly once more. And I will fly *away from here and never return.*"

Rhosyn's mouth snapped closed. Her sputtered objections lived at the back of her throat.

"Mother never had the power to stop it. But she can send me forth into a new life."

"Where... where will you go?"

Arwenna shrugged. "I cannot say. And I wouldn't tell you, for Rendyr has uninhibited access to your thoughts, doesn't he?"

"Not anymore. Not here." Beads of sweat pricked the flesh of her neck, traveling down. "But he also has access to yours. He'll know you've tricked him."

"Eventually," Arwenna said. "But not quick enough to do anything about it. By the time he realizes my thoughts haven't ended with me, I will be clear of the Northerlands and his range. I'll start a new life, somewhere, with an unremarkable name. Perhaps I'll work in the kitchens, or be the maid of some great lady." Her smile stretched across her face. "I mean that. I can think of nothing better than being the woman who blends into the tapestries, whose name no one can remember."

Rhosyn ran through her objections, but each one collapsed. Did it matter how Arwenna had left, as long as she was gone? As long as Rendyr still had what he most wanted?

"Come with me," Arwenna pleaded. "You could go ahead of me, find a place for us, while I await my sentence. We could start a new life together!"

Rhosyn's heart broke in between the spaces of each of her sister's hopeful words. What she wouldn't give for this future! The two of them, sisters in more than blood, finding their path in their freedom.

She shook her head, her sadness deepening with every back and forth pass. "He might not risk his life to follow you. But without me, he'll be nothing. He would burn these lands from mountain to sea. He would bring war to us, to them, and destroy everything."

Arwenna didn't insult her with objections. They both knew the truth. Arwenna had known it before asking, but some pleas had to be made.

Rhosyn folded herself into her older sister's arms. In another world, another life, they could have been so much more to each other.

Arwenna kissed the top of her head. "If you ever find yourself free of this life, come and find me, Rhosyn. I will save you a place at whatever table I build."

Rhosyn watched her sister erupt into feathers and soar away to meet her fate.

"Rhosyn?" Morwen sounded timid as she crunched through the snow just beyond their hill. "Is everything okay?"

"No," she whispered, falling into this truth. "We should get back."

84

ELEVEN
WULFSGATE

Meira had never seen such snow. She'd heard about the endless winters of the north, but that was not the same as being immersed in miles of nothing, a sea of white and the occasional peek of green from the tops of the tallest trees she'd ever seen. Evra's chattiness waned more and more as they left the verdant landscapes behind, but she'd also turned her thoughts inward.

It started as soon as they'd hit the east-west Compass Road bisecting the Westerlands from the Hinterlands. Once they'd angled north, there was no longer much of interest to sway their attentions, and it wasn't until they hit Dunwoode that they'd even set eyes upon another town. They'd passed a night there before making the final push to Wulfsgate.

"You've said little since last night's supper," she offered once Dunwoode was behind them. The only thing worse than empty conversation was none.

"My words only get swallowed by the snow," Evra grumbled. She could hardly hear him, because he was right. The snow had a way of absorbing everything around it.

"I hope you've saved some for Lord Dereham. I told you we should have sent word ahead that we were coming. He might not even be there."

Evra waved a gloved hand around. "And just where is he gonna go in this?"

"They're used to it. It's what they know. If they waited for the snow to clear, they'd never go anywhere."

He shivered, hunkering lower on his horse. "Don't worry, Meira. I'll know what to say when we get there."

"I'm glad to hear it." Meira pointed ahead. Through the squall, a set of massive gates welcomed them. "Because we're there."

"About damn time," he muttered, though she didn't miss the hint of fear lifting the edges of his tone.

Evra grew smaller away from home. Gone was the bold young man who'd faced down his nefarious council. He was once again the little Evra she remembered playing with in the River Rush, fashioning swords out of branches and daring one another to eat suspicious berries before they both lost their nerve and moved on to some other new challenge.

Though it was not this little Evra who flushed so dark last night in the inn when he'd turned away to let her change into her nightclothes. She was still getting to know *him*.

Wulfsgate was a proper town, smaller than Longwood Rush but busier. Commerce greeted them immediately upon passage through the tall gates, stalls teeming with dozens of different wares and just as many eager buyers. No sooner than they cleared the gates did her mouth water at the rich scents of meat and baking bread, rendering her dizzy in her hunger. This welcome sensation was beset by the acrid stench of hot metal forged into weapons and armor, becoming more pungent as they passed slowly by what would be the first of many armories in the Northerland capital.

In their Longwood regalia, they didn't blend in at all. They might as well be running through town splashing colored dyes in the dirtied snow to mark their arrival. Men, women, and children bundled into their furs and layers watched them in guarded curiosity. Some smiled. Most pushed their carts or children along a little faster. She heard one woman whisper to another, *witch burners.*

The north were once their allies. It was the Westerlands' fault this was no longer so.

They needed no sign to direct them to Wulfsgate Keep. It sat upon the tallest hill in the capital, a vast but practical stronghold of dark stone, topped in a fine mist. Smoke from the kitchens sent dark plumes spiraling into the air, disappearing into the low cloud cover.

Neither commented on their turn down the upward path leading them to the stronghold of the Derehams. Meira hoped Evra was carefully revisiting his strategy because if he had nothing of use to say, their journey would meet an abrupt end. Dryden Dereham's reputation did not include a penchant for patience.

At their approach, four guards stepped forth in a line before the gate.

"I hope you're ready," she said.

She trusted she didn't imagine Evra nodding from her side.

Evra and Meira accepted the steaming mugs of cider with palpable gratitude. Evra lowered his face over his drink, as if it possessed the power to warm him straight to his chilled bones. He had another reason for keeping his eyes to himself, as he tried to ignore the suspicious glares of Lady Asa Dereham, bouncing a cooing infant in her arms by the hearth.

Lord Dryden Dereham straddled the bench across from them, one leg in, one leg out. He wasn't much older than his young wife, but his experiences lived in the lines around his eyes and mouth. His heavy look was absent of the suspicion his wife carried, but there was another kind of wariness there. The choked grunt he made as he sized them up was for himself.

"These colors haven't been seen in the north in many years. Not in my lifetime, anyway," Dryden said finally. He lifted his other leg over the bench and faced them. "Cannot say I'm thrilled to see them for the first time now."

"We convey our apologies for not sending word ahead that we were coming," Evra said. He tried to read Meira, but her anxious gaze was fixed on the Lord of the Northerlands.

"We? Is this Rush Rider your wife, then?"

"No, she's..." He watched her from his peripheral. "A friend."

"A friend?"

"His bodyguard, sir," Meira corrected. "I'm a fledgling Rider of the Rush, and I've joined Lord Blackrook to aid him in any way he commands."

Lady Asa hid a snicker against her baby's scalp.

"Any way he commands," Dryden repeated. The corner of his mouth twitched. "I didn't know they made female Riders."

"They don't 'make' them, sir. I trained for this."

Dryden grunted. He slowly rolled his head back to Evra. "Where's the rest of your retinue?"

"It's only the two of us."

"The two of you, both barely out of your swaddling, traveling about in daylight like untrained assassins? Why don't I believe that?"

"Our business didn't require a full guard, Lord Dryden. Nor did we want our intentions confused. With luck, we'll not be here long."

"I still don't understand why you're here at all." Dryden emptied his cider and slid the mug across the table. A servant girl emerged from the shadows to refill it. "I wasn't sorry to hear of your father's fate. Any lord who murders his own people is less than a man."

"None in the Westerlands would disagree with you, other than perhaps his council."

"And your brother. I remember him. We were both summoned to Termonglen for the King's Feast when we were boys. He wasn't made for the tougher stuff, was he? If the Blackrooks have business with the Derehams, why is he not the one sitting here?"

"Lord Astarian has also succumbed to the sickness," Evra said. "Leaving me to sort out the mess left in both their absences."

"I didn't realize Aeldred had a second son until you showed up. Your problems are in the Westerlands. Why are you here?"

"What my husband means to say," Asa said, stepping forward. "Is that we have our own problems. Such as the uprising in Salthill due to having to prohibit their lucrative trade agreement with the Westerlands, on account of your plague sticking to everything you touch."

Dryden held up a hand. "I said exactly what I meant, Asa. Go on, put Torrin down for his lie-down. I'll sort this."

"I'd like to hear what they have to say for themselves."

"And you will. When I relay it to you, later, after our guests have returned to where they belong."

She held her son tighter and aimed a sharp nod at Evra and Meira. "How do we know *they* don't have the sickness, then?"

"Because it comes on swift and takes even quicker. They would've arrived to us dead if they had it. Go on, then, love."

Evra felt the hard look Lady Dereham leveled on him as she—slowly—did as her husband asked.

"Even if you had it," Dryden said when his wife and son were gone, "we'd never let it spread here, would we? For we have no fear of what is needed to cure it."

"I'm not afraid of magic," Evra defended. He shifted on the bench. "While it is perhaps the business of heathens—"

Dryden pounded his fists on the table as he threw his head back in a laugh.

Evra flushed, waiting for the man to finish. Dryden at last waved a hand, red-faced, urging him to continue. "As I said, while it may be..." Meira grabbed his leg, and he changed course. "May not be what we believe in where we come from, it's magic that brings us here to Wulfsgate."

The humor melted away from the young lord's face. "You've come here for magic."

"Yes."

89

"Magic. After you've burned half your Reach to the ground for the hatred of it."

"My father did this. Not me."

"Are you not his son?"

Evra's shame deepened. He'd expected this, but what shocked him was how the words wounded him. He may have abhorred his father's choices, but he understood the man's fear. Magic didn't come from the Guardians. Not even from the much-reviled Guardian of the Unpromised Future, which would have been bad enough. If it didn't come from the Guardians, that meant it came from something darker, fouler.

These men of the Northerlands didn't care, though, did they? Their lives were enriched by this profane gift.

If Evra let himself think about it too much more, he'd talk himself out of availing himself of the same thing.

Saving his Reach—his beloved Edriss—had to be bigger than his wariness of magic.

"I wasn't meant to be the lord. I was happy enough at university." Evra opened his palms, remembering how a book felt. "I was going to take the Scholar's Path." He glanced back up, closing his hands into fists in his lap. "Until I was called home."

"I cannot tell if you're after sympathy or something else telling me that. I have no care of your hopes and dreams, Lord Blackrook. Your father stole the same from thousands of men, women, even children, I hear. A lord's duty is to look after his own. Not burn them from the inside out."

"I'm not my father!" Evra exclaimed, slamming his hands on the table. Meira jumped. "I'm not Aeldred. I'm not even supposed to be here, but I am. And if you'd help me try to make this right for the Westerlands, I'd be in your debt for the rest of my days."

Dryden cocked his head. "Help you? How could I help you?"

"I'd like to borrow a Ravenwood and bring relief to my people."

Dryden's lips parted. His mouth widened in shock and then bemusement, then he was again laughing, pounding his fists on the table.

90

"What?"

"Did you say borrow a Ravenwood?"

"Yes. I understand they're in your employ, and—"

"In... our..." Dryden doubled over. "Ah, I wish I hadn't dismissed Asa. How she'd enjoy this."

"Sir, Lord Blackrook's words may seem strange to you, but we have no such equivalent in the Westerlands as the Ravenwoods. Please understand he means no harm," Meira attempted.

"I don't need help," Evra hissed under his breath. "If I've misunderstood the situation, Lord Dereham, kindly correct me."

"You misunderstand much," Dryden said after he'd calmed again. "The Ravenwoods are our friends. We command nothing."

Evra was confused. "Yet they come whenever you need them."

"Yes."

"Why?"

"We keep them safe. They aid us in return. Our arrangement benefits us both equally." Dryden nodded at their untouched mugs. What had seemed so soothing to Evra now felt foreign and unwelcome. "Go on, drink. The Derehams make this cider with our own hands." He waited for them to do as he asked. "You want aid from the Ravenwoods? You'll have to ask them yourself."

Evra wiped the froth from his mouth. "All right. How would I do that?" He pushed his mug away and leaned in. "Do you have a map to their keep? What's it called?"

"The Rookery," Meira answered.

"A map," Dryden said, shaking his head. "A map would do you little good. Only one way up that mountain, Lord Blackrook." Dryden grinned and mimed his arms as wings.

Meira spoke before Evra could. "You must have some counsel on the matter, my lord? Them being your friends."

Dryden tapped his foot against the stone. His eyes traveled between them, wearing a look that belied his indecision in helping them. He dropped his elbows on the table, folding his hands in. "All right, then. Frost owes me a favor he's late in repaying. It's Midwinter Rest you want. There's a Ravenwood there now, proffering aid to the stewardess in her confinement. She won't be there long, but perhaps long enough."

Evra brightened. He nudged Meira, but she looked less excited than he felt. "Perfect. Then we'll go there! The Guardians are with us after all."

Meira nodded into her mug.

"I'll send a raven. The steward will make a room for you. He has about a hundred to spare in that mausoleum." Dryden extricated himself from the thick bench. "Lady Asa will see you fed, bedded for the night, and Guardians help you both, trussed in something more appropriate for the north. I'll send some men with you long enough to clear Torrin's Pass, and then I trust you'll find yourself the rest of the way on your own."

Evra nodded as he stood to join Lord Dereham. "I can't thank you enough. I know what the kingdom thinks of my father. Of the Westerlands. I will change that if I can."

Dryden took his hand briefly, then dropped it. "I reckon it will take more than sneaking around in the darkness to change all that, Lord Evra. I wish you success just the same, even if the odds are higher that fresh flowers spring up out of the snow and announce an early springtide. If nothing else, Oswin will have an amusing story to tell us on the next Torrin's Day."

"Thank you, Lord Dryden."

Dryden nodded. "If that's all, I've business here awaiting me. Lady Asa will be out quick enough, she'll see to the rest." He cleared his throat and tapped his chest. "Find me again at the first snow, Lord Blackrook. Rider Ashenhurst."

TWELVE
FLY FAR

Naryssa Ravenwood paced the stone corridor with one eye beyond the mass of Ravenwoods. She kept her movements calm, deliberately tempering her stride to seem controlled and resolved, when she felt neither of those things. All those solemnly gathered watched her with their own assumptions, and that was their right. Her heart was her own.

"Where is she, Mother?" Rendyr shifted anxiously near a pillar. The beaming smile he gave the other Ravenwoods was a foil contrast to the somber mood. No one *wanted* to do this. No one *wanted* to be there. Tradition demanded it, and tradition was bigger than them all. If they didn't have tradition, they'd have chaos. They'd have nothing but the same darkness they'd fled in their old world, all those years ago.

Rendyr was the standout among them. He didn't even attempt to disguise his glee.

"She's coming. Be still." Naryssa held her head high, lengthening her neck, reminding others she still held the power even if she was neutered of it in what they came to do that day. She'd had

93

more years as High Priestess than most and would have more still, for Rhosyn would reset the Langenacht, all of it. When Arwenna was gone, it would begin again.

Dead, not gone, she thought, reminding herself to be careful with her words even in the palace of her mind.

"There's still time to change this," her son, Augustyn, whispered. Not to her, though. He'd never say it to her. The words were for his younger brother, Vradyn, who only shook his head as he nodded, eyes closed. At least two of her sons were decent men. But decent men died decent deaths. There was no future where either of them bested Rendyr and gave Rhosyn a fair life.

Augustyn was wrong, though. There wasn't time. Time was precisely the one thing they no longer had.

A wave of gasps sounded, followed by the snaps and flurries of robes and leather as all shifted their eyes toward the far end of the corridor. Arwenna made her way in a billowing black gown with a look that hovered between defiant and defeated. At her side, her grandmother, Avadora; Naryssa's mother. Naryssa had heard her mother crying the night before, but had no comfort to offer. If the older woman knew she'd heard at all, the wedge between them would only deepen.

When Arwenna was near, Naryssa reached for her daughter's hands and squeezed them. She dared not embrace her. Arwenna was a traitor now, a failed High Priestess; the most hollow of all crimes she could imagine, but also the highest. They'd said their goodbyes the night before. Today was about the inexorable finality.

"*Finally!*" Rendyr thundered in a whisper intended for everyone's ears.

"Arwenna Ravenwood, daughter of Naryssa, granddaughter of Avadora," Naryssa began. She channeled her fear into rage, which steadied her words, turned them to stone. "You are gathered amongst your blood to face penance for your crime. Do you understand the nature of your sedition?"

94

Arwenna's brave face curdled Naryssa's resolve. "For failing to produce the next of our bloodline. For forsaking the gods who have created us."

"Yes," Naryssa said, breathless. She gathered herself. "And do you know the punishment for this crime, Arwenna?"

"My wings clipped." Arwenna's eyes swam with tears, but her jaw was tight with strength. "For my flightless excommunication from Midnight Crest."

"Do you accept this punishment now? Will you come to my arms willingly, so that I may strip you of this sacred magic, magic you no longer deserve?"

"I'll do it," Rendyr said with a snort. "I'd like to know how that feels, her magic leaving her. I want to see it in her eyes."

Naryssa ignored him. "Come to me, Arwenna, and let us soften your sentence with this last act of fealty. Surrender, so that you may go in peace."

Augustyn's howling sob ricocheted off the stone. She would hear the sound in her nightmares.

Arwenna stepped forward. She moved past Naryssa and wrapped her hands around the icy balustrade. From behind, Naryssa slid her hands over her daughter's belly and leaned in long enough to whisper, just for them, "Fly far."

Arwenna gasped, just as Naryssa had told her to do. She flailed back, wearing a look so lost and terrified that even Naryssa wondered if she'd failed, and really taken her daughter's magic after all, sealing her fate.

Naryssa performed the irrevocable act. She bound her daughter's hands, making a show to all that she'd not gone light on the knot. She only exhaled when she caught the glimmer of the steel she'd given Arwenna last night peeking from the end of her sleeve.

"Now," Naryssa said, voice higher as she fought with herself. "Now, you may choose. To fall on your own, or be sent over by my hands. But go, you must. Your time here is ended."

"I'll go myself," Arwenna said. She didn't look back as she pulled one leg up on the railing, floundering for purchase without the use of her hands. Naryssa helped guide her into place. As Arwenna lifted the other leg, Rendyr shoved past Naryssa and sent both palms into his sister's back. She screamed as she flew over, the sound fading into the abyss of cloud and storm.

Naryssa choked down a sob, trapping it in her chest.

Fly far.

"That's done. Now get on with it and bring the other one to my bed," he said and stomped off through the crowd of horrified Ravenwoods.

Arwenna's gut lived in her throat, trapped there, choking her. The fall was swift, and she'd thought she'd have a few more seconds to draw her breath, to hold it in and gather the last of her strength. And then Rendyr had taken that, too.

But he hadn't taken everything, had he?

Arwenna's fall hastened, but she waited, waited until she had passed through the clouds before calling upon the magic that was hers at birth, and was hers now. Before she carefully shook the dagger out of her sleeve and sliced through the rope.

Midair, she shifted into her raven form, leaving a dangerous world behind for an unknown one.

THIRTEEN
THE TRAP

"A ye, we got the raven," Steward Frost was saying. He passed conspiratorial glances to his son, Thornton, or Thorn, as he called him. Where Evra came from, thorns were sharp, cutting you if you weren't attentive enough. Frost's heir seemed aptly named.

"It said we were coming?" Evra asked. "Lord Dereham—"

"Lord Dereham was quite clear in his message. So clear you might say we had to read it a few times, to be certain of the meaning," Thorn said. He paused at the end of the long corridor. Evra wasn't surprised to see there was another corner to round, though they didn't take it. Midwinter Hold was the largest keep he'd ever been in. A man could easily get lost in the maze of halls and rooms. "Your guard can stay here."

"Are these the guest apartments?"

"Servant's quarters."

Evra flashed an offended look at Meira, but she was already on her way in. He started to tell Thorn and Oswin that Meira was no servant; she was a distinguished Rider of the Rush and a

97

daughter of House Ashenhurst. The words caught on his tongue as she nodded in thanks and closed the door on them.

Rest and a warm bath sounded better than more handshaking and tours to him, too.

For all its mass, the stone and tapestries of Midwinter Hold held court in solitude. The stark absence of life was the prevailing impression as their footfalls echoed down halls devoid of conversation or laughter. Even with the mess Evra's father had made of the Halls of Longwood, you couldn't take ten steps without running into someone else.

"How many of you live here?" he asked.

"Seven," Oswin answered.

"Seven people?"

"Seven Frosts, yes."

Evra shook his head. "Right."

"Will be six," Thorn added. "My sister, Morwen, will depart with her bridegroom for Dunwoode soon."

"We passed through Dunwoode on our ride north."

"So you did."

"Should I have the rest of my things brought in?" When they'd reached the village of Midwinter Rest, they'd been informed their horses—even Meira's majestic warhorse—would not make the steep climb to Midwinter Hold. After some strong convincing, Meira paid the stable triple to give her mare the proper care, and they'd gone the rest of the way to the keep riding in the back of a rickety cart pulled by rented mules.

"Already taken care of," Oswin said. "They'll be in your apartment. Our finest one, for our finest guest. The one Lord Dereham made quite clear you were to have upon your arrival."

"I see. Thank you."

Oswin's small, annoyed head shake was meant for himself, but Evra caught it.

"Have you eaten?" Thorn asked.

"We grabbed some stew and bread at a tavern in town."

Thorn smirked. "Then you'll be wanting a proper meal. I'll ask the kitchen to heat something edible while Father takes you to the armory. Though I daresay you'll find it less satisfying than the elaborate feasts you enjoy in the Westerlands."

Setting aside the obvious slight, Evra wanted to ask about the need for an armory, but was tired of the way his voice sounded since he'd left Oldcastle. Like he knew nothing. Like everyone around him was all too aware of this terrible fact.

He'd been sweating inside the warm keep, still bundled in his furs, but as the steward angled him out the back and into the storm once more, the chill that sliced through his bones nearly sent him to his knees. He struggled to keep pace, landing in the man's heavy footprints instead of a clear path.

The steward suddenly came to a halt. Pulling his hood tight, he turned to Evra. "Too many ears inside. Tell me true, Lord Blackrook. Why are you here?"

"We're not going to the armory?"

"Oh, we most certainly are. I don't even need you to draw that scrap metal from your rusted scabbard to know it's not suitable for a lord. What happened to your father's sword? Don't you have ancestral steel?"

"I don't know," Evra confessed. He'd never thought to ask. His brother would have known. "I just took what I could find in our own armory at Longwood."

"Scraps," Oswin confirmed. "So, then. What's the truth?"

Evra stammered.

"The *truth*, Lord Blackrook. I may be indebted to Lord Dereham, but I'll not abide a trickster under my roof, either. What is your business with the Ravenwoods?"

There was something about Oswin Frost. Something cool, yes, but also kind. He wasn't leading Evra into a trap; he was presenting an offer. A means of discarding the pretense and a safe place in which to do it.

Even if he was wrong about the man, he'd get no help with lies.

Evra shivered, wrapping his arms tighter around himself. Fresh snow tickled his nose. "My father was a tyrant who murdered his own people. Those who didn't die at his hands have and will die at his ignorance. I don't trust magic, Steward, but I won't allow more blood to stain the Blackrook name."

Oswin nodded. "That doesn't explain to me why you're here."

"I think the Ravenwoods can help me."

"Setting aside, for a moment, that the Ravenwoods have no cause to help you, if you truly want to undo the terrors of your father's reign, then why would you not approach the Sepulchre? Mend that alliance? They could have the Westerlands free of plague in days."

Evra hung his head. "I cannot."

"Cannot or will not, Evrathedyn?"

Evra was taken aback at the steward's familiarity. It also eased him. "Evra. Please."

Oswin watched him. He ran a gloved hand over his nose. "Well, Evra, if it's my hospitality you're after, I'm not known for it, but you'll have warm nights and a full belly, for as long as your business keeps you in the far north. I'll fit you for proper steel, as your father should have. Any more, I cannot do. The Ravenwoods do not answer to me. Even if they did, I'd never send them any farther south than Wulfsgate. It's not safe for them out in the kingdom. It's why they're there, and why we're here."

"But you have one here, do you not?" A hard wind ripped through them, causing his teeth to chatter.

"Rhosyn," Oswin said. "But if you even look at her sideways, it's me you'll answer to, boy. Lord or no."

The trek to the armory stretched on for so long, Evra wondered if the steward was leading him straight into the mountains. He closed his eyes against the assault of wind and icy snow, cautiously opening them every few steps to regain his bearings.

100

He used to enjoy snowstorms, but that was because he'd never been in a proper one.

Another fierce wind knocked him from his feet. He reached for something to push himself back up, but sank farther into the snow. The steward hadn't heard him cry out, and now he couldn't see the man at all. Only oppressive walls of white, closing in on all sides.

Evra rolled forward onto his knees. He hadn't hit ground, but he maneuvered on to a patch of ice between the snow layers. He heaved himself forward, stumbling back into a half-jog, but he no longer knew where he was. He couldn't recall which way they'd been headed, nor where they'd come from. He was snow blind.

"Steward Frost!"

He slowly inched forward, straining his eyes to the front and sides for any sign of the steward. His scream was trapped in the storm.

"Steward Frost! I've lost my way!"

His next step sent a thrill of blood straight to his head. The pain took a moment to catch up, but when it hit, his howl erupted into the evening air. He made the terrible mistake of glancing down. The snow around his ankles wasn't white anymore, but deep red. A light tug revealed his foot was only partly attached.

He screamed.

A trap. He'd stepped into a trap.

Evra fainted.

An ochre light flickered around the edges of his vision. A shadow passed by, splitting the aura, and then it was dark again.

Evra groaned into his stretch. His muscles coiled tight inside his limbs, screaming against his need to move. He closed his eyes again, and when he opened them once more, something silvery and fair, a brighter light, stepped into the tawny glow.

A young woman.

When she leaned in, her shimmery hair tickled his chin. His mouth parted in wonder, in awe, in *something*, but her gaze only lingered a moment before she traveled away from him. He didn't know where she'd gone until he felt her soft hands on his mangled foot.

The trap.

"My foot..." he managed, but his throat felt stuffed with wool, and he was still so tired, so exhausted. "My..."

"Your foot is well enough to stand on." The voice, like the petals of his grandmother's roses passing across his arm, spread a strange but not unwelcome sensation across his chest. "I'll need more time with it before you're walking as you were."

"You healed me?" Evra wondered, not quite meaning to say the words aloud. "With your hands?"

"Well, yes. That is how one heals."

"But my foot... it was hanging... it was..." Evra winced. He tried to sit, but the exhaustion hit him like a wave.

"I saw it. You lost quite a battle with the snowbeast trap. You're lucky you didn't lose your life, bleeding out as you did. If that had happened, you would've been beyond the help of *my* magic."

Evra slid higher on the bed. He tried to get a better look at the silver-haired woman running her hands across the top of his foot, rolling around the outside of his ankle, like silk. "Who are you?"

"Who are you?" she countered with a light flip in her tone at the end. "I know Midwinter Hold is a village unto itself, but I'm confident I know every last"—she laughed, ticking down her fingers—"two dozen or so who live here."

"I thought there were only seven."

"Frosts, maybe."

"You're not a Frost?"

She laughed again. "No."

Evra blinked through the last of his confusion. The orange light faded as the young woman set the candle on a nearby table. Now, he could see her. Her hair *was* silver. After all, he hadn't imagined it. Her long hair framed a pale face, porcelain skin trailing down into a black gown with even blacker feathers drawing lines down the sleeves. "Raven," he said, once more without meaning to let the words leave his mind. *This* was Oswin's raven.

"Not at the moment," she said. She glanced back from the table with a light, devious grin. "You're not from the north, are you?"

Evra tried to answer her very simple question, but all he could do was shake his head. He rotated his ankle, trying to conjure the whisper of how her flesh felt against his.

"Emerald and silver. I wish I could say something clever right now, about how I'd recognize that standard anywhere, but I've never been south of Wulfsgate."

"The Westerlands," Evra choked out. He stretched a grin across his face that made her smile fade, and he wondered how he'd messed that up, too.

The young woman nodded. "Emerald. Right. I've heard tell of your gardens. Most don't bother with them here. Except in Wulfsgate, they have this garden... the Wintergarden, they call it, for it grows the most vibrant, beautiful... cherries, if you'd believe it, in midwinter." She laughed to herself. "I'm sorry. You know more about gardens than we ever could."

"I'd like to see it," Evra said, even though he had. Meira had been the one who insisted they wander through it after supper that night. Why hadn't he said *that*? Why was nothing coming out right?

"Then you should, on your return." The young woman spun around and leaned against the table, watching him. "My name is Rhosynora. But you can call me Rhosyn."

"Rhosyn." He liked how the word sounded as it rolled neatly off his tongue. He liked even more how it sounded coming off hers. Steward Frost's warning came back to him. "I'm... Evrathedyn Blackrook. Son of... it doesn't matter. My family calls me Thedyn, but I prefer Evra." He winced after what seemed more explanation than was needed.

"Ahh," Rhosyn said. She cast her eyes to the ceiling, nodding. "If you prefer that, why do they call you Thedyn?"

"They say it's a king's name. That Evra is a boy's name."

"But you're no Rhiagain. You'll never be king."

"Anyone can be king, Rhosyn." His father's words. He didn't know why he'd said them.

"I may not know very much, Evra, but I know the name. Blackrook. You're not just from the Westerlands. You're the son of their lord."

"I am the lord now," Evra said. As he spoke, his heart turned over in his chest. It was the way she watched him. She hung on his words, not the polite attentions expected of conversation, but out of real, genuine interest. "I wasn't supposed to be. My father spent his promise, and then my brother."

"Spent their promise. I've heard the Frosts say that. Then you mean..."

Evra nodded. "Dead."

"That must have been horrible. I'm very sorry."

"It wasn't," he insisted, only understanding how that must sound after the words were out. The pause between them grew heavy, and then she brought a hand to her mouth and laughed. "What?"

"I see your relationship with your family is as pleasing as mine," she said as her laugh trailed to a chuckle. "Few would ever say so, though."

"I never quite know what to say and what not to say."

Rhosyn's face darkened as she approached him, the light now behind her. She knelt at his side, and he could not fathom how, but she seemed even less real, an even more perfect figment of his crafty imagination, up close. "I prefer people who say what they mean. You don't have to wonder who they really are." She stretched her hand to the nightstand and handed him a drink. "Have some wine."

Evra watched her over the mug as he tilted it back. Her smile, beset by brilliant violet eyes, left him unable to properly swallow.

The garnet liquid ran down his chin, spilling against the blanket. Her mouth parted in humor, and then she folded the fur cover over the evidence, hiding it; their own shared secret.

"Better?" she asked.

Evra nodded, despite not having actually drunk a drop.

"And what brings you so far north of anything green, Evra Blackrook?"

"I..." Like Oswin, her invitation to the truth was sincere. Unlike Oswin, he was terrified of saying anything that might fade her smile again. "I have business with Steward Frost."

"I see. Well, Steward Frost would also like you to know that when you're feeling ready, there's food in the banquet hall. It's a rather long table to sup at alone, but you get used to the quiet if you spend enough time here."

Rhosyn set the mug back on the table, but she stayed at his bedside. His arm accidentally brushed the edge of her gown. The sensation shocked him. Leather and velvet, and the feathers. The feathers were real. She smiled down at his series of revelations, and he forgot why he'd come to Midwinter Rest. It didn't matter anymore. Had it ever?

"Guardians, Evra, you gave me quite the scare!" Meira's excited voice cut through his daze. Instinctively, he turned toward the sound, but his attention was pulled back to the girl, the Ravenwood, as she left them alone.

No! Don't go! He cried out, but this time he hadn't said the words aloud. As Meira knelt at his bedside to fuss, Evra reached back into his memory, to only moments ago, and his first surge of happiness since leaving his promising future behind.

FOURTEEN
MANY TALENTS

Morwen watched her friend with alternating curiosity and bemusement. Rhosyn practically glided from room to room as she moved between her two patients. Nearing the door, for the newest one, she pressed her hands down over her gown, and buried a smile.

"Rhosynora Ravenwood," Morwen accused with playful censure in her tone. "I know that smile isn't for my mother."

Rhosyn's grin died as fast as it had been birthed. She looked around either side of Morwen, then shook her head. "Do you never smile to yourself, Morwen Frost?"

"Not like that," Morwen said, tilting her head. "I won't even ask because I already know, and if you deny it, I'll be hurt."

"There's nothing *to* deny," Rhosyn said. She had her hands up before Morwen could rebut. "The only men I know are your family, and Lord Dereham, who I met only once. I've never known anyone from the Westerlands. That might as well be another world to me."

"You've been in another world ever since you saved his foot."

Rhosyn's smile returned, painting her rosy face. "I did save it, didn't I?"

"Be careful," Morwen warned. She drew her sigh inward. It was so nice to see joy written on her friend's face. How she wished Rhosyn could feel as she did now, always. Morwen would do anything to help fight back against the future awaiting Rhosyn. But not even her father could keep the Ravenwoods away forever. "I know you believe you've held Rendyr off, but—"

"I can feel him when he's there," Rhosyn insisted. "He cannot sneak about without me knowing. But there's nothing there to anger him, other than me being here. I've done nothing untoward. Nothing I was not *asked* to do by your father."

"And why is the young lord even here, anyway? What could a man of the Westerlands need of us? Not even our own people venture up this far, except Lord Dereham, and that's only because he has no choice. A lord must visit his own lands."

"You're being silly, Morwen. It's only... only that it was nice to exchange words with someone who doesn't know me. Who doesn't want something from me." Rhosyn reached for the door. Morwen's heart skipped; her friend had never seemed so eager to be rid of her. She reminded herself she *was* being silly, though not about that.

"Am I? Has he told you, then, why he's come all the way to Midwinter Rest in the middle of our hard season? At a time where even Northerlanders won't travel beyond the essentials?"

"Why would he? His business isn't with me." Rhosyn glanced toward the door again. "We've hardly talked at all, anyway."

Morwen crossed her arms. "Go on, then. Play with his foot or whatever you do."

"Morwen!"

"But tonight at dinner, while you're sitting with Mother, I'll be finding out why the young Lord Blackrook and his very pretty Rush Rider have graced the far north with their conspicuous presence."

"If you insist," Rhosyn said. She reached for the door. "But you'll be doing it to satisfy your own curiosity. I care for nothing except his well-being."

Morwen rolled her eyes. "Allow me to care for the both of us."

Rhosyn found the young lord sitting at his desk. She started to chide him for being out of bed, but a limp didn't stop a man from doing business. Especially not a lord.

"Ahh," he said, turning. His smile brightened the dim room. She gave him one in return, then eased up as Morwen's warnings came back to her. "Rhosyn. I was hoping you might return."

"Of course I'll return, as long as you require my healing," Rhosyn said, turning her words to sound more like a concerned sister than this other, stranger feeling that tried to take precedence. "It won't do to have you riding back over the pass without a fully healed foot."

Evra set his quill aside and beamed even brighter. "Shall I lie in the bed?"

Rhosyn squeezed the fabric of her dress in her fists, fighting the flush that rose up from her toes. "Uh... if that pleases you."

The corner of Evra's mouth curved up. She shifted her glance downward as he hobbled from the desk to the bed.

As Rhosyn moved toward him, she noticed the half-written letter on the desk. "Writing to your wife?"

"Wife?" Evra laughed. He leaned back on his arms, folded above his head. "No."

"Have you none?"

"No, nor do I have any intention toward marriage."

"Oh?" Rhosyn pulled the chair to the end of the bed and sat. "Are lords not required to marry? To produce heirs?"

Evra's head fell to the side. "The Westerlands would be better off if the Blackrooks faded into obscurity."

"Why's that?"

"Why do you want to know so much about me, when your life must be far more interesting?"

"Interesting, perhaps," Rhosyn said, working her hands over his swollen flesh. "But beyond that..."

"What?"

"If not your wife, then who were you writing to?"

"A friend," Evra said. "From university."

"University! What's that like?"

"So many books you could drown in them." His smile was different now; he went somewhere else. "Men, and women too, who only want to learn. To know more, and to use that knowledge to further more knowledge and more learning. To help the kingdom with it." He turned to watch her. "Do you have books where you come from?"

Rhosyn shook her head. She disliked this feeling that came over her then. Of shame.

Evra scrambled to prop himself up. "I suppose you wouldn't need them, with your magic. Books are my magic. But yours..." He nodded. "Nothing I could learn, not in a hundred years, would teach me that."

"I do read," Rhosyn said. She cleared her throat and said it once more. "I do read, Evra. I like books. Steward Frost has a library here and has said I can take whatever I please, though I'm careful to only take one at a time. I know books are valuable to men."

"What do you read? Do you like stories?"

Rhosyn continued her ministrations on his foot. Her healing magic had never tired her before, but she was learning now that she had limitations, with two to look after instead of one. "The more fantastical the better."

Evra sat higher. "Dragons?"

Rhosyn grinned. "Especially if they breathe fire and have troves and troves of gold."

"I have something in my bag." He nodded to the bureau. "I brought a few books with me. If you want..."

"You'd let me borrow your books? You hardly know me."

"I know where you live," he said with a teasing smirk.

"What if I flew away with your treasured stories? What would you do then?"

"I'd find another way up the mountain."

"What if there was no other way?"

"I'd make one."

Rhosyn's heart fluttered so intensely that she had to steady her breathing to keep the dizziness at bay. She'd never talked to anyone like this, except Morwen, but even Morwen didn't leave her feeling as if she'd left her heart outside her body. "I suppose a lord is capable of anything he pleases," she remarked, exhaling the last words with her eyes closed.

"Feels much better," Evra said. "My foot, I mean."

She tried to laugh. "What else could you have meant?"

"Oh, I don't know. Perhaps I might have meant that I feel at peace for the first time since my father and brother died, and I inherited their job. That, for the first time in weeks, I can lay my head on a pillow and be asleep in moments." Evra sat up, drawing his legs with him. Her hands slid away. "I want to repay you in some way, Rhosyn."

Rhosyn shook her head as she quickly stood. "No. I wouldn't think of it. Nor would Steward Frost."

Evra rolled off the bed, landing upon the foot she'd saved. His limp as he stumbled toward her was still there, but receding with every touch of her hands. "But this isn't anything to do with the steward. It's about what you have done for me."

Rhosyn turned toward his desk. "That's what Ravenwoods do, Evra. We come to the aid of men when called."

Evra reached for her. She pivoted away, then regretted it, only to be glad of it again seconds later. *What is happening here? To me?* "Your agreement is with the men of the north. Not with me. So, I thank you, Rhosyn Ravenwood, and it would be my honor to give you my service in return, whatever that might be."

111

"I'd never deny anyone aid if I had the power to provide it. I need nothing in return."

Evra slithered into his boots, using the bedpost as leverage. He winced when his wounded foot settled in. There was yet work to do there. But by the time he returned home, she'd be sure that snowbeast trap was only a distant memory. "Still. Think on it."

"You're not going to finish your letter?" she asked as he approached the door.

"Seven can wait. As of just now, I feel the urge to be useful." He nodded at her, gifting her one last smile before leaving.

Evra's eyes moved between the three doors leading in and out of the dining room. Steward Oswin was the first to settle in, seating himself at the head of the overlong table. Thorn joined with his wife, Brin, but their little one was not with them. When Morwen appeared alone, his hope at seeing Rhosyn dwindled further. Another set of footsteps lighted his optimism, but it was only the steward's youngest son, Rylan, nudged forward by his governess, who disappeared as soon as he was in the room.

"Looking for someone?" Meira quipped.

"Just, eh, wondering which door the food comes out."

"Right."

"Now that the unfortunate accident is behind us, you'll see how northern men take their meals," Oswin said. His cheek twitched in the start of a smile, but he grunted instead and moved his fork to the other side of his plate.

"How are you feeling?" Brin asked, eyes wide with earnest concern. At her side, Thorn rolled his eyes, but she was oblivious or inured to it. "That must have given you quite the scare. The only other person I know who's stepped in a snowbeast trap didn't survive to speak of it."

Evra nodded, swallowing a sip of his wine. He tried not to choke as he ingested the tart drink, which was even *drier* than the wine they'd been served in Wulfsgate. He wondered if he had any of the sweet cordials of the Westerlands in his satchel. "I'm feeling quite fortunate right now, Stewardess Brin."

"Please, you may call me Brin, and my husband, Thorn. We both prefer the less formal greeting at this stage of our lives. It will hopefully be many years before we are the ones in charge of affairs at Midwinter Hold."

Thorn rolled his tongue along the inside of his mouth, watching his reflection in his empty plate.

"Did it hurt?" The young one, Rylan, watched Evra with wide, intent eyes. "Did it hurt a great deal?"

Evra stretched his lower jaw as he winced into the memory. "A great deal only gets us halfway there." He glanced under the table, rolling his booted foot. "You'd never know now, though, would you? Rhosyn's talent is really remarkable."

"She has many talents," Morwen said. She twirled her long, dark waves with her finger. "It's yours I'd like to know more about."

"Morwen," Brin chided under her breath, passing a chastising glance to her sister-in-law. "Lord Blackrook is our guest. He should not be subject to your incessant inclination for chatter and questions."

"It's all right," Evra insisted. "I don't have many talents, I'm afraid. I wanted to be a Scholar, but that path is no longer available to me."

"But you are here for a reason?" Morwen pressed, turning her head to avoid even more indignant looks from Brin. "Surely, Midwinter Rest was not topping your list of desirable holiday destinations?"

"Ahh, at last someone has lured a boar out in winter!" Oswin cried, throwing his head back as he inhaled the rich scent drawing closer to them.

A small retinue of kitchen staff entered from the back of the room, forming a line as they carried the feast toward the table. Evra's stomach churned in kind. He'd heard the food was gamier, tougher up north, but the smell mingled with his vivid imagination had his mouth watering.

Thorn finished off his wine and a kitchen maid refilled it. He waved at her to stay, emptying his mug a second time, and waited for her to again perform her task before flicking his hand to dismiss her.

"This looks incredible, Steward. Thank you for your hospitality and your kindness," Evra said. He couldn't help glancing again toward the door the Frosts had all entered through. Meira shook her head.

"That business of yours," Morwen said as their plates were stuffed with food. "What was it again?"

"There is no again, sister. Lord Blackrook has not shared his business, and that is his choice. That matter is between him and your father," Brin said with a prudent nod. In the stewardess' absence, she had stepped into the role with neat precision, Evra thought. Her husband had no mind for anything that was not on his plate.

"But do you not think it *strange*, Brin?"

"That's enough," Oswin boomed, mouth stuffed with boar. The juices ran down the sides of his lips, clinging to his jowls before plopping onto his leather. "Let the man eat."

Evra started in on his meat, but Morwen's eyes burned holes in his forehead, making him aware of everything from the way he gripped the bone to the speed with which he brought the succulent meat to his mouth.

"Well, his Rush Rider didn't almost lose her foot. Meira, is it?"

"Yes, ma'am."

"Morwen is fine. You're his guard, then?"

"Guardians, Morwen, let up!" Thorn called without slowing his chewing.

"I am." Meira passed a cautious, sidelong look at Evra, but he was too caught in his thoughts to acknowledge it. Morwen was Rhosyn's friend. He knew what she was doing. He'd done something like it for a friend at university; sizing up the suitor, making sure their intentions matched their attentions. But thinking of himself in such terms only rendered him more confused.

He wasn't Rhosyn's suitor; he'd come to solicit her aid. Yet being around her not only caused him to forget this need, but to desire being rid of it altogether. He couldn't want and need her at the same time. And why did he want her at all? Why could he not simply do what he'd come to do?

He asked these questions in Meira's voice. They weren't so different from the ones she'd peppered him with the night before.

If he was clear with his intentions, Morwen would tell Rhosyn, and whatever strange magic swirling between them would end. If he hid his purpose, he could hardly call himself a man of honor.

"He needs magic," Thorn said, chewing through his words. "Because his father and brother ran his Reach into ash and smoke for their hatred of it."

Morwen's eyes grew wide as she turned them back on Evra. "You're here for magic?"

"I... yes, I suppose that's the sum of it."

"You have more than you deserved, Morwen. Now be a lady and eat," Brin hissed.

"Magic," Morwen repeated, her voice wondrous. "You're here for Rhosyn?"

"Morwen!"

They were well on the path now. There was no leaving it. "I'm here to solicit aid from the Ravenwoods, in exchange for payment of their choosing."

"Does Rhosyn know?"

Evra felt his cheeks darken. "We haven't had... we haven't discussed it, no."

"And good luck to him when he does, eh?" Oswin said, raising his mug. He brought it back to his mouth before anyone could join in.

"Luck." Morwen drawled the word, pressing her tongue to her teeth as she sounded it out.

"Morwen, for all that is good, will you please stop?" Brin set her fork aside, exasperated. "For the life of me, I cannot ascertain whether you are interrogating this man or flirting with him!"

Thorn cackled. He picked something out of his teeth, grinning at Morwen. "Someone oughta teach you how to flirt properly, sister."

"You weren't exactly a skilled tradesman in the craft," Brin muttered.

"I am *not* flirting," Morwen insisted, though her haughty demeanor was decidedly more demure now. "I just think that if Rhosyn is to be *used* for nefarious purposes—"

"Used?" Evra repeated. He stopped eating. "Morwen, that is *not* my intention at all! If she does help me, it will be to mutual benefit. Whatever she needs, she can have."

Morwen snorted. She squinted her eyes to hide the tears. "The only thing Rhosyn needs is the one thing no one can give her. Least of all you."

"What?" Evra leaned in. "What does Rhosyn need?"

Morwen crossed her arms and flopped back in her chair, shaking her head.

He looked around at the others. They'd all stopped eating, except Thorn. "What are you all not saying about Rhosyn?"

"The Ravenwoods have a different path than the one we walk," Oswin explained, suddenly solemn. He drained his mug of wine, slower than the fervor he'd attacked it with earlier. "It is not for us, or for anyone, to get involved. That isn't the way."

"Why are you all being so elusive? What path could she be on that has you all looking... like that?"

"You really know so little about the Ravenwoods?" Meira asked. Her streak of annoyance was paused for the moment.

"I only know they come from... from Beyond," Evra said, now aware of all the eyes turned toward him, dinner forgotten. "That they possess magic. That..." He had nothing more to say, for he knew no more.

"Rhosyn," Thorn said, ignoring the warning look from his wife, "is going to be High Priestess soon. Much like you, she wasn't born to lead, but fate has other ideas sometimes, doesn't it?"

Evra's smile returned with his relief. "But that's a good thing, isn't it?"

"Was it a good thing for you, Lord Blackrook?" Thorn countered.

"This really isn't suitable supper palaver," Brin attempted, looking at her palms in defeated indignation. "Nor is it fair to speak of Rhosyn with her not present."

"Do you know how a Ravenwood becomes a High Priestess, Evra?" Morwen's question was a trap that he had no choice but to walk into.

He shook his head.

"Mor*wen*," Brin warned, with much less energy than the prior attempts.

Rylan followed the conversation with wide-eyed interest.

"Why not tell him? Maybe it'll knock that lovestruck look off his face before it gets them both in trouble," Thorn said. He sucked the last of the meat off the bone and dropped it with a clang.

"Rylan is sitting right there," Brin whispered from the side of her mouth.

"Rylan will be a man soon enough. Why should he not hear this, too?"

Brin closed her eyes and beseeched the Guardians.

Thorn glanced at his father for approval. Oswin set his utensils aside and gazed into his plate.

"The Ravenwoods' High Priestess is chosen from birth," Thorn said. "The oldest daughter of the High Priestess, and so on. Rhosyn isn't the eldest, but her older sister failed her test and has been cast out."

"Failed?" Evra repeated the word more for himself.

"Just leave it at that," Brin pleaded.

"Why? He needs to know that his behavior isn't harmless. That she could be killed if they find out she's been wagging her eyelashes at him."

"They try that, let them see what my line is for getting involved," Oswin muttered.

"Rhosyn might be selected by their gods, or whatever, but her High Priest is chosen from within. And it's the *how* that would make your blood curdle, Blackrook. For if it wasn't bad enough that she'll wed and bed one of her own relations, she'll first have to bed a dozen or more of them to decide which one has *earned* his place at her side." He paused to see how his words had landed. "They call this warped ceremony the Langenacht. Arwenna Ravenwood once told me this translates to 'long night.' Long night, as if it's funny to them, the horrors they'll put their chosen one through?"

Evra paled. The sourness of the wine curdled in the back of his throat. "That sounds like fishwife gossip to me."

"No," Oswin said, shrugging off the brief pall of darkness that had overcome him. "It's not gossip, Evra. That is their way of things. As arcane as it sounds, it's true, and it's neither our place, nor our right, to get involved, or to judge. Hard as it may be for us to watch someone we care for endure such a fate."

Meira sighed into a groan. "How can it be that their High Priestess is revered above all the others, but then is forced to do something so horrible?"

Oswin held out his hands. "Rhosyn asks herself these same questions. And, I fear, her asking them will lead her into dark places."

Evra pushed his chair back. "If you care so much for Rhosyn, why would you allow her to return to that? If she doesn't want it, then what you're describing, it's... it's..."

Thorn laughed. "Allow? You misunderstand the nature of our relationship with the Ravenwoods. There might be a mutual benefit there, or so you'll hear us say, but under the surface, there has always been a war brewing."

"Evra, please. Sit down. Thorn, ease off," Oswin urged. To his left, his youngest son's mouth hung open. He hadn't touched his meal since the conversation shifted to Rhosyn's fate. "Our feelings about this do not matter. Rhosyn is like a daughter to me. If she asked me to raise arms for her, there would be no hesitation from me. There would be no fear of what it would invite. But unless she does, we will do as we have always done and stay within the boundaries of the sacred agreement."

"Then I'll talk to her. Tell her to ask!" Evra's face flushed so hot he had to grip the edges of the table. "No one should ever be forced into such a life against their will!"

Brin's soft sigh cut through the tension. "She would never ask. Rhosyn's heart is too big. She would never wish for another to come to harm for her sake."

Morwen remained surprisingly silent.

"I don't care what she wishes, then." Evra's knuckles whitened as he dug his nails into the table. "I'll raise my own army."

"Evra," Meira warned. "Don't forget why we're here. If you want the aid of the Ravenwoods, starting a war with them is a fine way to be sure that never happens."

Evra's silence thickened in his chest. Meira's eyes burned him clear through as she waited for his reassurance that he hadn't forgotten their task; that he'd never throw aside the care of his entire Reach for a girl he just met.

"Evra?"

"Don't you dare say a word of this to Rhosyn." Morwen at last found her voice again. It shook with her words. "It would break her heart to see the pity in your eyes. Just as it will break her heart when she discovers you've come to use her, making you no better than her family in the end."

Oswin caught them in the hall. Meira angled the two of them in the steward's direction, Evra hobbling just a little faster than he was earlier that day.

"Forgive Morwen's words. She and Rhosyn have been close since were girls. My daughter's protectiveness is how she shows her love."

119

"There's nothing to forgive," Meira insisted, while Evra was deciding how to respond. She'd failed him by not stepping in more, not guiding him with a firmer hand. She'd not seen how much slower he'd matured than she had. Now he was in well over his head, and she had no choice but to steer him back to the right path. "Morwen is right. We were misguided in coming here. We'll make plans to return to the Westerlands as quickly as travel allows. Right, Evra?"

Evra didn't get the opportunity to argue. Oswin's frown silenced them both. "No, I'm afraid you won't be doing that. Not until the worst of midwinter is behind us."

Meira shook her head. "We had no troubles getting here only days ago."

"And in those days, you've seen the storm descending on us. It will be the first of many. You might clear Midwinter Rest without troubles, but you'll never cross the pass like this. No one travels in the thick of midwinter. I'm surprised Lord Dereham didn't inform you of this before you troubled yourself."

"Then we'll veer south from the east side," Meira challenged, frustrated with herself that she couldn't hide this from the steward and Evra.

"Only the Compass Roads are passable in this weather, and the Compass Road of the North is west of the pass, not east. You'd find yourself in fair trouble, with no one to get you out of it."

"It's fine." Evra looked as exhausted as he sounded. "I'm in no condition to ride yet, anyway. We'll wait it out, then return."

Meira wanted to fight them both, but there was no winning against an unforgiving and unknown path. She'd heard the stories of Rush Riders caught in a Northerlands midwinter, never to return. She might risk it for herself, but she was sworn to protect Evra, not lead him deeper into trouble. "We've agreed on one point, though, yes?"

Both men looked at her.

"The Ravenwoods are no longer an option. We'll find another way to save our world, without ruining another."

Both men looked away.

Once the door was shut, Evra released the tension he'd been collecting since Meira declared their fate in the corridor. He flattened his back against the door, sensing her lingering on the other side. What more could she want? She'd made a fool of him in front of the steward. She'd reduced him to a boy, requiring a firm hand. And now she had the nerve to decide *for him* what *he* would do?

The rest of the night churned through his thoughts. Rhosyn's terrible fate awaiting her. The Frosts' loving complacence. The way Morwen eyed him like he was a predator on the prowl.

Morwen would tell Rhosyn why he was there, and then Rhosyn would see him through that same clouded mirror.

And no matter how strangely and viscerally he'd reacted to Rhosyn Ravenwood, she *could* save his Reach. All of it. If he could set aside his own fears and prejudices in a way his father and brother could not, he could put an end to this all. He could still save Edriss' life. Rhosyn was all he would need.

Perhaps he was no less a monster than his father and brother, only one wearing a different colored cloak.

Evra jumped at the sound of raps against the door. He stepped away from it just as it swung inward. Rhosyn's smile decimated all the dark thoughts preceding her arrival. He could live in that smile, die in it; be resurrected, over and over again, and never know he'd been anything but hopelessly alive.

"I wanted to check in on you once more before I retire." Concern spread across her face. "Are you all right, Evra?"

"Much better now," Evra answered. He set aside his fears and doubts. He set aside Morwen and Meira, and the Westerlands. They could wait.

Rhosyn was here, and he had never been so eager to exist in any moments as much as the ones he existed in with her.

121

FIFTEEN
THE UNTIMELY ARRIVAL
OF STEWARD HADDENFOOT

Evra awoke with a lightness he didn't recognize. A peculiar peace stole over him, finding no resistance from the usual tension that greeted him with the day. Despite the utter absence of them in the midwinter of the desolate north, he could swear he heard the sweet trilling song of birds just beyond his window. As he pulled himself higher, a peak of sunlight washed over his face, and he wondered if he was still dreaming.

He closed his eyes and opened them again. Curled each toe, one by one, and then his fingers, just as his mother once taught him when the nightmares were nightly visitors. No new reality replaced his current one, and so this feeling, this rare and wonderful sense of purpose, could only be real.

If the sun was high enough to light his room, then the day had already moved on. Evra threw the furs back and started to dress when he heard what sounded like screaming. As he shimmied into his clothes and boots, he recognized it more accurately as crying. There were other voices, too, and he went still to make sense of them, but he wouldn't solve this mystery from his bedchamber.

When he reached the hall, Meira was already heading toward the melee. He almost called to her, but he wasn't ready to surrender the strange joy of this morning to her skepticism and judgment. He limped along behind her until she disappeared at the end of the corridor. She'd taken her longbow with her.

"What's all this?" he heard her say.

Evra used the wall to push himself along faster. The chorus of sobbing was louder now, competing only with two male voices, one he recognized, and one he did not.

Oswin Frost and another man stood off to the side, engaged in terse conversation. They passed furtive glances at Rhosyn and Morwen, the source of the conjoined cries. The two clutched each other in a desperation that Evra couldn't relate to. He had never known the kind of love that could elicit such sadness.

"Morwen's bridegroom has arrived from Dunwoode," Oswin explained to Meira. His eyes were on his daughter, his focus on the newcomer.

"I feel terrible," the young man said. His brows furrowed as he watched his soon-to-be wife howl against Rhosyn. "I confess, I haven't spent enough time traveling the northern half of our Reach. I greatly underestimated the pass."

"Most men do," Oswin said. His frown deepened, becoming a scowl. "You'll forgive my daughter's melodrama. As you know, we are sheltered up here, and she has not the experiences of the young women of Wulfsgate or Dunwoode."

"Still." The young steward ran his fingers over the corners of his mouth.

"Ahh, Evra." Oswin seemed neither glad nor regretful to see him. He existed outside the moment, despite his great effort to be at the helm of it. "Steward Haddenfoot, this is Lord Blackrook of the Westerlands."

The steward's eyes shot wide. "Lord of the Westerlands, all the way up here?"

"On business," Evra explained as he took the man's hand, eyes still on Rhosyn. "Steward Haddenfoot."

"Call me Edelard," the steward said, with a light chuckle that seemed out of place in the somber moment. "I'm not yet used to the formalities."

"Evra," Evra returned, still caught between the arrival and the departure. "I am also newly ascended to the role."

Edelard sighed in light relief. "Then you understand."

"I do." He forced himself not to listen to the devastated whispers passing between the young women. A goodbye, he understood, after the revelations of the prior evening, that would be permanent.

"Well, as I was explaining to Steward Frost, I regret we must leave so soon. I would have liked to get to know Morwen's family, but the storm in the pass took two of my men, and I hear there's another coming in mere days."

Oswin nodded. "There'll be nothing but until the springtide comes whispering her false hopes." He opened his arms as little Rylan came running toward him. "If you don't time it just right, Edelard, you'll find yourself in worse circumstances on the return."

"If we have to travel all the way to the south instead, we will. It will be a rougher path, for sure, but my men know the way."

"Are you sure I can't talk you into staying until the season breaks?"

"I can think of nothing more pleasing, but my father left me with more work than I know what to do with, and if I'm away so long, I fear managing a revolt will be next on the list."

Oswin nodded in understanding. "A steward's job is never done."

Edelard passed a glance at the girls, still crying in one another's arms. "I'm almost more afraid to break that up."

"Go say hello to Thorn. I'll manage Morwen." Oswin sighed as he watched his red-faced daughter. "She'll come around."

"It's too soon. It's too soon," Morwen sobbed. Rhosyn held her, one hand pressed to her friend's matted hair. She hadn't had time to run a brush through it. It was all happening so fast.

"It will always be too soon, Morwen. This day was always going to be like this. But you must be strong now!" Rhosyn peeled back and kissed the corners of Morwen's eyes. She rolled her lips inward, inhaling the salt of her tears. If her magic allowed her to pass strength, she would give it all to Morwen. "You'll finally be a bride, just as you always wanted. And he's so *handsome*." Rhosyn whispered this last. "This will be no burden for you."

"I thought we had more time," Morwen cried. "I thought... I thought I would have to watch you leave, and that's what I prepared myself for, not this..."

Rhosyn held her at arm's length. For herself. For Morwen. If she could not be strong for herself, Rhosyn would have to do it. "We're women now. There is no going back. Wishing for that, for what can never be, only wounds us. There's enough in this world to hurt us. Let's not hurt ourselves, if we can help it."

Morwen's splotched face gaped back at her. Her sobs turned to small, shuddering gasps. "I love you, Rhosyn. I would set this kingdom on fire from sea to sea for you. And yet, when you need me most, I can do nothing but watch, helpless, and then be dragged away to a place where I cannot even reach you with my comfort."

Rhosyn's flesh tingled with her grief. There would be time to address it later. Morwen had only moments left in Midwinter Rest. "Then do this one final thing for me."

"What?"

"Be brave." Rhosyn kissed her mouth. "Be brave and embrace your future with the happiness it deserves. For all endings are also beginnings, are they not? Just as midwinter will eventually fade to springtide, so the season of our youth passes. There are only two choices from here. To collapse under the weight of it, or to soar in the promise. And I, Morwen, want nothing more than to watch my sister soar."

A change came over Morwen. The tears stopped, though her grief reflected in her eyes, glistening like spun glass. "There's something else... I was going to tell you, but..." Morwen looked past Rhosyn at some fixed place that darkened her face. "Not here. I'll send a raven once we're safely in Dunwoode. But since you've made one final request of me, I have one of my own."

"I'll happily oblige."

Morwen leaned in and whispered, "Be shrewd with your trust."

Evra observed Rhosyn watching the train of wagons disappear beyond the iron gates and into the fog. Oswin gathered his two sons in each arm, waiting, it seemed, for Rhosyn. But she only stared stubbornly ahead, and eventually they turned to go in.

"Come on, Evra," Meira urged. He waved her away. He felt her pain as the blow of his indifference landed, but his apologies remained buried in his chest, in the same place where his confused feelings for Rhosyn lived. When she stormed off after the men, it was relief he felt, not the regret that should reside in its place.

It was the relief he followed when Rhosyn started moving again. She didn't return to the keep, however, but ventured beyond the same iron gates Morwen and her new husband had exited. Evra worried she might take to flight and go after them, but once clear of the property, she angled herself to the south and entered the woods.

He followed her past the first dense copse of needled trees, fighting against snow that was thigh deep and his still sore foot. When she didn't turn to confront him in the clearing, he kept on after her, panting through every labored step, wondering if she had a destination in mind. It was solitude she was after, and he should give her that, and not whatever he thought he might offer when at last he caught up to her and found the courage to say something that would fall short of adequate.

She turned toward another clearing and a short hill, and that was when he saw what she must have known all along. At the top of the mound was ground untouched by snow. Above, a dense canopy of trees provided the shelter for this haven.

Rhosyn knelt on a blanket someone had left. Without turning, she called to him, and he nearly jumped out of his skin.

"There was no need to follow me, Lord Blackrook. I'm perfectly fine out here on my own."

"I'm not... I wasn't..." He began to explain his uselessness at defending even himself, but it was nice, for a change, to be around someone who knew none of that. "I know you can defend yourself."

"Against what?" she sniffled, laughing, as she waved her arms around. "Nothing out here but that which walks on four legs instead of two."

Evra moved closer without encroaching on the careful distance still between them. "What about snowbeasts? They must be massive. That trap nearly took my foot off."

"Snowbeasts aren't real."

"Not real?"

"Myth. Legend. You do have those in the Westerlands?" From where she knelt, he could just make out the jut of her pale chin resting against a mantle of feathers.

"Everything without explanation is myth to a Westerlander," Evra quipped.

"Steward Frost told me about your father's disdain for magic."

Evra swallowed. He pulled his meager cloak tighter, but it was no help against the morning chill. "What else did he tell you?"

"That your business is your own." Rhosyn lowered herself all the way down to the blanket, unfolding her legs in straight lines before her. "You can sit. Unless you prefer the snow to eat through your trousers."

Evra hobbled the rest of the way up the hill and lowered himself next to her. It *was* warmer here, and it wasn't only the break in the snow. Some of it was her; rising off her flesh like an invitation. Briefly, the memory of kissing Seven flashed through his mind and he wondered, if he were to kiss Rhosyn, would it feel as empty? Or would it be precisely the thrill that would lead him to question everything?

But he wouldn't kiss her. She needed a friend, and he needed a reprieve from his racing thoughts.

"Morwen and I used to ride here. Well, *she* would ride, and I would ungracefully slide across my saddle like a midnight goat."

"I thought horses couldn't come here. We had to leave ours in town. Or was that just to mess with us?"

"These horses are born here. They know nothing else," Rhosyn said. She seemed to go somewhere else. "They never leave. Like the Frosts."

"I'm sorry about Morwen," Evra offered.

"Sorry?" Rhosyn leaned back on her palms, shaking her head. "Morwen travels toward a future she was born for, one that will coat the rest of her years in happiness, in whatever form it comes."

Evra sensed the underlying comparison. The Frosts didn't want him telling Rhosyn he knew her future, but her unspoken words issued an invitation. "I know little about your world, Rhosyn, but I understand you're not happy about what awaits you."

Rhosyn stiffened. Her throat ebbed, the feathers from her collar moving with her flesh. "I know you're offering kindness, but you could never understand."

"I never wanted to be lord, either."

"That's not the same."

Evra bowed his head. "I know."

"I like talking to you." Rhosyn closed her eyes and sat up straight. "You don't already know all there is to know about me. I can be whoever I want with you."

Evra folded his hands in his lap with a smile. "I was just thinking the same."

"Were you?"

"Everyone at home has already decided who I am. Who I'll be there. Here I can be... anyone."

"You can be yourself," Rhosyn said. She leaned in and briefly nudged him with her shoulder. "Not who *they* think you are. Who *you know* you are."

Evra nodded, still looking down. "But it is also true, for both of us, that these freedoms of self are ephemeral. In the end, we'll both follow duty, and we'll both be whoever *they* need us to be. Won't we?"

Rhosyn rolled her head back in surprise. "Evrathedyn. I did not figure you for such a cynic."

Evra lifted the corner of his mouth in a chuckle. "I came out here to make you feel better. I can't claim to possess comfort as a talent now, can I?"

Rhosyn's fingers traveled slowly across the blanket. The tips of hers brushed the tips of his. If she had run him through with a sword, the shock of this sensation would not have been half as powerful as touching her like this, on their terms. Not to heal. Not from duty. From the desire to exist in just one moment where there were no *theys* to keep them from being who they wanted to be, in the space of their hopes and dreams.

They both looked down at the same time. Rhosyn climbed her fingers over his flesh, and he slid his palm closer until their hands formed a perfect union.

"Comfort is more than words," she said to him, and for a glimmer in time, Evra thought he could see past the barrier Rhosyn had constructed to keep herself safe. "I came to Midwinter Rest for a reprieve. I never expected to find a new friend."

Evra couldn't break his gaze away from their hands, still linked. Nothing had ever felt so right to him, but it was wrong, *wrong*. If she knew he, too, wanted something from her, that light in her eyes would die, and she would again turn to her own shadows for solace.

Rhosyn tilted her head to the side, her silver hair falling away from her face. The ends tickled the tops of his hand, and he stifled a gasp. The tears from before had dried, and now her violet eyes were shining from the remnants, brilliant flecks of twilight. Instinct guided him closer, drawing his face to hers, and her response bade him continue down this path, until—

130

"Evra?" Meira's accusing tone cut between them. Rhosyn snapped her knees to her chest as if she'd done something wrong. Evra brushed at his leather armor and jumped to his feet.

"We, uh... that is, I..."

"I don't care what you were up to." She looked past him, eyes fixed on Rhosyn. "I care that neither of you heard our calls."

"Calls?"

"The steward, his son. Me. We've been looking for you both. The stewardess has begun her laboring, and she needs her healer."

"So soon?" Rhosyn took Evra's hand when he offered it, rising to join him at his side. "She should have weeks yet. Are you certain?"

"Me?" Meira scoffed. "I know nothing about bringing a child."

Rhosyn turned her panicked face to Evra. "I have to go to her."

"Go on," he urged. The knot in his chest dissolved, replaced by fear, but of what? "Go see to the stewardess."

She glanced down at his foot.

"Don't worry about me. I'll catch up."

"What if you fall?"

Meira groaned and joined Evra at his side, flopping his arm over her shoulder. "He won't. He has me."

Rhosyn slowly nodded, regarding them both. To Evra, she said, "Thank you again. I'll see you..."

"Yeah," Evra whispered. "I'll see you."

Rhosyn lifted her dress and bolted off.

"What are you *doing* out here?" Meira asked when she was gone. "What is going through your head, Evra? What could you possibly be thinking?"

"Why are you so angry with me?"

"How can you not know? We didn't leave the Westerlands and come all the way to"—she waved a gloved hand—"this, so you could sneak into the woods with a sorceress."

Evra hobbled back and faced her. "We came here to learn how we might save our people. She's the key to that."

"We agreed—"

131

"No, Meira," Evra said, shaking his head. "You said we'd find another way. Not me."

"You're not learning anything from her. You know she can't help you. The steward and his son made it perfectly clear. So if you're not searching for another way, then what are you doing?"

"We've only been here a few days!"

"And you've wasted every one!"

Evra pointed both hands at his foot. "I didn't exactly *plan* to get mauled by a snowbeast trap. And did you know they're not even *real?*"

"What?"

"Snowbeasts, they're—"

"I don't care about the bloody snowbeasts!"

Evra fell back another step. "What's really going on here, Meira?"

Meira dropped her hands to her sides. He finally noticed she didn't have her longbow, and she looked strange without it. Like Rhosyn might without the feathers that reminded him, always, who she was. "I came here not only to protect you, but to *aid* you. I'm more than your guard, Evra. I'm your *friend.* Your oldest friend, even if you don't remember."

Evra lowered his eyes. "I remember."

"I don't blame you for running off to university and leaving the horrors behind, but some of us? Some of us stayed. Some of us had no choice. So while you play happy families with the raven, all I can think about is that every single day we're away, more people are dying. More people will die tomorrow, and the day after, and only you have the power to stop that."

"I know that," he said. "I know that, Meira. I just... I thought it would be easier than it is. That I could offer her some enticement, and she'd ride back to the Westerlands, and that would be that. I *know* how naïve that sounds. But now, what I feel, is fear for her. She doesn't deserve what's coming."

"Your people don't deserve to die! *Edriss* doesn't deserve to die!" Meira countered. "I, too, feel pity for the sorceress, but *Evra.*

132

Evra, you cannot save her. You heard the steward and his son. It isn't the place of men to judge or interfere with the ways of the ravens. And if you can't get your head on straight, you'll fail both her and your Reach, because you can only save one, and trying to save the other will keep you from succeeding at that."

Evra moved away from her. This was all true. It changed nothing. "I just need time."

"There isn't time."

"There isn't another resolution, either."

"You know there is. The Sepulchre."

Evra shook his head. "You wonder where my head is at. How could I ever tell you, when yours can only think of one thing?" He turned his head over his shoulder. "You say you don't want our people to keep dying? What you suggest would bring war to our lands, and then there'd be no one left. There *has* to be another way. There has to, or we'll trade one war for another."

"Whatever the answer, it isn't here. Not anymore."

Rhosyn passed the filthy basin to the kitchen maid. It wasn't until the girl was gone that she realized she was still holding the rag. She set it aside and sank into the rocker at the stewardess' bedside.

"How is she?" Brin appeared at the door, apron in hand. Her hair had fallen out of the braids. Some stuck to the sweat on her brow. She'd stepped out for air but looked no better for it.

"Sleeping," Rhosyn said. Only now, when it was over, and both the stewardess and her unborn child safe, could she appreciate how close she'd come to losing them both. It hadn't been Ethelyn's time to bring the child, and her body had fought on both ends of this battle. "I'll stay a little longer before I retire, just to be sure."

"You were very brave," Brin said softly. "More than I've ever been. If you hadn't been here, I... I think I would've just huddled in the corner and cried."

Rhosyn gave her a tired smile. "That's not true."

Brin stepped farther into the room. The candlelight brought her exhaustion into full view. "Rhosyn, I know the two of us are not close, not as you are with Morwen. But I feel as if I should still say something, like I would if you were my own sister."

Rhosyn stopped rocking. "What do you mean? Say what?"

"It's not my place to speak on behalf of Lord Blackrook. So I will only say, please consider caution in your dealings with him."

"My dealings with him? I have none. Not beyond his injury."

Brin cocked her head. "You'll get no judgment from me. Nor is it necessary to ply me with the same denials you'd use on my husband or father-in-law. I'll say none of this to them. For this is the business of women, isn't it?"

Rhosyn didn't have that answer. She'd known so few women who bothered to speak to her at all. "I suppose."

"You have more wisdom than me," Brin said. She leaned into the doorframe with a light sigh, the last of the evening's stress. "I just hope you'll be careful and guard those parts of yourself that no one else can guard for you."

"There's no..." Rhosyn exhaled. "I like Lord Blackrook. I enjoy talking to him. Beyond that, he's just another thing from a world that doesn't belong to me. I appreciate your words, Brin. I do know better. I know better than most."

"It doesn't belong to anyone," Brin said with a sleepy smile. "I'll tell the steward and Thorn how your quick hands and mind saved Stewardess Ethelyn tonight. That without you, both she and her child would have spent their promise."

"That's not necessary."

"We never know what might one day prove necessary."

SIXTEEN
SWORDS AND INTENTIONS

It's true, then? You know nothing about your ancestral steel?"
Oswin remarked as he resettled the heavy metal bar into the
forge. Sweat beaded across Evra's flesh, the inside heat shocking
compared to how frozen he'd felt moments before.

"My father had little time for me," Evra said. When he came
to help, the steward pointed to the bench.

"Some blacksmiths prefer extra hands. I do not." Hands on
hips, he watched the metal heat. "And anyway, there's nothing to
do except wait, for now. It's not hot enough yet, and I laid my
tools out before I came to you." He turned. "Your father had two
sons?"

Evra nodded, folding his hands over his lap. "He would say he
only had one. It wasn't so bad, though, not when I was little and
my mother was still around. She shielded me from the worst of it."

Oswin leaned back against his anvil. "His reasons?"

Evra opened his palms in a shrug. "I wasn't strong enough.
Not bold enough. Brave enough. Didn't have the belly for the war

he was waging against his own people." He twisted his mouth into a wry grin. "I liked books better."

"Nothing wrong with books," Oswin said. "Except the gold needed to buy them."

"We've never lacked for that in the Rush. Imagination, though..."

"And you've come here, why? To prove him wrong, or to right a wrong?"

"Can't it be both?"

"Anything can be more than one thing. But a man always has a cause that starts from within and compels him. I've been trying to figure yours out since you arrived here. I can see plainly enough that you're not your father or your brother. You wouldn't have needed to leave home at all if you were. Beyond that, I still don't quite know who Evrathedyn Blackrook is." Oswin watched him closely. "Do you?"

Evra looked down at his hands.

"No." Oswin decided for him. "Perhaps you're here to find that out. How goes your quest to borrow a Ravenwood? All I've seen is you follow her around with twinkles in your eyes." When Evra tried to protest, the steward chuckled. "I had to have a talk with my own son about it, more than once. But you're not here to fall sideways for the girl, and even if you did, she's not the one. Not for you. Not now. Not ever."

"I've tried to tell her why I'm here," Evra said, and he realized, as the words left him, that they were a lie. He'd fought himself *not* to tell her, to purchase every available second with her before it was taken. All this, for someone he didn't even know. "I don't know how, Steward. Now that I know... what you've told me..."

"Gives a man some perspective about his own troubles, doesn't it?" Oswin shook his head and pulled a pipe from his boot, lighting it with the forge. Evra held his breath until the steward withdrew his hand safely. "Rhosyn is strong. Stronger than her mother. She'll survive this, just as you will."

136

"I can't stop thinking about what she has to face. How *awful* it must be, to be a Ravenwood, surrounded by tyrants and abusers. If that's the cost of their magic, it's not worth it."

"Is that what you think? Careful where you take that thought, Evra. It's dangerously close to the ideals you came here to be rid of." The steward inhaled a lungful of smoke. "They're not all like that. Most aren't like that. Even the bad ones are only finding their way in a system their forbears built. As you are now."

"I hadn't thought of it that way."

"What will you do?"

"What do you think I should do?"

Oswin checked the heat in the forge once more. "You didn't come here for my advice, Evra. Nor would you like it very much."

"Because you think I should abandon the idea of the Ravenwoods?"

"I cannot see any of them willingly going any farther south than the capital. You'd need to act with great dishonor, binding their hands so they have no fight against you, and I know that's not who you are."

"You said you didn't know who I am."

"You're not that. You have to understand, they've lived safely in the north for hundreds of years. The concerns of your Reach may as well be the concerns of another world."

Evra frowned. "Then why have you helped me?"

"I've shown you kindness, as I would any guest of the Hold. I know better than to tell any man what he can or cannot do. Those are things he must discover for himself." Oswin pressed at the metal with a poker. "I've work to do, and this won't be a proper weapon until the morning." He leaned back and withdrew his own sword, angling the hilt toward Evra as he approached. "In the meantime, you'll be in the back room, practicing against the hay."

Evra laughed. "You want me to stab hay?"

"I want you to become used to the feel of wielding a sword. Of swinging a sword, and then the strength and persistence needed to bury a sword and retrieve it again."

Evra reluctantly accepted the weapon. He sagged as the heft tugged against his palm, straining his wrist. "Why are you doing this for me?"

"A thriving Westerlands is a thriving kingdom. A thriving kingdom leads to the resumption of trade, which puts richer foods on my table and will provide for a better marriage for Rylan than I was able to give Thorn." Oswin wrapped Evra's other hand around the one already holding the hilt. "You came here to be a man. A man should have a sword."

Rhosyn fell back in the chair, spent. She mopped at her brow with her sleeve, wishing for the more practical gowns the women of Midwinter Hold wore instead of the ornate costume forced upon the Ravenwood women. The leather bodice of her dress clung to her flesh. The feathers stabbed at her neck. She could borrow from the wardrobe Morwen left in her rush for Dunwoode, but then she'd only feel more like a Frost, not less. It would be even harder to shrug off the shroud of man.

But Stewardess Frost would survive another day.

"You're still here, dear." Ethelyn rolled her gaunt face to the side and smiled weakly. "You'll be recalled soon. You shouldn't spend all your time in here, with me."

"I don't," Rhosyn reassured her. "But you gave us quite a scare, Stewardess. It was almost beyond my magic to save you while calming the babe a while longer."

"What will be, will be," Ethelyn whispered. Her eyes fluttered as she fought off needed rest. "No one knows that like you, though, I suppose." She stretched her hand toward the nightstand. Rhosyn rushed forward to bring the wine to her, but Ethelyn shooed her. She finished off the remnants herself and let the goblet fall to the stone floor. "It wasn't the silver-haired witch who stayed the babe. It was the child's mother."

Rhosyn leaned forward. "You? How?"

"When you're a mother, you'll understand. This is the closest I'll ever be to my last son. Once he's born, he'll go to the wet nurse, and then he'll be subject to his father's whims until he's sent off to wed a Weatherford, or, if Oswin can swallow his pride, a Dereham, even. I told Castian it wasn't time, and he listened to me. It's no simpler than that."

"Castian is a wonderful name." Rhosyn had sensed the child would be a boy as well, but she didn't know the stewardess knew. "It's good he heeded his mother, even just this once. You'll both fare better if he makes it further along."

"I didn't do it for Castian."

"No?"

"I asked you for one thing. You did it without question. I can remove Morwen's future from my long list of worries."

Rhosyn balked. "There was no need for you to ask me at all. I would've never come between Morwen and her happiness. Love isn't about keeping the object of your devotion in a box. It's about helping them be free of it. She will always be the sister of my heart, no matter where her life takes her."

Ethelyn chuckled. She rolled her head back. "You've always had a poetic way of seeing the world, our silver-haired witch. Brin tells me you've been spending time with the steward's guest. The young lord from the Westerlands. Does he like your poetry, too?"

"He stepped in a snowbeast trap and it nearly took his foot. If the steward hadn't found him when he did, it would have taken his life, too."

"Save your defensiveness for those who would begrudge your happiness. I won't order you to be careful, Rhosyn, but I will ask you to be mindful that your whims do not bring another un-win-nable war upon Midwinter Rest. Your fate lies beyond any power we wield. Let it be enough that we would wield it, if we could, and then respect that we cannot." Ethelyn yawned into her pillow. "Let me rest a bit, dear, and then we can begin again."

Evra let the sword tip fall to the hay-covered floor as he nursed the fire burning in his shoulder. He'd been at it for the better part of an hour, and still he couldn't swing the steel any more than a few times without taking a break, winded and aflame with a soreness he'd never known before.

Why *had* he never seen his father's sword? Was this a failure of Aeldred, in choosing not to fold him in, or in himself, for failing to be curious enough? What must the council have thought, when he'd never even asked about these things all men should know?

Evra took a step back and returned his free hand to the hilt, gripping it tight enough to feel his weak wrist scream in protest of the coming assault. He winded back, not from any training, or knowledge, for he had none of either, but from a scorching desire to make even one pass at the hay bale that didn't leave him humiliated.

Evra closed his eyes and screamed into his swing. The steel connected sideways, cutting a clean line through the twine and exiting the far side without so much as a sigh.

He stumbled back with a laugh. "Well, would you look at that?"

The sound of delighted clapping squelched his joy. He knew who it was. He didn't need to turn. Now he saw the past seconds through her eyes, no longer a young man overcoming, but failing, returning to the weakness he'd been born out of and was destined for.

"That was a clean cut!" Rhosyn exclaimed. Hay crunched under her feet as she drew closer. "That's the steward's sword, isn't it?"

"Uh, yeah. Yeah, it is." Evra willed the embarrassed flush in his cheeks to subside, but that was about as likely as the floor swallowing him whole, though equally desirable. "He's crafting one for me. Wants me to practice."

"Well, that's no practice sword," she said as she stepped around him. She hadn't looked up at him yet. She only had eyes for the steel. "This weighs as much as Rylan, I'd wager."

"I hadn't noticed."

"Liar."

Evra grinned. She grinned back. He forgot he was supposed to be embarrassed. "I should know... you know... how to do this."

"Swing a sword?"

He nodded.

"I can't either." Rhosyn's flippant shrug drew a laugh from him. "There are a lot of things I can't do." She nodded at the ground. "I came to check on you. Took me a while to track you all the way out here. How's your foot?"

"Better. And what does skill matter when you have magic?"

Rhosyn rolled her head back. "You misunderstand magic if you think it's a replacement for skill. For experience. For talent. For wisdom. For *anything*."

Evra wagged his finger at his foot. "No physician could have saved my foot. No experience, no wisdom, no talent he possessed could have done what you did."

"That's one thing," she conceded. She pulled the sword from his hand and sagged into the heft as she circled him. "It's not everything. And what good is magic if you cannot even use it to save yourself?"

"Your brother, you mean." The words came easier now. He wasn't afraid to say them, or how she might react when he did.

"Yes."

"This sword would be no better at stopping him."

"I never said it would, did I?" She watched him from the side as she dragged the sword around him, drawing a circle in the hay. The steel tip scraped on the wood as she moved. "Some things are what they are, and there is no defense. Knowing this is its own form of survival."

"You'd be well suited to a lord's council with that way of thinking."

"Lords only have one use for someone like me, Evra."

"I don't think of you that way." Only days ago, this would have been a lie.

"So you've thought about it?"

Evra spun with her, turning as she made her way around him. "So that's all you can do, then? Heal?"

"No."

"Are you going to tell me or make me guess?"

"What *would* you guess if I were to give you one?"

Evra pretended to think about it, but he already had his answer. In his fantasies, a true sorcerer was one who could conjure fire with their hands. "A fire dancer."

"Fire dancer? Is that something that happens in the kingdom? People dance with fire?"

"That's what we call it. A conjurer, I guess."

"Incorrect."

Evra pushed against his dizziness and kept up with her growing pace as she circled. "Do I have to keep guessing? Because I'm terrible at it."

"I can read minds," Rhosyn answered. She was behind him now. "And intentions."

Evra's newfound courage faltered. "What about mine?"

"I could," she said with a devious grin. Her eyes twinkled. "If I wanted."

"Have you already? Looked into my mind, gleaned my intentions?"

"I have not."

"Why?"

Rhosyn came to a halt. The steel ceased its shrill scraping along the uneven floor. "It feels like an invasion, to do it without permission."

Only a fool would say this, he thought, but it didn't stop him. "I'm inviting you to."

She turned. "You're what?"

She'll see straight through to the reason you're here. She won't understand things have changed. She won't understand you. Or she will understand you, and that will be worse. "Inviting you. To read my intentions."

"You don't mean that."

"I do."

"You're certain that's what you want? You do know what you're asking?"

Evra wasn't certain at all. It was his worst idea yet, in a string of bad ones. He bit his lip and nodded.

"Why?" Rhosyn handed the sword back to him. "No one's ever asked me this. No one's ever been foolish enough to want their thoughts bare to another." She stepped closer. "I'd never want anyone to see mine like that."

"I didn't think I would, either," Evra said. "Until I met you."

Rhosyn's mouth parted. She searched for her next words but never found them.

"It's all right. I know what I'm asking. I want you to."

Rhosyn came closer. She raised her hands and settled them on either side of his face. Her palms cupped the flesh of his cheeks, forming a warm, soft canopy. He stopped breathing until she pressed her forehead to his and closed her eyes.

"This is how you do it?" he whispered. "Not just with your hands?"

She shook her head against his. "I just wanted to know how you felt."

Evra brought his hands over hers, tangling their fingers. Her eyes were open again, and he could see into them, through them, and she was... she was... "Rhosyn."

"Evra."

"So, tell me." He pushed the lump down his throat. "What are my intentions?"

Rhosyn's eyes filled with tears. She flexed their hands against his face, and as her palm slid down, his lips caught the edge.

143

"I..." Rhosyn's hands slipped and fell away, breaking their entanglement. She backed up. "I have to get back to the stewardess. I'll... I'll come check on your foot later."

"Rhosyn!" he cried, but her footsteps were already in the armory, and then, seconds later, the outer door swung closed.

SEVENTEEN
THE BETRAYER

Evra found the library easily enough. The stretch of the broad double doors belied a behemoth within, but what greeted him was a starkly decorated room. The expected shelves and books were there but crowded into a shadowed corner, away from the muted light of the tall windows.

This room instead seemed to be an homage to Frosts of the past. Portraits taller than Evra stretched along the walls, men and women alike judging him from their eternal perches. He recognized Steward Oswin at the end of the line, a blank space beside him waiting for Thorn.

Whatever the answer, it isn't here. Not anymore.

Meira's words hadn't left him. He wished she wasn't so single-minded because he needed guidance, now more than ever. But she was incapable of the objectivity needed for that conversation. He pretended instead to take her advice, while taking his own path in secret.

The answer wasn't Rhosyn or her kin. Meira *was* right. But that didn't mean there were no answers here at all. When they

145

left here, they couldn't simply return to the Rush. Not without a plan.

Evra wrapped his hands around his chilled arms and went to the shelves. It seemed almost *too* simple to learn about magic from books, but to possess such a book in the Westerlands was a death sentence. Even at university, they'd refrained from bringing the subject into lessons. That's what the Sepulchre was for.

He made a dust trail with his fingers, running them along books that probably hadn't been touched since before Oswin had children. None of the titles jumped out at him until a glance to the right startled him.

Rows and rows of chapters from *The Book of All Things*. Evra stopped when he came upon this collection. There were so many chapters, he could hardly believe what he was seeing! To possess so many, in a personal collection, was unheard of. And to leave them here, unused? Unread? It was like shoving trunks of gold in a closet. Even one of them could feed a village for a year.

Chapter of Beasts, Creatures, and Winged Animals. Chapter of Flora, Trees, and all Other Plant Life. Chapter of Customs. Chapter of Gods and Prayers. Chapter of Armies and Battles. Chapter of the Great Timeline. Chapter of the Northerlands. On and on it went, Evra's wonder growing with each title read. He'd once had the great honor of observing the Scholars work in their chambers as they slowly and meticulously transcribed the chapters. Theirs were the only transcriptions allowed. Reproductions were so few, it was shocking to see them in a private collection. And of a steward who'd been tucked into the corner of his Reach?

Chapter of the Westerlands. Evra reached for this one, but a voice stopped him from opening it.

"You've found Father's collection." Thorn walked up beside him. He leaned in and blew hard, but his efforts barely touched the layers of dust. "Impressive, isn't it? He's only missing a few chapters."

"I don't understand," Evra said in a reverent whisper, eyes still moving over the titles. "This is unheard of. There are hardly any transcriptions of *any* of these, and he has so many of them. The Reliquary believes our histories and ways should be protected, not spread to every corner of the kingdom."

"Say what you mean."

"I meant no slight." Evra backed down. "But this *is* surprising."

"Has your time with my father not shown you he's a surprising man?"

Evra still didn't know what to make of Oswin. "But why... why have them, if they're only going to rot on a shelf?" He pulled out the Westerlands chapter. "And so old. You know it's a crime to possess copies more than one generation out of date, don't you?" He sat the book on a nearby table and flipped to the end. "See? This still has my grandfather, Andarian, as Lord of the Westerlands."

"Is this why you wanted to become a Scholar? So you'd have an occupational excuse for your pedantry?"

Evra sighed. "He should apply for updated chapters if he can afford it."

Thorn furrowed his brows. "You gonna report him if he doesn't?"

"That's not what I meant."

"What did you mean?" Thorn reached past Evra to close the book. He replaced it on the shelf, patting it in. "If it's a library you were after, you should have returned to your beloved university. What we have here, we've worked for. You know their worth."

"But why? Why collect them at all, if they're only here to sit and rot?"

"Must be the Scholar in you, all your questions." Thorn leaned against the table, watching him. "You already know what's in those books. What are you really looking for?"

"I was wrong coming here," Evra confessed, despite knowing Thorn wasn't his friend. "I couldn't have known that before, but I know it now. Still... I can't go home without *something*. I thought, perhaps, you might have books here that were forbidden in the Westerlands."

Amusement glinted in Thorn's eyes. "Magic? You want to learn about magic, from a book?"

Evra flushed. "I realize how that sounds."

"There are no books on magic, Evra, beyond what that *Chapter of the Sepulchre in the Skies and Magic Practicers* holds, and clearly you've already read that. Consummate pupil that you are."

He nodded. "It's all dry facts, like all the chapters. Lists of famous Enchanters, Grand Magi, their curriculum over the years. It tells you nothing."

"Magic isn't meant to be understood like plants and animals and men. It's everywhere. Man. Ravenwood. Medvedev. Even the Rhiagains brought magic with them to our kingdom. It's all around us. It *was* all around your kin until your father and grandfather made bloody work of the practice."

"Which is why if I return home, I'll know even less than I know now, here, where people aren't afraid of it."

"What is it you want to know?"

"How to save my people!" Evra exclaimed. "How to save them, without more falling to the inevitable civil war that will follow when I betray my council."

Thorn scoffed. "How can a lord betray his council? They're there at your service and pleasure."

"They've had many years to convince the people to follow their ways. I've already spent more of my time as lord here than at home. If I return with nothing? No relief? No way forward?"

"You have to go home eventually, Evra."

Evra glanced back at the shelf of dusty books. "I know."

"If you're staying for her, you're staying for heartache." Thorn turned his eyes back to the books. "You wouldn't be the first to try."

"You, right?"

"Father set me straight. Mind you, she never so much as turned her eyes on me. But then, that means I was never a danger to her like you are."

"I've only just met her," Evra protested. "I don't even know her."

"You're right. You don't know her." Thorn clapped a hand on his shoulder. "And that makes what you're doing more dangerous than you'll realize until it's too late to unwind it. You want to know about magic? Make it safe for the Enchanters in your Reach still left. Or decide to be a man and make amends at the source. Because, the Ravenwoods? We don't get involved in their affairs. We don't pretend we have any power over what they do, when, and with whom. If you learn that lesson the hard way, it will be too late for her." Thorn shook off his solemnity and grinned. "I came here for a purpose. Father has requested your presence in the armory."

"It's done?"

"It's done. I told him he's a little ahead of himself when you haven't even grown hair in the places that make you a man, but he insists you'll miraculously transform once you have a proper weapon. I've wagered against you, so I'd appreciate if you fail to meet his lofty expectations."

Evra glowered at him, but he was laughing, too. "I'd bet against me, too."

"There you are." Oswin rotated the hilt and passed the newly crafted steel to Evra. "Take your gloves off, son. You need to feel it. Feel the way the leather wraps. Where it sits best."

Evra dropped both gloves to the ground. With a nervous intake of breath, he retook the sword. He winced in preparation for the inevitable pull, but it didn't come. There was a good weight to it, but it didn't overwhelm Evra as the steward's steel had. This one was just right.

He rotated the sword in his hand, feeling, as Oswin commanded, for the way it sat best, smiling as he became acquainted with his first proper weapon. He looked up. "I don't know how to thank you."

"You'll name it, for starters. Any respectable sword needs a name."

Evra chuckled. "How would I choose? Does yours have a name?"

"Frostbringer," Oswin answered. "Named by my great-grandfather to show the wind and snow they cannot break us. For we belong here, as much as they do." He laid a hand on his sword hilt. "He'd lost his wife and three of his children that year. That's when he built the armory. Crafted his own steel, with help from his surviving son. He left his father's sword stuck into the mountainside. It's still there today. Wedged in so tight I don't think anything could free it."

Evra set the metal on his palm, careful not to connect with the sharp edges. "He named it for his enemy, then."

"He named it," Oswin said. "For what gave him strength. What brought you here, Evrathedyn? It was more than saving your Reach or your sister."

"I wanted things to be different," he answered as he slid the steel into the sheath. He drew it again. "Which seems so strange now that I say it aloud. Because it was my desire for nothing to be different that kept me away from my land and kin to begin with. I wanted to fall in line with an easier path. To know what to expect from every second."

"You're coming closer. Go on. You came because..."

"I wanted something different... I wanted to be, if not better, then at least not worse... to be..."

"To come here, you went against your council. You made your own way."

"They would say I betrayed them," Evra said. He rolled the metal, catching the detail in the slim beam of light pushing through the boarded window. "They're saying it right now."

"Betrayal is not always an act of treason. Nor evil. Betrayal can be the instrument of change."

Evra met the steward's eyes.

"I think you have your name, then."

Evra raised his sword to the side. He enjoyed the strain in his upper arms as he drew it higher; enjoyed more how he fought this and emerged victor. "The Betrayer."

Oswin nodded, grinning. "With a name like that, you'll have to work to live up to it. No obscurity for you, eh?"

"It was never obscurity I wanted," Evra said, more to himself. "Only stability. Consistency. I wanted to know what awaited me with each waking day, and that when I went to sleep at night, that too would be predictable."

"No man has that luxury, Evra. Life isn't like that."

"Life always catches up, doesn't it? My aunt Alise, she once said to me that the world always heals itself when things have gone too far. If a predator takes over a forest, the forest will fight back to protect the smaller beasts, making it inhospitable for the larger ones. When a plague takes over a patch of plants, the plants will learn to defend themselves, becoming resistant. Life catches up, she said. My people are dying. I can say it a thousand times and it doesn't soften at all. And they are *my* people, aren't they, Steward? I might be the third choice to the council, but life and fate have made me first. I don't have to like it. I just have to... to embrace it. To accept that if it isn't me, it will be no one else. If I don't fight back against the plague and the predators, then they win."

Oswin started to respond when the door flew open. They both turned.

Meira panted as she gripped the wood frame. "Congratulations, Steward Frost. Your son entered the kingdom only minutes ago. Castian is healthy, a fair weight, and the stewardess is in good spirits as well."

Oswin sighed, sagging. He caught himself on the bench. "Ethelyn is fine? She'll be fine?"

"Rhosyn asked me to let you know she'll stay another couple nights to be sure, but... yes. She was quite confident in the stewardess' prospects."

"Thank the Guardians." He looked up with his eyes closed, hands folded. "When can I see them?"

"You can go now, sir," Meira answered with a tired smile. "Brin and Rhosyn are tidying up the chamber, but the stewardess is awake and awaiting the arrival of the wet nurse."

Oswin clapped Evra on the shoulder. "Practice. You'll find it comes more natural because it was made for you."

Evra nodded, but his thoughts had already swung to Rhosyn. *She'll stay another couple nights to be sure.* And then... "Thank you, sir. And congratulations."

He waited for the steward to leave so he could be alone with his thoughts, so he could *think*, but he wasn't alone. Meira lingered. His heart leapt in the back of his throat, fighting against the rise of anger that now accompanied her presence. She never had any words for him except the unhelpful ones, and right now, right now, there were bigger problems than her reservations, or the Reach, or—

"It's time, Evra. I'm leaving. I won't waste my words trying to force you to come with me, because that's all they'd be. Wasted. But you *should* come. You should return with me because there's nothing for us here, is there? Not even your little raven. Don't bother denying it. I'm not a fool, and neither is anyone else here. But her time here is ending, too, so what could be your reason for staying? Your foot is healed well enough. What else could there be?" Meira said it all in a rush.

Evra pointed at his foot. "Well enough? I still can't walk without a hard limp."

"You'll ride just fine with it, and I'd be there to help, where you need it."

"I owe her a life debt, Meira! She saved mine. I have to repay that."

"There's nothing you could give her that she would need, and you know that."

"What about the snow? The midwinter, the—"

"I'll hire a guide to take us south, over the pass. No one can tell me it's impossible now, not when I watched Steward Haddenfoot leave here in such a rush. No, we wait any longer, and the damage in the Rush will become that much harder to mend. We go now."

"I..." Evra looked down at the sword in his hand. "I can't."

"Why? Why can't you?"

"I can't shake off the sense that I'm here for a reason. If I just have a little more time, if I—"

"You take the time you need, then," she said, spreading a smile across her face that was about as welcoming as the ones his council gave him. "I'm leaving in the morning, with or without you. Rush Riders were never meant to be the personal guard of the Lord of the Rush. I came as your *friend*. I come to you now as your friend, when I tell you that your time here is wasted. Every moment you spend trying to find that reason is a moment more will die."

"You're the one who suggested this!" Evra countered. "You! The Ravenwoods had never crossed my mind until you pointed us here, showing me that there might be a way without bringing war to the Reach!"

"I was wrong! Okay? I was wrong, Evra." She stretched a hand toward him, recoiling before it landed. "I was wrong. I thought I knew about them, but I know nothing. I see it hurts you to think of Rhosyn's future, but you'd be sentencing her to death if you tried to take her away from her family and bring her back to the Rush. And if you think the same people who would kill their own daughter would *ever* help us? Then you haven't listened to a word the Frosts have said."

Everything she said made sense, and yet... "I can't leave yet. Don't ask me to explain it, because I can't. I'm sorry."

Meira wrapped her arms tight across her chest. "I'm sorry, too. For setting you on a path to ruin. But you do understand what choice you're making now, don't you? Because this *is* a choice. Her or your Reach. There isn't a world where you can have both. And if you choose her, it will be her ruin and yours."

Evra wanted to say so many things. That she was wrong. That it wasn't only about Rhosyn. That he still felt like there was something he needed here before he could put Midwinter Rest in his past.

Instead, he watched her shake her head and leave.

EIGHTEEN
THE STORM CALLER

Rendyr had come for her. He was inside her head. Only the
distance and her solid will had kept him away. And if he was
in her thoughts...

*Come now. Come alone. I don't have to tell you what happens if
you don't, do I?*

Rendyr didn't hold the same fears as the other Ravenwoods.
War didn't frighten him. She suspected it thrilled him. She'd tried
to tell her mother, to warn her that if Rendyr became High Priest,
he would bring an end to it all, but her mother dismissed her
words as overly and unnecessarily dramatic. But Naryssa had not
spent sleepless nights listening to Rendyr's unhinged rants about
the 'new way' and the 'new order' coming when he no longer had
to heed his mother. When he had a wife he could crush under
heel.

Rhosyn slipped quietly out of the stewardess' chambers, careful not to let the door settle too loudly in its frame, lest her steps
signal her presence to any nearby. She'd been mulling over her
encounter in the armory with Evra when Rendyr arrived, and she

155

took this feeling with her, this strange marriage of exhilaration and terror, out into the snowy evening.

Rendyr waited just beyond the iron gates. From habit, she glanced up at the words that greeted all visitors to the hold, but the snow had settled into the curves and bends of some letters, and from here, reading it backward, she could only make out: OLD WIN. Something about this combination of words unsettled her, but she didn't have time to think about it long.

Rendyr's dark cape caught the wind like an enemy banner. He didn't come any closer. He waited for her to come to him. Had he ever been inside a house of man? Had he ever been invited?

"Did you not trust me to return when my duty was fulfilled?" Rhosyn had to yell to hear herself over the wind. "Could you not have given me these last days?"

"You're fortunate I gave you anything at all, Rhosynora. Your duty is to *me*. To us." He pointed his arm past her. "It was never to them. I don't care what foolish alliance our predecessors bowed down for. Our days of putting men before Ravenwood are in our past now. You and I, we'll change that. Together." He dropped his arm. "Or alone, if you prefer to be only a pretty face. Wouldn't be the first High Priestess to cede power to her more capable husband."

Rhosyn choked out a bitter laugh. "More capable? You think yourself more capable than me? Than Arwenna? Has that anything to do with who we are, or is it simply the way you've always viewed all Ravenwood women?"

Rendyr rolled his eyes. "You can make your petty conjectures when we're returned to The Rookery."

"Why are you in such a hurry to go?"

"Why are you in such a hurry to stay?"

"I remember how you were as a boy. You were cunning, even then, but you were kind. How did this happen, Rendyr, that you have become so consumed by your hunger for power that I see nothing of the boy I once played with? Once loved?"

"Love is a notion of man, and any Ravenwood searching for it, let alone expecting it, has nothing but the misery of fools at the end." He cocked his mouth into a dark grin. "Is that why you stay here? You've finally been snared by their ways? You think them better than ours?"

"I think you'd be a better raven if you knew what it was to be a good man, too."

"Good? Another precept of man that's *tainted* you, Rhosyn! We have no use for these brands in Midnight Crest! What is good and evil, but a way to divide us? We never even *spoke* of such things before we came to this kingdom."

"How would you know?" Rhosyn met his intense gaze. "How would you know how it was before we came to this kingdom? It's only the High Priestesses who hold the visions of the past." Did he know the matriarchal visions were a lie? No, she decided. The slight falter in his arrogance was confirmation.

"If not for the visions, it would be the High Priest in the highest seat, choosing his priestess according to his own desires." He took a single step closer. Then, with a glance upward to the gates, stopped. "The visions are the only thing that makes you special. But you forget, Rhosynora, that I can read your mind." He grinned as he nodded. "With enough time and patience, I'll have these visions for myself. And then what need will I have of you?"

"Is that..." Rhosyn's breath caught. The matriarchal visions were a concept created by her ancestors, a means of holding the power through the female line. It was said only the women could see their past before the kingdom, and that this gift of sight was proof of their godliness. Proof the gods had chosen *them* and them alone to carry this gift. But Arwenna had never had hers. And then Naryssa had said something... something *odd*, that Rhosyn hadn't understood then, only later, as she was older, and had seen her world through more jaded eyes. "You abandoned Arwenna because you couldn't get to her visions. And now you think you can get to mine?"

Rendyr shrugged. "I've never been able to read Mother, either. But you? Something's always been special about you, and it's more than that silver hair and the prophecy that comes with it."

"There's no prophecy."

"There is," Rendyr said. "And you and I are going to prove it. Together."

"No matter what happens from here, there will be never a 'you and me.' There will never be a 'together.'"

"You and your big dreams. That's all they ever were. You lack the spine to see them through."

Rhosyn turned back toward the keep. She couldn't see past the gates, but she knew what she'd find. A family gathered around a warm hearth as they welcomed their newest addition. Even the stewardess would be out of her bed now that her reward for all her suffering was at last hers. Rhosyn had imagined herself a part of this scene, and that this celebration, this beautiful act of kinship, would be her final memory of a life that was never going to be hers, but was still, even now, always, a part of her.

"If you care for them..." Rendyr made a gagging sound. "If you care for those men inside, then you won't fight me, Rhosyn. This was never going to end any other way, but it doesn't have to end in a tragedy."

Tears burned in her eyes, but she wouldn't give him the pleasure. "*This* is a tragedy. But I won't bring that darkness to their doorstep."

Rhosyn spun at the intrusion of boots crunching in the snow. They came on suddenly, so fast that even Rendyr did not immediately realize that someone had joined them. "Evra, what are you doing?" She heard steel against sheath before she saw him, but she knew it was him. She knew it, same as she'd known when she placed her hands on his face that she'd see only kindness. "Go back to the keep!"

Evra flashed her only a fleeting look before moving past her and planting himself directly between her and her brother. He held his sword out to the side, hand trembling. "You are not welcome here, and it's time for you to leave."

"This is no Frost," Rendyr said. "This one's soft, Rhosyn. Look at him, he's not hardened to the cold! Where did you find this one?"

"Evra!" she hissed, but there was no reaching him. However misguided, however wrong, he was spellbound by purpose.

"You are not welcome here," Evra said again. He shifted his feet, settling into his stance. The sword sagged but didn't fall. "And it's time for you to leave."

"Is he serious? He wants me to kill him?" Rendyr stepped to the side, shrugging his hands at Rhosyn. "He's *inviting* me to kill him. See, Rhosyn, this is why men are not fit to share a table with us."

"I'm giving you a choice." Evra spaced his words evenly, but Rhosyn heard the shaking in between them, and if she had, then so had Rendyr. "You can leave on your own. Or you can leave on the end of my sword. But you *will* leave."

Rhosyn stepped forward, but Evra shot his other arm out to block her. "I know you think there's only one way for you, Rhosyn, but no one, man nor Ravenwood, should have to walk a path they didn't make for themselves."

"What's he blathering about?" Rendyr demanded.

Evra tilted his head just enough for her to see his mouth move. "I know you're afraid to stand up to him. But I'm not. You saved me the day I arrived here, and I owe you a life debt. I won't watch you fly off to misery when there's another way."

"There *isn't* another way, Evra! Don't you understand? I'm not going because I'm too weak to stand up to Rendyr. He's a fool, and he's not as strong as he thinks he is. I'm going because, fool or no, he would bring war to this land without a second thought. He would undo everything the Ravenwoods and the men of the Northerlands have worked for. If I don't go, others will die because I couldn't summon the strength to put my own needs and wants aside."

"I wasn't born to be a lord. And you weren't born to be a High Priestess." Evra turned back to Rendyr. "If no one else here will stand for Rhosyn, then I will."

"Stand him down, Rhosyn. You won't like my methods if you leave it to me."

"Leave."

"Evra, I'm *begging* you. You don't know what Ravenwoods are capable of. You don't know our magic!"

"I know firsthand what your magic can do, Rhosyn." His grip on the sword tightened.

"You know what I've shown you. But there's more! There's more in all of us, and it's darker and harder, and some things, some things cannot be undone!"

Evra dropped into a fighting stance, joining his free hand to the sword. "He can't say I didn't warn him."

Time stopped. Rhosyn *felt* it stop, her consciousness now existing in the spaces between the seconds as she observed Rendyr subtly raise his hands to call down death, as Evra began his reckless charge, as the tingle—the one she'd been told to ignore, to push down, to never address—twitched her fingers into action. Rendyr's hand glowed as the deathbolt surged to life, ready to be released to its master's bidding.

Rhosyn thrust her arms to the side with a roar. She planted her feet just as the earth upended in a massive groan, knocking both Evra and Rendyr sideways. The brutal wind she'd summoned whipped her hair around her face, but she didn't need her sight to finish her call.

"Rhosyn!" Rendyr screamed from underneath his cape's protection. "This is forbidden magic!"

"So is murder!" Rhosyn pointed her outstretched fingers to the sky just as the wind reached its peak. A dense, powerful snowfall rained from the clouds, but the rest would follow. It was only a matter of time before she rained her own death.

The first snowbolt landed to the left of Rendyr, splitting the earth. He rolled to the side, narrowly dodging another.

"Evra, come to me!" she cried, and now he finally listened. When he was close enough, she yanked him into the swirl of wind shielding her from the assault. In here, it was still, unlike her heart, which had never beat with such ferocity.

"You've gone too far, Rhosyn! You'll be punished for this when they find out! You think I'm the one to fear? Wait until I tell them what you've done!"

She returned no answer. All her energies were consumed in her defense of the brave boy who had made a foolish choice. She didn't think about tomorrow when Rendyr would return and kill him. Everything inside her fused together to protect the now.

"Rhosyn!" Rendyr howled, eyes swollen with rage.

"Rhosyn," Evra whispered, eyes wide in wonder.

"You left me with no choice!" she cried back as the world shuddered in response.

"You've made your choice!" Rendyr shielded his face, stepping slowly toward her. "And you've bought yourself *nothing* except more angst! More pain!"

"I will show you pain!" Rhosyn screamed. She barely noticed Evra's arms slide around her waist. "Now, leave here!"

Rendyr's smirk sent spikes down her spine. He turned it on Evra. "And you. *You* will be the first one to die when this world comes falling down."

Evra gasped as Rendyr burst into a spray of feathers. Together, they watched him spiral into the sky, dodging the snowbolts she no longer controlled. Everything now was so far beyond her control, she didn't know whether she was up or down.

When she could no longer see his figure against the stormy skies, she sagged into Evra's arms and, together, they sank into the snow.

"Why is this still happening?" Evra cried as they ran. He had hold of Rhosyn's hand, or maybe it was the other way around. Everything was a blend of mess and confusion. She gripped him so tight it sent shocks through his arm, but it was nothing compared to the icy boulders plummeting to the earth, to the right and left of them, some missing them by only a hair. If he hadn't seen her call them, he wouldn't believe they were real. "Why won't it stop?"

"I don't know!"

Evra shut out the assault and focused only on Rhosyn's long silver hair. Her black feathers bounced as she bolted. He had no choice but to trust she knew what she was doing.

"Where are we going?"

"We have to get out of this!"

Evra couldn't look down. If he looked down, he would see the snow level rising. That the path Oswin had cleared only earlier that day was now an inch deep and would only push higher and higher as long as this terrifying storm continued. He tried not to think about how bad it could get. How, if it went on long enough, the snow would swallow the keep, the town, the entire Reach.

"Evra!"

Her panicked scream brought him back to the moment, to her urgent tug as they veered away from the keep, passing it until they were behind it and aimed toward the armory.

"Where'd he go? Your brother?"

"Don't stop!"

Rhosyn heaved herself against the armory door and they stumbled in together. Evra's knees threatened to buckle, but Rhosyn had him moving once more, urging him to help her bar the door. When that was done, he tried to sit, but she tugged him into the back room, where only earlier that day he'd raised his sword in such confidence. It was that same confidence that bade him raise it against Rendyr Ravenwood, knowing, even as the steel quavered in his grip, that he stood no chance against the sorcerer.

"Is he coming?" Evra asked, spinning to face her, but his words were cut off when her arms looped around his neck. He started again, and her kiss silenced him.

The warmth of her mouth, desperate and demanding, was enough to quell the chill in his bones. He gasped at the intrusion of her tongue, the urgent press of her body against his, the firm command of her hands moving across the back of his neck.

162

This was not like the kiss he'd stolen. Rhosyn was not Seven. She was not only a friend. She was not just anyone.

Evra wrapped her in his arms and deepened the kiss, disregarding the screaming in his head that this only drew her further into danger. Rhosyn moaned when his fingers spread across her back, tightening, digging in against the leather dividing flesh from flesh.

"You silly boy," she whispered through her kisses. "You stupid, foolish boy."

"I know. I know it was foolish. I know it was reckless. I know," he interjected.

Rhosyn pulled him down to the hay-covered floor. He thought he'd fallen in love with her before, but he was wrong. It was now, in the gleam of her violet eyes and a gaze that started from somewhere deep within her. It cut through to the very center of him, leaving him weak in the glow of her strength.

"No one." Rhosyn swallowed and tried again. Her throat moved with her slow words. "No one has ever done anything like that for me."

"I'm not no one," Evra answered. "And neither are you."

"That's the trouble," she said. She reached for his hands and laced them into hers. "We aren't no one. And we'll never be allowed to forget it."

"I don't know what I'm doing," Evra admitted. He tried to smile. "I don't know why I'm here now with you. I know less than nothing. I..." Evra kissed her. "I know only what I want right now, and that's you."

Rhosyn pressed her hands against his chest, gently shoving him into the hay. She bowed over him. Her silver hair tickled his lips, his neck, tracing a new chapter in his story as he came alive beneath her. She reached between his legs with a flash of surprise, but this only lit something even more urgent in Rhosyn, and before he could catch up to the moment, she had him freed from his trousers.

"He'll kill you," was all he could think to say as her mouth parted in pleasure, as she took him in, all the way in, bringing him out of his world and into hers. "Ah, Rhosyn. Rhosyn, Rhosyn, Rhosyn."

"Then I will have died knowing the difference between love and power," Rhosyn said, and these were the last words either of them spoke as she brought them away from their fears and toward a light of their own creation.

NINETEEN
SAY IT FOR WHAT IT IS

R hosyn wasn't there when Evra woke. It was just after dawn, he guessed, by the way the morning light spilled in through the slats of the boarded windows.

Nothing about the prior night felt real. As he shrugged off the rest of his sleep and embraced the splitting headache that greeted him promptly after, he was reminded of the time he'd gotten into his mother's brandywine stash. How he'd imbibed the dark burgundy liquid with startling lucidity, only to see it through hazier eyes the following day.

Evra caught sight of his trousers farther down, tangled in a swatch of hay. His shirt... ah, well, he was lying on that, and when he yanked at it, the soft fabric was replaced by the scratchy straw beneath.

He shrugged the shirt over his shoulders. The muscles underneath screamed at even this basic chore. Now he thought of the sword, trembling in his grip as he faced down someone infinitely more powerful than him. Straining for his trousers, another soreness, farther down, reminded him of what had happened after.

"Rhosyn." Each time he'd spoken her name, it had meant something different to him. His voice was lost in the cacophony of snowbolts hitting the thatched roof. A storm she'd created, but somehow could not stop.

I'm sorry for ever suggesting this and setting you on a path to ruin. But you do understand what choice you're making, don't you? Because this a choice. Her or your Reach. There isn't a world where you can have both.

Meira's wisdom haunted him. It landed harder, weighing him down when she wasn't here to say the words herself.

She's not here because you drove her away. She was right to leave. You can lie to yourself, but she saw right through your reasons for staying.

But that wasn't fair. His whole life, he'd been accused of being aimless. And though he wasn't meant to save Rhosyn—all the reason he possessed howled this inside his head—he'd at last understood what it meant to *have* a purpose. He'd come here with the lofty vision of saving his sister, of saving what remained of the Westerlands, but how was that any more or less crazy than thinking he might save Rhosyn?

The hard truth was, he stood no chance of either.

And yet... despite knowing this, despite everything, he still picked himself up off the floor and braved the storm to return to the keep, and her.

"You have been a blessing to me now not once, my dear, but twice." The stewardess shook Rhosyn's hands in hers. The tears seemed real. Ethelyn had always been hot and cold with her, but this convincing show of grief only ate deeper into Rhosyn's courage. "If there were a way to make you ours for eternity, you know we would do it."

Rhosyn had to look down to nod. Oswin's quick but fatherly hand on her shoulder broke her down to the little girl she'd been when she'd first flown to Midwinter Hold, responding to a call for service and finding so much more.

"You sweet girl." Brin sobbed off to the side. Thorn's weak attempts to console her were more humorous than ardent. "Life can be so unfair. So very unfair."

"Please, save your tears." Even now, she would reassure them. Especially now. "You have been like a family to me, and no matter how many years will come to separate us from this moment, I won't forget it." She passed a tight smile to each of the Frosts. They'd all come to see her off. The nurses had even brought the little ones. "I won't forget you."

"If I thought..." Emotion choked Thorn's voice. "You know where we are, Rhosyn. You know you can come to us, for anything."

"For anything?" Evra's stunned, high voice cut through the goodbyes. "Really? Anything? Does that anything include watching her fly away to a brother who will spend the rest of her days torturing her?"

Rhosyn shook her head at him, but his eyes were on the others.

"Like family to you, is she? But not *quite*, is that right? Not *nearly* enough to upset the comforts you've come to love. Maybe if she were Morwen, or—"

"Enough!" Rhosyn pleaded. "It's *my* choice to leave, Evra. Mine."

"Only because you see no other choices put before you!" Evra flew his hands out to the side as he regarded them all, aghast. "How many of you has she healed? Has she aided? Has she comforted? Say it for what it is, then. It's not love. It's need. And when you need her again, and this time she can't come, you'll shower another Ravenwood with these false platitudes!"

Rhosyn sighed into her hands. "You don't know as much as you think you do. You really don't."

Thorn shook off his wife and stepped forward in a burst of anger. "You would scold *us*, Lord Blackrook? When you stand before us because of your own selfish needs?"

Evra tried to rebut but could only shake his head.

Thorn rubbed his hand across his mouth and laughed. "All your big words. Your accusations. You didn't tell her, then, why *you* came? Why you came all the way up here?"

"Evra, what's he talking about?" Rhosyn passed her attention between the men, the tense moment locking them all in.

"You didn't come here to save her, Lord Blackrook. You came here to convince her to be your magic slave, so she could spread her hands all over your Reach and make you a hero."

Rhosyn's gasp caught in her throat. She whipped her head again to Evra so he could assure her Thorn had it wrong, but he couldn't look at her. All he could do was shake his head at Thorn.

"Evra?"

"It's not true," Evra finally said. He knit his mouth together, his lower lip trembling. "It's not true."

"Of course it's not true," Rhosyn whispered. "It cannot be. You would've told me, you..." But what *was* his business here? Why had she not pressed him for it? What else could have brought a Westerland lord all the way to the barren north, as Thorn said, when no one else ever came?

"Tell her." Thorn aimed his arm at Rhosyn. "She deserves to know. After what... what you did to her."

"Thorn," Brin warned. "We said we'd leave it be."

"Did we? That was before he came in running his mouth about things he doesn't understand. What do you think that brother of hers will do when he discovers he's not the first to her bed? What if a child comes, too soon? What then?"

"Oh, Guardians," Ethelyn moaned. "Thorn, you shouldn't repeat such rumors."

"They're not rumors, Mother. Why do you think neither of them slept in their own bed last night?"

"I thought..." Ethelyn turned to Rhosyn. She pointed at the roof. "After what happened last night, you were only being cautious. That you were hiding."

"Tell her," Thorn pushed. "Tell her why you're here."

"I was going to tell her. I was *going* to, I..."

A dark sob rolled forward, catching Rhosyn up to the rapid exchange, to the reality of what Thorn had shared, and what Evra hadn't denied.

Her breaths shallowed as she watched the Frosts and Evra volley their questions, accusations, denials. She was both there and not, watching from her own eyes and from someone else's.

"You." The word lodged in her chest as her grief at last crested. "You came for my magic? All of this... everything we..." Rhosyn sucked in both of her lips to steady the sobs. "You would go so far, when all you had to do was ask?"

"That's not exactly right, Rhosyn. I swear to you. Yes, it..." Evra lost his courage. "Please, come to the armory with me. I'll tell you everything but not here."

"Not here, where we can counter your lies with truth, you mean?" Thorn snorted, passing a look to his wife.

"I'm not going anywhere with you. Ever again."

"Please." He reached for her, but she rolled back. "I'm begging you, give me a few minutes. A few, no more, and everything I tell you will be the truth, but I need you to hear this in my words. From me. Not from them."

"I told you, Evrathedyn, that this was a fool's errand, did I not?" Oswin shook his head and ran his eyes over the others in silent command to follow him. Ethelyn and the children did, but Thorn stood firm. Brin sighed at his side.

"After..." Evra tried not to look at Thorn. "After everything, you don't want to leave with this unresolved. I'll answer any questions you have, but not here."

Rhosyn's heart rose to dizzying beats, matching the pace and frenzy of the storm she couldn't turn off. She glanced at Thorn. He looked ready to take his sword to Evra, but he waited for her to answer.

"Fine," she said. She pushed ahead of Evra, not waiting for him to follow. When she entered the icy, catastrophic morning without so much as a cloak, he was right behind her. She threw her hands out, willing the snowbolts to land farther from their path, and they obeyed, but her call fell silent when she asked them to stop altogether. It was bigger than her now, this creation. Only when she left would relief return to Midwinter Hold. Or would it?

She smashed her palms on the doors, crashing them open. Evra went to bolt them behind her, but she grabbed his arm and pulled him farther in.

"Say what you mean to say," she commanded when they stepped into the back, into the same room that... that...

Evra bowed his head, sighing. "I came here to see if there might be a magic strong enough to save my people. I was told the Ravenwoods had stricken the plague from the north, and I thought, maybe, you could do that in the Westerlands, too."

"Because that's what we do. We rise to the service of men. That's all we are," she countered.

"No! No. I didn't know you. I knew nothing about your family, your... any of it. And then I met you, and I forgot my purpose altogether. I forgot about my people, even my poor sister, on her deathbed. Meira *left* because of how far I'd fallen from my goal. But I'll tell you what I told her." His head shook as he spoke. He stepped forward, but she stepped back. "We'll have to find another way because this isn't it." He bit his bottom lip. "This isn't it. You aren't going to save my people. I am."

"Oh yeah?" Rhosyn wiped her eyes on her sleeve. "How?"

Evra shrugged. Tears rolled down his cheeks. "I don't know. I'm more lost now than I was before I left home. I don't know anything anymore. I just know..." He squeezed his eyes shut. "Guardians, Rhosyn, I'm so sorry for not telling you. But every word we exchanged, every moment we stole that wasn't ours, I fell deeper in love with you, and—"

Rhosyn slapped him so hard it sent a bolt of pain through her wrist. "Don't you *dare* speak to me of love. You offer me a betrayal of only a slightly different color than what my brother has waiting for me."

Evra's cheek flamed bright red, but he didn't reach up to nurse it. He only watched her with his sad eyes, out of words.

She spun away from him. The silence turned the air dense around them, becoming more oppressive with each unsaid, desperate word. Behind her, Evra shuffled around, and she wondered what he was doing, but she couldn't look at him anymore. *I fell deeper in love with you.* No! Why, *why* had she let herself slip so far away from her path? Why, with him, a man she hardly knew then, and now knew not at all? Whoever had moved above her as the moonlight alone bore witness, he was only an illusion. A tease to test her resolve, and she'd failed. She'd—

Rhosyn cried out in sudden pain. Her wrists felt like they'd been lit on fire, but then she was jolted forward, her arms drawn back, and she understood... she understood why he'd been so insistent they come here, alone. That he'd once more lied to her, so he could...

"Rhosyn," he sobbed. "Forgive me."

Rhosyn tugged at the rope binding her wrists, but it was a solid knot. He must have known... someone must have told him she'd have no access to her magic without her hands, that it would leave her defenseless. Now she knew what he'd been searching for in the hay. She caught him from the corner of her eye just as he secured a longer end of the rope to the wooden pillar nearby.

She should have been ready for this, should have *seen* it. "Forgive you?" she repeated through her sobs, more incredulous with each torturous moment that brought her closer to seeing Evrathedyn Blackrook for who he really was. "*Forgive* you?"

"I swear to you, Rhosyn, I swear to you, I'm not doing this because I want your help. I've moved past that, because I love you, because—"

"Stop saying that word!" she screamed, so loud the snowbolts were momentarily silenced.

"You can't go back there." Evra came around the side of her. His tears disgusted her. They fired the rage that had replaced every other weak-minded, silly emotion she'd allowed herself to feel for

171

this *man*, who had proved to be exactly what the Ravenwoods said men were.

Rhosyn yanked at the rope with a dark laugh. "You're forcing me from one prison into another. And you're calling it love, so you'll sleep tonight, but we both know what this is. What you are."

"I would have killed him. Rendyr. If you hadn't called that storm."

"If I hadn't called that storm, you'd be dead!"

"Then I would've died doing something that finally mattered."

"Honor? Is that..." Rhosyn released a scream. "Leave me alone! GO!"

"I swear to you, I will make this up to you. I'll fix this—"

"GO!"

Evra stumbled sideways in the hay. He cried harder now, and she hated him more for how he could still speak to her sympathy, after what he'd done.

"You want to save me from Rendyr, Evra? Well, you're too late." She spat at his feet. "You've become him."

THE SHROUD
OF MIDWINTER

176

TWENTY
PROVISIONS

E vra was late for the break of the morning fast. The Frosts gathered at sunrise, as they'd done every day. None raised their head or eyes in greeting, nor even curiosity at his tardiness. Thorn's head hung over his porridge as he took quick swings at the contents. His wife had pushed her bowl to the side and gazed off toward the wall of windows and the storm still raging. The others ate in silence.

"Get to it, Evra," Oswin gruffed. "Eat. The gruel will be hard enough to build a wall with soon, and there's nothing to be done about that."

"Nothing to be done," Evra repeated as the past night washed over him in startling clarity. But as the events replayed in his mind, he felt more like an observer, watching a play in the town square. The Tragic Ballad of Evra and Rhosyn.

He took his seat, and one of the kitchen maids slid the bowl in front of him. "Can I have two today?" he asked. He felt her judgmental shift from one foot to the other, but it was Thorn who stopped gazing into his breakfast to give him an incredulous look.

"Two bowls?" Thorn repeated. He tilted his forward. "Of this?"

"Enough about the porridge! Provisions will come soon. We'll eat better when they do," Brin said.

"I was going to take the second bowl back to my chambers, for when I write my letters," Evra explained. "If that's all right."

Thorn gaped at him in pure disgust.

"He's still growing," Ethelyn said, eyes on her eldest son. "He's barely a man yet. If his mother were here, she'd be stuffing him so full we'd have to roll him out of the dining hall."

Evra was surprised to see her at the table. There was no sign of the infant. The little one must be wherever they took Thorn and Brin's child at mealtime. Ethelyn was nearly glowing. No evidence of her arduous lying in. Of the delivery most in the household expected to spend her promise.

And not one of them, speaking of why. Of *her*. Of the one who made it all possible.

No, but they're thinking about her. Look at them. They're miserable. What would they say if they knew what you'd done?

He heard the question in Meira's chastising tone.

"There won't be any provisions." Oswin cut through the threads of tension. "The storm has made the roads impossible to travel. Landslides washed part of the main road out, and there's work to be done to make it passable again. If the Guardians have not entirely forsaken us, Morwen and Steward Haddenfoot were well clear of it before the worst hit. As for you, Evra, I hope you're in no hurry to get home." His spoon clanged in the bowl. "We'll have to make do with what we have, until midwinter is past, and we can begin again."

"The storm," Thorn repeated, eyes closed, shaking his head. "Is that what we're calling it?"

"Is it not a storm, Thornton?" Oswin pointed his hand at the windows without looking beyond them. "Or are you used to seeing snowbolts in the heart of springtide, too?"

"I'm not used to seeing snowbolts at all, Father. They're *supposed* to die in the mountains, never reaching our ground. Until last night, I'd only seen them once before."

"What are they?" Evra asked. He pushed his spoon through the hardening porridge. He didn't want to talk about the storm. About her. But this was left of the point. Safer. "Snowbolts?"

"Poorly named, for one," Oswin answered. "There's no snow in them. If there were, they'd not be so dangerous. They're boulders of ice that hurl from the skies. Usually they melt off as they descend from the clouds, breaking apart into hail when it reaches us. Hail, well, that's enough to knock a rabbit senseless, but no worse. Snowbolts can kill a man. They don't care what your name is, where you're from. My grandmother was taken by one. Most around here know at least one person who lost a battle with a snowbolt."

"I didn't know Rhosyn could do that," Brin mused. "Call a storm."

"Her mother used to call storms," Oswin said, elaborating no further. "Anyhow, Rhosyn has left her storm behind for us, and that leaves work for us to do. We'll need to board up the windows on the ground floor of the keep. The barns, the storehouse. And the armory... I've put off shoring those windows up too long. It won't last midwinter if her storm doesn't abate. But this leg..." Oswin glanced under the table with a wince.

"I told you not to go out in it, you old fool," Ethelyn chided. "You never listen to me, do you? And now, you can hardly walk at all."

"I'll be fine. Just a sprain."

"Tell that to your boots. You cannot even get half your toes in."

"Hmph."

"I'd like to help," Evra said too quickly. "I can take the armory. I know the path well now."

Oswin's sideways glance carried suspicion. "I'll need more hands in the keep."

"I already know what needs to be done in the armory. I've seen it myself and won't need the hands like you will. And if... if your leg isn't well, then it would be unwise for you to take that path if you don't have to." Evra swallowed the lump at the

179

back of his throat. He tightened his grip on the spoon as a bout of dizziness smacked him. "It's the least I can do for your hospitality. And for taking up more of your resources when you're forced to ration."

"Hmm," Oswin said. "It's not a small building when you account for the back room. The whole thing needs to be redone. I keep putting it off. I had a mind to put a spinning wheel in the back one day, for Ethelyn, but it's in no shape for that."

Evra nodded, trying not to think too much of the back room. "I saw the windows that need tending. When I was practicing."

"I know what you practiced in there," Thorn accused. "The whole keep knows."

"Thorn," Brin and Ethelyn warned in tandem.

"It's done. She's gone. Leave it be," Oswin said with a soft, sad sigh.

"We're not to speak of it, then? Of the Lord of the Westerlands, falling in love with her, like a fool?"

"He wouldn't be the first, would he?" Oswin shot back. "Only the first who received her return affections."

Thorn looked away. "I never wanted her return affections. I knew better than to solicit them." He waved behind him, to the windows. "I knew no good could come of it."

"It wasn't intentional," Evra said softly. A tear dropped into his hardened porridge. With a thousand more, he could soften it again, make it edible. "I wasn't trying to bring... all this... down upon you."

"There's nothing to be found in blame," Oswin said. He tapped his hand twice on the table. "You're not from here. You don't have our history. You don't know..." He grunted. "Leave it in the past, Evra. That's what my father told me, and his father told him. Leave her in your past. There's no place for her in your future. 'Tis a harder lesson, for some, than the ones brought to us in the shroud of midwinter."

Brin cried silently, wiping her tears as she looked away from them. Little Rylan sobbed openly.

"We won't speak of it again," Ethelyn said with stony decisiveness. "We have more than enough requiring our attention now, without wasting it upon a whim."

The stewardess rose and left.

Rhosyn heard the outer door to the armory swing open. She cried out, hoping it was the steward, or even a worker, but the clumsy fumble that followed—the struggle to bar and latch the door, the frustrated grunts—killed her hope.

She turned away from the sound. Away from Evra, whose boots crunched in the dry hay as he drew closer.

The door to the back room creaked. He stepped inside. She crushed her eyes closed and reached for her rage, which was safer than all the rest.

"Rhosyn?"

She didn't answer. Her toes curled in anger. Tears slid down her cheek.

"I brought you something to eat. I thought you might be hungry." He came closer. When he knelt at her side, she raised her arm, and he backed off. "You're awake."

"I don't want your food. I want nothing from you."

"I didn't make it. If that helps."

"Of course you didn't make it. When have you ever done anything for yourself?"

"We've both had others do for us. We still need to eat."

"There is no 'both' of us, Evra. You know nothing at all about the world I come from. If you did..." Rhosyn squeezed her eyes to rid them of more tears. "You don't know what you've done."

She heard him settle the bowl on the bench. He sank down into the hay but didn't attempt a closer approach. "I don't know what I've done. I agree."

"Then let me go, you fool! Or do you want everyone around us to die?"

"What I want..." Evra faltered. "Is for you to live."

"This will end the same way it was going to end. It can end no other way. Except now he'll be worse. He'll..." Rhosyn didn't want to think of this. To speak of it. The words were wasted upon this *man*, who had decided he wanted something and taken it, making him no better than all the others. Who had taken *her*, not considering what it might mean to anyone but him. And to think... to think she'd...

"I don't know your world. I know that," Evra insisted. "But unlike the Frosts, who say they love you like a daughter, but then let you go off into misery, I... well, I cannot, Rhosyn. I've seen the hatred in your brother. He'll spend it on you, the rest of his days. He'll do it with gladness."

"And now he'll spend it tenfold. You've only delayed my pain, making it worse. At least he gave Arwenna a swift death. You remember me telling you this, don't you? He *killed* our sister."

"Of course I remember. It's all I can think about when I imagine you going back to him."

"Well, he won't kill me, Evra, because he needs me, but he'll make me wish he had. Every second that passes, every second that I'm not there, I will pay for."

"Why not leave?"

Rhosyn burst out laughing. She twitched her bound hands.

"That's not what I mean. Forget me. Us. Any of this. Why not just fly away and leave it all behind? All of it?"

"You're such a boy."

"Do you mean that as an offense? Because I've much preferred my life as a boy than the one so far offered me as a man." He lowered his eyes. "Excluding my time with you."

"You know next to nothing. You have me bound here for your own wants and needs. You've taken for yourself."

"No! No, I—"

"Why don't I fly away, Evra? Because I *love* the Frosts. I love the gruff Oswin, the cold Ethelyn, and the sweet, sweet little Rylan. I love Thorn, and Brin, and all of them. And if I fly away, it's them who will endure Rendyr's rage."

182

"Oswin said neither side wants war."

"Rendyr doesn't see things like most Ravenwoods. The alliance means nothing to him. He wants what he wants. He cares not who suffers in his quest to achieve it."

"Why does he need you for this?"

"Well, I'm to be the High Priestess, now, aren't I?" Rhosyn answered with a snicker, but she'd realized that it was more than that. Rendyr had finally hinted at it, the night before, with his words about a prophecy. What did he know, that she did not?

"But he already had that with your sister. So why would he kill her?"

"As if you could ever understand."

"Is it because you don't know? Is it because, even asking that question, why a brother would kill his own sister, has no sense in it? Not knowing should scare you, Rhosyn! If you don't know why he killed Arwenna, then you cannot be certain he wouldn't kill you, too!"

"I don't have to explain this to you!"

"Why has the storm not ended?"

"I don't know!"

Evra reached for her, but she rolled farther away. She heard him sink deeper against the wall.

"Why are you doing this to me?"

"I'm doing this because I love you, foolish as that sounds to both our ears," he said. "Perhaps love looks different to a Ravenwood than a man." He softly laughed. "Not that I'd know what it looks like to a man, either."

"If you mean those words, you'll let me go."

"It's because I mean those words," Evra said, rising, "that I won't release you into what I know will amount to great suffering for the rest of your life, however long of one Rendyr grants you. I don't know what to do. I truly don't. But I know I can't do that." His voice hitched. "I'll figure it out. I will." His shadow fell over her, and she buried her face in the rough hay.

But all he did was lay the bowl next to her face.

She waited until she heard him latch the armory door from the outside before opening her eyes.

TWENTY-ONE
A BUCKET OF WATER RISING FOR THE SEA

How long had passed? How many short days had turned into long nights? How many meals grudgingly half-eaten, while she ignored the one who delivered them?

Rhosyn hadn't counted. She'd started to, but it only reminded her of yet another piece of her life beyond her control, which caused the fury to spin itself into agony, damning her to more restless sleep. If she thought too long about the storm that wouldn't end... about the snow piling higher, and higher, the drifts almost completely covering what little light was allowed through the windows... about the sound of Evra's grunts as he, every few hours, shoveled the path so he could pound more nails into more boards... about any of it... madness would soon replace rage, and she really would be lost.

He was there most of the time. She fired off words caked in anger, ensuring he knew how vile he was, but most of the time, he never came to the back room at all. She heard the repeated, excruciating sound of metal upon metal as he worked to replace the rotting boards that Steward Frost kept saying he'd get around to. A task that had only become necessary because of *her*, and her inability to destroy what she'd birthed. And what if she could now? What if she only needed to be free, to have use of her hands again, and it would all be over?

Evra was resistant to her pleas. He only watched, with growing fear and consternation, as the snow rose higher; as his work grew more urgent.

Did he feel the wrath of Rendyr, slinking about in the skies? She doubted it. Rendyr was here for her, and with what little magic she could employ without her hands, she forced him from her mind, drawing him away from the Frosts.

He'd leave, then return the following day. Or night. She'd lost track of that, too.

Rhosyn licked at the edges of the bowl. She used her teeth to draw in the hardened, cracked porridge. Evra always offered to feed her and seemed surprised, even disappointed, when she'd refuse his help. As if he hadn't bound her hands and turned her into his prisoner.

Clatter. Clatter. Clatter. Clatter went the hammer in the other room, wielded by unskilled hands.

Her belly turned with hunger. She rolled away from the piles of food she couldn't eat without her hands. She tugged at her arm and got it close enough to hide her scream against.

Clatter. Clatter. Clatter.

Rhosyn sobbed without sound. With every drop of the hammer, she sensed Evra's fear, channeled into his work. She hated him for it. She hated herself for still loving him. For spending her restless nights rationalizing his choice to keep her here, using his words to convince herself.

All the while, Rendyr. Swooping low, listening for her, while she pressed him from her mind, knowing she could not keep him away forever.

Clatter. Clatter. Clatter.

Are you done? She wanted to scream. To howl the words from a place deep within her, where the darkness rotted her from the inside out. This was worse than being alone, this cacophony of Evra's torment turned to sound that she couldn't escape any more than she could escape the makeshift barn at the back of the steward's armory.

Steward Frost wasn't coming for her. He didn't even know she was here. Nor did Thorn, Brin, or even the icy stewardess, who seemed to love Rhosyn with one hand and loathe her with the other. They believed her to be long gone, and Evra had shored this belief with his work out here, protecting the small structure from a storm that wouldn't end. He'd made certain none of them had a reason to be here. None but him.

All this he'd told her through his tears. She'd listened through her own, pretending to be asleep.

Rhosyn kicked at the hay, pivoting until her head was where her feet were. She sent her boots flailing into the pile of dishes. They slammed into the wooden wall, shattering in tandem with her scream, the pieces coming to a final rest on the hay and stone.

The clattering stopped.

Rhosyn slept.

Rhosyn woke to the sensation of being watched. From the corner of her eye, she caught Evra leaning against a stack of hay across the room. He wore an indecipherable look as he turned the spoon through the gruel, keeping it from hardening, while he waited for her.

"You're awake," he said before she could hide it from him. "I brought some supper."

"I don't want it."

"You need it." Evra crawled forward, holding the bowl up high. He settled in next to her and lifted the spoon. "Can I?"

Rhosyn shook her head. The sob in her mouth kept her from saying the word to match.

"Please? I'll leave, after. I just... you need food, Rhosyn. I know you've touched very little of what I left."

187

"I can feed myself if you untie me."

Evra lifted the spoon higher. Rhosyn set her jaw and willed the tears back. But she *was* hungry. She was so hungry, even her rage was no longer so formidable, and she couldn't have that. She opened her mouth wide, glaring.

Evra looked away as he fed her. He did this as if affording her some dignity, which was laughable, really, given where they were and why. When she'd finished, he quickly backed away again and returned to his place next to the hay pile.

"Have you seen him?" Rhosyn asked. She laughed. "Or are you blind, too?"

"Who?"

"Rendyr, you fool. He's been coming every day. He'll keep coming."

"Ahh."

"Ahh? Is that all you have to say for yourself?" Belly full, her anger returned. "Is that all you *can* say, or are you really that dim?"

"I don't know."

"You don't *know?*"

"I don't..." Evra winced. His eyes stayed closed. "I really don't know. I spent my entire life in search of knowledge, only to discover I know nothing at all. Nothing that matters."

"Are you angling for my sympathy? You won't find it. You've killed it." This wasn't true. She hoped he couldn't hear it in her voice.

Evra dropped his face into his hands.

"You don't get to be the sad one, Evrathedyn! You're the one who brought us here! You're the only one who can stop this!"

"Tell me," Evra said, sniffling as he looked up. His face bloomed with red. "Is that really what you want? To go back to Midnight Crest? To be with him and others like him? To suffer at his hand, helpless?"

"What I want doesn't matter."

"That's not what I asked you."

188

"It's what you should have asked me, for the question you asked has no place here."

Evra shook his head. "Would you answer it, anyway?"

"Would I..." Rhosyn scoffed. She inched her way back against her own hay pile, struggling to sit. "Why would I do anything for you, when you've locked me away?"

Evra didn't answer. He waited for hers.

"I..." She bit into her bottom lip, drawing blood. "That's never been what I wanted. I decided, when I left, that I'd... that I'd die before allowing him to ever lay hands on me."

"Then what's changed?"

"Those were the words of a girl. A woman understands duty."

"Duty to him?"

Rhosyn laughed. "To Rendyr? Gods, no. To the Frosts. To the people who have loved me, cared for me... in ways,"—she shook her head—"you could never understand."

"You like to say that," Evra said with a sigh. "But you never offer to explain."

"Why should I?"

"Because I'd like to know."

"Know what?"

"Everything. Anything. About you. Your world."

"No, you don't. No one *really* wants to know. Not even Morwen. She'd rather imagine me flying away like some heroine in the books her father bought her. Because if she really had to consider the alternative, then she'd have to do something about it. Wouldn't she?"

Evra shifted. "Are you comparing me to Morwen? Because I *have* done something, Rhosynora. It might be the worst thing I've ever done, but it's the only thing I've ever done that was for someone other than myself. If you return to him, he *will* kill you. If not in body, then in spirit. And though I suspect at least some of you can reverse death, this will not be the kind that can be undone."

"Better, then, for you to have the honor?"

Evra dropped his eyes to his hands. "I'm sorry. I am. For not knowing a better way to save you."

"Save me," she repeated. She didn't like how it sounded in her own voice. She liked less that his love had turned to pity, and she had no defense against it. "All right, then. Why did you want to become a Scholar, when you were the son of a lord?"

"You really want to know?"

"Not especially," she lied. "But you'll tell me. It's the least you can do."

Evra leaned back. "There was this feeling. It started when I was a boy, and it only grew, festering, as I matured, and showed signs of who I'd become. It was this sense that... that although I was surrounded by everything I could ever want or need, I was the most alone person in all the kingdom."

Rhosyn snorted, but his words had struck a nerve. She knew precisely the feeling he was describing.

"I had one friend. Meira. She was always shaking sense into me. She never let me wallow for long. She and Edriss. My sister, that is. They were both cut from the cloth lords were made from. Not that it mattered. They weren't born men." He splayed his fingers, regarding each one. "And my father, he, well, he expected me to grow out of the things I'd loved as a boy. Books. Time alone with my thoughts. Dates with my imagination. When I didn't, he tried to force them out of me.

"One night, he came into my room. The rest of the keep had been sleeping for hours, except for the guards. He ordered me to follow him. I asked where we were going, and he wouldn't answer. I reached for my cloak, and he swatted it from my hand." Evra swallowed. His words grew thicker as he spoke. "He led me into the Whispering Wood, exposed. It was midwinter, and there was a chill in the air, and we all knew it would grow colder still. He knew it, and brought me out there without cover, without protection. I should have run, then."

Evra inhaled a shaky breath. "I don't know how long we walked. Long. Far. When I turned away from him, he withdrew a whip, and he took it to the back of my neck. I knew he was cruel, but this, this shocked me. So much that I didn't have time to defend myself against the assault that followed. And when it was over, and I lay bloodied, eyes swollen shut, unable to walk, he said... he said if I tried to follow him, he'd kill me. If I survived the night out there, he'd let me live another day."

Rhosyn was aghast with horror. "Do you think he wanted you to die?"

Evra laughed through his tears. "Very much so. Yes. I think he wanted me to die, so he could bathe in the sympathy of his subjects and have his greatest trouble solved at the same time."

"Why not just kill you himself, then?"

"I guess even an evil man has limits. But that makes him a coward, doesn't it? He can't rise to finish what he started." Evra wiped at his eyes. "*Made* him a coward. He's dead. And to answer your question, Rhosyn, clearly I survived the night, but I didn't return to Longwood Rush or my father. I limped down to Windwatch Grove. It took me days. When I arrived, Meira took me in, cleaned me up, and gave me a horse. I rode that horse all the way to Oldcastle. I enrolled in university, and I waited until my death had been announced in the kingdom to send my own raven home. I sent the message not only to my father, but to his least loyal stewards, so that he couldn't hide the truth that I'd lived, despite his efforts. But I knew that if I returned, he'd finish what he'd failed at before. Whatever hatred he had for me when I was a boy burned so much brighter after I'd humiliated him before all his Reach."

Rhosyn could hardly believe his words. She'd heard of the cruelty of men but never seen it. The Ravenwoods had their own kind, of course, but it settled upon her in a different way, to hear someone else speak of such dismissive love.

She said none of this, though. "Well, that's all very sad, Evra. Truly."

Evra turned from her. He was embarrassed by his emotion now, in a way he hadn't been before. "That's how I became a Pupil and why I decided to give my life to it."

"And how did you become an abductor, then? How did you make *that* leap?"

He looked at her again. "If you tell me that returning to him is what *you want*... if it's what *you want*, not some misguided sense of duty toward others, then I won't keep you here a moment longer. I'll untie the rope right now."

"You'll untie me." She repeated the words slowly.

"I never wanted to keep you here. I mean that." Evra's face strained as he tried not to cry again. "I panicked, and it happened, and I'm sorry. I'm *sorry*. But if you tell me, tell me truly, that it's what you *want*, then I will let you go. Because this isn't about choosing me. I already know that what we shared is in the past, and it can never be again. I know that. It's not about me or us. It's about choosing life."

Rhosyn's hope surged forth with the lie. It rolled to the front of her tongue as she prepared to speak it to life. But as her lips parted, the lie died. She closed her mouth again, wondering when she'd become so weak.

Evra nodded, as if he understood the battle she'd just waged and lost with herself.

"Let me go," she pleaded, the fire in her voice spent.

"I can't."

"You *won't*."

"My life has been defined by my indecisiveness. My failure to rise for everyone I've ever loved."

"Is that what you think this is?" Rhosyn shot back. "You, rising for me? A man, rising for a priestess? That's like... that's like a bucket of water rising for the sea."

"Now that I know he's been coming around, I'll know to look for him." Evra dusted himself off as he stood. "Thank you for telling me."

"You make no sense to me. You can barely swing a sword, and now you want to take on a sorcerer?"

Evra nodded, looking toward the windows still needing his tending. "Yeah. That's what I intend to do."

TWENTY-TWO

SOFT BRISTLES

Rendyr paced the Courtyard of Regents. His path was oft-interrupted by midnight goats, but was it not these very goats that had brought him here?

"You can't keep going down there. To the world of men." Augustyn. What a good heart his little brother had. How he'd fantasized about tearing it from his chest as he enjoyed the last scandalized look of shock he'd ever wear. "You're veering dangerously close to violating the alliance."

Rendyr pictured himself punting a goat off the edge of the courtyard, into the abyss, followed by his brother. Later, perhaps. "You should leave *here* before someone finds you. You're not allowed. You'll never be allowed."

"Nor are you. Arwenna is dead. Only Mother and Father can be in the Courtyard of Regents now. Even if Rhosyn does come home, you'll have to compete once more. Until then..."

"Until then. Before then. After then. It's all the same to me." Rendyr stopped at the base of an icy tree. It was said to bear fruit every hundred years. As rare as the silver-haired Ravenwood.

Perhaps the two were connected. That he couldn't know, without *her*, was vexing. But he would know. She would give it to him. He would take it from her. "Why *are* you here? To lecture me? Your words are wasted, Augustyn. You'd fare better spending them on the air."

Augustyn's boots clicked on the ice as he stepped farther in. This was odd behavior, coming from his normally reticent brother. It unsettled Rendyr. He'd never liked when things ventured beyond what was known and expected. Not unless he was the architect of such change. "I know why you did it. Perhaps no one else does, but I do."

"Did what?"

"You wanted Arwenna to fail. You wanted her to fail before you even cast your lot for her, but you *had* to cast it, because if any other man would have won the night of her Langenacht, you'd be pushed aside. She would've borne their child, and the line would have continued, as it always had. You wed her and then waited patiently to kill her, so you could have your true prize." Augustyn sounded appropriately disgusted at his choice of words. "You did that to our *sister*."

Rendyr's chest tightened. He reached for an icy branch, steadying himself. "Arwenna was a traitor who was never meant to be High Priestess. She suffered a traitor's death. Rhosyn will rise in her place. She *must* rise in her place, which is why I go down there, as you say. If she does not, chaos will ensue. Someone has to do it. To stand for our ways. *Someone* has to bring her home."

"What I'm saying, brother..." Augustyn paused with a sigh. "What I'm saying is that I know why it's Rhosyn you wanted all along. I was there, too, that night. When Grandfather told us his stories."

Rendyr constricted his grip on the branch. It snapped in his palm. "I don't recall any stories."

"You do," Augustyn said. He kept his distance. "I think about them all the time. Especially this one. Every time I look at Rhosyn, I cannot help but wonder."

"Then you're speaking of yourself. Not me."

"It's not true, you know. It cannot be true. How could it be?" Augustyn dropped to his knees, cooing at a midnight goat passing by. "Rhosyn is special, but she's not... she's not what Grandfather said she is. Those are just stories, Rendyr. That's all."

Rendyr both heard and felt the pop as he bit through his tongue. "Leave before I tell someone you were here."

"There are no prophecies. Only tales passed down. Rendyr! Think! Even if Rhosyn was your way to wrest power from the women, does the rest of it make any sense? Her being sired by the magic of the midnight goats? That's absurd. It's *silly*. Just because her hair is silver, like theirs? You would do all this for the careless whisperings of old men?"

It wasn't silly. It wasn't silly at all. Rendyr had never even used the word. He hardly knew what it meant, because he'd spent most of his life being the opposite of silly. No, what it was... what it was, was a way forward. A means of ending the matriarchal rule that had devastated the Ravenwood legacy for centuries. Every hundred years, it was said, the midnight goats intervened in fate, fathering a half-breed, instilling their immortal magic in every drop of her blood and strand of her hair. Though she herself was not immortal, she was possessed of something even more valuable. Known by her silver mane, it was through her, through her alone, that a man could take the sacred visions for himself and become the true leader of the Ravenwoods of Midnight Crest. Rendyr would be the father of a new age. The one by which all that followed would be measured. They'd never answer to a woman again. He would be The First. The One. Nothing else would matter.

"If you were wise, you *would* cast your lot, brother." Rendyr turned. He let the remnants of the broken branch fall to the icy floor. "But you think too small. Your love for our sister blinds you. Shackles you." He grinned. "More for me, then."

Rendyr exploded into feathers and aimed himself for Midwinter Rest.

195

Sweat rolled off Oswin in waves, despite that it was as frigid as the Guardian of the Unpromised Future outside. Coldest he could remember in a long spell, though it wasn't the Guardians that had sent this mess, was it?

This cursed leg was his problem. He'd caught the twist in it trying to get to Evra and Rhosyn. She'd already called the storm by then, and the wind knocked him about and then straight into the side of the keep. There'd been no crack, but there might as well have been, for all the use the limb offered him now.

He refused all help offered. He ordered the staff to join Thornton in the other wing. Even Rylan was down there. Here, alone, Oswin could work in peace, without the pity he'd seen in their eyes when he'd come limping in that night.

It would heal, as all things did. But the storm...

Oswin pressed the last board to the window he worked on when he saw the dark figure at the end of the path. The man lingered just beyond the iron gate, a choice that made his identity clear. Rendyr had never come beyond the gate.

There'd been a rumor among the Frosts that, generations back, one of them had mingled with a Ravenwood. That the Ravenwood had placed a protection on the keep, protecting them against evil. But evil in their parts came from the skies, not the ground, and he'd never placed his trust in stories.

Oswin swallowed a deep breath and hobbled to the door. He'd already boarded the nearby windows, so he could no longer see the intruder, but he was there. He'd be there until Oswin addressed him. Why he'd come, though, was still unknown.

The hard wind rushed up and knocked Oswin back inside. Only Rendyr's cape surrendered to the gust. The feathers at his shoulders fluttered. He seemed otherwise unaffected, standing tall and solid.

Oswin steeled himself and aimed himself down the path. The snow was ankle deep already, and Thornton had cleared it nigh an hour ago. The snowbolts had eased off, though one or two still slammed into the earth in the distance.

Rendyr came no closer as Oswin limped toward him, trying to keep his pain from the monster without causing himself further injury. No one knew he was out here. Had he the need to cry out for aid, none would hear him against this wind.

"Slow old man," Rendyr accused when at last they were face to face. "Where is she?"

"She?" Oswin leaned against the gate to find his breath. "You cannot mean Rhosyn?"

Rendyr's eyes burned with a depth of hatred Oswin had never possessed for anything or anyone. "Who else could I mean?"

"Why are you coming here, when she's returned home? She left us the morning after she called the storm down upon you."

"This storm, you mean?" Rendyr asked, pointing both hands at the sky. "If the storm is here, she is here."

"I told you. She's not here. She flew away."

"If she flew away, she did not come to me," Rendyr hissed. "But I very much doubt she flew anywhere, Steward Frost."

"She's not here."

"Invite me in, and I'll decide for myself."

"Invite you in?" Oswin half-turned, gesturing behind him. "The door is right there. You can see for yourself."

"Is that an invitation?"

"No." He should be afraid, but all he felt was anger. For Rhosyn. For the ones who'd come before her. "It is not."

Rendyr's tongue rolled around the inside of his mouth. "You don't want to deny me, Steward."

"I've denied you nothing. Rhosyn came to us as part of the alliance, and she left us when her duty was fulfilled. If she's not returned home—"

"She has not."

"Then she has gone elsewhere."

Rendyr grinned. "Or she never left."

"Look here—"

"Save your threats. Send them into the wind for all I care. I'm not the one who should be afraid right now, Steward."

"Me, you mean? I don't fear you, Rendyr. I don't fear any Ravenwood."

"You should."

"Your magic is king here in the north. But if you had no men to shield you, you'd be dragged down from that mountain in chains. Enslaved. Studied. Murdered. We're all that stands between you and that fate, so yes, you could best *me*, but the Northerlands would rise if you did. And then where would you be?"

Rendyr's mouth distorted, reminding Oswin of the tantrums Thornton would throw when he was a small child. Perhaps that was why he had no fear of Rendyr, in the end. He was only a willful boy playing a man.

"I will ask you once more."

"And I," Oswin said, drawing closer, "will answer you once more and then never again. Rhosyn isn't here. And as she's not here, your business here is concluded. If we have further need of Ravenwoods, it will not be you we will call upon, Rendyr."

Rendyr turned into a raven and swirled into the air.

Oswin's heart leapt and lodged into the back of his throat. He gripped the gate to keep from sagging.

Had Rendyr read beyond his hard words? Had he seen how Oswin's heart was sore for his shadow daughter, now lost to the world?

For if she hadn't returned to Midnight Crest...

"Where are you, Rhosyn?" Oswin whispered.

Evra ran his fingers over the text as Rylan slowly moved through the words. "The light rises in the... in the..."

"Morning," Evra said gently. "The light rises in the morning."

Rylan nodded and focused harder on the page. "The light sets in the e... evening?"

"Very good." Evra smiled. "You're a quick study."

Rylan beamed. "Brin taught me my letters, but she hasn't had the time for me lately. Not since Wystan was born. Will you be here long, Evra? Long enough to teach me?"

Evra looked toward the boarded window. "I don't know. Until the pass clears, I expect."

The little one laughed. "Forever, then!"

Evra ran a hand through Rylan's hair. "I have my own land to return to, so let us hope not."

"I've never seen another land." Rylan cocked his head. "Is the Westerlands as green as they say?"

"Greener."

"Greener?"

"So many hues we don't have names for them all. And the flora? Colors like you've never seen. The women, they have this garden in the Halls of Longwood, and there they can grow wonders you'll find nowhere else in this kingdom." Evra's smile faded as he listened to himself speak so fondly of the same land he'd thought he had no place in.

"Like the Wintergarden? At Wulfsgate?" Rylan's eyes widened into saucers.

"A little," Evra said. "Have you been to the Wintergarden?"

"No," Rylan said. He glanced back at the book. "Father says when I'm older, but I heard him tell Mother that Lord Dereham hasn't extended an invitation since Father offended him."

Evra grinned. "Were you eavesdropping, Rylan?"

"No!" Rylan insisted, scandalized at the suggestion. "I was brushing Mother's hair. She gets tired and can't do it herself anymore. But I think she just likes it better when *I* do it. Women love to have their hair brushed, you know."

"That so?"

"Mhm. She says it feels better when someone else does it for her. I like making Mother happy. She's always so sad. I don't like it when she's sad."

"She seems very happy now that your little brother is here."

Rylan jerked his jaw into a frown. "I'm not."

Evra began to ask Rylan about the unfortunate arrival of his little brother when their attention was pulled toward the door. Oswin's large form cast a long shadow.

"Rylan. Go on, then. I need to speak with Lord Blackrook."

Rylan shot another proud look at the book and Evra, then scuttled out.

"What's wrong, Steward?"

"I need to know, Evra. Did you actually *see* Rhosynora fly off that morning? After the two of you... after you went to talk?"

Evra paled. This question hadn't come from nowhere. "No, I didn't... I didn't *see* her fly off, Steward."

"What happened out there? When you took her to have your talk?"

"We talked." Evra swallowed the lie, mingling it with a touch of the truth. "She was angry at me. That was how we left it."

"Hm. So you didn't see her go? Didn't see her take to the skies?"

Evra shook his head.

"Guardians," Oswin whispered. He sank into the large chair in the corner of the room. "Guardians help her if he finds her before we do."

"Rendyr?"

"He came for her today. She's not been seen at Midnight Crest. She never returned." Oswin scratched at his beard. "If not for this storm, I'd send out a search for her, but I'd be commanding the men to their deaths, combing through that mountain. And I can't..." He pointed at his foot with a pained look. "Ah, Rhosyn. Where could she have gone? What was she thinking, running off?"

"Perhaps she was thinking that there could be a better way for her."

Oswin closed his eyes as he scoffed. "Would that this were true, Evra. There are some truths in this kingdom that are beyond dispute. Hard truths. The Derehams, you know, they enjoy the spoils of their alliance with the Ravenwoods and can close their eyes and harden their hearts to the fate they send them back to. But us? We know better. We have no haze over our own eyes. We know who the Ravenwoods are. We know what sentence awaits the women 'fortunate' enough to be born for their highest role. And yet, send them off we do. For there is no other choice. There is no other path for Rhosyn. Her fate was written in the skies long before she was born, just as yours was or mine."

Evra stood. He was tired of the steward's complacent acceptance. He was tired of the word fate, which he'd never thought much of. What was fate, but an excuse to fail? A justification for doing what you've always done. A reason against change for the better. If he'd had room in his life for fate, he would've died in those woods and never made it to Oldcastle.

"I hope she's well free of him, Steward. For you might rest at night knowing what he'll do to her, but if I thought she was back in his hands, I'd never sleep again."

Rhosyn was roused by the realization something was stuck in her hair. Reflexively, she made to swat it away, only to remember she had no use of her hands.

Now awake, the sensation shifted. Soft bristles ran the length of her hair, with only gentle tugs against the snarls that had formed in her fugue. When had someone last brushed her hair? Arwenna, when they were girls. Before either of them understood anything, and these small joys were still big ones.

Evra's soft grunts anytime he hit a snag almost made her laugh. He was almost too gentle, using his hands before the bristles to keep his path smooth.

Rhosyn pretended to sleep so she would not be required to confront the confusion this tenderness created in her.

"I stole it from Brin's chambers," Evra said. Her breath hitched until she realized he was speaking to himself. He didn't know she was awake. "Borrowed, actually. I'll take it back. But she had this entire row of them, lined up like my sister used to line up her dolls. I hardly think she'll even miss it."

He continued his ministrations. "We can't stay here. I know you said he was creeping around, but he's threatened Oswin now, and... the storm be damned... we have to leave. I'll take you wherever you want to go. Anywhere. You never have to see me again. As long as I know you're safe, I'll... I'll do anything to know you're safe. That you won't end up like poor Arwenna. I'll endure your hatred until my last breath if I just know you're beyond his reach."

Evra leaned in and kissed the crown of her head. Rhosyn sucked in her bottom lip to subdue the swell of emotion tingling through her chest and limbs as Evra lay down next to her in the hay.

He pressed his head against the middle of her back and said no more.

TWENTY-THREE
SUMMON THE STRENGTH

Evra had been working on boarding the same window for the better part of the afternoon. His pace was purposefully sluggish. Rhosyn didn't need to read his mind to see the conflict brewing within him. Even if she wanted to read his mind, her hands...

But she could, couldn't she? She didn't need her hands for everything. When he was close enough, she could hear him so easily if she wanted to. So why didn't she? Was it the fear she might confirm he was keeping her here for a nefarious purpose? That he didn't love her?

Or that he did?

What did I see when I read his intentions before?

Kindness. Adoration. Innocence.

What would I see now?

Rendyr had come again. This time, she hadn't pushed back quick or hard enough.

Evra stumbled back and sat on a stone bench, spent. He huddled over his knees, facing away from her.

"What excuse will you use now that you're done?" Rhosyn called out. Why was she doing this? She'd asked him to leave her be, and he had, so why was she goading him? "Steward Frost knows good and well you have no skill at the forge."

"Can you stop this storm?" he called back without looking up.

"You know I can't. Not without my hands."

"Then I'll unbind you." He shook his head in his palms. "I have to, don't I? I thought if I spent time with my thoughts, the answer would come to me, but it hasn't. He knows you're here, and that means you aren't safe here, either. I've tried to think of a place I could take you beyond his reach, but that place doesn't exist, does it?"

"If you unbind me, I'll fly away. Back to him." What was *she* doing? He was going to let her go!

Evra nodded into his hands. "I asked before if that was what you wanted. You told me you didn't, but it's not that simple, and perhaps that's what you were really trying to tell me with your half-answer."

"I didn't owe you an answer at all."

Evra spun half-around, watching her with a harrowed look. "You don't owe me anything at all." His smile died before it formed. "I don't want to be this man, Rhosyn. The one who would claim the end was reason enough for the means. I panicked when I did this to you, but what can I say about every moment since, except... except that I'm so afraid for you. I know how foolish that sounds. I have not half the strength you possess, so who am I to be so bold to assume I can offer you anything in the way of protection?" He laughed as he gestured around. "In a *barn* in the back of an armory."

"You're going to unbind me, then?"

He nodded. "If that's what you really want."

"What if I say yes?"

"Then I'll be a man of my word. If not, I can't call myself a man at all, can I?"

"And if I say no?"

Evra turned all the way around. "No? Why would you say no?"

Rhosyn trapped the gasp in her chest. It burrowed there with her confusion, her clarity. What was she suggesting? That he keep her there, bound and imprisoned? It was madness! She didn't want this. How could she?

"Rhosyn?"

"I hate you," she choked out.

"I..."

"How dare you love me?" She tried to stand, but without her arms, she only fell back into the hay. "How *dare* you show me what it is to be loved? And then... and then this..."

Evra rushed over and helped her to her feet. She wriggled away from him once she had her balance, but the tether snapped against the pillar, stilling her.

"Rhosyn, I don't know what I'm supposed to say to that. What would you like me to say? That I don't love you? Would that be better?"

"I hate you!" she sobbed. The salt of her tears slipped into her mouth as they made their way down her cheeks. "Why did you let this happen?" *Why did I let this happen?*

Evra's hands fumbled, wanting to touch her, afraid to. "I didn't mean for it to happen. I didn't come here expecting... you."

"No," she blubbered. "No, you came to *use* me. To whisk me away to your land like an animal brought to heel."

Evra stood straighter. He dropped his hands back to his sides. "I was wrong for that. I was wrong about many things. I've been wrong my whole life, and I'll keep being wrong, I expect, because if the Guardians could bring you into my life, only for me to watch you fly away into danger and sorrow, then what can *right* be? What use is right and wrong when the pain is greater than both?"

"You're rambling. Carrying on about nothing."

"I'm breaking." Evra's hands trembled. "Into pieces. Into someone I don't know anymore."

"I know you," Rhosyn asserted, head pulled back. "I know who you are."

205

Evra watched her with heavy eyes. "Who am I, Rhosyn?"

Her voice trembled. "Come closer, and I'll tell you."

Evra took a step.

"Closer."

He moved forward until his cheek was pressed to hers. The heat of his breath against her neck elicited a sharp, quick moan. When his hands traveled around to her back, to her own hands, as he fumbled with the rope, she whispered a single word.

"No."

He stopped. "You don't want me to do it?"

Rhosyn shook her head.

Evra pulled back to look at her. "What *do* you want? Tell me, and I'll do it."

Rhosyn pressed her mouth to his. The soft warmth of his lips felt like silk wrapped around her heart. Stifling her. Filling her.

Evra backed away with a reluctant sigh. "I won't do this with you bound."

"I'm asking you to." Rhosyn backed into the hay pile. "I'm *telling* you to. You said all I needed to was tell you, and you'd do it."

"Rhosyn." Evra stepped to her once more. He ran his hands down the sides of her torn dress and back up to her shoulders, her neck, her face. "I'm going to let you go now."

"Don't." She leaned into him, knocking him back into the hay as she fell upon him. His desire for her pressed through his trousers, but he wouldn't see it through. She'd known that before beginning this madness.

Evra's soft, uncalloused palms traveled up the flesh of her thigh. His slow blink; his ebbing throat; these were agony. She guided his hand to voyage inward, and it did, and she cried out as his fingers slipped inside her. Her hips rose and fell against his knuckles as he strained beneath her, fighting himself. She *wanted* him to be weak. To turn her over and take her from behind, proving that he was no better than who she'd said he was. That he was just a man, filling a need.

Rhosyn climbed higher and higher in her ecstasy until she reached a peak that sent black swirls into her vision. She cried out as she collapsed over the edge and then fell beside him, spent, confused.

Evra watched her with the same emotions. He looked down at his hand, covered in her, and then brought it to his mouth, touching his fingers only briefly to his lips.

"I thought you wanted me," she whispered through her uneven breaths. "Hasn't this all been about wanting me?"

"That's not what it was about. And no, not like this."

"You could have had me. As many times as you wanted. In any way you wanted. I would've been powerless to stop you."

"I'm going to let you go now, Rhosyn."

"In the morning," she said, turning away from him. "So that I can summon the strength I thought I had all along."

TWENTY-FOUR
THE FIRE CALLER

It was impossible that he'd slept until morning, but he must have, for it was light. Except this light was... it was...

Too bright.

Evra checked on Rhosyn, but she was still asleep. He extricated his arm without waking her, and quietly rose. The light was blinding, even from behind the boards. But it wasn't just the light. It was the smell.

He stumbled into the front room of the armory. That unbelievable orange hue was even brighter here. He held his arm to his eyes and made for the door.

Evra flung it open to find the world on fire.

"Brin!" Thorn screeched her name so loud something broke in his lungs. "BRIN!" He dodged flaming timber as it crashed around him, but each scald across his flesh only pushed him harder. Half his breaths were choked with smoke. He screamed anyway. Brin was still inside with Wystan, and the fire could take him, too, if he couldn't get to them.

"Rylan!" his father howled from another wing. It might as well be another world. Half the keep was already gone, but the fire was only ramping up. That wicked Rendyr was only getting started. "Rylan Frost, don't you play with me! I'll have you whipped for it!"

He glanced up through a gap in the roof to see the raven swooping back and forth, pouring his fire down upon Midwinter Hold.

"Brin! Call out for me, and I'll find you!" Thorn's sleeve caught fire, and he slapped it against his leg in a panic, slowing but not stopping. The smoke turned his eyes to milky orbs. Sight was nearly impossible now, but he didn't need all his senses. "Brin!"

"Fire caller," Ethelyn hissed, clutching her son to her breast. She paced in the snow with the few furs she'd seized on the rush out of the flaming keep. There'd been no time. Oswin shook her awake so roughly she thought, for a moment, it might be a thief, come to murder them for their gold. Before she could even ask, he had her scooped up into one arm, Castian in the other. He'd forgotten his wounded leg, moving so fast she almost remembered what it had been like to watch him rule the other boys in the jousts.

She had no time for such memories as she watched her entire world burn.

"Ethelyn! Have you seen Rylan?" Oswin's voice, from somewhere. She couldn't see him through the haze of black smoke.

"Rylan? He's not with you?"

"I'll find him!"

"Oswin! He's not with you? Oswin!"

He didn't respond.

Ethelyn slid the furs over her head to protect her youngest son, leaving her fear for the two still inside unaddressed, for now.

"Shh, easy now, Wystan." Brin comforted her son with soundless tears. The door was blocked. She'd tried it three times now. Two times she'd been met with flames. The third had burned her hand to the bone. It should be painful, she thought, but it wasn't.

There were the windows, but the glass was thick, crafted to withstand the very worst of their volatile weather. She'd thrown a chair and had not even splintered it. She tried to lift the desk, but the wood was solid; heavier than she was. All the while, Wystan's screams were a reminder he was still breathing. She was still breathing.

They would die in this room. Brin hadn't confronted these thoughts so directly, because she still needed strength to endure it. For Wystan, if not herself. She was his mother. She could not allow his last moments to mirror her own.

Ethelyn would blame this on the Ravenwoods, but Brin knew better. Rendyr might be the one breathing fire from the sky, but it wasn't for nothing that these assaults had become a generational tradition.

She pressed her face to Wystan's light curls, inhaling her favorite scent, as if it was enough to replace the sting burning its way through her breath and blood.

This was their penance. For their indifference. Their placid acceptance.

"It's all right now, love. It will be over soon," she comforted, imagining the glass breaking; envisioning her scaling the gap in one smooth leap, clearing the shards, delivering them both to the safety of the storm.

Brin closed her eyes as the door exploded.

Oswin had to step outside. It was the last thing he wanted to do, but his lungs were crowded with smoke. If he collapsed, he'd never find Rylan. Thorn was after Brin and the baby. Ethelyn was safe outside with Castian, and knowing this was the closest he'd come to peace on this night.

The servants had forgotten their charge in their own panic, scattering into the fields. There was no one else.

He prayed Evra had found his own escape, for there was no one coming to save them.

Oswin coughed out the poison and inhaled as much cold air as he could stand. But before he could reenter, he caught the sight of Evra trudging through the snow, coming from the armory. Is that where he'd been all night? Is that where he'd been all these nights? And did he, Oswin, deep inside, know why?

It didn't matter. Only one thing mattered.

Evra dodged a ball of flame on one side, a snowbolt on the other, and pushed harder.

"Tell me how to help!" Evra cried out.

"Rylan!" Oswin tried to scream it, but it came out as a squeak. "My boy!"

"We'll find him!" Evra called back and pushed past the steward and into the flaming keep.

Rendyr flew his path in haphazard loops, dizzy with joy as he rained his fire upon the unworthy. He watched them scatter and flee. He heard their screams, unanswered.

It was their fault, all of it. All they had to do was give her back.

You beautiful little fool, thought Rendyr as he fantasized about Rhosyn's defeated retreat home. Her contrition that would be rewarded with a cruelty beyond her imagining. It didn't have to be this way. She made it like this. Made *him* like this.

It wasn't coincidence that he'd been born in the era of the silver-haired sorceress.

His energy at last spent, Rendyr climbed back into the skies and made for Midnight Crest.

There was no point in waiting for his sister.

She'd come on her own now.

Evra dropped to his knees as he huddled with the Frosts and their servants in the courtyard, watching their great keep turn to smoldering ash and fragmented stone. Behind him, Wystan cried in his mother's arms, while Thorn screamed his agony into the still-going storm. Oswin struggled and failed to calm his own wife as she howled Rylan's name to the Guardians.

Rhosyn's storm had overcome the flames in the end, but Rendyr's fire had been birthed from animosity bigger than them all, and the trauma inflicted on this night would last for years. Generations.

"We'll take the war up the mountain!" Thorn was saying. "We'll take every last man in the kingdom to that cursed castle and cut them all down!"

Oswin didn't discourage his son. He was in thrall by the cries of the women and infants, and when Evra looked back at him, the man, too, was crying.

Evra cast his glance back into the carnage, and beyond, to where the little armory still stood, untouched.

214

TWENTY-FIVE
RUINS

Evra stepped through the blackened, crumbling rubble, cutting an aimless path through the ruins, as the others did. Now and then, someone would call out for Rylan, but it was a call beyond the reach of hope. Oswin kept the others away from where the family chambers had been, to spare them a gruesome discovery. Evra joined him because a man shouldn't have to come upon something that terrible alone.

"I can't reckon how the servants' quarters made it unscathed," Oswin mused. He turned sideways to step over a pile of debris. His foot caught it and a plume of choking ash flew up into their faces. What had that once been? A desk? A bed?

The stone floors and walls remained mostly intact, and from a distance, one might not notice the missing roof. The charred kisses. The stench that couldn't help but remind him of home.

"Is that where you'll stay?"

Oswin nodded. "Where we'll all stay, for now." He covered his face as he kicked at another charred pile. "A hundred rooms in that wing. And how many servants do we have? Fifteen? Twenty?"

215

He coughed into his sleeve. "But you'll have a bed, a privy pot, and a small cabinet for your belongings. It will be enough until we can rebuild."

"I wasn't thinking of myself, sir." Evra had the urge to cry, but he had no tears left. He'd spent the night, into the morning, waiting for the heat of the fire to die down enough for them to reenter and begin their recovery mission for Rylan. Little Rylan, who had been so proud, mere hours earlier, at his accomplishment in reading.

"Would be natural, if you were. I know you're eager to return to your home, Evra. But with this storm..."

"Are there any in town who might be after some coin in exchange for a crossing?"

"Perhaps. Plenty of trackers and trappers find their way up here from time to time." Oswin paused, looking left and right to orient himself. "I'd say this was Thorn's chambers. Can't be certain."

"Then Rylan's would be the next one."

Oswin nodded.

The hazy morning cast a surreal pall. Evra grappled to reconcile the before and after, how quickly reality had shifted. He'd been unfair in his assessment of their cool apathy, never understanding how they could claim to love Ravenwoods like Rhosyn and yet let them suffer. But as he'd watched Rhosyn sleep, before the night turned to fire, he saw the color of his love for her shift, too. He'd forced her into a gilded box that fit his own narrow understanding of the world. All his life he'd done this, in his desperation to find sense in the bad things and to excuse his inaction in them. His father was evil and could not be bested. His brother was weak and could not be strengthened. Evra was a second son, neutered and useless. Easier to believe these truths than to change them.

Rhosyn's cause was the first to challenge this self-belief, but he'd taken a hard swing in the other direction, not grasping that most of life existed somewhere in the in-between. Evra was still a second son and still half the man his forebears were, but neither of those things made him less liable. Neither of those things made room for the future he'd wanted.

Rhosyn might not embrace her fate, either, but it was *her* fate, wasn't it? Just as he must return and attempt to find some peace in being the Lord of the Westerlands, Rhosyn's options were just as limited. They could love each other until the world fell apart, and it changed nothing.

She'd understood this from the beginning. It was what she'd been trying to tell him. *You don't know what you've done.* Ahh, but he was so sure!

She'd known that Rendyr would bring his vengeance here. That it wouldn't be Evra or Rhosyn who paid the price, but the people they both had come to see as their family.

This is my fault, he started to say to the steward, but he didn't deserve what Oswin would offer in return. Comfort. Reassurances. It *was* his fault. He saw it in the eyes of each of the harrowed Frosts, even if they'd never speak the words. He'd failed his own people, then come here to fail a world he was so certain, in his arrogance, he understood better than they did.

He yearned for Meira and her unflappable wisdom, but she'd be almost to Longwood Rush by now. And he didn't deserve her, either. What he did deserve was this raw agony gnawing at his bones, drinking his blood. That, he had earned. That was his.

Evra wouldn't seek their forgiveness, because they'd give it.

"Did you hear that?" Oswin stopped and cocked his head. "Was that Ethelyn?"

Evra turned halfway, listening. He heard Ethelyn calling for Oswin. Unlike her cries before, this one sounded hopeful.

Both men cut a speedy, messy path back the way they'd come. Oswin took the lead. He no longer shielded his face as he ran into everything he'd avoided on the way into the wing.

"Oswin!" She was clearer now; her joy indisputable. "Oswin, it's Rylan! It's Rylan! He's alive!"

"Oh, Guardians. Oh, sweet Guardians," Oswin panted as they cleared the last of the ruin and broke out into the daylight.

And there he was. Little Rylan Frost, wrapped in his mother's arms. Evra's voice cracked as he laughed with Oswin, the only reaction either of them could find for this miracle.

"Where were you?" Oswin crushed his son to his chest with a guttural moan. "Where *were* you, Rylan? Where did you go?"

"I wanted to help Evra." The boy stopped to address a coughing fit. "I went to the armory."

"I didn't see you." Evra's breath halted. "You weren't there when the fire started."

Rylan shook his head. "After. I saw you run toward the keep, and I looked back and everything was red and orange. I was afraid, so I went inside."

"Is that where you've been all night?" Oswin demanded. He hadn't released his hold on his son. "Didn't you hear us calling for you?"

"I heard you," Rylan sobbed. "But I was afraid. I didn't want to burn."

"That's enough, Oswin," Ethelyn chided. She used her sleeve to dry her tears, drawing a sooty line across her cheeks. "He's safe. That's all that matters now."

"The armory..." Evra was stunned.

Rylan tried to smile. He beamed at Evra with wide, tired eyes. "I kept everything safe inside. Everything."

"That's a good boy. That's my good boy," Oswin managed through his clenched jaw. He sniffled. "That's my boy."

But Rylan only had eyes for Evra.

The sun was high in the sky when the villagers arrived with their carts and tools. Oswin cracked at the sight of them, trudging through the snowy path as they fought the cold and stormy skies.

"Time to get to work, Steward," one man said, and the others nodded. "Can't be leaving this mess for the springtide to handle."

A woman, probably the man's wife, stepped forward and held her arms out to Ethelyn, who allowed the gentle comfort. "We have a cart with blankets for the women and babes, to take you into town. Get a hot meal in you and a warm bed. Doesn't that sound nice, Stewardess?"

Ethelyn sobbed. Brin clapped her free hand to her mouth, clutching little Wystan tighter to her chest.

"Where is she?" Evra pulled Rylan aside as the men and women negotiated the remainder of the day.

"She's still there, Evra."

"You didn't free her?"

Rylan shook his head.

"Why not?"

"Because she was safe there."

"Rhosyn can fly. She could have been safer anywhere."

Rylan shrugged. "But you didn't think so, or you wouldn't have bound her."

"What did she say to you?"

"I told her how you helped me to read better. She said you're a wise man, and I should listen to you." Rylan averted his eyes. "And that I shouldn't think poorly of you for what you'd done."

"She said that?"

Rylan nodded.

"You should think poorly of me." He brushed away a mat of hair covering Rylan's eyes. "It's the worst thing I've ever done."

Rylan shook his head. "I saw what her brother did. I saw him in the sky. Big black bird breathing fire." He shivered. "If you let her go, that's what he'll do to her, too."

Evra pulled the boy in for a hug. "She's stronger than that, Rylan. We have to trust in that strength. In her." He released him. "Why don't you go take her some dried fruit from the storehouse. The fire didn't touch that, either."

Rylan brightened. Nodded.

"And then, if she'll let you, unbind her. Please."

"You don't want me to wait for you?"

"No. It's been too long already. Go on, then. I'll come to the armory after I've helped the men with cleanup."

219

Evra watched him run off and went to join the others.

It wasn't until the sun dropped behind Icebolt Mountain that Evra took a break. They'd barely made any headway, but the men had hauled cartload after cartload into the forest, dumping it all in a pile to be dealt with later.

They scoured the rooms for anything salvageable and found more than they'd expected. Evra's own belongings were a loss, but when he'd seen the scorched edges of the book peeking from under a pile of stone, something inside him brightened.

He slipped it into the back of his trousers and went about the rest of his work.

Oswin showed him to his new room in the servants' wing. The women had returned with clothes for the family, and Evra had a pile of pressed shirts and clean trousers waiting for him. A new set of furs hung on the back of his door. They'd all be too big; he could see that straightaway. They'd done it not from duty, but because they loved Oswin Frost and his family. Evra had a hard time conjuring what that must be like, for none had served his father with anything deeper than fear. The kindness of the act left him drained and hollow.

Once he heard the sound of all the doors closing for the night, Evra slipped out of his room and stepped quietly down the hall, wrapped in the donated furs. By instinct, he tried to navigate toward where the double doors should be, but at the end of the hall, he stepped into the quiet cold of the evening.

Evra glanced up into the night sky. The smoke from the fires had cleared, and he could see all the tiny lights again. The Guardians, people liked to say, but there were too many for that to make any sense, and he didn't know if he even believed in the Guardians. Too many used them as a reason for their actions, or an excuse for their grief.

He would have to face his actions and his grief unabated to move forward.

TWENTY-SIX
CONFUSING LOVE WITH FONDNESS

Evra's heart constricted as Rhosyn turned her head into the hay pile to hide her grief.

"It wasn't your fault. It was mine. I should have listened to you."

"Does it matter where the blame lies, Evra? It changes nothing. I *told* you. I said—"

Evra folded his hands over his lap. "I know. You were right."

Rhosyn shook her head, aghast. A band of silver hairs stuck to the corner of her mouth. He wanted to free them. He didn't. "But that was *days* ago. Why were my words not enough to sway you? Why did the Frosts have to lose everything for you to see?"

Evra nodded into his lap. "I've been asking myself these same things."

"And?"

"And nothing. There is no satisfying answer. None that changes anything."

"It took a tragedy for you to see!"

Evra's sigh shuddered as he looked up. "You're right."

Rhosyn rolled her shoulders back. "What's wrong with you? You're not... yourself. You're different."

"Different?" Evra wiped at the soot on his face. "Watching people you care about lose everything will do that. Knowing you caused it will do that, too."

"I meant," Rhosyn said slowly, "you're different toward *me*."

He held out his palms. "How would you like me to be, Rhosynora? When I love you, you curse me for it. When I try to let you go, you tell me not yet. You insist I know nothing, and I can't argue with that, but when I say to you, yes, you're right, I know nothing, you tell me I'm treating you differently."

"You're the one who bound me and kept me as your prisoner, Evra. I don't owe you an explanation of *my* intentions."

Evra turned away, shaking his head. "No. You don't. Why didn't you let Rylan release you?"

"And let you slink away, answering for nothing?"

"I thought that might be easier for you. Not seeing me again."

"Tell me," Rhosyn challenged, bowing forward. "How did you think this would end? That I would see through to the heart of you and love you back? That I'd leave the Frosts to the whims of Rendyr and follow you to your home and become your wife? Your prize, paraded for all to see? Savior of your realm?"

"You know that's not what I thought."

"Isn't it? I can see no other conclusion from your actions."

"You wanna know what I thought, Rhosyn? You really wanna know?" Evra jumped to his feet and paced away from her. He couldn't look at her. His confessions would die alongside his courage, and he *had* to say these things. If not now, then he'd never get the chance. "I thought that if I could love you so much, so quickly, that... that a love that powerful could fix any complication put before us. Go on and laugh. Those are the words and whims of a boy, not a man. I know how it sounds."

"Ahh. And so now, thinking like a man, you can simply shrug these feelings away, like an old fur."

"No!" Evra screamed. He turned again to her, chest heaving. "The way I feel for you is... it's the only real thing I've ever felt. But that feeling led me down a dark path." He sniffled. "I can't save you. I can't even save myself. I couldn't even prevent your brother from burning Midwinter Hold to the ground, and I thought I could cut him down with a sword I can't even wield for long without pulling my shoulder out?"

Rhosyn leaned back against the hay again. She watched him through tired, glassy eyes. "I never needed you to save me, Evrathedyn."

Evra shrugged, laughing to cover the sob. "I'm not sure you ever needed me at all. And now I've made a mess of your life, and the Frosts'. I can't even apologize, because how inadequate would words be at a time like this?"

"I never wanted your pity, or your apologies, either."

"What's left, then?"

Rhosyn tried to stand, but stumbled back to her knees. "It won't be so bad, Evra. Rendyr, he's a terrible creature, but he can only be so terrible to me. He *needs* me. Without me, he's nothing. Without me, he'll die nothing. He raises a hand to me, he'll be struck down by the other Ravenwoods. I will be as god to them, and he, only my consort."

"Are you saying this to make what I'm about to do easier?"

"What are you about to do? I can't tell through your ramblings."

Evra crossed his arms and moved to the boarded window across the room.

"Evra?"

"Is it true? He wouldn't hurt you?"

"No more than he already has."

"But you'd have to..." Evra swallowed his disgust. "Wed him."

"Ravenwoods have always wed Ravenwoods, Evra. It's all we have." When he took too long with his response, she said, more urgently, "There's no world where the Ravenwoods exist alongside men. We have no choice but to wed our own if we want to survive. Is that not what men want, too? Have men never made questionable choices for this reason?" She sighed. "Was it not one of these questionable choices that brought *you* all the way up to the base of my world, desperate?"

"I already said I was wrong."

"You were wrong," Rhosyn agreed. "That does not make *us* wrong."

Evra had been summoning the courage for this since before entering the armory. He was still summoning it. But he'd never have all he needed for this. He didn't have another few days to convince himself he was doing the right thing because a few more days and the Frosts might lose more than their home.

"Rhosyn," Evra said, turning. The knot in his stomach tightened, growing. "I want you to go now. I should have never assumed I knew better. I should have never..." *Now or you'll never say it.* "What love could ever exist between a man and a Ravenwood? Oswin tried to warn me. Thorn, too. Meira left because of how foolish I was."

Rhosyn's mouth parted. It widened as his words rolled out, as the cruelty of his lies washed over her.

Tears stung the back of his eyes. If they fell, he'd be lost.

She'd be lost.

"I will never forget you, Rhosynora. But my people are waiting for me. Your people are waiting for you. I know I said any apology would be inadequate, but I *am* sorry. For confusing..." His throat bobbed as he pushed down the small moan of pain. *For her. This is for her. For a world you only pretended to understand so you could have what was never yours.* "Love with fondness."

Rhosyn's low voice cracked as she said, "I see."

"So I'm going to undo your bindings. I'm going to watch you fly away and return to where you belong. Because that's what you've been trying to tell me all along, while I was too busy acting like I knew better. And whatever... whatever has been wounded between men and Ravenwood, it will heal, once you're home, and I'm gone."

"All right," Rhosyn answered, breathless. She blinked her eyes, freeing the rest of her tears. "I suppose this is what I've been trying to make you see these past days."

Evra nodded. "I'm sorry for not listening. I truly am."

She cast her eyes down into the hay. "Well, you've listened now."

"Turn around, then."

Rhosyn's eyes pierced his heart. She hesitated, giving him the chance to confess he'd meant none of what he said. When he didn't, she turned with a short sigh.

"Evra!"

They both whipped their heads toward the front of the armory.

"Evra! Mother has asked for you! The men are felling trees, and Father is going to get himself killed, she said!"

"Rylan," Evra whispered. "I'll sort this and be right back. I promise."

"I'll be here," she whispered back.

226

TWENTY-SEVEN
THE LAST DRAGONS
OF THE SOUTHERLAND PENINSULA

Rhosyn hadn't meant to fall asleep. She'd waited for Evra to return for what seemed like hours, and when he didn't, she closed her eyes for a moment. But a moment was all that was needed for her exhaustion to steal over her.

She prepared for the familiar scream in her shoulders as she tried to stretch through her bindings, but it never came. Instead, her arms rose. Out to her sides. Above her head. They ached from the lack of movement, but that didn't last long. They were happy to be free.

Behind her was the rope, severed in pieces.

But no Evra.

Rhosyn scrambled to her feet and rushed to the door leading to the front room. Unlike before, it wasn't bolted but wide-open. She darted through, swaying on her unsure legs as she reached the forge. She paused for breath and looked around, seeing now, for the first time, Evra's fine work on the windows. He'd done well, despite the clattering.

No light spilled through. She had no sense of time.

"Rhosyn?"

She gasped and turned toward the voice, but it wasn't the one she wanted to hear. "Rylan?"

"He said to be here when you wake."

"Who said?" she demanded, as if she didn't know.

"Evra."

"Why? Where is he?"

"Gone." Rylan shifted in place.

"Gone? Do you mean helping the men with cleanup?"

Rylan shook his head.

"Well, where did he go, Rylan?" she cried.

"Back to the Westerlands." Rylan ventured a step closer. "He said to tell you goodbye."

"Goodbye. That's all? Just goodbye?" The tension spread across her chest. "He had nothing else to say?"

Rylan reached behind him. He pulled something out of his back pocket and handed it to her.

It was a book.

"What is it?" she asked as she accepted it. The edges were charred, but when she flipped through the pages, the words were untouched. "Why would he give me this?"

"He didn't say. Only that it was important to him you had it, and that you shouldn't be alone when you woke up."

"Shouldn't be..." Rhosyn inhaled her gasp. "He's really gone, then?"

Rylan nodded.

"And your father? Your mother? Do they know I'm here?"

"No. That's why you must be quick about flying away, Rhosyn. We mustn't let anyone see you."

Rhosyn tucked the book inside her gown. Anything in her hands would be lost when she shifted. "Thank you, Rylan."

"For what?"

"For being here when I woke up. For this book. And for keeping Evra's secret." She swallowed. "And mine."

Rylan flushed, embarrassed. "He's my friend. And you're my friend."

"I'm so sorry about your home, Rylan. I really am."

He looked up again. "It's not your fault. And it's not the first time a Ravenwood destroyed our home."

"It's not?"

He shook his head. "Father helped rebuild Midwinter Hold when he was a boy. Grandfather helped his father do the same. There's always a Rendyr who wants to hurt us. There's always a Frost who knows it would be worse if we fought back. That's what my father says."

"Your father is a wise man," Rhosyn said. "A *good* man."

Rylan smiled. "Do you really have to go back there?"

Rhosyn nodded. "I do."

"Can I hug you?"

Tears blurred her sight. "I would like that."

Evra shoveled the stew into his mouth, keeping his face low to the bowl. The candelabras were dimly lit, reminding him of the taverns of Oldcastle, but the pubkeep here had simply grown tired of relighting the candles with every fresh wind.

He was nearly finished with his meal when the other patrons went silent at the same time. One gasped and then another. The pubkeep threw his rag on the bar and darted out into the morning with impressive spryness.

"The Guardians have arrived! They've saved us!" he yelled, and all the cheers that followed made Evra aware, for the first time, how many had gathered inside the tavern. He turned to see what the fuss was about, and the sight sparked his own amazement.

The storm had ended. The air was crisp but clear.

He swallowed the rest of his ale.

A meaty hand slapped down on the table across from him. He looked up to see the pubkeep returned. When the man removed his hand, a sweat-stained roll of vellum sat upon the wood.

Evra pointed his spoon at it. "And what's this?"

"You're the Westerland lord, ain't ya?"

Evra slowly nodded.

"Right, then, this is for you."

"It looks like a raven's vellum."

"You have good eyes, then. Next you'll tell me you know how to read."

"If a raven came for me, why wasn't it sent to Midwinter Hold?"

The pubkeep twitched his nose. "Only one kind of raven will fly to the keep, boy. And anyway, I would've sent a messenger with it, if not for the storm."

Evra reached for it. The pubkeep leaned in before he could take it. "Your men will be ready in a half tick of the sun. Your coin bought you the best trackers we have this far north. But if you have it in mind to push 'em harder than their wisdom tells them to go, lord or no, they'll abandon you to the wulves. Your name means nothing to us. Even less to them."

Evra nodded at him. "I'm content to keep the pace they deem best, publican."

"Good lad. I'll leave you to it, then."

Evra held up the badly re-rolled scroll. "Someone read it?"

The pubkeep shrugged, grinning to reveal both front teeth missing. "If I did?"

Evra sighed and dropped his head again. A raven, for him, meant someone knew where he'd gone, when they'd told no one of their destination, other than Edriss, who'd gleaned the truth in a less traditional way. He supposed it could be Meira, returned, but his gut told him this was something else.

He pulled at the edges of the vellum to flatten it and skipped to the end to see who the sender was.

Rider Blackfen.

Lord Blackrook,
While you did not disclose to us the nature of the business
taking you and Rider Ashenhurst away from our Reach in our

darkest hour, I cannot think that purpose is greater than the last hours of your sister, Edriss. Lady Alise has sent for Grand Minister. It could be days. Weeks, if the Guardians still smile upon her.

You'll forgive her for betraying your confidence regarding where you've gone, but that secret will go no further.

She will want those dearest to her at her side when her promise is at last spent. I am only a Rider of the Rush, not a lord, or even a steward, but I am a father. And I know the weight of blood.

Your return, if it is to come, should come with haste.

Yours in service, First Rider Thennwyr Blackfen.

Evra waved the letter at the pubkeep. "When did this arrive?"

The man shrugged as he sloppily poured some ale. "The days run together in the far north. Couldn't say."

Evra closed his eyes, measuring his breaths. "You have your own ravens, publican? This far north, and all?"

"Some are missing an eye, and others take to flying in circles as it pleases them, but I can have the ravener here before you finish that stew."

"Do that. Please."

"Not all ravens are up for all tasks. What's the distance? The Westerlands?"

Evra shook his head. "Farther."

The man nodded. He snapped his rag at a boy sitting on a stool, and the boy jumped to life, running off.

"Don't think I've forgotten you've yet to pay for that stew."

Rhosyn landed upon the damp stones of The Rookery, dropping to a crouch in exhaustion. The light storm battering the ramparts was her welcome home. She was alone, for now, but Rendyr had surely sensed her.

She pressed herself against the inner wall as she slinked, soundless, down the hall, settling her boots in light, careful precision with each landing. When clear of the outer ramparts, Rhosyn turned her pace to a sprint and raced to her chambers.

Once inside, she shut the door and leaned into it. Her face was wet from the rain and her tears, and her gown hadn't fared much better. She needed a warm bath, but to acquire the heated water, she'd need to wake someone, and she intended to spend at least one night alone with herself before the attendants commanded her hours.

She bowed down over her dressing table, glimpsing herself in the mirror. The figure staring back was not someone she recognized. This Rhosyn was older, harder. She'd seen things the old Rhosyn could never understand and was safer not to.

Something poked at her ribs as she tried to sit. She reached in and withdrew the book, turning it over in her hands. The leather binding the pages was very old, the vellum soft. She flipped back to the beginning and read.

For Evrathedyn. May you always believe in everything your father tells you not to. Love, Mother.

Rhosyn brought a hand to her heart. Why had he given her this?

She turned another page. The title was scrawled into a neat script: *The Last Dragons of the Southerland Peninsula.*

Rhosyn laughed in stunned glee, but it turned to a sob. She moved her hand from her chest to her mouth and trapped the sound there.

In a panicked rush, she shoved the book in her drawer and locked it with her magic. Only she could open it now. But she never would.

Rhosyn rose and backed away from the dressing table. She let her cape fall to her chamber floor without kneeling to settle it somewhere proper. Both hands pushed at the shoulders of her dress to remove it, but she stopped halfway through the gesture.

Green eyes peered at her from the corner of the room. The light revealed the rest of the monster as he stepped forward.

Rhosyn pulled her dress back up and crossed her hands over her chest. "How long have you been there?"

"I felt you when you broke through the clouds." Rendyr stepped closer. "I've always been able to feel you, Rhosyn."

"Don't touch me."

"You're mine to touch."

"You'll get your chance. At the Langenacht. Along with all the others." Saying the words aloud made them real. She wanted to retch, but she had nothing left to give but the last of her hope. "If you try before then, you'll be eliminated from competing. Then where will you be?"

Rendyr's fingertips brushed the soft flesh of her shoulder, but he didn't land his touch. "For someone who turns their nose at tradition, as you do, I have a hard time believing you care so deeply for this rule."

She lifted her chin. "You know nothing about me and what I care for."

Rendyr pressed into her, backing her up until she hit the wall. He spread his hands over the stone above her head. His breath stung her eyes. "If you tell me how he touched you, I might let you pretend I'm him. If you're good, that is."

Rhosyn spat in his face. Her immediate, surging regret didn't quite overshadow her delight at having done something she'd only fantasized about. "You could *never* touch me like he did."

Rendyr ran his tongue along the shape of her lips. She turned away, but he grabbed her face in his hands and finished his trail. "This could have been fun for you. You might have even been happy. But now? Now, you've given me no choice but to show you what happens when you betray me. When you forsake me."

"You can't touch me for weeks yet. The calendar is sacred. It cannot be changed."

Rendyr nodded. "For every hour I have to wait, for every hour you *make* me wait, I will conjure terrible ways to remind you that you'll never belong to anyone but me. Your mind. Your heart. Your body. Your spirit. I'll take it all before the end, Rhosyn. But all of those things put together still don't equal the real gift you'll give me." He laughed. His spittle dotted her face. "And the best part is, you don't even know, do you?"

"Leave, Rendyr."

"You don't!" His grin widened. "Fascinating, how you could be what you are, and not have an inkling of it yourself. In the end, that only makes it easier for me, doesn't it?" He lifted her face and kissed the center of her neck. "And if your dalliance with that man has left you with child, I'll heave the infant from the ramparts while you watch."

Rhosyn wrenched free of his grip. She charged into him, pushing him back and away from her, glaring through her rage. "If you don't leave my chambers, then I'll throw *myself* from the ramparts, and then what will you have? Nothing!"

Rendyr backed away, hands raised. "I wouldn't touch you as you are now, anyway. You reek of *him*. Of farm filth. Of men." He grinned. "Of the scorched ruins I delivered to show you that, for all your bold words and declarations, you're still nothing."

Rhosyn's mouth twitched. She moved closer, backing him out the door. "You wouldn't go to such trouble for *nothing*, Rendyr." She pushed him out and slammed the door, bolting it.

She felt him linger a few moments longer. He did it for her. A reminder that he was only outside because he wished to be. That no door could keep him out.

In a few weeks, no door would ever keep him out again.

THE DEATHS
WE DIE

TWENTY-EIGHT
YOUR DUTY, YOUR CHARGE

The council waited for Evra to take his seat before doing the same. The rapt faces gaping back at him as he prepared his first words for them in many weeks were different from the ones he'd seen when he first addressed them as Lord of the Westerlands. The distinctions lived in their careful expressions, but also in the men themselves.

Aelric Tyndall, Roland Ashenhurst, Lewin Wakesell, and Walter Glenlannan were no longer his counselors. Two of them— Aelric and Lewin—had perished from the plague, a result of both their carelessness and their cruelty. The other two, Evra removed. He'd decided this when sitting across from the Grand Magi of the Sepulchre, in the old man's office in the high tower of the Consortium, at Briarhaven.

Before he'd left for the Northerlands, doing such a thing would have been dangerously preposterous. What could they do to him that would matter now?

He'd sent the ravens that very night, so they'd arrive ahead of him.

239

In their places sat Edriss, Aunt Alise, Cressida Wakesell, and Enchanter Grimoult. This last addition was one of over a hundred Enchanters to return with Evra to the Westerlands. Once they'd reached the borders, the Enchanters broke off to their prescribed assignments, as per the peace accord signed by Evra and Grand Magi Rutland. Before Evra, Grimoult, and the six other Enchanters with them even reached the final path to the Rush, word of the healing crossing the Reach had spread to all corners of the Westerlands. Two of the men sitting before him—Osman Derry and, surprisingly, Leonarde Bristol—had already availed of the magic themselves, narrowly escaping a similar fate of their peers.

"If it's war you want," said Leonarde. "You've done more than a fair job calling it down upon all of us."

"You have no authority to speak ahead of your lord," Evra snapped back. "Nor will I grant it until I've said what I needed to say."

He was too numb to enjoy the shock bouncing off the remaining men of his father's old guard. The hidden smiles of Edriss and Alise did nothing for him, either.

Bristol fell back in his chair with a sneer, arms crossed high on his chest.

"As you're now all aware, there is now peace between the Sepulchre and the Westerlands, and with that peace comes the salvation of our people." He ignored the scorching glares and continued. "By now, their healing hands will have reached most of our land. Many will return to their duties at the Sepulchre, while some will become honorary residents on permanent assignment. I have asked for an Enchanter to be present in every Great City, and the Grand Magi has obliged." He gestured to his right with a tight smile. "Enchanter Grimoult is now a man of the Rush. He will also be my trusted counselor. If any of you expect to remain the same to me, you'll welcome Grimoult with the respect he deserves and defer to him where he knows better than we do. He has much to learn and just as much to teach."

Evra locked eyes with Meira. She blinked into a curt, approving nod.

"You will by now also have seen there are other new faces on this council. Rider Meira Ashenhurst, who has now passed her trials, will become the second Rider to help guide this Reach. Her wisdom has never steered me wrong, not as children, and not now. Cressida Wakesell, replacing her late father, hopes to restore her family's good name in service to the Reach. My sister, Lady Edriss, now much recovered, takes her rightful place here with us, as my equal. Lastly, Lady Alise, who is perhaps the wisest of us all."

"You set aside experienced men," Tedric Blakewell said under his breath. "Good men. For... for women?"

"Good men watched other good men die and still slept at night. Good women have been calling for a truce with the Sepulchre for years. We could have saved some of those good men, had we listened to even one of those good women." Evra turned away from the steward. "And there are at least two of you in this room who have taken for themselves what you have denied others."

"You abandon the Rush at the moment of its greatest need to spend weeks with the Sepulchre and now you're one of them," Osman Derry accused. "Bristol is right. Whether or not you want war, the Reach will not stand for it."

"The Reach is only standing at all because they've received the magic needed to heal and be well. As you are, Steward Derry, being one of the men who secretly accepted the magic in replacement of death."

Osman dropped lower in his seat with a scowl.

"What does it matter who took the magic? We all know you did it for your sister," Bristol rejoined, with a dismissive hand gesture aimed at Edriss. "You'd throw aside over fifty years of reform, for her."

"Reform is your word." Evra turned his head toward Bristol. He blinked through his disaffected weariness. "Murder is what most would use."

"Punishing heathens is not murder. It's *just*. It's our charge, our duty, if we are to be a lawful society."

"Heathens is also your word," Evra said. "And one we will not again use here, unless speaking of ourselves and the accompanying legacy that will take years for us to unravel. Let us not confuse priorities. *That* is our duty. Our charge."

"How can we help?" Rohan James asked.

"Help?" Bristol stood and spread his arms as he dropped down on the table. His chair toppled behind him. "You're barely out of your swaddling, Lord Thedyn, and you want to tell *us*, the men who have given our lives to this Reach, what our charge is?" He ran his fist across his nose, looking at the others. "You're one man, Thedyn."

"Lord Blackrook," Evra coolly corrected. "And you're alive because of me. Gratitude would suit you better than whatever this is."

Bristol flushed dark. "You'll still be only one man when we return to our people and tell them what you've done."

Evra exhaled and calmly unfolded the scroll he'd brought with him into the room. "And what will you tell them?" He nodded at the vellum. "That I have not already?"

"What is that?"

"I'll read it to you, though your own copy is already sitting on your desk back in Valleybrooke," Evra said. He read. "A message from Lord Blackrook, to be read in every tavern, every hearth, every guild before the end of the night. By now, you will have seen the presence of the Enchanters of the Sepulchre in our Reach. Perhaps, even, had the pleasure of acquaintance with one. These Enchanters have entered homes and healed the sick, from farmers to blacksmiths to noblemen. Men, women, and children. These Enchanters will eradicate the plague from our lands, once and for all." Evra's eyes traveled across the council with a firm look, then he continued, "But it will return if we allow the men who murdered our healers to do it again. These same men who accept the magic for their own illness in secrecy would keep it from all of you. No one will

242

be safe in the Westerlands, not without peace, not without magic. Henceforth, there will be no limitations on the practice of magic in the Westerlands, except that which has already been established under the guidance of the Consortium of the Sepulchre in the Skies. All men in this Reach are equal, and the assailants of any will be treated with the appropriateness of criminals."

Evra dropped the scroll, letting it roll up. He folded his hands. "I had the scribes send five hundred of these messages across the Westerlands. Tell me again, Steward Bristol, about the war I should expect, from people who no longer have to watch, helpless, as everyone they love dies?"

Thennwyr Blackfen twitched his jaw to keep from smiling.

Bristol's fingers trembled against the oak. "It was our men who burned the heathens to begin with. You think a vellum from their child lord is enough to stir them to your cause?"

"I suppose we'll see, won't we?" Evra stood. In uncertain concert, the others followed. "You all, those few remaining to the old guard, stand before a choice. When we meet next, you'll make it. That is all."

"Evra!" Edriss cried when most of the council had left. "I wish you could have heard yourself! That was incredible."

"Formidable, even," Alise added. She leaned against the sill of one of the tall windows. "One might say you've returned to us a new man."

"You provoked them." Rohan James paced sentry near the door. "Their pride has been wounded."

"Let them lick their wounds," Evra said as he sank back in his chair. His weariness clung to the velvet. "Or let them fester. I don't care anymore. I'll find new men to fill their seats." The corner of his mouth lifted in an attempt to smile. "Or women."

"Really, I think that's what has their knickers all blotted," Alise said. "That you had the audacity to replace some of them with some of us."

"You did the right thing, Evra." Meira dropped to a crouch at his side. "No one knows as well as me what you gave up doing it."

"I gave up nothing," Evra answered through clenched teeth. "I only did what I should have from the start."

"Shall I have the kitchens prepare supper, then?" Edriss gathered her skirts and moved toward the door. "Lamb tonight. Your favorite."

Evra nodded, waving her away. Alise hesitated before following her.

Meira lingered.

"Was there something else?" Evra gazed at the lines on his palms. The patterns they formed, where they diverged. Enchanter Grimoult had told him on their ride back that there were those said to be able to read these lines, but it was not magic sanctioned or recognized by the Sepulchre.

"What is it, Evra?" Meira leaned in closer. "Are you still cross with me for leaving you there?"

"You're on my council, aren't you?" he barked, not looking up.

"So are some of the men who stood against you."

"Enemies are safer kept at your side. I learned that from my father. One of the few things of worth I learned from him."

"So I'm your enemy now?"

Evra snaked a hand across his arm, holding it out for her to take. "You're my truest counsel, Meira. But right now, I don't have it in me to speak of right or wrong, of heroes and villains and sacrifices. All right?"

Meira slowly nodded. "All right."

He released her. "One last thing. It's Thedyn now. Not Evra."

Most were deep in their cups before the kitchen maids had even poured the first wash of ale. And why shouldn't they be? Edriss had been restored to life, moments from death. The Reach was healing, and would, with the leadership of their beloved Evra—*sorry*, Meira corrected herself, *Thedyn* now—continue to heal, ushering in a new era of peace and prosperity. A land where women, too, had a place beyond the bedroom and hearth, like she'd heard tales about in the parts of the Northerlands, or even some of the harder-spun corners of the Southerlands, like Blackpool.

"You should have seen the look on their faces, Mother! I've never seen men so constipated, not even when they've had into it with the Windwatch cheese." Alise's drunken smile stretched from ear to ear. Her cheeks flushed with the wine and ale, even though everyone knew you never consumed both together. Alise did. She'd done as she pleased all her life, and now Evra had blessed her to behave this way under protected authority.

Meira swallowed her bitterness in a huge slug of ale. She didn't mean it, anyway. Women like Alise, like Meldred, they belonged in places of power. So why did she feel this way?

Meldred chuckled as she dabbed her mouth with a napkin. It was no use. She'd missed half the crumbs. "What I wouldn't have given to see that." She shook her head. "But we mustn't ever let them see us celebrate their losses." Suddenly solemn, she passed her gaze around the table. "There's never been a more dangerous man than one who finds himself the fool."

"Maybe I *will* accept Roland James' offer to marry," Alise mused. "Who knew he had it in him to stand so tall against the reeds?"

"You'll never marry again," Meldred countered.

Alise chuckled to herself. "No. I won't. I'll never give up anything more than I already have. Especially not now."

"Especially not now," her mother repeated.

Alise had arranged the intimate dinner. She'd invited the women closest to Evra, including Meira, who was grateful to have been remembered in what was otherwise mostly a family affair. The only other outsider was the Enchanter, Grimoult, but she had a keen feeling he was about to become an essential coil in their inner circle. He observed the bold, drunken women with alternating surprise and bemusement.

Meira passively tracked the boisterous exchange, but her eyes kept falling back on Evra.

He sat in his rightful place at the end of the table. Having done even that seemed a substantial burden to him. He slumped in his seat, stabbing at the chunks of pink lamb without landing a clean blow. The others hadn't seemed to notice his melancholy, other than Edriss, who sat at Meira's left with concern etched in her brows.

"What happened to him, Meira?" Edriss turned toward her. "What happened to my brother up there?"

"That's not for me to say, my lady."

Edriss slid a hand over Meira's upper arm with a quick, sad smile. "Please. Edriss. As it was when we were girls." She made a soft sound. "I know you were Evra's friend, not mine, but I do still think of those days with fondness."

"He prefers to go by Thedyn now," Meira said, unsure about what to do with the delicate hand still gripping her forearm. With a tight smile, she offered it an awkward pat, then tugged her arm back to her lap.

"He couldn't even say that word before without looking ill," Edriss returned. She glanced back at her brother, then down. "If you bear me ill will, for—"

"I bear you no ill will, my lady."

"For," Edriss went on, "what he did, going to the Sepulchre..."

Meira raised her brows. "You think I was against him making peace?"

"I don't know what to think. I only know the disdain you look upon me with."

"Disdain? No, Lady Edriss, I think nothing poorly of you. I *wanted* him to ride for Briarhaven. I wanted him to go there all along, before... before we ended up where we did. Whatever you're reading in me now, it's nothing to do with you."

"I already knew he wasn't in Briarhaven all these weeks, and you've just confirmed it."

Meira flushed in her shame. Even at home, she was failing him. "He'll tell you when he's ready."

246

"What I should have said, Meira, is that I know precisely where he was. I've known since before you left. What I don't know is what happened to him there, and why it's led to him returning to us, as he is."

"All I can say is, I believe..." Meira cleared her throat, picking carefully through her words. "I believe Evra... that is, Thedyn, needed to take this journey to end up in the right place."

Edriss cast another longing look at her brother. "But at what cost?"

"Wasn't it you who argued that the value of one life was not greater than the lives of all?"

"What are you saying, Meira?"

Meira shook her head. "I don't know. I don't have the answers you seek. And I doubt your brother does, either."

"Why won't you tell me what happened to him there? He's my *brother*. I want to help him."

"Trust me when I tell you that what happened to your brother isn't something you can help with."

Edriss leaned in. "Then who can, Meira?"

Evra flattened his back to the door. They'd cleared the chambers belonging to his father—and, briefly, Astarian—but he wasn't ready to ignore their ghosts. He preferred the apartments of his childhood, where he could hide away when the demands of court life were more than he could bear.

He reached behind to pass the latch across before stepping into the room.

Though he had no heart for celebrating, he'd stayed with the festivities until even the women could no longer stand on their feet. He heard what they said. *Sometimes you have to break something to fix something.* His grandmother, that one. As long as he'd fulfilled the needs of his Reach, whatever had happened to him—and he heard this, too, the rampant speculation into his new hollow frame of mind—was an acceptable loss for the Westerlands.

No one had even whispered to him of marriage because they had Alise and Edriss now. He'd seen to that when he drafted his articles of succession, and there was no longer a problem of an heir. Edriss would marry soon, even if Alise didn't, and—

"Stop being so cursed cynical," he hissed at himself. His aunt and sister loved him. His grandmother loved him. They were merely giving him the space he'd asked for. He'd earned that, at least.

He paused at the edge of his bed. Frowned. Not exhausted enough. Not nearly enough, if he wanted to shut all the rest out and just sleep.

His attendant had left a stack of letters on his desk. He already knew what they were. Mostly praise and gratitude, from farmers in the fields beyond Greystone Abbey to millers and blacksmiths in Commerce Row of the Rush. He had half a mind to respond to every one of them, insisting he didn't do it for their gratitude or their praise, and that both left him feeling so powerfully empty that he didn't know where to go to fill his cup.

Evra slumped into his chair, sifting through the stack. Snippets of their words filtered through to him, but nothing grabbed hold. He was nearly through the entire pile when one *did* snare him. But this letter didn't come from the Westerlands.

Evra pushed the rest aside. He flattened the soft vellum with his palms and read.

> *Evra,*
> *Or should I call you Lord Blackrook?*
> *It never much mattered to me who the lord of my own Reach was. I've never even met Lord Quinlanden. Any of the Quinlandens. But you were born the son of a lord, and now you're one yourself. So I suppose I do know a lord now, don't I?*
> *If I know you, you'll be sulking about in your huge castle, looking for excuses to throw spectacular tantrums. Barring that, you'll brood. I would expect nothing less and will be disappointed if you tell me otherwise.*

Yet, what you have done has altered the future of not only the Westerlands, but the kingdom. And as your dear, yet poor and unfortunate friend from the dredges of Oak Hill, I would be remiss if I did not write to tell you how proud I am that you found your courage in the end. The kingdom rejoices. On your behalf, of course, as we both know you've never rejoiced about anything.

You could never be the son of no one, or one of many, as you once claimed. But you may now return to your sulking and brooding. You've earned it.

Master Quinwhill would like to extend his felicitations. He, too, is proud, and says he always knew you had it in you.

Your friend,
Seven Thorsen

Evra read the letter again. When he was done, he balled it in his fist and hurled it at the wall.

He grabbed his cloak and left the room.

"You couldn't sleep either?" Meira sidled in beside him. Evra leaned over the stone balcony overlooking the singed remains of the forest's edge. Deeper within, the Whispering Wood was still the heart blood of the Rush. It would be again one day. Because of him. She didn't say this.

"You look tired enough," he replied without turning his head. "I'm sure you'd rather be sleeping."

Meira leaned over the stone and inhaled a gulp of fresh air. What a delightful feeling this was, to breathe again. "I'll sleep when you sleep."

"I'm not my father. I won't order you to serve me in ridiculous ways."

"I am capable of making my own choices, you know."

"Of that I'm well aware."

Meira tilted toward him. "You *are* still angry with me."

"I told you I wasn't. Now you won't take me at my word?"

"Evra." Meira sighed. "You did the right thing."

Evra waved a hand in the crisp air. "So you mean all these festivities, painstaking dinners, stacks of letters weren't enough to tell me this? You had to stay up into the wee hours to make sure I knew?" He shook his head and went back to gazing into the forest. "And I already told you. I prefer Thedyn now."

Meira dropped her voice low. "I'm not talking about the Sepulchre."

"What else could you be talking about?"

"You know."

"Ah, Guardians, Meira, you can't be serious." Evra spun away from the balcony and her. "I didn't think I needed to tell you, we don't talk about that here."

"You had no choice! You did the only thing you could do." Meira stepped behind him. "She wasn't yours."

"I don't want to talk about it!"

"But it's all you can think about. I read it in your eyes."

"Am I so transparent?" he snapped.

"You made the right choice. A *hard* choice, but you made it yourself, of your own accord. It's pride you should be feeling now."

Evra crossed his arms tight. His head bowed. "Then why do I feel like *this*?"

Meira was so shocked to hear him address his emotions she didn't know what to say.

"Why can't I stop thinking about her? Day, night." He laughed. "I can't even escape her in my dreams anymore."

"Evra... Thedyn... it will take time. That's all. All hurts eventually heal."

Evra turned. His eyes were glassy with tears. "What if I don't want this to heal?"

"What—"

"What if healing means forgetting her?"

"I don't understand. I thought that's what you were doing. Trying to forget her."

"When, Meira, have I given you the impression I know what I'm doing?"

Meira cooled her rising blood. She came here to comfort him, not upset him. "I'm only trying to understand. How could you love someone so fast? How can you be so sure it's love?"

Evra kicked at the stones. "When it happens to you, you'll know."

Meira's heart thumped against the back of her chest. She had to say it, for herself. It wasn't the reason she'd left him in Midwinter Rest, but it was part of it, wasn't it? Lying to herself was a betrayal of the worst kind. "I'm a fool, I suppose. I thought... when we saw each other, on the road to the Rush, that it was..." Meira cleared her throat. "Me you wanted."

He looked up with a start. At first it seemed to be pity washing over his face, but as she watched him watching her, she saw there *was* love there, just not the kind she'd thought there was. "Meira! You're my best friend! Of course I love you. I'd be lost without your friendship." He sighed. "I thought there might be something more there, too. You do look awfully nice in that new Rush regalia."

Meira dropped her eyes with a flush. "They dress me like a man."

"You don't look like a man when you're riding your mare, your longbow kissing the ground." Evra reached for her hands. "I would make a terrible husband. I'd never subject you to such torture."

Meira laughed, shaking her head. "I never wanted to *marry* you."

Evra's eyes widened. "A bit bold, don't you think?"

Meira shrugged. "I'm a Rider now. Riders don't marry. They don't follow the familial path." She chuckled. "The men, at least, are rather free in their associations. Why not the women, too?"

"Your offer is more appreciated than you know," Evra answered with a small smile. "But your friendship is the last real thing I have. The only thing that still presents itself as exactly what it always was. I can't look at Edriss... at Alise... and my grand-mother? She doesn't even know I'm in the room. I fulfilled the role they needed. I'm no longer so important to any of them."

"They love you, Evra. They're relieved, is all. To them, it's as if they've been freed from prison."

He didn't correct her use of his name this time. "And now, I've taken their place."

TWENTY-NINE
THE DRESS

"You can stop gawking at the door, Rhosyn. He can't come in here." Naryssa stood just past the room's center. Rhosyn felt her appraising look searing lines into her bare back as another Ravenwood, one she'd never met and likely would have no occasion to know when this was over, fitted her for her gown. "Even Rendyr has limitations."

Rhosyn winced as the young Ravenwood pricked her with the needle.

"Oh, no. Forgive me, High Priestess."

"I'm not the High Priestess yet, and I think I'll survive a pin-prick. What's your name?"

The young priestess dropped her hands back to her sides with a cautious look. She braced herself for reprisal. "Elynarra."

"Elynarra. Who are your mother and father, Elynarra?"

"That's enough. I think we're done here," Naryssa said as she glanced around the room with an air of disdain. "We'll send the gown to you for needed adjustments and we'll do this again in two nights. That will be enough time, won't it?"

Elynarra nodded at her feet.

"Of course it will. Now go."

"High Priestess." Elynarra moved backward out of the room and bowed so low she nearly tripped over the door's frame.

"You didn't have to be so unkind to her," Rhosyn said when she was gone. She stepped down off the platform and shrugged the dress to the floor. "She's only doing her job."

"If my discontent was that obvious, the seamstress wasn't the intended target." Naryssa crossed her arms. "Rhosyn, she is not your equal. You *have* no equal here, other than me, and soon, even I will bow to you. You cannot make casual palaver with just anyone. Not anymore."

Rhosyn pulled a robe from the rack to cover herself. "I don't know what you mean."

"You, chatting her up this whole time, when she was only trying to work. You confused the poor girl. She isn't your friend. She could never be."

"She's a Ravenwood, no different from you or me."

"She's a Ravenwood," Naryssa agreed. "But she could not be more different from you and me."

Rhosyn dressed in a rush. She had no interest in hearing her mother chide her for becoming thinner while she was away, but it was more than that. Her sins were carved across the surface of her flesh. Naryssa was hard, but she was wise. With enough time, she'd read them.

"What's going on in your head? Where do you go when you leave me?"

Rhosyn was surprised to hear her mother use such direct words. "Nothing." A half-truth. It was nothing, as far as her mother was concerned. It was nothing because her mother would do nothing. Offer nothing, beyond useless platitudes and false smiles painted on her placid face.

"Lies. That's what lives in your head. You used to talk to me."

"What good ever came of that?"

Naryssa's heels clicked on the stone. "I could have sent Augustyn down there. I sent you because you asked me. I thought it was what you wanted. I *thought* you would represent our family with honor, as you have in the past. Instead, you consort with some *boy*—"

"You did *nothing* when Rendyr burned their home to the ground!"

"No one knew what Rendyr had done until it was done. He's been chastised soundly, rest assured."

"Rest assured?" Rhosyn couldn't decide whether to laugh or cry. "Chastised? He's still allowed to compete at the Langenacht, Mother! How has he not been removed? Why are there no consequences for what he's done? The Frosts would be well within their right to take war to The Rookery!"

"They will not," Naryssa said, crisp and decisive. "Just as they never have in the past. They will rebuild. Tensions will ease. And once more, one day, we'll rain our fire down upon them for the crime of some perceived slight, and they'll do the same as they always have. There will never be war, Rhosyn, because neither side can win."

"Rendyr still freely walks our halls while Arwenna was cast off the mountain!"

Naryssa bowed her head. She inhaled a long breath. "It does not now, nor has it ever, served a reigning or future High Priestess to dwell upon the inequities between our brothers and us."

Rhosyn rushed to her mother and cupped her hands over her shoulders. "You have the power to remove him! *You!* Why won't you?"

"You have some nerve, Rhosyn, asking me such things, after what you did down there."

"Why won't you?"

Naryssa lifted her arms and gently pushed Rhosyn away. "It has always been the brothers. The others will expect it to be your brother. The magic *always* picks a brother, unless there isn't one."

Rhosyn scoffed. "The magic. We both know—"

"Mind your words. They will expect this, Rhosyn. Augustyn won't cast his lot, and Vradyn is too young. It will be Rendyr. You must prepare yourself for that. You must *forget* about this boy from the kingdom."

Rhosyn bit through her lip. The popping sound shocked them both. She pressed her hand to her mouth to stem the bleeding while her mother searched for some cloth.

"You beautiful little fool. Why did you have to do such a stupid thing?" her mother chided as she pinned the cloth tight to Rhosyn's face. "Hold it there, unless you want it to be worse than it has to be. When it's stopped bleeding, I'll heal it for you."

"What if I do?" Rhosyn challenged. "Want it to be worse?"

"Oh, Rhosyn." Naryssa sank onto the dark velvet bench. "It doesn't have to be so hard for you."

"Did you know?"

"Did I know what?"

Rhosyn ran her tongue around her lower lip. Blood pooled in her mouth. "Why Rendyr is so determined to have me?"

Naryssa folded her hands together. "I think we both know."

"I asked, Mother," Rhosyn continued slowly, "why he wants *me* so badly."

"When Arwenna failed—"

"You know I'm talking about this supposed prophecy!"

"All right, Rhosyn. You can calm down."

"Did you know?"

"You're working yourself into a pique."

"Did you know?"

Naryssa angled her palms up. "Men, they... they've always sought ways to feel less insignificant, and so of course, they've... well, *they* created this prophecy, and I believe that's a very strong word to use for something that means nothing at all."

"Tell me."

"It's nothing, Rhosyn, it's the whisperings of old men—"

"TELL ME!"

Naryssa leaned back against the tapestried wall. "Very well. But you'll soon see why I say it's silly. Why it's nothing." Rhosyn stared at her, stone-faced. "There are some, very few really, but they believe there's more to your silver hair than chance. That priestesses with your hair appear once every hundred years or so, and with your arrival comes an opportunity. They believe you are, somehow, infused with the same magic the midnight goats possess that makes them immortal. Eternal."

Rhosyn snorted. "If I took a dagger to my neck, I can assure you, I'd bleed out."

"They don't believe you're blessed with immortality, but another magic. A magic that, if left vulnerable, allows someone stronger to come and take something from you. Something unique to you, as a High Priestess."

"I already know he wants my vision. He told me as much when he came to Midwinter Hold."

Naryssa nodded.

"He doesn't know that—"

"Don't say it."

"He doesn't," Rhosyn said with a short, hard laugh. "Or he'd know I have nothing worth taking."

"Some men, the ones who are disenchanted with our ways, see it as a means of reversing our customs and restoring men to the highest perch. A way out of a world that celebrates women. Regardless of what they can and cannot take from you, it's what they believe. Nonsense, as I said, for reasons you and I know better than most."

Rhosyn backed away, nearly tripping over the raised stage where she'd been poked and prodded for hours. "You *knew* this, and you're still allowing him to come near me?"

"It's thread spun into air! It's meaningless. You're special because you're you, not because some immortal goat has 'blessed' you with their magic." Naryssa laughed. "It's madness, and I don't know how you've convinced me to give it more life with words!"

"It's not madness to Rendyr, Mother. He believes it. He's staked his life on it being true, and once I'm his..." Rhosyn recoiled. "Once I'm his, what's left to stop him? Once he knows it's all a lie, and he's done all this for nothing at all?" She hurled the bloodied cloth into a corner. "What's to stop him from discarding me, as he did Arwenna?"

Naryssa's practiced joy faded. She rose. "If I don't let Rendyr cast his lot, he'll bring every last stone down upon our heads. He'll call a war we cannot win. He'll do this because if he cannot have what he most wants, then he'll make sure none of us has a thing left. He cares about nothing more than his own self. He doesn't possess the fear that keeps most Ravenwoods in line."

Rhosyn's jaw dropped. "So you *want* him to take my power?"

"No, Rhosyn. And as you very nearly pointed out, what is there for him to take?"

"He doesn't know that!"

"No." She sighed.

"You're going to let him discover this for himself, and then destroy me when he finds there's nothing for him."

Naryssa reached for her, but Rhosyn bent away. "He wants what he wants, and no one can dissuade him of that. Even if we told him the truth, he'd not believe it. But in his greed, he has failed to see *you*. Prophecy or no, he will do what he believes he must, to achieve his desires. But you are who you are, Rhosynora."

"Yeah? And who am I?" She no longer bothered to withhold the tears. They burned her eyes, her flesh, a searing reminder of how her weakness had taken her back to the one place that could crush her.

"The strongest among us."

"I'm a second daughter. I wasn't born for this."

"You of all of us must know that has nothing to do with the magic we're given." Naryssa again reached for her, and this time Rhosyn didn't fight it. "I saw the storm you called. Your use of forbidden magic. It's bigger than you. That's why you couldn't call

258

it back to you. You have not reached the peak of all you can do. Not yet. But you will."

Rhosyn flexed her hands at her side. Blood ran down her chin and onto her gown.

"He thinks it will be easy to subdue you," Naryssa said with a slow, sly grin. "But when you strike him down, he will know how wrong he was. He will know that for all his perceived wisdom, none of it served him when it mattered."

Rhosyn flinched. "You want me to kill him?"

"I want," Naryssa said. She didn't immediately finish, sighing instead. "I want you to triumph."

"If he touches me..." Rhosyn brought her fist to her mouth, biting down. "Even one hand..."

"He will touch you. They'll all touch you. Some strength we are born with. Others are born from pain. You'll take one with you to the Langenacht and emerge with both." Naryssa straightened her spine. "Now wipe your eyes. We have to pick out your jewels."

THIRTY
THE WHISPERING WOOD

Over ten years had passed, but he still knew the way. There were some things a man couldn't forget.

For Evra, this would forever be the place where he'd died and was reborn.

Despite what awaited him, he breathed a welcome sigh of relief when he stepped past the charred edges and slipped deeper into the Whispering Wood. His memories here were tainted by what had happened, but he hadn't always hated the trees, the undergrowth, the strange blossoms that sprang from the old white bark. Once, before his father had taken it from him, it had been the font for his imagination, and the source of his rare joy.

So many of his stories involved those words. *Taken from him.* He wasn't helpless. Not then. Not now. It was easier to believe he had no choice than to make one.

He stepped into the same clearing where his father had once paused and turned with a look that had chilled Evra's blood. He'd known it then: His father meant to kill him. Why hadn't he fought back?

Evra approached the stump. He shouldn't be surprised it was still there. Dead trees didn't grow. The stain forged from his blood had faded over the years, but the memories lived within the rings.

With a wince, Evra lowered himself and sat down upon it.

"This was the place, Rhosyn. It doesn't seem so frightening, does it? It's just a clearing in the woods. Just a stump from a dead tree." Evra bowed over his knees, hands folded together. "I've often thought of this as my death, and what happened after, my rebirth." He squinted through the pins of light dotting the canopy of trees above. "But it was only my first death. No one told me I would keep dying, keep shedding the older, weaker versions of myself."

A cool wind whistled through the trees. Even this sound was wrapped in that terrible night, but perhaps those memories no longer had such a deep hold on him, because instead of fear, he felt release. "Do you have a place like this at Midnight Crest? You told me once that you knew how to turn fear into power. But what about grief? Where does that fit? Can it be altered, or are we meant to feel every last painful drop?"

Evra cleared the brush at his feet with his boots. He carved a smooth arc into the dirt, a clean canvas. He had a strange and sudden urge to lean down and write his name in it. Beside it, Rhosyn's.

He messed the soil up once more and stood.

Another breeze whipped through the trees, but this time it bounced from branch to branch, creating a circle of echoes. He turned into this, spinning as he strained to define the source. The sound came to a decisive halt behind him.

Hand on his sword, he whipped around to find himself face to face with a Ravenwood.

"Hello, Evrathedyn."

"Which one are you?" he asked. He passed his gaze through the trees, looking for more. "And what are you doing all the way down here?"

"So you know who I am."

"I know *what* you are," Evra answered, breathless.

"Who do I most remind you of?" Her dark, ethereal waves cascaded down from her shoulders, tickling her waist as she moved closer. If they were silver...

"I'm no good at games. Tell me who you are. Tell me what you're doing in the Westerlands." He swallowed the dry patch in his throat. "In my woods."

"Yours, are they? I knew men were territorial, but was not aware they possessed the authority to lay claim to the trees themselves."

"Arwenna," Evra decided. He set his mouth in a tight line. "Am I right?"

Arwenna nodded. She stopped moving when she was close enough for him to feel her breath on his cheek.

"I thought you were dead," he said. She was as bewitching as her younger sister. This effect brought it all back for him. How Rhosyn's flesh had felt against his hands. The sharp demand of a stolen kiss.

"As far as the Ravenwoods are concerned, I am. Only Rhosyn and my mother know better," Arwenna answered. "Please. Sit. It's you I've come to see. Is it Evra you go by, or do you prefer Lord Blackrook?"

"Thedyn is fine." Evra watched her in bewilderment as she settled upon a moss-covered log. She waited, wearing the same patient smile, while he returned to his seat on his stump.

"Thedyn," she said, tilting her chin as she considered the name. "That's a king's name."

"So they tell me."

"Is that what my sister called you?"

"Why are you here?" He cocked his head to the side. "And how is it you've flown away from your fate when Rhosyn could not?"

"That answer is as simple as it is complicated," Arwenna replied. "I could fly away for the same reason she could not. Rendyr had no use for me for the same reason he had use for her."

"I fail to find an answer in any of that."

"There's a reason Rendyr needs her, Thedyn. Why he conspired for me to fail and be cast out of my home. My mother's love was greater than her fear of treason, so she helped me, but she would never do the same for Rhosyn. Rendyr hasn't come for me, and he won't, but he would come for her. For the silver-haired priestess, he'd fly to every corner of this kingdom. She'd never be safe anywhere. Nor would any who dared to aid her."

Evra curled his toes inside his boots as he struggled to maintain his calm. "Why does he want her so badly?"

"There's a prophecy, so it is said, that the silver-haired priestess will rise every hundred years, born of the immortal magic of our magnificent beasts. Through her will arrive an occasion for a male Ravenwood to take what has been the burden of the women for centuries."

Evra recoiled. "Can he do that? Take power from her?"

"If it's even true. And whether it's true, Thedyn, is not what matters here. *He* believes it, and everything he has done has led him to this moment, right now, where she's finally his. And when he wins her hand at the Langenacht, and he will, he'll attempt this seizing of power. If he wins, he will kill her, for how can he not? Most Ravenwoods will cling to the old ways, so he'll have no choice but to destroy her, and with it, the last of their hope. If he doesn't win, and he will not, for what he most wants to take does not even exist... I fear his rage will produce the same outcome."

Evra inhaled a trembling breath. "Does Rhosyn know this?"

Arwenna shook her head.

"How could you not tell her?"

"Mother thought it best. To protect her. To allow her at least some joy and peace before she stepped into this inevitable future. And it was inevitable, Thedyn. There is none among the Ravenwoods who would stand tall enough to be seen and heard. We survive in our world by remaining well divorced from the truth, and the quibbles of right and wrong."

Evra leapt from the stump. "How is this protecting her? She'll be unable to defend herself if she doesn't know what's coming!" He ran his hands down his face. "Do you all speak like this? So disaffected? So uncaring? Rhosyn is your sister! She deserves better!"

"Rhosyn is strong, Thedyn. Stronger than either of us knows. Stronger than she knows."

"I've seen what Rendyr can do. He'll destroy her, which was exactly..." Evra reached up and wrapped his hair tight in his fists. His breaths pulsed so hard his eyes felt like they might leave his head. Every day since he'd let her go, he'd told himself, another day, another month. Another year, and he'd be free of his pain. That he was no better than Rendyr, when he'd held her against her will, afraid that letting her go would mean the end of her. "Why are you here?"

"In my travels, there've been whispers of the strange goings-on at Midwinter Rest. Of the foreign lord and the raven princess."

"Did these whispers tell of how I'd kept her against her will, like a fiend?"

Arwenna shook her head. "It's more than I've done for her. As long as Rendyr lives, she cannot." She closed her eyes and drew in a slow breath. "I came because..." She bowed her head. "I wanted to be near the man who had spent that time with my sister. To feel close to her again."

"But not to help her? Not to save her?"

"If I return, I'll be killed before I can come anywhere near him. I'm supposed to be dead, remember?"

Evra sighed. "It was wrong, what I did. Not just holding her against..." He closed his eyes. "It was wrong because she never felt as I did."

Arwenna shook her head. "No, Thedyn. Rhosyn told me herself she was going to run away if she was called to take my place. She was set on it."

"But she didn't, did she?"

"If she changed her mind, there's a reason." Arwenna nodded to herself. "She had good reason."

"Are you going to tell me or make me guess again?"

Arwenna let a thoughtful pause fall between them. "I don't know what went on with the two of you at Midwinter Hold. But only one thing could have persuaded her to change her mind."

"What?"

"If she thought that someone she loved would come to harm because of her choice. If returning home was the only way to protect them from Rendyr's wrath."

"That already happened. Rendyr burned Midwinter Hold to the ground. Or was that not part of the rumors you heard?"

"She loves the Frosts," Arwenna said. "But it was not for them she would have thrown her life away. Despite their love for her, they would not throw theirs away, either."

Evra balked. "This can't be about me. Have you heard what I said?"

"Do you love her?"

"It doesn't matter now."

"It matters to Rhosyn," Arwenna said. "It can still matter to you."

"She didn't want my interference. All I did was make things worse. All I did was... was *hurt* her, and she said herself, I'm no better than he is."

"You are nothing like Rendyr."

He snickered. "You don't even know me."

"I don't have to. Rarely does pure evil exist naturally in this world. My brother is rare."

"What are you saying?"

"As long as Rendyr breathes, neither Rhosyn, nor anyone she loves, will ever be safe."

Evra sank back into the stump. He bowled over, catching his breath. "I have to respect her wishes, Arwenna. She was clear with them. She didn't want my involvement. She doesn't want me anywhere near her. She doesn't... feel as I did. Do."

"She was afraid for you."

"You can't know that."

"I know my sister."

Evra rolled his head back. The clouds had darkened overheard. A storm was coming. "The rain won't wait much longer. Where do you call home now?"

"Nowhere."

Evra nodded. "You can stay here as long as you like. I'll have an apartment prepared. No one will bother a guest of the Lord of the Rush."

"That's very kind. Thank you." Arwenna's words were tender, but within them, disappointment, and he didn't know what to make of that.

"Of course," Evra said, pulling ahead of her as he led them down the path back to the keep. When he was certain she could no longer see his face, he squeezed the rogue tears from his eyes before they could grow and fester into the familiar pain of what he'd left behind.

He should have known one of them would be in the Hanging Gardens. Maybe he did know. Maybe that's why he went there.

"Thedyn, then," Meldred said with a bemused grin. "Is this because you believe you've become a man your father would respect, or in some ironic defiance of him?"

"Hello, Grandmother." Evra slid his leg over the stone wall protecting the azaleas. "It was time, is all." He wrinkled his mouth into a wry smile. "And we both know Father is glowering down at me from the Guardians for what I've done."

"Serves him right," his grandmother said. She pressed her cane into the fine dirt and hobbled closer. "No, don't get up. One of my harder days, is all, nothing to be fussed about. I still have less of these and more of the better ones."

"We have healers now, you know."

"There's no cure for getting old, Evrathedyn."

Evra hung his head, shaking it. "No, I suppose not."

"Did you come to greet the twilight or hide from it?"

He lifted his gaze to the violet sky. "I just wanted to be alone."

"If you wanted to be alone, you'd be in your chambers."

He dropped his eyes and smiled. "But then I wouldn't be able to enjoy your beautiful flowers, Grandmother."

Meldred eased herself up on the wall with a light grimace. She set her cane aside. "Twilight arrives well past my time to retire. My pillow calls to me, and her song is loud. You'll forgive me for getting right to the point."

"There's a point?"

"I've read your heart, boy. No, not in the ways of old crones who claim to know all. In the simplest way. My magic came from my mother, and I gave it to Alise. I suspect your father had some in him, too, and that may have been what fed his hatred. The fear." She shook her head with a wistful look. "I've read your heart. You left it in the north."

Evra shifted his gaze away again. He focused his eyes on the sea of white flowers he didn't know the name of. "You're right. I did."

"It's changed you. Love has changed you."

"Love is why I'm here now. Why the Enchanters are here, and the Reach is healing." He forced himself to break his reverie with the flowers and turned to her. "If I'd followed my heart, I don't think I would've ever returned."

"You would have," she said. "Eventually. But to truly love another involves a sacrifice of self. Had you kept her for yourself, your love would have shriveled and died, and with it, her. You as well."

Evra's heart throbbed in his chest. He pressed the heel of his palm to it, as if that alone would be enough to suppress the pain that had been demanding address for weeks. "If letting her go was the right thing, then why does this hurt so much? Why can I not move on? Why..." His foot tapped against the wall. "Why has saving our people given me nothing but emptiness?"

Meldred reached a hand over to still his shaking knee. "You know why."

"No, Grandmother, I don't!"

"Your Reach is whole now. But you..."

"She doesn't want me! Not me, not my aid, not my love, not my pity, not my admiration, none of it."

Meldred clucked her tongue and grinned. "The lies we tell ourselves."

"Even if they are lies," Evra said, calming. "She's already made it clear to me that I cannot save her."

"Who said anything about saving her? Child, have you learned nothing from the women who raised you? We don't need your chivalry."

"Then what?" Evra threw his hands up in surrender. One trembled against the air, and he clasped the other around it to make it stop. "What am I missing? What can I do that I have not done? Why is this so hard for me to understand?"

"What if all you needed to do... all she *needed* from you... was to stand at her side?"

Evra's words rolled to the front of his mouth, but that's all they were. Words. What his grandmother spoke of was so much more than that. And there it had been, all along. *You cannot save me, Evrathedyn.* She'd returned because of him. And he'd let her do it, never seeing... never understanding...

"I have to go back," he whispered, breathless. "Don't I?"

"Yes." Meldred offered an approving nod. "Yes, you do."

"To show her she's not alone. That I don't need saving, either." Evra hopped off the wall. His flesh tingled from head to toe, alive with energy and youth and hope. It was so simple! How had he not seen it? "I'll bring an army. Not for me..." Evra pressed his fingers to his temples. "Not for me, no, but for the Frosts, because I cannot let them suffer even a moment more. I regret not staying to help them rebuild, but I can do that now, too, can't I? I'll take the whole of the Westerlands over that pass, and he'll have a new keep by springtide. That's what I'll do."

"If you don't know by now that you can do anything, then you never will." Meldred reached for her cane. "You know the risks, so I'll not insult you by reciting them."

Evra nodded, pacing away from the wall and back. "Edriss will be Lady of the Rush, if I don't return. I've signed the decree. It's the women alone who have given me any wisdom in this family. Why shouldn't it be the women who rule?"

"It stirs my stony heart to hear you speak, for once, about something with such passion." Meldred used her cane to slide off the wall. "What will you do when you charge up that mountain to your Rhosyn?"

Evra shook his head. "That's for her to decide. All I can do is confront her fear and put it to bed. If Rendyr is gone... then she can choose the life she wants for herself, and I..." He trailed off. He didn't yet know the end of that sentence.

"It will not be easy."

"No. It won't."

"When will you leave?"

Evra glanced again at the darkening sky. "At first light."

THIRTY-ONE
IN THE ABSENCE OF A SET OF WINGS

Evra's arrival at Midwinter Hold was different from his last, just as he was.

They'd not solicited aid from Wulfsgate in clearing Torrin's Pass this time, nor was their stop in Midwinter Rest longer than a brief respite. If he and his men couldn't do these things on their own, there was no chance of them making it up that mountain.

Convincing his men wasn't the problem. He'd never seen the Westerlands so invigorated. They passed their excited, animated predictions between them on the ride north, and, at some point, these turned into song.

Ah, ice and cold, a history untold, a magic to unfold, this is the house that Rhosyn built!

Oh, salt and wheat, food so sweet, all kiiinds of meat, this is the house that Thedyn built!

The ballad had taken on many iterations, bouncing through his excited men on their ride north. He wanted to tell them it was the gardens that made the Rush, but the song wasn't *for* him or even Rhosyn. They had already deified her. She was the mythical

271

raven who had captured their lord's heart and turned it back to his Reach. They'd never see her as anything else.

"There's nothing special about our meat in the Westerlands," he'd muttered to himself, only for Meira to pick it up and, as usual, have an answer prepared.

"Well, it rhymes. And besides, it's an elbow at the Ravenwood ways. They don't eat meat. Didn't you know?"

No, he didn't know. He'd known so little about the woman who had stolen his heart, and the realization pained him.

He rode at the front of his retinue, Meira on one side, Thennwyr on the other. The road to Midwinter Hold had been rebuilt in his weeks away, and he hoped that meant other fortunes had turned their way as well.

The Frosts were already waiting with widened, disbelieving eyes as first Evra and then two hundred others passed through the achingly familiar iron gates.

He'd died here, too. He'd died a dozen deaths in Midwinter Rest. But it wasn't death on his mind today.

"Lord Blackrook," Oswin said with wonder as he dropped into a light bow. Only to his own lord were these formalities required. Evra flushed at the sign of how much had changed between them. "You aren't here to tell me you're just passing through?" He leaned to the side to look past him with a disbelieving shake of his head. "You and half the Westerlands."

"Steward Frost." Evra nodded. He dismounted his horse, handing the reins to Meira. "As it is, I *am* just passing through."

Oswin cocked an eyebrow. "To where?"

Evra pointed his gloved hand toward the mountain. "There."

Oswin turned, whistling through his teeth. "I see. And you think all these men you've brought this time will make it easier to do the impossible?"

"Not all these men," Evra said with a quick smile. "Most are here to assist with your rebuild, Steward, once they've finished defending the Hold. Many hands make—"

"Lighter work," the steward finished. He rubbed the back of his neck. "You didn't have to do this, Evra."

"The most important things happen when we do more than what we must," Evra said. "You'll tell me what happened to the keep wasn't my fault, but it was. Had I not come here, ignorant of your ways, and of theirs, Rendyr would not have done what he did."

"Rendyr is a monster," Oswin said. "But there's always a Rendyr."

"Let me help, Steward. I *want* to help."

"I'd be a fool to turn aid away, with all we have ahead of us." Oswin nodded to himself. His eyes again went to the large company still mounted behind Evra, swarming the courtyard. "I see you're still making use of your sword. Didn't find a better blacksmith, craft you a better one?"

Evra slid his fist around the hilt of The Betrayer. "This is my ancestral steel now."

Oswin flushed with pride he tried to bury by looking away. "Have you someone to pass it to now?"

"My sister, if I don't make it home."

"You know what I mean."

"And you know what I mean as well." Evra nodded to the mountain. "I didn't come here for that. But I'll never find peace or move on, unless this is settled."

Oswin nodded. "The rest of the family is already at supper. Tell your men they can set up camp wherever they like. You and Meira join me." He frowned up at Thennwyr, standing to Evra's left. "And this one, if it pleases you."

"It pleases me," Evra answered, smiling. He looked around, his eyes catching up to his memories. Weeks he'd spent here, but it felt more like home to him than anywhere he'd ever been. "We'll be right in."

Evra spent the first few minutes happily indulging the family in hugs. They all wanted to know what he'd done since he'd left them, how he'd been. These were not merely polite questions, but the eager demands of people who loved him.

They'd rebuilt their dining hall first, and though they didn't explain this choice, he understood it just the same. It was a symbol of their familial bond, which had survived the worst and endured.

"You did it, after all," Thorn mused when they were all seated. "What changed your mind?"

"It was the right thing to do," Oswin answered for Evra. "He realized that, in the end."

Evra dove into his bowl of stew with ravenous attention. How he'd missed their hearty meals. When he came up for air, he answered. "There wasn't another option. I thought I might find one here, but..." He wiped the broth from his mouth. "You could say coming here showed me that peace with the Sepulchre was the only way."

"And Meira," Brin said, setting her spoon aside with a pleasant smile. "I don't suppose you played any part in this realization?"

"I regret to say none of my words did any good at all," Meira said with a teasing glance Evra's way. "Our lord is a stubborn man who listens to no one."

"Is that true?" Rylan's look was stunned. "Father, have you ever said such a thing to Lord Dereham?"

"I'm not Lord Dereham," Evra said, grinning. "Meira can speak as she likes to me. As can anyone, so long as they speak true, and with the interest of our people at heart."

"You're different," Thorn said. He tapped his spoon against the side of the bowl, thinking. "Something happened to you."

"We know precisely what happened to him, Thornton, but such talk is really not appropriate when we're enjoying our supper," Ethelyn countered.

"How are the little ones?" Evra asked after swallowing another mouthful of the delectable stew. "Castian and Wystan?"

"When they're not shitting, they're screaming," Thorn said. "When they're not screaming, they're, mercifully, sleeping."

274

"Really, Thorn." Brin pressed her fingers to her forehead, shaking her head.

"And how would you describe it, Brin? Is it flowers that come out of their asses, then?"

Evra laughed with the others. Time stood still. If he could capture this moment, just as it was, for all of time, he would. He'd take it from his pocket when his heart was sore or defeated and live it over and over again. This was the table he wished he could build in the Rush. Lined with the people he wanted around it.

His joy was tamped by the realization there was still something missing.

Meira passed him a knowing look. She grinned.

"Thank you for your kindness, Steward Frost. For the place at your table." Thennwyr broke through the reverie just as it was dying down.

"I regret I cannot offer you more," Oswin said. "When we're whole, I could have housed the lot of you."

"Fields have always done us fine, Steward. We've made tents of skins, as we've done on other rides north. If there's anything left to hunt in midwinter, my men are faster than any hare or deer. If there's not, we brought our own refreshment, and more still, for the family. We understand many won't make the trek up the pass to your keep to deliver more, so we've done it instead."

"That was unnecessary," Oswin responded, a hitch in his voice. "But appreciated, just the same."

Thennwyr nodded low.

"You're really going up that mountain?" Rylan asked. He hadn't stopped staring at Evra. Admiration reflected in the boy's eyes, and he wasn't sure he'd done anything to deserve it.

"I am," Evra said. "We are."

"How?" Thorn challenged. "Will you build a staircase of a million steps? Even that would not be enough."

"There has to be a way up," Evra responded.

"Even if there was, you'd never fit all those men."

"I'm not taking all of my men up the mountain," Evra said. He was aware all the eyes at the table were settled on him, waiting. "I'm taking a dozen. The rest will remain here, for the defense of Midwinter Hold and the village. I won't have my actions causing you or your people further harm."

"Defense!" Ethelyn pressed her palms to the table, swinging her neck around. "Oswin, you said nothing about a war!"

"There won't be a war," Oswin muttered.

"Can we not just enjoy the fact that Evra is again at our table?" Brin shot back. "I, for one, am so happy to see him. We never got to say a proper goodbye. He's come back to us, so let's not spoil it."

Thorn tensed in his chair. He fought back a response.

"Brin is right," Oswin said, forcing a pleasant smile. "Our Evra has returned to us, and while we cannot know what tomorrow brings, tonight we can celebrate his place at our table." He nodded at Evra. "And these gifts he has brought us."

Belly full, Evra observed the animated exchanges passing across the table. The laughter, the gentle ribbing. Meira caught him in his musing and asked him what he was thinking.

"Only wishing this could be my life."

"It can. Why couldn't it?"

"There's only one Frost family."

"No family begins this way," she countered. "Oswin built the house he wanted. He sets the way for them, and they follow happily. You could do the same."

"I don't think so, Meira."

"Why?"

"For one, I doubt I'll ever marry."

"Not marry? Why?"

"You know why."

Meira nodded. She turned back toward the others as she fingered the cloth napkin in her lap, tearing at the corners. "You said yourself, you didn't come to take her home."

"I didn't." Evra exhaled.

"You're still secretly hoping she'll come with you, though?"

276

Evra shook his head. "Hope like that will only get in my way, make it harder to summon the courage to go up that mountain and face her brother." He turned to look at her. "I know she won't come home with me. If I can only show her she doesn't have to accept a fate she doesn't want, I'll have accomplished what I came to do."

"Why can't she do that on her own?"

"Because she's gone back because of me. And so it has to me to show her I'm not afraid of Rendyr."

Meira scrunched her face in confusion. "That doesn't make any sense. She doesn't want you, but she does?"

"She's afraid he'll come for me if she runs away."

"I don't know, Evra. I've never been in love myself, but that sounds like love to me."

He shrugged, though indifference was not the prevailing emotion passing across his chest, tingling through his fingers and toes. "We both know there's more to love than that. I came to ease her mind on my well-being, so that she could choose the life she wanted without worrying about mine or anyone else's. Not to pin her into another dark corner."

"You have to forgive yourself. Desperation can drive us all to do terrible things."

"I'll forgive myself when she's free."

"That bowl has seen better days, Evrathedyn," Oswin charged. "You want some more?"

"No, sir." He rubbed a hand over his belly. "My trousers have seen better days, too."

Oswin laughed. "To the study, then. Thorn, you'll join us?"

Thorn perked up. "The study?"

"That's what I said." He turned back to Evra. "Seems we have quite a bit to discuss."

"So this is the study?" Evra mused as he accepted the overflowing mug of ale. He couldn't place what this room had been before the fire, though from the rich, lingering aroma still stuck to the remaining stone, he guessed it had been part of the kitchens. It was one of the few rooms in the old wings with a roof. Mismatched chairs were scattered about the edges, with a rickety table holding sentry in the center.

"For now," Oswin answered. He passed a cup to his son. "A man can do business anywhere, though, can't he?"

"I'm sorry about all your books. Those will be hard to replace."

"Father had his gold on the way to the Reliquary before the fires had stopped smoldering," Thorn said, rolling his eyes. "Priorities, you know."

Evra chuckled. "Can't say I blame him. Those stories were here before us. They'll continue after us."

"Without our histories, we don't know where we've been. We don't know where we'll go," Oswin said, a touch defensive. "Not everyone understands this."

"I understand your history well enough," Evra said. From here, he would either lose Oswin Frost as a friend or gain him as an ally. "It's rather predictable, is it not?" He set the mug aside and folded his hands, squeezing them tight. "Every generation or so, the Ravenwoods break the alliance. They burn your home to the ground, you rebuild, and you do nothing. Their crimes go unanswered. Your own lord pretends not to notice. History repeats itself. Nothing changes."

"Say that again," Thorn challenged. He stepped closer, chest puffed. "Louder, this time, so I can hear it the way you intended."

"Thorn," Oswin cautioned. He inhaled a deep breath. "It's considerably more complicated than that, Evra. If you truly understood our history, you'd understand that, too."

"What more is there to understand, Steward? You're on your own up here. The Ravenwoods know it. When no one comes to settle the score, they know it. They count on it. Rendyr surely knew it when he showered his hatred down upon you. And so you'll rebuild, Lord Dereham will again pretend nothing happened, and you'll wait for the next time the Ravenwoods feel slighted."

"The Ravenwoods lash out because they know that's all they can do. They'd never win a war against men. They can burn our homes to the ground, but their power stops there. If we came for them, that would be the end."

"Seems to me they win all their wars, as long as it's only the Frosts they have to fight."

"And what would you know about it, Evrathedyn? A foreign lord from the garden realm, fresh to the job?"

Evra absorbed the slight. The steward had to say these things, just as he had to say his piece. "I've learned more beyond my home than within it. I can see now where I've been wrong. You helped me to see that. Why can't you accept even a foreign lord from the garden realm might offer that same gift in return?"

"A night in the barn with a raven doesn't make you an expert," Thorn charged. "But it does make you a craven bastard with no concern for who you hurt."

Evra slowly nodded. "I know what I've done. I've come to make it right, if I can." He drew in a steadying breath. "You don't have to join me. I'll understand if you don't. But I'll leave my men in defense of your family and village just the same. I won't have others harmed because I've failed to understand the power of what I'm up against." He swallowed the knot in his throat. "Not this time."

"This has nothing to do with us," Thorn retorted. "You'd put us in the middle of this wick whetting we never asked for! Do you not have enough pleasing women in the west? Or do you just like to be on the wrong side of everything?"

"Enough, Thorn," Oswin warned. He squeezed his fingers at the edges of his forehead, breathing through his teeth.

"If you think that's why I've come, you haven't heard a word I've said," Evra answered. "I love Rhosynora. I won't let the lie rot inside me anymore. I love her in a way I didn't know love could exist, and I still haven't grasped what it all could mean. But I didn't come here to save Rhosyn and whisk her away to the Westerlands, where I can keep her all to myself. *That* would make me no better than the man I was when I left here. I love her enough that

I would give her the gift of ridding her worry of me from her thoughts, and in that, find her means to be free of the monster who will otherwise one day be the end of her."

"He'd never hurt Rhosyn," Thorn argued. "She means too much to him. To all of them. To their..." He curled his lip in disgust. "Ways."

"Would you stake your life on that? Hers?"

Oswin moved into the center of the room. His silence commanded their attention. "Evra, you are always welcome here. You're a friend of Midwinter Rest, and of mine, and my kin. It is for these reasons that I'm even entertaining your words, which have the potential to destroy what my ancestors have spent centuries building." He lifted his shoulders into his sigh. "But more than this, I cannot offer you."

Evra shook his head, scoffing. He gripped his chair as he rose. "Fair enough. I have what I need, and I thank you for the food, the bed, and the land."

"You'll never make it up that mountain," Thorn said. "Only one thing can take you there, and you don't have it."

Evra pretended to check his back for wings. "Ah, I suppose you're right."

"You'll be sentencing these men to their deaths. And you."

"None will be commanded to come who does not want to come."

"As if it were that simple."

"Thank you for your counsel, Thorn." He pulled his furs back over his head. "I'll be in my tent outside."

"I insist you take a room," Oswin pressed.

"I need to be with my men," Evra said. "They need to see me. And I have some planning to do, figuring out what will replace a set of wings."

Thennwyr and Meira secured the map at the other end of the wooden slab. Evra set the stones at the corners of his end before they could curl back.

"All right, what am I looking at?" Evra rubbed his hands together for heat. The fires outside the tents made little progress against the icy chill.

"We sent two parties out, my lord," Thennwyr said. He put his gloves back on and pointed to two spots at the base of the mountain. "One east, one west. Neither found a pass."

Evra ran his hand through his hair and leaned in closer. "How much ground did you cover?"

"More than we expected."

"What, then? What's our move?"

"Ev... my lord," Meira started. She passed an anxious glance at Thennwyr. "We'll keep trying, of course. Failure isn't one of our choices. But I fear that the longer we wait to ascend the mountain, the greater the chance that the Ravenwoods will see how many men we've amassed here on the ground." She frowned. "There's only one conclusion they could draw from that."

"Then we'll *make* a path," Evra said, undeterred. "Rylan told me animals come down off the mountain all the time. If they can do it, so can we."

"Men have died on Icebolt Mountain attempting the same," Thennwyr said. "No path exists on this map."

"Where did we get that map, Rider Blackfen?"

"I brought it from the Westerlands."

"Precisely. The Westerlands. Why would a Westerland map-maker know of the secret paths of a Northerlander?"

"If there was a pass, we would've seen it," Meira countered. "We'll go back tomorrow. We'll start again."

"No," Evra said. He crossed his arms, pacing back and forth before the map. "No more discovery missions. We make our earnest push tomorrow."

"You've not seen the terrain, my lord! If it were that simple..."

"I never said it would be simple." Evra dropped down on his hands, onto the map. The soft vellum wrinkled beneath his touch. "I won't force either of you to join me. I won't force any man out there to join me. But I *will* go."

Meira exchanged another look with Thennwyr. "We'd never let you go alone. You know that. Every man out there would follow you up that mountain, if that were your wish."

"Lord Blackrook? Might I have a minute?"

They turned toward the open flap of the tent to see Oswin. Both his Riders offered a quick, perfunctory nod and slipped outside without being asked.

"They didn't have to leave," Oswin said when it was just the two of them. Evra gestured for him to sit on a stump, and then he joined him on another.

"They think I'm a fool. They'll never say it." Evra accepted the warm mug of cider the steward offered with a grateful smile.

"Their role is to provide counsel to you that will keep you safe. They're afraid, is all. They cannot see the path you can."

Evra snickered into his cider, drawing a long sip. "Seems there isn't one."

Oswin hunkered over his knees, mug clasped between them. "That's what I've come to tell you, Evra. There *is* a path."

"What?"

"There *is* a path." He nodded at the map. "You won't find it on that, but it's there."

"Where? They scouted for miles today."

"Only a Frost can lead the way." He set his mug on the map. "No map will take you there. The way is protected by Ravenwood magic. It reveals itself only to one of us, their sworn protectors."

Evra shook his head in confusion. "Magic? What kind of magic is that?"

"Only a taste of what you'll see if you make it to the top." Oswin grunted into his sigh. "If *we* make it to the top."

"We?" Evra watched the steward closely. "You want to go?"

"I have to go, if you're going to succeed," Oswin answered. "And, the truth is, I do want to go. Your words struck a nerve with Thorn, because he's used those same ones on me, for years, only for them to fall empty upon the air. I've accepted our way of things because it's how I was taught. How my father, and his,

282

were taught." He whistled through his teeth. "There's so much more to it. You say Lord Dereham does nothing. Well, he would, if we were to ever raise arms against the Ravenwoods. But it's us he'd come for. Not them."

"Why?"

"He doesn't live our life up here. He has no inkling of the bonds we've formed, nor of the trials that transpire between two worlds so closely linked. To him, the Ravenwoods are a mystical blessing he can call upon whenever he needs them, and forget them as soon as it becomes expedient to do so." Oswin rolled his tongue around his lips. "He doesn't concern himself with our plight because he doesn't have to. If we were to ever stand against the Ravenwoods, we would stand alone. And then we would lose."

"In that way, he's not so different from my father."

"Lord Dereham is still a boy, like you. He does as he was taught by his own father, who died very young. But he'll train his own son in this way, and so on."

"Why would you want to come with me if this is the outcome you fear?"

"We're not standing against the whole of the Ravenwoods, are we?" Oswin asked. "We're only standing against one."

"We're standing *for* one," Evra gently amended.

Oswin nodded. "Thorn will come, too. I asked him not to, but he reminded me I still have two other sons." He clucked his tongue. "We can't take many men, Evra. Seven. Ten at most, and even that will only slow us down."

"You don't have to do this," Evra said, feeling a great sadness steal over him as he watched the man who had been a father to him wrestle with himself. "If I go alone, with my men only, you can still keep your peace with Lord Dereham. You can show me the path and then turn back."

Oswin didn't answer right away. "What does this peace bring me, other than more burden? I love Rhosyn like my own daughter. Thorn, Arwenna, Rylan, they're mourning the loss of a sister they'll never again see. *That* is what's real, Evra. Family. I don't deserve to rebuild my keep if I cannot stand tall against the forces that would burn it down, for they're the same forces that keep young women like Rhosyn tethered to terrible, terrible duty. If she wanted this, it would be different. Many of them do. Most of them do. But every couple of generations... one comes along who doesn't quite fit." He smiled sadly. "There's always a Rhosyn, Evra. There will always be a Rhosyn."

"But this Rhosyn is our Rhosyn."

Oswin nodded. "This Rhosyn is our Rhosyn."

Evra reached his hands across the table. Oswin looked at them, then back up at Evra before clasping his between them.

"You've grown, Evra."

"Because of you. You and your family."

"And so have we. Because of you."

The rest remained unsaid, and they finished their ciders in silence.

THIRTY-TWO
THE FEAST OF THE LANGENACHT

Rhosyn practiced bracing her jaw. She assessed the results in the mirror, clearing her tension and beginning again when her courage didn't look convincing enough. She would be safer if her agitation could be deflected into a shield. Her painted red lips pursed in response to this cynical self-appraisal. The urge to slice her silver hair off at the nape of her neck was intense. All this happened in the space of a single second.

She did this again, and then again, still undecided. Would these proceeding days be harder or easier for her if she herself was hardened?

There wasn't time for further reflection. Every Ravenwood was gathered in the Great Hall for the Feast of the Langenacht, waiting for her.

The first of three events.

Tonight, there was the Feast.

Then, there was the Solitude, where she was to be left in isolation for two full days.

Last, the Langenacht itself. The greenlight fires lighting the night all the men had waited so patiently for. Where she'd be paraded among them in this farce of a gown and pretend it was the gods responsible for what came next. As she pleasantly, pliantly allowed each of these men to climb atop her and have their chance to deliver the strongest seed, all knowing the outcome had been decided long before that night.

Rhosyn emptied her wineglass down the back of her throat. Some came back up, and she clapped her hand over her mouth just in time. A trail of garnet liquid ran down the corner of her mouth, and she watched in silent horror, breath hitched, almost hoping it *would* stain her precious gown.

The glass crashed to the floor just as she saved her dress from calamity.

Where had this fear come from, of sullying the dress she'd once thought of as her funeral shroud? A sign, more than anything else, that she'd fallen in line to the same practiced beats she'd sworn she'd never dance to. If she'd never gone down to Midwinter Rest, she would've followed Arwenna's brave lead and left all of this behind. If she hadn't worn her heart so plainly, Rendyr would not have known the means to crush it. She could endure almost any pain, except this one. To watch those she loved suffer for loving her was a burden too great to bear.

Rhosyn was mostly successful at keeping Evra from her thoughts. She was getting better at existing at the edge of the crevasse of this lie, where the two Rhosyns were split down the middle. One who had never met the young lord, and one who had loved and been loved in return.

Easier to remember his last words to her, rather than the ones he'd whispered against her flesh as they lay tangled in the aftermath of the best and worst night of her life.

There was nothing, though, that brought this lie of her heart into brighter relief than thinking of what Rendyr would do to him if she were to defect.

For though she knew the Frosts would prevail, it would not be the same for Evrathedyn. He would breathe his last, the fool, at the end of Rendyr's searing hatred and would approach this fate with youthful gladness.

That could never happen.

She couldn't allow it to happen.

Rhosyn looked up from her dressing table when the door slammed. The stab of ice to her bones was immediate. She had to learn to control this, or it would control her. This was her life now.

"I asked for a few moments alone before the Feast." The Feast of the Langenacht was the last time she'd consume any food at all for another three days, when at last the Langenacht celebrations had ended. No one would explain this strange tradition of starving the High Priestess, but Rhosyn understood well enough. If she was too weak to fight, she wouldn't. "You'll respect that if you want me agreeable in a few days."

"Rhosyn," the intruder panted. The pitch of his voice stilled her blood. It wasn't Rendyr. She turned, shocked to see Augustyn.

She spun around and rose to her feet. "What's wrong? What is it?"

He rolled his hand at her as he struggled for breath.

"Do you want some wine?"

His head shook. He backed into the wall, closing his eyes. "I've had a vision."

"If it's about me, I don't want to hear it," Rhosyn said, more bitterly than she intended. Augustyn had always been one of the few bright lights in the darkness of this castle. His unwillingness to sully their relationship by casting his lot reflected his purity of heart, which was not a strength in a place like Midnight Crest. "There's only so much—"

"It's your man," Augustyn blurted. "The one..."

Rhosyn paled. "How do you know about that?"

287

"Everyone knows, sister. It wasn't only the visions. Rendyr, he..." Augustyn drew a deep breath. "He wanted them all to know, to bring them to his side."

"His side?" Rhosyn repeated. "What side? Am I not the one chosen to lead us forward? What side is there, in that?"

"There's something you don't know about, Rhosyn. A prophecy."

"I know of it. It holds as much truth as goat piss tasting like wine." But this wasn't the point, was it? It all came down to what Rendyr believed. What he would do, at the sharp end of this belief.

"He will kill you," Augustyn said in a whisper. "I'm certain of it. I haven't seen it, but I feel it. He'll take everything he can from you, and when he cannot, he will take from you another way. He'd rather see the end of it all than a future where he's simply a priest, without title or renown."

"You aren't the only one who thinks this," Rhosyn answered. She looked at the dressing table for more wine, but she'd emptied the whole carafe. "In doing so, you all place your faith in Rendyr alone. You assume his strength exceeds mine."

"I know who you are, Rhosyn. It doesn't still my fear." Augustyn shook his head. "That's not what matters right now. What matters is that your lord, and other men, are on their way to Midnight Crest right now."

Rhosyn balked. "On their way? You're not making sense."

Augustyn drew closer. "Frost showed them the path. The secret path."

Rhosyn pulled her hands to her mouth in a gasp. "No! Why? Why would he do that?" She sank back onto the velvet bench. "Are you sure? Are you absolutely certain Evra is there? That he's coming here?"

Augustyn nodded. "Rendyr will kill them, Rhosyn. It will take nothing for him to do it."

"Are you so concerned with the life of men now?"

He leaned back into the wall, dropping his gaze. "I don't want to see you hurt any more than you have to. But..." He balled his hands into fists, pumping light flexes. "He would bring a war to us, Rhosyn. If he kills these men, this will not end in silence, like when he burned their keep to rubble. If he kills a lord, *other* lords will have no choice but to answer. The whole of the Northerlands will be called, perhaps the rest of the kingdom as well, and The Rookery will be no more."

Rhosyn wrapped her arms around her chest. She tried to steady her breathing, but it came rapid, hard, and there was no calming herself this time. Evra. Evra was *here*. Evra was coming for her, that stupid, silly boy, and soon he'd be neither of those things, because Rendyr would find out, and Rendyr would put an end to him.

"I have to go warn him," she decided, her words coming fast, with a sharp intake of breath. "I have to tell him to back down. He'll listen to me. If I tell him it's not what I want, that—"

"Rhosyn."

"You cannot stop me!"

"Rhosynora. If you're not in the gilded seat at the banquet in the next few minutes, every one of them will come looking for you."

"I don't care about a feast, Augustyn!"

"I know," he said. He glanced toward the door. "I'll go. I'll carry the message from you. I'll tell them it comes from you. I'll tell *him*."

"No." Rhosyn shook her head, jumping to her feet. "Absolutely not. This isn't your fight. If I go, Rendyr will punish me, but he won't kill me. I believe he would kill you if you warn these men, Augustyn. I believe he'd kill you for a lot less."

"I'm not asking for your permission." Augustyn reached behind him for the door. He flashed a quick smile. "There's still time for me to make it to them and back before anyone knows I've gone anywhere at all. The second you take flight, Rendyr will be right behind you. He tracks your every move."

Rhosyn ran through the game of steeling her jaw and easing it. The trembles started in her fingers, but now they were everywhere. All she'd done to protect Evra and the Frosts was coming undone, and there was nothing, nothing she could do except plaster on a forged smile and place herself on display as if her heart wasn't shattering inside her chest.

"If you can't convince them..."

Augustyn nodded. "I can. I will. Go! If you're where you're supposed to be, no one will care where I am. Not until it no longer matters."

Rhosyn rushed to him. She kissed his cheek. "Do nothing foolish. You go. You come back. You tell no one. Quickly, now."

He nodded once more. "I know what I'm doing."

She waited at the doorway, watching him catch the wind with his sprint, and then, at the end of the hall, her brother leapt and disappeared into the stormy sky.

THIRTY-THREE
DEATH TRAP

This isn't a pass. It's a death trap!" Thennwyr called back. He was at the front of the narrow line of men making sluggish progress along the narrow shelf. "When have you last taken this way, Steward?"

"Never," Oswin called back. "Wasn't our charge to take the path, only to protect it."

"Then I'd say you did your duty. This isn't passable."

Enchanter Ludwig squeezed forward, past each of the men as they flattened themselves into the jagged mountain wall. "Eh, watch it!" one of them yelled, others grunting similar responses.

"What's he doing?" Evra asked Oswin. He'd started out in the lead, but Thennwyr, Meira, and Oswin stopped him. He could lead his men from the middle, they insisted. Those better experienced should be at the helm, ready to face the unknowns ahead.

Oswin shrugged, huddling tighter in his furs as a snowy wind whipped through the line of men.

"I've taken the path," Thorn said from behind. "Not far, but enough to know he's right."

"Could you not have said that before we started?" Oswin said over his shoulder. His teeth clacked together. Evra shivered in anticipation of his own chill.

"Would it have done an ounce of good?"

"Any other secrets you're keeping?" Oswin murmured. He took a careful step closer to the steep ledge to try to get a look at what was going on in the front. "Where'd you find this Enchanter, Evra?"

"He came to me from the Sepulchre. He's not as strong as Grimoult, but I needed him to stay back with the women."

"Do you trust him?"

"Much as I trust any man leaving their fate to the Guardians on the side of an unforgiving mountain."

Evra reared back in time with the other men as a bright light sheared across his vision. The sound that followed pushed him to a crouch. He'd never heard anything like it, but he imagined it to be the sound the earth would make if rent in two.

"Isn't that something?" Thennwyr cried, laughing, and it was *that* sound that stilled Evra's fears, putting them back into the box where they belonged. "Can you all see this?"

"We can!" Evra shouted. "How's the path now?"

"Decidedly clearer," Thennwyr announced with one final chuckle. "Though no less treacherous. Stay to the wall! Watch every step. Don't trust a single one. Just because the man before you made it, does not mean you will be as fortunate. If you need to stop, you call it out. One stops, we all stop."

Nods rippled through the freezing line. Evra glanced back at Thorn and Meira, who had taken up the rear guard. She braced through her fear. Only in her eyes could he see her darkest thoughts.

"All good, then?" she asked when he didn't fall as quickly into formation behind the others.

"Yeah. Yes. All good." Evra used the wall to pull himself back to his feet and pushed on. Every step was laborious. The snow here never had occasion to be cleared, and it had as many layers as the mountain itself, slabs of snow covered in ice covered in snow and more ice. He'd watch the man in front of him, a Rider named Falstaff, studying the way he planted his boots in the footprints of the others. Only when he'd completed each advance did he allow himself to breathe.

They'd barely begun.

"I know what you're thinking," Oswin said behind him, through heaving, exhausted grunts. "But save your words. One step. Then another. That's all there is, until there's more."

Evra nodded and continued on. It was no longer a matter of if he could. He must, and so he would.

"We've company!" Thennwyr yelled a few hours later, and Evra heard the unmistakable stretch of bows being drawn. Evra reached for his sword, but Oswin's hand on his arm stopped him. "From the skies!"

"If it's him, don't hesitate!" Evra cried. "For he will not!"

"This one is landing. Not attacking."

Thennwyr's bow lowered out to the side. The men behind him shuffled closer. Evra leaned out to see, but Oswin pulled him back to safety.

"You're all in terrible danger!" The raven's voice carried, though Evra could see nothing but the tall, towering figure of Thennwyr. "You must go back!"

"We're well aware there are dangers ahead, raven. None more than Steward Frost, who has endured more than his share," Enchanter Ludwig answered. "This time you'll find the North more prepared."

"We're on the same side," the raven said, growing more desperate. "We want the same thing!"

Evra pushed ahead one more step and leaned to the side again before Oswin could stop him. "If we want the same thing, then you'll confirm that Rendyr has been imprisoned for his crimes. That he will stay imprisoned, and that Rhosyn is free of his tyranny."

"You must be her young lord from the west."

"You can't, can you?" Evra pointed to the sky. "You come to warn us, not because we're on the same side, but because your side cannot win if ours does not stand down."

"I cannot stop him, Lord Blackrook," the young man said. Evra got a glimpse of him, and he was young, slightly older than Rhosyn. His darker features were more in line with what his youthful imagination had conjured of Ravenwoods. More like Arwenna. "No one can."

"That's a lie. You *won't* stop him."

"Either way. It matters not." The raven turned with a furtive glance to his back. "There's no time. Go back, and everything will return to as it was. There will be no bad blood. No one will even know you started down this path."

"No bad blood? Tell that to the Frosts. And as it was?" Evra cried over the whip of the wind. "Can you truly tell me that's what you want?"

"Doesn't matter what I want. Rhosyn would have come herself—"

"Where is she?"

"You know where she is. She's where she must be. She'll never come down this mountain, Lord Blackrook. Don't throw away this alliance for something that can never be. I beg of you."

"The Westerlands have no such alliance with Ravenwoods."

Thennwyr craned his neck back. "Your command, my lord. What shall we do?"

Evra breathed deeply into his gloves for a shot of warmth. He looked at Oswin for the answer, but it had to come from him. "Our quarrel isn't with you, raven. Not unless you attempt to bar the way."

"Bar the way? I have no violence in me. I have no ill intent toward you. Quite the opposite! I come to warn you, but if you will not listen—"

"I have listened," Evra said. "And I've heard enough."

"Go on, then, raven." Thennwyr again raised his bow. "You heard him."

The raven shook his head in panic. "You don't know what you'll bring down."

"To the south!" Falstaff cried, drawing his own bow across the sky before Evra could finish his blink. "Another one!"

"It's too late. It's too late," the raven in the path said. His form disappeared from view, and a raven emerged in its place, cawing once before aiming directly for the raven Falstaff had scouted.

"This one's not so friendly," Thennwyr announced, nocking an arrow. "Guards up!"

"Rendyr," Evra whispered with a glance back at Oswin.

A ball of fire crashed down behind him. Meira screamed. Evra turned in time to see a flaming Falstaff flying downward off the cliff, disappearing into the fog.

"Go. GO!" Oswin yelled. "Harder to hit us if we're moving!"

The line pushed forward, but their speed was hindered by the impossible terrain. Screams sounded from the back to go, to move, go faster, but they were already going as fast as they could. Flames rained down around them, hitting the shelf above, melting snow that turned to flood. Evra lost his footing as the water flowed around his ankles, but the Rider ahead of him, Everhart, clasped a hand around his wrist without turning.

More screams. Another man. He heard Meira announce she'd been hit.

"Can you go on?" Thorn panted.

"It's just my arm! It's just... oh, Guardians, look out!"

A boulder of orange light landed ahead of Thennwyr. It died as fast as it landed, but the snow that stopped it rolled downhill, and now the flood was impossible to avoid.

"Cover ahead!" Thennwyr shouted. "It isn't much, but enough for some of you to take shelter while we try to pull him down from the sky."

"He'll have brought his tricks with him," Evra said. "He thinks he's far too clever to be taken down in his own battleground."

Thennwyr strained to pull ahead in a bend in the path. He waited for the line to reach him and then selectively pulled certain men to safety. Evra. Oswin. Thorn. Ludwig.

"The rest of you, nock your arrows. Line your sight!"

"Everhart!" Meira cried, just as they all turned in horror to watch him be plucked from the sky by Rendyr's talons. His weight was too much for the raven to bear, but he'd never intended to bear him long. They watched, helpless, as Everhart joined his fellow Rider in the emptiness of below.

"We're not helpless against magic!" Enchanter Ludwig cried as he grunted himself out onto the exposed path. "You brought me for a reason, did ye not?"

"Old fool's gonna get himself blown off this mountain," Thorn hissed. He tore through his satchel as if it might contain an answer to this disaster.

Ludwig planted his feet. His silver Enchanter's robe, the one he'd insisted on wearing despite its unsuitability to climbing the mountain, flapped in the wind. A flame caught the ends, but he didn't notice. Evra reached forward to tamp out the fire but was blown back by the force of Ludwig's magic.

A collective gasp rippled through the company. The Enchanter seemed to command air itself. His hands pressed against an invisible barrier, and the sky took form under his touch, bowing outward, toward Rendyr's hard approach.

Rendyr stopped his assault mid-air. His wings flapped in helpless defense against the shield of magic. Nervous laughter rippled through the men. The Ravenwood magic they'd all so feared was no stronger than what they could conjure from their own kingdom of magicians.

Their confidence died in a snap. The sound of the Enchanter's neck breaking in two quieted their hearts. His lifeless body arced outward and then flew into the open air.

"Evra! What is your command? What do we do?" Meira cried.

"Hold your ground!" Thennwyr boomed. "We take every shot, or we take no shot!"

Evra was jolted back to the cool darkness of the small enclave by the quick but steady grip of Oswin's hand on his thigh. The smile that followed was swollen with more defeat than any words could say. It was over. To Oswin, it was over. To Thorn, who silently cried to himself, it was over.

Evra rocked to his knees and crawled to the edge just in time to see the other raven swoop down and knock Rendyr from his course. The two tousled in the air, talons clawing at feathers, caws breaking through the din of wind and cold.

They both disappeared into the clouds.

Evra gasped for air as Meira pulled him to his feet. She gaped at him with the same slack-jawed look.

"Is it over?" Thorn called out.

"Not by far," Evra said, teeth clenched, sword hilt wrapped in his fist, the way Oswin had taught him.

He pushed ahead of Thennwyr and Meira and continued up the mountain.

THIRTY-FOUR
SWEET AUGUSTYN, FOOLISH AUGUSTYN

The feast had been postponed until the following day. This decision had not been made lightly. Ravenwoods lived and died by the Sacred Calendar. Deviations were failures. Cracks in the delicate façade patching everything together.

Everyone at The Rookery had been ordered to their chambers. Did they even know what was going on? Why it was happening? Did they care? Could they see beyond the veil of deception, through to the truth?

And what was the truth? It was simple, thought Rendyr. The Ravenwoods, as they once were, had come to the end of their purpose. The Ravenwoods, as they would be, well, *that* was coming. Because of him. How many would survive these hours to join him? How many would perish in their idolatry, stalwart to the last?

It was supposed to begin in three nights, but it would begin now. All because of sweet Augustyn. Foolish Augustyn.

Rendyr reached for Rhosyn's door but paused before opening it. The hard pull of a recent memory overtook him. Maddening it was, that anything had this kind of power over him still! And why should he be forced to entertain his younger brother's confused, wide-eyed plea, as he lay, mortally wounded, at the mouth of the cave? A glimmer of hope still burning in Augustyn's dying eyes as he watched Rendyr watching him. Rendyr could have healed him. His wounds mended and erased, as if brother had not attacked brother in the sky.

Rendyr... we can still make this right.

Making things right is why I'm here.

Had Augustyn been prepared for his push over the edge, he might have mustered some final strength to shapeshift and fly; if not home, then to safety. To the last, Augustyn believed there was still good in Rendyr, and that belief was his death sentence.

His blood is on your hands. Not Augustyn's words. Nor his own conscience. He heard this in the voice of Arwenna, dead but still commanding space in his thoughts. *Everyone will know. They will know who you are. No one will follow you now.*

Rendyr slammed his head into Rhosyn's door to expel Arwenna's low chanting. Once, twice, and then a third time, until fresh dizziness sent him into a swoon. Wood slid across stone on the other side. Rhosyn knew he was there.

Rendyr waited for the lightness in his head to pass. He felt Rhosyn's escalating pulse as if her heart were sitting upon his palm. Her fear was his strength. He'd need all he could get now to finish this.

Rendyr slammed the door open.

Something was wrong with Rendyr.

It wasn't that he was covered in blood.

Nor was it the strange way his chest rose and fell out of synch with his breaths.

It was the way these things nourished him, transforming him into the depraved creature he'd been so determined to become.

Rhosyn had never been more afraid of her brother. To let him see this would be a fatal mistake.

"Where's Augustyn?" she demanded. She couldn't take her eyes off the blood. It was all over him. His face, his hands. The blotted stains still forming in the dark leather of his pants and jacket. "Where's Augustyn?"

Rendyr held his hands out to his sides, wearing a grin that left no room for wondering. It stretched to the corners of his face, like someone had carved it upon him with a rusted dagger. "You shouldn't have sent him."

Blood rushed up and rendered her sick, only to plummet back to her feet. "*No.*"

"You have only yourself to blame, Rhosyn. Augustyn... fool that he was, was easily persuaded. The right words from you, and he'd be alive."

"No!" Rhosyn made a rush for the door, but Rendyr blocked her. Hitting him was like smashing into a stone wall, and it slammed the breath from her chest. "I don't believe you. Even you... no, Rendyr. Not even you would kill your own brother."

"I killed my sister," he said with a light shrug. His chin dimpled with the dismissive frown. "That wasn't so terrible." He laughed. "For me, I mean. It was perfectly fine for me."

She stopped speaking, realizing all her horror, her heartbreak, fed his malevolent vigor. He feasted upon the tears she willed from spilling over. The tremble in her hands she tried, ineffectively, to hide behind her.

Rendyr backed closer to the door. "None of this had to happen. None of it. I would have been content with just you." He stepped beyond the threshold, leaning forward for the handle. "But it was *your* discontent, Rhosynora, that killed your brother, and will kill your little lord from the west. Your *willfulness* that will be the death of every last man, woman, and child bearing the name Frost or allied with them. Many Ravenwoods, too, though you don't particularly care about them, do you?"

Rhosyn tried not to look at the door. She didn't want him to know that she knew what he was doing. Magic of the Accused, they called it, when they rarely named any of their magic. But it was aptly called, for it could only be cast upon those accused of a great crime. There was no defense against a lock applied by an accuser, to the accused. To apply this magic without evidence of a crime was treason. "You've overplayed your hand, brother." Dark spots danced behind her eyes. "They may forgive your crimes against men. But against me? Against Augustyn? You do this, and—"

Rendyr pulled the door shut. His inaudible whispers sounded from the other side.

Rhosyn threw herself at the latch, despite knowing what she'd find. Unbreakable magic, locking her in, away.

The howl started deep in her belly. *No. No, no, no, no. no. Not here. Not like this.* She dropped to her bed, tapping her feet in rapid pulses on the floor. It couldn't end like this. It wouldn't end like this.

"Augustyn." Rhosyn swallowed the moan that barely escaped her lips. Her sweet brother. Her foolish brother. Had he only let her go instead...

"No. Not now." Her cracking voice, the only sound in this stone prison, began an awakening inside of her. "Now, Rhosyn, you will collect yourself and stop him."

That's when she heard him.

Evra.

I won't ask any of you to follow me from here. You know what lies in wait for us. You know what will happen.

How brave and bold he sounded. How well his courage masked his fear.

As for me, I cannot turn back. There is no return for me if I don't finish this.

Why was she hearing this? Why was he in...

All at once, she understood.

He was a part of her now.

He was close.

She leapt to her feet. Turned toward the door.

"This has gone on long enough!" Naryssa whipped through the room without stopping to see whether her husband was alone. Aberdyn so rarely was. He enjoyed the company of younger Ravenwoods, and Naryssa enjoyed everyone's company but his.

"Why come to me about it?" Aberdyn feigned a yawn and sifted through the bowl of nuts at his bedside. He lifted one to eye level, frowned, and dropped it back into the pile.

Naryssa inhaled through her nose. "Where is she?"

"Indulging herself in a bath."

"Do you even know the name of this one? Or does it matter?"

"Do you care?"

Naryssa leaned in and yanked the bowl away. She threw it against the wall behind her, and they both listened in wonder as the nuts scattered to the floor.

"Was that necessary?"

"Your son is inviting war to The Rookery, and you ask me if *that* was necessary?"

"So strike them from the path!" Aberdyn mimed it. "Like we always do!" He shook his head. "Why come to me, Naryssa? Am I not still the most useless Ravenwood at Midnight Crest, in your esteem?"

Naryssa narrowed her eyes. She'd hated Aberdyn as a brother, and she loathed him as a husband. The best day of her life had been when she delivered her fifth child and never had to return to his table—or his bed—ever again. "Your reputation is not at risk. But your home is. Your children are. That whore in your privy is. And you laze about..." She really was astonished. He *was* useless, and that was Aberdyn at his best. But was he truly this stupid?

He spread his arms over the piles of pillows he'd stuffed about him. "Maybe it's time."

"Maybe it's *time*?"

303

"You heard me."

"Aberdyn, you old fool! I flew down to Midwinter Rest myself! There are hundreds of men. *Hundreds.* And those were just the ones I could see with my raven eyes. All were gathered in defense of their village. Ready, for us! This is not like the other times. They're fighting back this time."

This got his attention. He pitched forward. "That cannot be what you saw. Men don't respond. And Oswin Frost is a coward."

"It isn't Oswin Frost leading the charge up the mountain, down the secret path, now, is it?"

"I told you, Naryssa. I told you it was more than a flirtation!"

How she hated that he was right. It happened so seldom, but each one was a dagger to the gut, with a hard double twist. "The boy is misguided. You know how it is with the Ravenwood girls. There's always a boy. Oswin's own son—"

"Never touched her! He knew better. A man of the Northerlands knows better. But this one?" Aberdyn pointed at the window. "He's just dumb enough to make himself dangerous."

Naryssa crossed her arms. "So we agree, then. Rendyr is to stand down."

"No, we don't agree!" Aberdyn jumped off the bed. "He isn't the only one wary of alliances with lesser creatures. Of *serving* them, with nothing in return. We don't need them, Naryssa. Perhaps we never did."

"You don't know what you're saying," Naryssa pleaded, shaking her head. She would drop to her knees if she had to. No matter how it hurt her pride. Aberdyn was the only one Rendyr had ever listened to. If he couldn't reach their son... "Aberdyn. Please."

A noticeable shift came over her husband then. He spun to face her, and she knew, in her heart, that it was over.

"Too long I've answered to you, Naryssa. Too long I've walked a half a pace behind you, deferred to you, knelt before you." His mouth twitched into a smirk. He held it, eyes passing over her from head to feet. "You're nothing. You're nothing without your visions. Nothing more than—"

Naryssa slapped him so hard it sent a ringing through her entire body. She looked at her hand, then again at him, and this time he caught her wrist midair.

"Unlike Rendyr, I haven't counted my victories before they've landed at my feet. But touch me again and I'll snap your neck."

He released her and started toward the door. She gripped her sore wrist in the other hand. "Where are you going?"

"Where do you think? To rally the men." Aberdyn grinned.

He left. Naryssa clutched her belly as the air left her. This was her fault. All of it. Had she prepared Rhosyn better... had she only *seen* what Rhosyn was really up to. Not that she blamed her. Naryssa had once fancied a life as a Frost daughter herself, and Oswin was a good man. Rhosyn's life would be very different if he'd been her father.

But he was not. Just as Morwen was not her sister. And this boy, this *lord*, could never be more than—

"High Priestess?"

Naryssa looked up. "Yes?"

"The men are taking to the skies."

"All of them?"

"Not all, but..." The attendant Ravenwood dropped her eyes to her feet.

"Enough. Is that what you mean to say? Enough."

She nodded.

"There are more of us than them," Naryssa replied. "Gather everyone you can find. Tell them what's happened. Tell them... tell them that unless they want all of this to become a distant memory, their lives upended forever, that they have no choice but to take to the skies, at my side, and end this."

The attendant smiled through her fear. "With gladness, High Priestess."

Lorcan James, son of Rohan James, readied the men on the ground. They ate a quick meal in silence and returned to their posts, swords out and waiting. They'd already watched the skies light the clouds with fire. Their turn was coming.

He swallowed a swig of wine from his waterskin. He preferred water, but it was so cursed cold here that he'd freeze without something to warm his bones. With a hard exhalation, he turned behind him to check again on the archers. Riders. He'd wanted to be a Rider when he was a boy, but heirs didn't become Riders.

Fifty of them, at least, lined up in four rows, at the ready. The night could switch in an instant, but that's all they'd need, these bowmen whose skills were another type of magic. Before he'd even finished giving the order, there'd be arrows whistling through the air and birds dropping from the sky.

The swordsmen wrapped around the Riders in tight formation. This war would begin in the air and end in the air, and their charge was to keep the bowmen alive, so it didn't end on the ground. To make the hard choice between their own life and a Rider's.

The women and children had ridden south for Wulfsgate. That great roaring fire sounded good to him right about now, too. Lord Dereham's special cider...

"I don't trust the quiet," Finnegan Derry said, falling in beside him.

"Shh," Lorcan said, hand up. "I trust sound even less."

Finnegan shuffled in place. Their breaths swirled in white clouds, mingling into one. His friend checked again for his sword, as he had every few minutes.

Lorcan's feet ached from the stillness. He needed to move. He'd rather have battle than this, this *waiting*. He shifted from one foot to the other.

"Lor." He could hardly hear his friend over the storm, but the sound of his name was unmistakable, ingrained in him through the course of his short lifetime. He whipped his glance to Finnegan, but the other man was looking up, and he followed his gaze to immediately see what had left the other man breathless.

"Guardians," Lorcan whispered as they watched the cloud erupt, issuing black feathered beasts into the night. This was it. No more waiting. He only had to...

"Aim!" Finnegan cried out when Lorcan failed to. Panting, he drew his sword with a chilled nod at Lorcan to give the final order.

Eyes on the dozens of ravens swarming the dark sky, Lorcan raised his left hand. With his right, he began to draw his sword, though this was not that kind of fight. If the Riders failed, that would be that.

"Fire!"

THIRTY-FIVE
HANDS AND KNEES

They performed an inventory of their losses. Three Riders. Their only Enchanter. Meira could no longer make use of her right arm from the deep burn she'd sustained in the battle. Thorn's ankle was so badly swollen they had to remove his boot, but if they didn't replace it soon, he'd lose that foot to the frost. He and Meira took turns dressing each other's wounds, but their efforts were insufficient, with nothing to use but what they'd brought, and no healer left to mend them.

Evra huddled with Thennwyr and Oswin several paces ahead. The skies were clear, but this reprieve was temporary. It would begin again at any moment.

"How much farther, do you think?" he asked Oswin. "Are we close?"

Oswin whistled through his teeth. He glanced ahead, though the fog and snow obscured any assessment beyond a few dozen feet. "Hard to say. I try to pair what we're seeing with what I know of the map, but it's useless. Only thing I do know, higher we climb, narrower the path gets. More dangerous."

"How many did you take down?" Evra turned to Thennwyr.

The Rider ran his hands through his hair. "Three. At most. But for all I know, they licked their wounds and returned to the sky. They all look the same to me."

"I saw them heading south, into town."

"I saw that, too."

"Won't be so easy to pluck us off down there," Oswin muttered. "Your Riders will take them from the skies before they get close enough to attack. Not like here, where we cannot even see the bastards coming."

Evra looked past him to see Thorn biting down on an ice-covered branch as Meira set his ankle. "He's done. He can't go on. Will be hard enough getting him down."

"Meira will take him," Thennwyr said. "We may do better with less to distract us."

"Meira needs to go, too. You're right." Evra looked out into the sky. They were high enough to be a part of it up here, and he felt this in more ways than the ice in his bones. His head was lighter. His breathing more labored. They'd come farther than they realized.

The others had gotten him to this point, and several paid the ultimate price for that service. He couldn't ask for more. He wouldn't. "But the two of you will be the ones to escort them," he finished.

Thennwyr cocked his head, incredulous. "My lord?"

"Don't be a fool," Oswin scoffed. "Evra. If you make it to the top, and that's a very big *if*, you'll be no less a hero with men at your side." Oswin cleared his throat. He tapped it with his fist. "Men who love you."

Evra again checked the skies. Any moment now. He sighed. "We can't win this, not this way. If you retreat—"

"Retreat?!" Thennwyr exclaimed.

"If you retreat," Evra pushed on, calmly, "they'll stop attacking us here. They'll focus their attention on the ground, where we have our strongest defense."

Thennwyr shook his head. "That's a bold assumption, my lord."

"If they attack a retreating enemy, even Lord Dereham couldn't turn a blind eye to that." Evra's eyes traveled to Oswin. "You've taken me this far, Steward. You've done more for me..." He couldn't finish. "Give me your cloak."

"What?"

"We're going to switch." Evra pointed at his shoulders. "I'm wearing black. You're wearing white. Apart from the fact that the white will blend into the mountain better, Rendyr knows I'm wearing black. When he sees the man wearing the black furs moving down the mountain, he'll think it's me. He'll move south with you, drawing his eyes away from me while I climb higher."

"What if you're wrong about this, my lord?"

"Then I'm wrong, Rider Blackfen. But I'm not wrong about one thing." He pointed to the sky. "We have no defense against them, against *him*, when we're barely keeping ourselves on our feet. We can't see ahead of us. We can't find safe ground from which to let loose your arrows. It has to be this way, or we admit defeat."

Oswin exchanged a look with Thennwyr. "I don't like this."

"I know you don't." Evra grinned. "I'm not particularly looking forward to going on alone, either."

"Then don't!" Thennwyr insisted. "Let Steward Frost lead the others back down. You *need* a bowman. Your sword is useless against a flying assailant."

"If I can get high enough before Rendyr realizes I didn't return with the rest of you, hopefully I can find another way."

"And if you cannot, then you'll die needlessly."

Evra shook his head. "Not needlessly, Thennwyr."

"The path won't take you all the way, Evra," Oswin said. "It ends just shy of Midnight Crest. Only those with wings can go the rest of the way."

"Then I'll go as far as I can. There must be something at the top of the path?"

"Perhaps, but none of us have ever been that far. It's a risk, not knowing."

"Nothing about this isn't a risk," Evra countered.

Thennwyr sighed into his gloves. "If I didn't know better, I'd say you *wanted* to die."

"Your lord has issued a command, Rider Blackfen," Oswin said. He tried to disguise the tremor in his voice. Evra couldn't look him in the eye.

"What if you do die up there?" Thennwyr challenged.

"Then you have Lady Edriss to lead the Rush. I should think that selection would please you."

Thennwyr dropped his eyes. "Lady Edriss needs her brother."

"She needs her father more."

Evra switched his cloak with Oswin. This one was heavier, made for a stouter man, not a boy. He sagged under the weight.

"I'll never be able to thank you both properly for all you've done to get us this far. For your belief in a boy who has no business wielding a sword, let alone leading a campaign of war."

Oswin clapped Evra's hands between them with several hard, tight shakes. He sniffled with a light twitch, as if responding to the cold and not the powerful emotion swirling between all three men. "Thank *you*, Evrathedyn, for reminding us that there's more to life than our comforts. I won't speak my goodbyes, boy, because I'll see you soon. You hear me? I'll see you soon."

Evra nodded. He wanted to speak but was overcome.

"We'll do as you command, my lord. Your victory awaits you when you return to the ground."

Evra shook Thennwyr's hand, nodding. "And ahead of me. I'll either prevail, or I'll die on this mountain. I expect there's an equal chance of either coming to pass."

"I won't wager to give you my guess, sir."

Evra laughed with him. "I appreciate that." He turned into his fur and inhaled a deep breath. "Now, go. Before he realizes what we've done, and it's all for nothing."

Evra waited until they were gone before he acknowledged his fear that he was marching toward certain death.

If they'd seen it, neither Oswin nor Thennwyr would have let him go on. He wasn't sure they believed his confidence, either, but it was enough to get them moving back down the mountain. Enough to draw Rendyr's eyes away from Evra while he formulated a plan.

He had none. It was laughable, really, that he'd trekked up this unpassable mountain, only to have no idea what he was supposed to do when he reached the end of the path. Even if he evaded Rendyr until the very end, all it would take was a single ball of fire to end it all. There was no deflecting *that* with a sword.

He did need a bowman. Thennwyr was right. But picking an enemy off from afar was a coward's move. The Riders were trained in ground combat, but Rendyr had nothing without his magic. If forced to land and then to discard his magic, Evra might yet have a chance.

The trouble was how to get Rendyr to do either of those things.

Hours passed, and he'd had no sign of Rendyr. He wondered where all the ravens heading south had gone. Was there a battle raging on the ground? How many had fallen? Had it already been decided?

When his breaths turned so harried he became dizzy, Evra found a fallen log and wedged himself underneath it. It wasn't much cover, but he wouldn't be stopping long. But now that he was no longer moving, his feet screamed at him. Blisters pulsed against the sides of his frozen boots. His heels, down to the meat, frostbitten. He couldn't feel his toes, but neither could he think about what that meant. He couldn't think about anything up here, because all thoughts had the power to weaken him.

He dug into his satchel for the bread Ethelyn had packed him and ripped a loaf in half. He couldn't taste it. When he swallowed, it was as if swallowing a wad of vellum. When he was done, he could almost feel it, like a stone, sink to the bottom of his belly.

He leaned his head back against the underside of the log, and before he realized it, he'd fallen asleep.

Lorcan sank down against the broken stone wall and allowed himself his first deep breath. It stopped halfway, turning to a cough, but he kept on until he had a proper lungful. "Guardians," he said between breaths, then drowned one last swig of his wine. Empty, he chucked the skin aside.

The smoke and blood gave the air a sense of finality. An eerie calm at the end of a battle no one had won. He and Finnegan had used the pause in the air assault to tally their losses, and they were both greater than he expected, and less than. Greater, because he knew some of the dead. Had grown up with them. Less, because the Ravenwood corpses outnumbered the men.

It was a curious thing, he thought, as they filtered through the carnage. Finnegan even remarked on it, wondering about why, when they died, they returned to their human form. There they all lay, curled up in their black leather, and all those feathers. Why did they wear feathers, if they were ravens themselves? Wasn't that a bit like a man wearing human skin for a cloak?

Lorcan was sick to death of these inane questions. In the end, dead was dead. Aside from their dress, they looked no different from the men who had fallen.

"That's not all of them, is it?" A shadow passed over him. He didn't look up. He knew who it was.

"No."

"Less of 'em overall, though. We'll have taken more, in the end, if you look at it that way."

"Look at it however you like, Finn."

"How do you look at it?"

"We always said as boys that we hoped there'd be war in our days. That we could fight in one. Is this how you saw it?"

"Fire hurling from the clouds out of the mouths of birds?" Finnegan countered. "No, Lor. That's not how I saw it."

Lorcan squinted up at him through a cloud of smoke. He chuckled. Finn shook his head and did the same.

"You wanna know how I look at it?" Lorcan mused. He used the wall to pull himself back to his tired feet. "Lord Blackrook freed us. Eh, I've heard the speculation from others as to why. That it was weakness that sent him groveling to the Sepulchre, not bravery. But in the end, does it matter? Our mothers and sisters can live in peace now."

"Yeah. They can."

"So if the boy who used to run around the woods playing with none but himself now wants us to hold this ground so that he can free someone else? I don't know how we can say no."

"We can't."

"No." Lorcan dusted himself off. "So let's pull these bastards off of him once more, so he can do what he came to do."

His brief respite would be the death of him. These were Evra's first thoughts as he awoke in dread, frozen to the ground. He couldn't bend his legs. His arms. A scream rose, but he pushed it back down, because he'd die right here if he lost himself to his fear.

Grunting, he angled himself out into the open again. He inched backward, mindful of his proximity to the edge, and had to take a break after only a few shuffles. Wheezing, Evra forced his arms to obey. The resistance sent a surge of agony straight to his head, but he struggled through it until his arms could turn inward, and again out to his sides.

Now, for his feet.

It was another tick of the sun before he was again moving forward, but the best hours were behind him. Darkness waited ahead, and when it came, his pace would be no better than a crawl.

He'd slept long enough for his belly to cry out for more of the dry bread. He ignored it. There was no time for food. No time for rest. No time for considering how he might never walk again on these feet, nor the fingers he'd lose if he survived this.

Steeper with each step, he had to use the mountain wall to pull himself along the path. The way narrowed, drawing the edge closer. If he lost his balance or landed a step wrong, he'd have nothing to stop him from careening over the side.

A fresh storm descended, peppering the path. Heavy flakes landed in his eyes, obscuring his vision to only a few feet in front of him. He couldn't tell if the ground curved to the right or the left. He slowed further, inching along against the wall, each breath a new pain.

When he reached the point where the incline was too much, he dropped to his knees and continued his climb that way. Though slower, this was easier, no longer subject to the bouts of dizziness that threatened his balance. He clutched at snow, at gnarled roots, at anything, anything that would pull him higher. Grunting, panting, the spittle frozen against his lips and face, he prayed the end was near. His damp hair formed into icicles, dangling against his cheek, obscuring his vision. Death had called upon his promise, and he would spend it here, now, he was certain of this, but he'd go out climbing. The Guardian of the Unpromised Future would have to work for this one.

Evra reached his hands over his head, pulling, climbing. There was nothing left inside of him. He pulled anyway. One hand, then the other. Each movement required everything he had. They'd find him like this, he thought, one hand stretched over his head, the other ready to overtake it. If they found him at all.

His right hand again heaved upward for the next notch, but it landed right by his head. He raised his eyes to see he'd reached some sort of platform. He pitched himself over the edge of it and rolled onto his back.

Evra looked into the sky and saw nothing. Only clouds and snow falling in gentle waves, dotting his face, turning to ice upon landing. He blinked slowly. The world appeared and then disappeared. This would be a better place to die than the climb up. All he had to do was close his eyes. He'd feel nothing. Go nowhere. A lonely but peaceful end.

"Rhosyn." The word traveled no farther than his cracked lips. Even now, the sound of her name soothed him. Like running his face through a bed of silk. Rhosyn. Rhosynora.

Evra turned his face to the side. His breathing slowed. He watched the clouds travel across the dark canvas of the sky. Why did they move like that, he wondered? Someone must know. He might have learned this answer, had he taken the Scholar's Path.

A patch cleared, and something new appeared. At first, he thought he'd imagined it. Master Quinwhill spoke of men who conjured desperate images when nearing death, and it was almost amusing to finally understand this now, experiencing this phenomenon for himself. But as even more clouds passed by, and the sharp spires darkened, lengthening against the stormy sky, a new understanding came to him.

Midnight Crest.

The Rookery.

Rhosyn.

He'd made it.

Evra rolled over onto his belly. He pulled his arms underneath him and pushed until he was on his knees. Checking again to be sure the castle was still there, he heaved himself to his feet. He swayed from boot to boot, eyes never leaving the castle. It was still so far away, but it was there, and it was *real*. He could see, now, what Oswin meant. Though there was more path ahead, it wouldn't take him there. Even if it would, this was as far as he could go. Everything he had left he would save for Rendyr. The final minutes of his life would unfold here.

His hand fell upon his sword. It wouldn't budge. It had frozen into the scabbard.

With the last of his resolve, Evra scrunched his face and pulled as hard as he could. The sword broke free, knocking him back several steps.

He saw now he was standing upon a ledge of ice. It jutted out into the air, thinner as it went on. Only the illusion of solid ground, but it was exactly the reprieve he'd been searching for on his desperate climb.

Evra lowered his sword to the side, panting. When he had his breath back, he brought his free hand to his mouth to amplify his words.

"RENDYYYYYR RAVENWOOOOOD!"

THIRTY-SIX
LIGHTNING

Rhosyn didn't know how much time had passed since Rendyr had locked her away. At first, she'd slammed herself against the door, attempting to overcome his magic with force. When that did nothing, she searched for ways to counter his magic. When neither was enough, she resorted to pounding on the door and screaming for someone, anyone, to help her.

No one came.

Her chambers were windowless. She liked it this way, for the closer to the air, the wind, and the sky, the further her imagination took her. It was her imagination that led to her imprisonment. Punishing herself, though, had never helped her, either. Every choice she'd made had led her straight back to this room, and this moment, except for one.

To stand.

To fight.

Evra's journey played in the back of her mind over the long hours. He was alone now. There had to be a reason he was still alive, that Rendyr had not finished what he'd set out to do. She felt his arduous push up the mountain. How he cycled through his courage and acceptance of defeat. With each step closer, his thoughts became louder in her mind, until it was all she could hear.

But what she heard then did not come from her mind. It rode the wind, drifting up to The Rookery.

"RENDYYYYYR RAVENWOOOOOD!"

Rhosyn raced to the far wall. She pressed her palms to the stone, wishing, now, that there *was* a window, so that her eyes could confirm what her ears had heard. What her heart knew.

"Oh, no," she breathed out. "Oh, no, no, no. Evra, no!"

She charged again at the door. Her body bounced off the wood, sending her to the floor. She did it again. And then again. With each thrust, her rage took a new form. It spiraled through her belly, sending charges into her arms, her legs, her fingers, her toes. She slammed herself against the door again. Again. Each time, growing stronger. The electric light pulsing at her veins, threatening to break through. Again.

"RENDYR! I KNOW YOU CAN HEAR ME! I KNOW YOU'RE THERE!"

Slam. Fall. Again. Slam. Fall. Rhosyn screamed. Her bones ached from the self-inflicted pain, but with each rush, she gained command. The pain turned to light, turned to power. She reared back, ready to throw herself at the door once more, but as the scream left her, so did something else.

Her hands flew out before her and a white, arcing light surged from the tips of her fingers. She cried louder, and more emerged with every pulse of sound, separate swirling shocks of light, forming one by one until she had tendrils at the end of each of her fingers. She passed her hands back and forth between her face, gaping in wonder. The lights made trails before her eyes. They crackled. Snapped. Whispered to her.

Try again.

Rhosyn leveled her eyes upon the invisible lock barring her from freedom. The light stayed with her. She needed no focus to keep it present. It was here to stay. It was hers. And now she would find out what it could do for her.

Rhosyn raised a guttural howl from the back of her throat and sent the sound and her light into the door with one booming command.

"OPEN!"

Rhosyn again bounced off the door, this time flying clear across the room from the brunt of the force she'd carried with her.

Prepared to scream again, to try again, she reached for the cracks in the stone to pull herself to her feet. Swaying, vision split into two, she looked at the door. What she saw tempered the white rage readying for another command.

The door was open.

Rhosyn wasted no time wondering. She raced outside, only to run straight into her mother.

"Rhosynora." Naryssa's bloodied face gaped back at her. Her mother's hair hung limp and tangled around her face. "Where have you been?"

"Me?" She reached for her mother's face, afraid to touch it. "What's happened to you?"

"You know what's happened. You know how to stop it. Where *have* you been?"

"Rendyr locked me in, with the Magic of the Accused."

"That's treason," Naryssa countered, stunned. "Punishable by death."

Rhosyn rolled her head back and laughed. "Of all the things he's done, Mother, *that* is what finally shocks you?"

"But how? How did you free yourself?"

Rhosyn's hands twitched. She looked toward the hall and the ramparts. If she took flight now, perhaps she could get to Evra before Rendyr did.

Naryssa gasped. "Your hands. Your hands, Rhosyn!"

Rhosyn didn't look down. She was beyond this revelation. Desperate for the next. "What about them?"

"You can summon energy itself," Naryssa whispered. "That's how you did it. You pulled your magic from the light of the world, and you immobilized his."

Rhosyn's focus shifted back to her mother. "I immobilized his magic? You're certain of this?"

"There is no other way a priest or priestess could break the Magic of the Accused. There is nothing else."

"Splendid." Rhosyn stormed down the hall, gathering speed with each hard land of her boots. Naryssa called after her, but she had what she needed, and her mother had nothing more to offer her. The eyes of other bedraggled Ravenwoods, sore and spent from battle, traveled with her, but her kin were as unspecific to her as the walls, the stone floors, the clothes she'd worn as one of them. They called out to her, but their voices blended into her past, and when she had lost the sound of them altogether, Rhosyn took to the skies and left her world behind.

Evra was farther down the mountain than she realized. His voice had carried so far. As she passed through the first layer of clouds, she spotted him, standing amidst a clearing in the clouds, sword tip scraping the ice he stood upon. He hadn't seen her yet, but would he recognize her? Would he know her in this form, as he had known her as a woman?

Rhosyn angled herself against the wind, looping around to land from the side. It was then she saw Rendyr. His wings flapped with manic force as he closed in on Evra. Evra spotted him, too. He raised his sword to the side.

She quickened her pace and caught the end of the wind as it carried her down to the frozen shelf. She was already unfolding into her priestess form when she hit the ice, and she pitched forward from the force of shifting too soon. She scrambled back to her feet just in time to see Rendyr's beak light with fire.

Rhosyn spread her arms in a shield, covering Evra.

"Rhosyn?" Evra tried to step forward, but she sent her light in solid streams, to the right, to the left, forming a wall.

Rendyr's beak closed. He circled around Rhosyn and Evra, and the two of them turned as he followed in flight, surrounded by the white barrier she'd created.

"I hope you didn't come here to save me, Evrathedyn."

"No, Rhosynora," he answered, winded. He held fast to his sword. She felt him tense, ready to strike. *Not just yet.* "I came to stand at your side."

"Or behind me?" she teased with a quick glance over her shoulder.

"Wherever you'll have me."

Rendyr's dips were lower now, tighter. "He's going to land. When he does, stay clear of him."

"I didn't come all this way to do nothing."

"Will you trust me?"

"Do I have a choice?"

Rhosyn reached a hand behind her. He hesitated, breathing labored, and then took it.

"Yes. Just like you had a choice to move on with your life and forget about me. But you didn't."

"I tried," he said. "But it proved impossible."

Rhosyn squeezed his hand in hers and then released it. She spun away from him just as Rendyr landed. His hands were already forming the magic he'd chosen to end this, but she was ready for him.

She thrust her hands out and sent the charged light into her brother. His head and neck arched back when it connected and he rose off the ground briefly before landing in a crouch.

Rendyr coiled back and went to launch another wave of fire. His eyes widened when his magic failed to respond to him. He threw out his hands again and again, and still, there was nothing.

"You bitch," Rendyr hissed. "What is this, then? Some trick?"

"Shouldn't you know? Aren't you supposed to be stronger than me? Far superior?"

He rolled his hands in the air before his eyes. "And what will you do when this glamour wears off?"

"Who's to say it will?"

"He's dead, Rhosyn. Magic or no. But now you've ensured his pain will linger for days."

"It's me you want," Rhosyn challenged. "So come on, then. Catch me if you can." She shifted into her raven form and rose above him. Waiting.

But Rendyr couldn't shift. She hadn't foreseen this. Their raven form was innate to them all, separate from their magic. Wasn't it?

Rendyr's grin was chilling. He created it for her, then lowered it upon Evra, who stood only several paces ahead of him.

Rhosyn went to land again, but the wind caught her wings, pulling her higher. *No, no, no. Evra, run!* The words burned inside of her, unable to find voice in her raven form. *Don't do this! Don't fight him!*

She angled into the wind, but it carried her farther away. She wouldn't get to him before Rendyr did.

No matter how fast she flew, it was too late.

Evra and Rendyr were face to face.

Evra tightened his grip on The Betrayer. It may as well have been a thousand pounds, it weighed so heavy in his tired arms. Rendyr might be spent of his magic, but his fury fortified him, filling him with frenzied energy.

"Now what will you do, with your little raven flown away?"

"I'm not afraid of you," Evra asserted. His jaw flexed as he steeled his nerves. "I've never been afraid of you."

Rendyr cocked his head. "You should be. I don't need magic to kill you."

"You don't even have a sword."

It happened so fast, all Evra felt was a quick sting. He looked down in horror to see a dagger buried to the hilt in his belly.

Rendyr smiled. "You were saying?"

Evra stumbled back toward the mountain wall. The bloom of red on his armor had already spread across his torso. He used his sword to straighten his stance. How long could he fight off the pain? How long before it caught up?

He raised the sword before him, stopping Rendyr at the tip. Rendyr's surprise was momentary, but enough for Evra to change course, pushing Rendyr backward, toward the edge of the shelf. Copper flooded his mouth. "Did you know there used to be dragons in the Southerlands?"

Rendyr, disoriented by the odd question, stumbled back a step. "*What?*"

"There were," Evra said, talking faster now. He didn't have long. It was a strange thought, to know the moment of your death was imminent. If he could only hold it off for a few more moments. If he could keep Rendyr's attention on the story and not the rest. "They were much dreaded, these dragons. They were fearsome and wicked, and only the bravest of knights would dare enter their lair and attempt to best them. And they had no choice, did they? These monstrous beasts would eat their livestock. Sometimes even their children."

"Do all men speak such nonsense when they're dying?" Rendyr fixed on Evra's wound. He crossed his arms over his chest. All he had to do was wait. The fatal blow had already been struck.

"But," Evra said, fighting the swoon. They inched closer to the edge, but Rendyr was too clever to be so easily sent over. "What they didn't know was that the dragon, he wasn't so fearsome at all. He was as big as a guildhall and breathed fire, but he had no weapons beyond his size. He had these teeth that couldn't even tear through a leaf." His arm burned with the weight of his sword, but he didn't waver. He couldn't. "One-on-one with a dragon, man was stronger."

"Do you really want these to be your last words, then? Rambling on about dragons?" Rendyr nodded at Evra's belly. "Do you even know you're dying?"

"The dragon relied on his fearsomeness and wickedness to best a man," Evra continued, "but when man realized the dragon was all roar, no bite, everything changed."

"Dragons aren't real," Rendyr retorted. "And you have moments left to live. I hope she was worth it. All this pain. Death."

Evra spat out a wad of blood. It froze against the ice. "The dragon, though not strong, was still clever. For the knights, disarmed by this strange realization of a toothless dragon, counted their victory before they'd sealed it. They didn't know that the dragon won by waiting for such moments, lulling them into a false triumph."

They both looked up to see Rhosyn descending.

"All the dragon had to do was wait for the right moment." Evra rolled the hilt of The Betrayer in his hand, flipping the blade upside down so it pointed at the ice. Blood ran down the corner of his mouth, the final push to the end of his promise. "I cannot match you for strength. I'm far from equal to you in might." Evra raised his arms as high as they would go. With the last of his vigor, he slammed the blade down into the ice. "But I've read a lot more books than you."

His sword wedged in the ice, Evra collapsed to his knees. Rendyr smiled in appreciation of his work, not noticing the tiny splinters spidering their way to the right and left of The Betrayer. They traveled outward, at last sounding their cracks into the wind.

Rendyr's smile faded as he at last looked down to see the ice he stood upon breaking away from the mountain. He pitched forward, running up the frozen shelf just as Rhosyn landed next to him. Together, they disappeared as the landing fell away.

Evra stretched his hand toward the edge and surrendered to the pain.

"What..." Lorcan pulled his sword from the chest of a raven. "What is that? What are they doing?"

There were so many of them. The arrows had pulled the ravens from the skies, but it had been the task of the swordsmen to finish the job. He'd watched his childhood friends fall to flame, or ice, or some other foul magic, but the men had picked up on that quick enough and were faster with their strikes. He'd stopped counting the fallen. He didn't know who was winning. It seemed no one was.

But now, the ones still in the sky, they were... they were...

"They're retreating," Finnegan panted. "Look over there, it's as if... no, that can't be right. Are they *fighting* each other?"

"Who could ever explain any of this?" Lorcan answered. Finnegan was right, though. That's exactly how it seemed. Hundreds more ravens had arrived, pouring out from the clouds, but they'd turned their sights on each other. There was no telling friend from foe.

"Where are they going?" another man cried.

"They're leaving," Lorcan said, watching the newly arrived ravens escort the others away, back into the clouds. "They're leaving!"

Rhosyn landed beside Evra. She called his name over the wind, but he didn't answer. When she rolled him over, she saw why.

She rocked back on her heels as she assessed the damage. Rendyr had struck him with a mortal wound. One she could only heal if he was still with her. And even then...

She felt for his heartbeat. In her panic, all she could sense was her own.

"Evra!" Rhosyn slapped his face. "Evrathedyn Blackrook, I need to see your eyes open! I need to know you're still with me."

His lifeless face fell back to the ice. Rhosyn, rattled, landed her hands on the wound, but her focus was beholden to her fears. "Please, Evra, I need you to fight for yourself with the same strength you fought for me."

Evra's mouth parted and closed. That was all he had.

"That's enough," she whispered as the familiar warmth of healing passed down her arms and into her hands. *More. More! Take it all. Take it from me. He needs all of it.* "Gods, please let me be enough for him."

When she'd spent the last of her magic, Rhosyn collapsed at his side.

THIRTY-SEVEN

CHERRIES IN WINTER

The first thing he knew was warmth. It washed over him, wrapping him tight in the promise of protection. He stretched his legs under the heavy pile of furs, and they responded as if to say, *about time*.

The next welcome was a scent. Rich, stewed apples and freshly baked bread. The bread had a yeasty acridity to it, not like his mother's sweet loaves, but nothing had ever smelled so inviting.

Evra opened his eyes. A room he'd never seen before came into uneven focus. A fire roared in the hearth, elaborate tapestries lining the walls to trap precious heat. He twisted his head against the pillow and saw a window. Nothing but white beyond the panes.

"You're awake, sir." A clatter of boots pulled his notice back to the other side of the room, where he found a young attendant scrambling to attention. "How are you feeling?"

Evra pushed up on his elbows with immediate regret. He lifted layers of cloth to reveal his last memory: Bleeding into the frost of Icebolt Mountain, Rendyr's dagger still stuck tight in his gut. The dagger was gone now, but in its place was a bloodied bandage needing changing. "Ah. I don't know. Where am I?"

"Wulfsgate Keep, Lord Blackrook."

"Wulfsgate?"

The attendant's anxious eyes kept traveling to the door. "I should really fetch Lord Dereham. Or the steward."

"Why am I in Wulfsgate?"

"Midwinter Hold is no fit state for a healing lord," the attendant answered, as if this was obvious.

"How bad was the damage? After the assault, I mean."

"No worse than before. It was well defended," the attendant said. He relaxed some, happy, it seemed, for the relief of simple answers. "The steward and his family are treasured guests of our Lord Dereham until proper repairs can be made. He wouldn't have it any other way."

"Wouldn't he?" Evra tried to laugh, but it sputtered to a cough.

"Are you sure you're all right? Can... can you walk?"

"I'm not sure."

"It's just, your healer... she says you need to walk if you can."

"My healer," Evra repeated. He rolled over and swung his feet over the edge of the bed. *I need to see your eyes open. I need to know you're still with me.* "She's still here?"

The attendant nodded. "She's in the Wintergarden. Would you like me to take you to her?"

"Yes," Evra said, reaching for the fresh pile of clothes left for him on the table. "I would."

The Wintergarden was not as she remembered it. But then, she'd seen it for the first time as a young girl, through eyes yet to be tainted by the understanding of who she was and what it would come to mean. Back then, she could enjoy swinging from the trees, playing with Lord Dereham's younger siblings. They liked to feed her fruit from the winter blooms, making her guess what she was eating. She never got an answer right. No fruits grew at Midnight Crest. But she'd liked the cherries best.

Cherries, they'd told her, never grew in winter. Except here.

Magic, they'd said, laughing in delight, and she wished her own magic could produce something so wonderful.

For three days, when she wasn't healing Evra, she sat beneath a cherry tree, on a bench, reading *The Last Dragons of the Southerland Peninsula.* She'd gone back for it, ignoring the incredulous gapes of other Ravenwoods as she did nothing, said nothing, and then once again, left them all behind, this time forever. She had no words for any of them. Not even her mother.

The book was a real yarn, as Steward Frost would say, a tale presented as truth but written with the silver touch of fiction. Embellished though it was, she couldn't put it down. She imagined herself as Evra, lying in bed to hear the words read to him by his mother. She practiced reacting to the more salient parts, using words she thought he might use.

When she was done, she tucked the book on the table at his bedside, where it belonged.

Rhosyn turned toward the sound of boots crunching in the snow. Her eyes were cast at the ground, but she knew his uncertain gait; the hint of hesitation he brought to nearly every moment, as if he couldn't decide if he belonged there.

Evra swatted at the chunky white flakes falling from the sky. She laughed and pointed to the bench she sat upon, free of snow. He limped the rest of the way, a mingling of injuries new and old. There was healing yet to be done, and she would stay until he was fully mended if he let her.

He nestled in on the far end of the bench, shivering as he ran his hands over the furs draped about his shoulders. "It's deceptive, how warm it is inside! Such a trick doesn't ready a man for this at all, does it?"

"You needed warmth to keep infection away."

"What happened to his dagger?"

"I threw it over the edge, right behind him."

331

"He's really gone? He won't inexplicably reappear and announce himself, popping out of the apple tree over there like a specter?"

Rhosyn shook her head with a soft laugh. "We don't believe in specters, Evra. Gone is gone."

"And now you're free."

"Now I'm free," she repeated, still unsure what that meant. What she wanted it to mean. "You never got the chance to tell me why you came all the way up the mountain."

Evra shrugged. He wrung his hands together in his lap. "I went home, and I..." He laughed. "Would you believe I actually saved my people?"

"I would believe it," Rhosyn said. "How did you do it?"

"I made peace with the Sepulchre and signed an armistice on the burnings. No magic will be punished in the Westerlands as long as I'm Lord." He tugged at his fingers. "It's what I should have done all along. But then I wouldn't have met you."

Rhosyn looked down.

"But I felt no joy. No victory. The celebrations ran for days, and I couldn't even pretend I wanted to be there," he went on. "I'd never felt so alone. I suppose I knew why, deep down, but it took some time for me to get to a place where I accepted it. Arwenna was the one who helped me see it in the end."

"*Arwenna?* My sister?"

"She came to the Rush to see me. It was from her I learned about what your brother really wanted from you. Why you'd really gone home."

Rhosyn was speechless. "Where is she now?"

"When I left, she was still there. I told her she could stay as long as she wanted. And that, if she did leave, I'd help her in any way I could."

"That was very kind of you."

"It was the least I could do after what happened." He dropped his head to the side and looked at her. "All I've made with you are mistakes."

"No," she said softly. "That's not true."

"It is," Evra insisted. "Was a hard lesson for me. Wanting something badly enough doesn't make it mine."

Rhosyn flushed. "You're being hard on yourself. That's not why you kept me in the armory."

"Not the only reason," he said with a small smile. "What brought me back to the north was realizing you'd gone back to him because of me." He tapped his knee. "Not only me. The Frosts, too. But because of *us*, the same men who would love you, and enjoy you, and use you, and then send you right back."

"I do have more autonomy than that, you know."

"I know that," Evra said. "But am I wrong? If Rendyr had never turned his eyes on us, would you have gone back to him?"

Rhosyn inhaled a lungful of the cool air. "I had a plan to fly south, to the Easterlands. To the Sepulchre, actually."

"Really?"

She smiled to think of it. It was still a good plan, even if it wasn't the one she wanted to follow now. "There's never been a Ravenwood at the Sepulchre, so they say. I thought they might appreciate having one."

"They would die for a Ravenwood there."

"Ah, perhaps. Or perhaps I'd just be another curiosity, like I am to most men."

"Not to me," Evra insisted. He shook his head and turned toward her on the bench. "Not anymore."

Rhosyn reached a hand over and laid it across his. "Stand beside me, you said. On the mountain. What does that mean?"

Evra made a light tsk sound as he laughed. "I thought we might take him down together. As equals. I do still owe you a life debt, after all. But I should have known you could handle him yourself."

"But I didn't handle him," Rhosyn countered. "*We* did, together."

"I didn't even see that dagger coming, Rhosyn."

"Nor did he see your clever move with the sword and ice. Yet only one of you is still here to reminisce about it."

The silence that fell between them was familial. She'd never sat so comfortably in the quiet, not even with herself. When Evra reached up to pluck a cherry from a low-hanging branch, she saw he had two. He dropped one in her palm.

"What do you want, Rhosyn? Now that you're free, and you could be anything. Go anywhere. What do *you* want?"

"As you said, I suppose. To be free." She rolled the red orb around in her palm.

"What does that mean to you?"

"Free to choose." She separated the stem from the cherry, twisting it between her fingers.

Evra shifted nervously as he regarded the fruit in his hand with unusual interest. "Choose me." When she looked at him, he had the other cherry by the stem, holding it out to her. "Choose me, Rhosynora, not because you have no other choices, but because what happened between us at Midwinter Hold was real, and it mattered. And if I'm wrong, and I've misunderstood everything, then you can let me down with cruelty or kindness, but if I haven't... if I'm not wrong... if—"

Rhosyn reached for his face and brought it to hers. His lips parted at the insistence of her tongue, drawing them closer, each desperate to close any distance still between them.

"Be my husband," Rhosyn whispered when she pulled back. She pressed her forehead to his.

"That's not fair," Evra replied, grinning. He passed his tongue over his lips, tasting the remains of their kiss. "I was *trying* to ask *you*, Rhosyn. You ruined my awkward speech and everything."

Rhosyn forced herself to sit back, patient. She held her head high. "Go on. Finish, then."

"Well, now, I don't know..."

"I want to hear it. You must have saved the best for last?"

"Prepare for disappointment if that's your assumption." He laughed. "An entire lifetime of it."

"I mean it!" She nudged her shoulder into him. "Please, tell me. I want to know."

"There wasn't much more," he insisted. "Only that... I want you to be more than my wife. I want you to be my equal in all things. I want there to be no inequity of power hanging between us, no question that you will ever answer to me, or anyone, ever again. I'll never need anything from you that you don't give willingly. But anything you ever want from me, it's yours."

Rhosyn reached for his hands. "How could anyone ever say no to that?"

"You missed my whole point, Rhosyn," he teased. "I can handle you telling me no."

She shook her head. His smile was the only invitation she'd ever been certain she'd regret not taking. It was the promise of home. A *real* home, one she'd chosen with her whole heart. "Not this time." She crawled into his arms when he held them out, drawing her legs over his as they curled together beneath the cherries in perfect silence.

EPILOGUE

Thus begins the reign of Lord Thedyn Blackrook and Lady Rhosynora Ravenwood. A new house, henceforth to be named Blackwood, in celebration of the union of these two blessed souls, without which there'd be only dark days ahead for the Rush and the West. A new era begins for all the Westerlands. For all the kingdom."

Evra held fast to Rhosyn's hand as they were showered with flowers plucked from his grandmother's garden. The carriage moved slowly down the road that took travelers to and from the Hall of Longwood. Poles, twined with brilliant ribbons of black and green, with more brilliant floral arrangements, replaced what had greeted him on his first return home, a reminder of how much had changed.

That wasn't all that had changed about this path. This time, the faces surrounding them on all sides were kin, some by blood and others by choice. Edriss, Alise. Meira. All the Riders he now knew by name. The Frosts, who were staying until springtide. Even

337

Morwen, ripe with child, had come with her husband, Steward Haddenfoot. And Seven! She'd scraped together enough gold for the ride to Longwood Rush and refused to accept his offer to pay for the ride back.

They were all here.

Arwenna stood at the side of Lorcan James, who had first been her friend and guide, and was now, perhaps, more. She was a resident of the Rush now, no longer just visiting.

Evra waved with one hand. The other he laid upon Rhosyn's swollen belly. She'd cried upon discovering she was carrying their child.

I never imagined being a mother could be a gift, rather than a sentence.

In his own way, he understood, for the Evra of only months ago had stolen a kiss to content himself with the loveless, monastic life that seemed his only path to contentment. Joyful marriages were a myth. A happy accident. Reserved for greater men.

"They all love you," Rhosyn said through her smiles and waves. "They adore you, Evra."

"They love *you*," he amended. He pulsed his hand against her belly and then lifted it to her chin, stealing a kiss from the only one who could ever make him want more of them. The crowd cheered and crowed in response. "They see you for who you are."

"And who is that?"

"The Mother of the Westerlands. My equal. The way forward." He brought her hand to his mouth. "The one who saved me."

The Ballad of Rhosyn and Thedyn started somewhere in the back, but it quickly made its way through the celebrants, and soon, everyone was singing.

Rhosyn, glowing with joy, blinked through glassy eyes, her smile lingering as she mouthed the words along with them.

"Men certainly love their celebrations, don't they?" Arwenna cooed. Rhosyn twirled, arms in the air, as her sister unbound her from the many layers of ribbon. She spun until she was dizzy. "Ah, there we are. To the pyre with all this?"

Rhosyn laughed. She sat on the edge of the bed and massaged her aching feet. "I don't think that's part of the tradition, Wen."

"Perhaps your influence will bring exciting change to the Rush. Starting with an instruction in fashion."

"I know it's lavish, but it *was* a beautiful day, wasn't it?" Rhosyn flopped back against the soft bed, arms spread. "I could not have conjured it in my wildest of imaginings."

"You certain about that? Your imaginings have always been wilder than most." Arwenna came and sat near her head. With the back of her hand, she brushed matted hair off Rhosyn's tired face. "He's a good man, Rhosyn."

Rhosyn's face spread into a contented, lazy smile. "He really is."

"The women in his life have accepted you, without question. They don't drag their eyes over you in envy, as their competition."

Rhosyn nodded. "Are all women of the kingdom like this, I wonder? They can't be, can they? Edriss is so full of warmth and love. Alise is cunning, shrewd, but also kind. I want to learn *everything* from her. And Meldred..." She laughed. "Evra has the best qualities of all of them."

"He's fair on the eyes, too, though I'll deny it if you tell him I said so. He's already so cocksure now that he's landed you."

"He didn't land me."

"Ah, yes." Arwenna clasped her hands together. "He climbed a mountain, on hands and knees."

"I'll never forget how he looked, standing there." Rhosyn's smile faded. "So brave. So painfully mortal. Standing between life and death, and so utterly unafraid."

"They aren't all bad, I suppose," Arwenna conceded. "Men."

Rhosyn opened her eyes. "Lorcan is pleasing as well."

Arwenna's mouth parted wide in indignation. "Just because you married the first man to show interest, doesn't mean—"

Rhosyn popped up and smacked her with a pillow. Arwenna responded in kind, and they erupted in a playful battle before dissolving into soft giggles.

After, they lay side by side on the bed, gazing up at the satin canopy. "What will they do now?" Rhosyn asked quietly. She hadn't allowed herself to think about it too much. To leave that world behind was to leave all of it. Her worries. Her lingering attachments. They'd never really been hers, anyway. Nothing had until now.

Arwenna knew what she meant without clarifying. "Mother is still young. Maybe there could be another daughter, if the gods willed it. Aunt Nerian has all daughters. *Five* of them. Uncle Langdyn has two. There is no shortage of women who will be more than happy to do what we were not."

"Yes. Perhaps."

"You can't let such questions weigh upon your heart. Be satisfied with never knowing the answers."

"I guess you're right."

"Have you any regrets?"

"None," Rhosyn answered. "Not a single one."

Arwenna rolled her gaze back to the violet tester. "No. Me either." She sighed. "Your groom will be here soon. I should let you finish."

Rhosyn grabbed for her sister's hand as she rose. Arwenna turned back.

"I'm so glad you're here, Wen. I do have one regret."

"Oh?"

Rhosyn rolled forward and enveloped her older sister in a hug from behind. "That I let you leave so easily, without knowing if I'd ever see you again."

"Don't be silly," Arwenna said. Rhosyn felt her sister's tears trickle onto her forearm. "I'm here now."

Oswin raised his glass. Evra joined him, followed by Thorn.

"To the House of Blackwood. May your legacy reign strong in all who come after you. May their curiosity fill them with the unflappable courage of a man who does not know any better than to charge forward into certain danger," Oswin said. They all emptied their glasses and slammed them on the oaken table.

"We're proud of you," Oswin said as he refilled the amber liquid, topping them all up. "I'm proud of you. Ethelyn is proud of you. Thorn is proud of you. Brin is proud of you. Rylan is proud of you. Morwen is undoubtedly proud of you. I'm reasonably certain both the infants are proud of you." He swallowed another sip. "Now that we've gotten that out of the way."

Evra laughed. He settled back into the tall leather chair that had once been his mother's favorite. He'd kept it during renovations, for Rhosyn, but right now he was happy to be the one to warm it. "I'll bet you're itching to be home."

"More like itching to go spy on all the laborers so he can tell them what a piss-poor job they're doing," Thorn said.

"Don't want a steward supervising your work, don't do piss-poor work," Oswin countered. He raised his glass again.

"We're happy for you, Thedyn," Thorn slurred. He'd had more to drink than any of them, but he was jovial in his cups, and it was nice to see. "For Rhosyn."

"I refuse to call you Thedyn," Oswin added. "You're forevermore Evra to us."

"To Rhosyn, too," Evra said. "She won't call me anything else. She said, 'I fell in love with Evra.'"

"Aww!" Thorn cajoled. "*Love!*"

"Love," Oswin murmured. "When can we expect the two of you to visit?"

"Once our child is born and strong enough for the travel, I promise, we'll come."

"Holding you to it."

"I'd expect nothing less, sir."

Oswin grunted. "Sir. Call me Oswin, or call me Father. Never sir."

Evra bit down on his tongue to suppress the fast wave of emotion. He nodded.

Thorn passed his father a knowing look. He waggled his eyebrows.

"What?" Oswin gruffed. "Have you something to say, boy?"

"It's their wedding night. We need to let Evra get on with... it..."

"Have you had a look at Rhosyn lately? They're not fresh maids on the eve of the springtide festival, now, are they?"

"Father." Thorn shook his head. "You've had more to drink than I have."

Evra rose to his feet. He went to shake Oswin's hand, but the man who'd just asked Evra to call him Father moved in for a solid hug. Thorn joined from the back, and after a few hearty squeezes, they let him go.

Evra watched his wife through grateful eyes as she removed her nightgown and joined him in bed. He shivered when her bare flesh brushed against his. His head fell back with a long sigh when her hand traveled farther down.

"I had all these things... I wanted to say to you..." He moaned. "Important things."

"Important things?" Rhosyn purred, breath hot and welcome against his neck. "More important than this?"

Evra rolled her atop him and let her assume command. He had no defense against this, nor had he any desire for one. Every time with Rhosyn was a voyage to some new and wondrous place. Every kiss he placed upon her in exploration added something fresh and powerful to his knowledge of her; his need of her.

"Well? I thought you had something very important to say?" Rhosyn asked as she rode him in perfect, agonizing rhythm.

"I love you." Evra whispered the words through each breathless stride. "I love you, Rhosynora."

"I love you, Evrathedyn," came her response, but what she did next with her hips clipped all the rest of his unsaid words, turning his thoughts inward.

How grateful he was that she'd come into his life.

How he'd spend every day remaining to him ensuring she never regretted leaving her world for his.

How utterly enchanted he was to wake up next to her, for her face to be his last vision before falling asleep.

Evra wrapped his arms around her hips, pressed his face to the swell of her belly, and released his words into feeling.

The Book of All Things continues with a new story in *The Sylvan and the Sand*.

ALSO BY SARAH M. CRADIT

KINGDOM OF THE WHITE SEA
<u>KINGDOM OF THE WHITE SEA TRILOGY</u>
The Kingless Crown
The Broken Realm
The Hidden Kingdom

<u>THE BOOK OF ALL THINGS</u>
The Raven and the Rush

THE SAGA OF CRIMSON & CLOVER
<u>THE HOUSE OF CRIMSON AND CLOVER SERIES</u>
The Storm and the Darkness
Shattered
The Illusions of Eventide
Bound
Midnight Dynasty
Asunder
Empire of Shadows
Myths of Midwinter
The Hinterland Veil
The Secrets Amongst the Cypress
Within the Garden of Twilight
House of Dusk, House of Dawn

<u>MIDNIGHT DYNASTY SERIES</u>
A Tempest of Discovery
A Storm of Revelations
A Torrent of Deceit

THE SEVEN SERIES
Nineteen Seventy
Nineteen Seventy-Two
Nineteen Seventy-Three
Nineteen Seventy-Four
Nineteen Seventy-Five
Nineteen Seventy-Six
Nineteen Eighty

VAMPIRES OF THE MEROVINGI SERIES

The Island

THE DUSK TRILOGY
St. Charles at Dusk: The Story of Oz and Adrienne
Flourish: The Story of Anne Fontaine
Banshee: The Story of Giselle Deschanel

CRIMSON & CLOVER STORIES
Surrender: The Story of Oz and Ana
Shame: The Story of Jonathan St. Andrews
Fire & Ice: The Story of Remy & Fleur
Dark Blessing: The Landry Triplets
Pandora's Box: The Story of Jasper & Pandora
The Menagerie: Oriana's Den of Iniquities
A Band of Heather: The Story of Colleen and Noah
The Ephemeral: The Story of Autumn & Gabriel
Bayou's Edge: The Landry Triplets

For more information, and exciting bonus material,
visit www.sarahmcradit.com

ABOUT SARAH

Sarah is the *USA Today* and International Bestselling Author of over forty contemporary and epic fantasy stories, and the creator of the Kingdom of the White Sea and Saga of Crimson & Clover universes.

Born a geek, Sarah spends her time crafting rich and multilayered worlds, obsessing over history, playing her retribution paladin (and sometimes destruction warlock), and settling provocative Tolkien debates, such as why the Great Eagles are not Gandalf's personal taxi service. Passionate about travel, she's been to over twenty countries collecting sparks of inspiration, and is always planning her next adventure.

Sarah and her husband live in a beautiful corner of SE Pennsylvania with their three tiny benevolent pug dictators.

www.sarahmcradit.com

SARAH M CRADIT

WEAVER *of* WORLDS

Made in United States
Troutdale, OR
09/28/2023

13254755R10219